Redemption

Paula Bowers

TATE PUBLISHING
AND ENTERPRISES, LLC

To Ben, my dear friend taken way too
soon. Keep heaven warm for me.

Redemption

Cindy —
Always remember that
with each dawning day comes
a new chance for Redemption!

In gratitude
Paula Bowers

ACKNOWLEDGMENTS

First and foremost, I would like to thank my Creator and Forgiver, whose still, small voice whispers words of comfort and guidance daily.

To my mom and dad, the most influential people in the world to me, thank you for the love, laughter, guidance, support, and help over these past thirty-nine years. I am the most blessed woman on the face of this planet to have the two of you!

Lovey, Brett, Aubryn, and Braylon, you four are my very breath. Without you, I would be nothing. Thank you for loving me in spite of me, for the snuggles, the words or affirmation, the laughs, heartfelt talks, and crazy fun we have! With no other four people would I want to walk through this life.

My siblings, nieces, nephews, and in-laws, if I were granted the opportunity to handpick my family, I would pick each and every one of you! You mean the world to me.

My dear friends, too many to name, thank you for believing in me and being my stability, rationality, and source of levity on a daily basis. There is no greater blessing than friends. And to my church family, I love you all dearly.

Probably most important at this point in my life is my shrink, without whom I would never have had the focus and clear mind to finish a sentence, let alone a whole novel. Thank you for keeping me alive and (somewhat) sane, Dr. M. I treasure you!

A very special nod to a woman who has made me feel so incredibly warmhearted in regard to my writing and who has encouraged me to keep plugging away on Redemption as she is my biggest Accessible fan. Jan Lynne, I am blessed beyond measure by you, and thank you so much for confirming that Redemption was an exceptional title for this novel!

Finally to Allie, Sam, Nick, Chris, Jen, and Greg, I'm going to miss you guys so very much! Thanks for coming to life for me and writing the story yourselves. Each of you holds such a treasured space in my heart.

Folks, no matter your struggles in life, each and every one of you have the innate capacity to find Redemption!

PROLOGUE

Dear Jen,

I wish I knew where to begin with this letter. First, I guess congratulations are in order. I applaud you for sacrificing your integrity and that of your so-called best friend in exchange for your fifteen minutes of fame. Was it worth it? By the looks of your most recent photo in *OK!* magazine, I would dare say your answer may be a resounding "No!" I have to admit, at first I thought I was staring at a picture of Kate Gosselin during her dark, haggard, post-divorce period. I would like to say that look doesn't suit you, but given recent events, I am afraid it is spot-on.

I heard Greg left. Boy, I just can't imagine why! I mean, what man would ever leave a woman who became so obsessed with a celebrity that she sacrificed her integrity and that of her family and friends out of pure spite and jealousy? That's hot, Jen—*hot*! Doesn't Greg know a good thing when he has it?

Oh, and Annabelle? How is she? I am sure she just loves going to school and hearing all the kids talk about her psychotic mom. I mean, what kid wouldn't? I heard that Greg had to send her to a private school because of all the threats she was receiving. You must be so proud. Bravo, Jen. Bravo. You are doing a bang-up job!

I may have lost a battle of which I didn't even realize I was a part, but you, my friend, have lost the entire war. I hope it was worth it.

Sincerely yours,
Allie Holly

1

Okay, so I didn't actually send it. I wanted to, believe me. In fact, it took every fiber of my being to literally pull my hand away from the mailbox at the post office with the addressed, stamped letter still clutched in between my fingers. I had fantasies for days of her reaction when she received the letter. Would she cry? Would she tear it up? Would she concoct a rebuttal? Or would she just use it as further ammunition to try and sabotage my already demolished reputation? Good luck with that one, Jen. I can't go much lower.

But alas, I did not send the letter, choosing not to place myself at her low level. I did, however, send the one I wrote to Nick's mother. No matter how much Jen despised me, the hatred spewing from Nick's mom was actually tangible and far more damaging to my soul. Unfortunately, I only got the opportunity to witness her wrath through a full spread in *People* magazine. Awesome.

Naively, I truly thought my full admission, which was published in hardback and featured in every magazine from *People* to *Time*, would somehow redeem me to Nick, to Jen, and to myself. I wasn't as much worried about the public reaction, except for as it pertained to my family. While the majority of women everywhere used my piece to further exacerbate their hatred, I did develop a bit of a cult following, consisting of those who wanted nothing more than to become my new "best friend" in an attempt to be one step closer to the ever-elusive Nicholas Price. While my stellar agent did set me up with a nice website and a Facebook account (by the way, I am now up to five hundred thousand "friends" or "followers" or whatever you call those weird people who want to be closer to a no-name liar like me), I avoid those multimedia venues like the plague. My agent calls me once a week to remind me that I "have a duty" to my "fans." Are you kidding me with this?

It is like saying Monica Lewinsky has a duty to her fans. How does someone so infamous have fans? Such is the disgusting state of the human psyche, and I have no desire to communicate to these so-called fans that I should never have in the first place. I am not proud of anything about my story, other than the fact that the writing has been described as witty and smart. Who would have thought I would be a writer?

When I finished the story of my journey with Nicholas Price, I had quite the time finding a media outlet dumb enough to believe my story, let alone buy into it. It took telephone records, e-mail proof, and snapshots of the flower nursery in my basement for anyone with any sort of significant pull in the publishing world to recognize the moneymaker that lay before their eyes.

While the writing had been extremely therapeutic for me (more so than years of therapy), I was ready to dump it out of my hands and into someone else's so that I could get back to some semblance of normal with Sam. Of course, as soon as Jen's story came out, every media outlet and publishing house in the world coveted my "version" of the story, and alas, "normal" was not to be had for…well, forever.

Once the British tabloid, *The Sun*, released the awful story Jen had allowed to be "leaked" to them (apparently she had taken pictures of Nick leaving my house with her telephone and used the photos to corroborate her story), it was literally a matter of minutes before the entire thing was plastered on the Internet and only two friggin' days before *People* magazine shoved it onto every store shelf in the world. *Entertainment Tonight* was almost an afterthought. I had no idea how fast a story could get out—thank you, technology—until I was grabbing a gallon of milk at the local Price Chopper and Nick's glossy face was staring back at me in the express aisle, a photo of me and another of a scowling Jen cropped together in the upper right corner. In bold white, it read, "Nicholas Price Vanished," and underneath was a subheading describing, "The woman behind his disappearance and the friend she betrayed." The photo they had found of me was absolutely hideous, my staff picture on the school's website at which I taught. I remember the day the picture was taken like it was yesterday. My fellow teachers often made fun of me for not remembering important school events, like picture day. In all the years I had taught, I had never once managed to remember it was picture day until I arrived and got a glimpse of my students in their Sunday best. On that particular picture day, I didn't hear my alarm blaring until five minutes before I was supposed to be out the door. It was a Friday, and although "casual Fridays" were not routine, I decided to take a chance that particular Friday and was wearing one of Chris's (my deceased husband) oversized sweatshirts and baggy jeans. My hair was a greasy mess, leaving me no choice but to pull it back in a bun. I mean no disrespect when I say that the way I looked, with the oily strands plastered against my head, resembled a bald chemo patient. I had always hated that picture, and of course, it was the one *People* grabbed. I had strong suspicions that Jen may have been the one to direct the editors to that photo. After all, she had thousands of pics of me in her possession that she could have forked over.

Despite my intentions to steer clear of message boards and editorial commentary, in my weaker moments I found myself scrolling to the bottom of website articles written about the whole situation to read what nasty things people were saying about me. Following the *People* publication, a common reaction among haters was bewilderment about what Nicholas Price would possibly be doing with such an old, ugly hag. I must admit, even though I deserved every ounce of criticism, it stung badly. People were merely noticing something I had been declaring all along—something Nick had dismissed time and time again, assuring me that I was gorgeous and that our ten-year age difference didn't matter. In black and white, I read what I already knew: "That geriatric ho-bag is nowhere near good enough for Nicholas Price!"

I spent the entire month of February doing damage control. Of course, I decided to head off my family and Chris's family at the pass before the original story broke, giving them as much information as I could while still maintaining some piece of dignity. My family was wonderfully supportive. Chris's… not so much. His holier-than-thou mother decided to use my indiscretion as a weapon with which to torture me and lecture me about the importance of honesty and the sin of deceit. (Like I didn't already know!)

Come to find out, sweet little Judy, my mother-in-law, had actually secretly hoped her son would marry Jen one day, a little tidbit I realized when she chose time and time again to defend Jen when the situation was discussed. Baffled, I stormed out of her home, only to realize once I got to my car that I had left my keys inside. I hated the fact that I couldn't let my dramatic exit be the last taste in Judy's mouth after her accusatory, demeaning tone and blatant lack of understanding. Remembering that the keys were just inside the front door lying on the foyer table, I decided to forego knocking and attempted to rush in and out without being noticed. It was then that I heard Judy ragging on me to John in the hallway, her words slicing through my stomach: "This is why Chris should have married Jen to begin with. I never understood why he would leave such a sweet, compassionate, sensitive girl…and a *believer* to boot!"

I couldn't believe what I was hearing. I had half a notion to storm into the living room to proclaim once again the venom that Jen had spewed at me, but my pride was too hurt and my eyes were stinging from tears that I refused to let spill over. I had to remind myself on the drive home that they didn't really know Jen like I knew her and that their son chose correctly. There was no doubt about that in my mind. We were meant to spend the short amount of time that we had together, and Samuel Christopher was not a mistake. Even though I was unsure of most everything else swirling around in my life at the time, I was certain of two things: Christopher Holly was always supposed to be my husband, and Samuel Christopher was supposed to be my son. *Screw you, Judy!*

My biggest motivation and main reason for penning my side of the story was to protect my son. After surviving the tragic death of a husband and being a single mom for seven years, I was not weak. I may have been nutty, a little loony perhaps, even suffering a severe lack in judgment, but I was not weak. I could handle the wrath of the world against me. I could not, however, stomach the thought of my son having to suffer because of my indiscretion, and I would keel over and die trying to protect him from unfair torment and ridicule.

Let me give you the lowdown on the reaction of my family when I spilled the beans, just two days prior to Jen's *Sun* debut. Now granted, I had already prepared them for what was to come, calling everyone together at my parents' house to avoid having to retell the sick story four different times. Sam was being entertained in the basement with his cousins, and so I had the undivided attention of eight adults, all seated in a semicircle facing the console television in front of which I stood.

Lisa, my oldest sister had her head resting against the back of the loveseat, her eyes closed, obviously bored by the whole gathering—or maybe she just had another headache, something she had been suffering from as of late. She was holding hands with

Mark, who was texting someone on his phone. They obviously didn't sense the urgency of the situation nor the severity.

Maggie was on the other couch with her legs draped over her husband, Paul, her hands folded nicely in her lap, wearing her "cat who ate the canary" grin. I knew she thought the news I was bearing was probably good news. I mean, in my family the only time we call an official meeting is for weddings and babies being born; and Maggie, being the well-adjusted middle child (second born), was forever the optimist. Later I found out that she thought I was going to tell her that I used more of Chris's sperm to get pregnant again, and she was set to be over the moon.

Adam and Christy were standing inside the doorway to the kitchen, Adam always unable to just sit and relax; my dad was fully reclined in his La-Z-Boy with my mom sitting one-butt-cheeked on the arm rest, her arms folded expectantly and her foot kicking nervously. My dad began to snicker, as he had a habit of doing in uncomfortable situations, and my mom elbowed him in the ribs, giving him her "Shut up, you dummy!" look.

I cleared my throat and, looking down at my feet for a second before glancing up into their expectant eyes, began to regurgitate my reason for bringing them all together. "Well, so I am sure you are all wondering what could possibly be important enough for Mom to ask you to come tonight—"

"I just came for the free food," Adam interrupted.

A nervous chuckle ensued amongst everyone except Lisa (who was rubbing her temples, her eyes still closed) and Mom, whose anxiety had taken on a physical form. I released the air I hadn't realized had been building in my chest dying to escape and gave my own little laugh as I combed my fingers through my unwashed hair. My family thrived on teasing and humor, and seeing me standing upright on the verge of delivering some sort of important news left them feeling obviously overwhelmed and tangibly uncomfortable.

Instantly aware of the tension, I plopped down on the floor Indian-style. "Okay," I began, "So here's the dealio, peeps." I had to speak the same language we had grown so accustomed to as a family in order to save them undue stress and anxiety as well as to cut myself some slack. These people loved me, and if anyone would understand…well, they had no choice but to understand. I was blood. Plain and simple. "What I am about to tell you is going to seem so crazy bizarre, sick, and twisted. It is truly the stuff that movies are made of…or Jerry Springer or something." I was stalling.

"Oh, get on with it already," Mark pushed.

"Now you are scaring me," Maggie chimed in, her optimistic smile quickly betraying her. "Is someone dying?"

"Oh, please," Lisa began. "Hasn't she had enough death for one person in her life? Get a grip, Maggie." Lisa finally looked at me, impatient. "What is it, sis? Just spit it out already. You will feel better once you do."

As my mom gave a reassuring nod, I blurted, "Okay, do you guys know who Nicholas Price is?" Not waiting for them to even answer—because who the hell *didn't* know who Nicholas Price is, and also because at one time or another, every female in my family, including Lisa's daughters, had heard me gush about the ever-palatable Nicholas Price—I continued, "Well, I don't know if you remember when I went to Omaha, but I didn't just go for my own R & R. Jen asked me to go because they were filming one of the *Exemption* movies there, and she had hoped we would be able to get a glimpse of the set. Jen wasn't able to go after all because, well, Jen is psycho, and so—"

Mom cut me off. "Wait, Jen is psycho? When did Jen become psycho? She is your best friend."

Maggie agreed. "Oh, I love Jen. What do you mean?"

"Please, guys, let me finish. I am begging you." And I began to cry. At my tears, Maggie instinctively cascaded her legs off of Paul and with two feet barely planted on the ground began to rise to console me. I immediately put up my hand, stopping her. Which reminds me, why does a hand up with five fingers indicate "stop"? That is a question Sam has asked me a few times, and I have yet to look into it. Anyway, I continued, "Maggie, please don't make it worse. I am walking on thin ice here, and any sympathy will destroy my resolve. For real." With that she sat back down, more erect and aware than ever.

I inhaled deeply and exhaled, my family staring intently at me, the "baby" withering on the floor. Straightening my back, I forced, "Jen couldn't go on the trip because she had become so crazily obsessed with Nicholas Price that her husband was not comfortable with it. I am not going to go into detail about it because I refuse to stoop to her level, but I believe Greg made the right call. I did go, however. And when I went I wasn't even really thinking about Nicholas Price anymore, I was thinking ab—"

"Okay, this is annoying. Why do you have to say his whole name every time?" Adam inquired. Christy gave him one of her death looks, but it didn't dissuade him from continuing. "I mean, seriously. You sound like a stupid teenager."

I chose to ignore him. Adam was a very impatient man when situations became uncomfortable and, like my dad, never could stand the sight of tears. "Okay, so I went to Omaha just to get away and because I had already paid for the hotel. The first night I was there, however, I did run into Nicholas Pr…I mean, Nicholas. I did. And I met him at a bar, and we hit it off immediately, and we talked all night and all day the next day, and I spent every waking moment with him while I was in Omaha." I paused, first to catch my breath and second to assess their reactions, which were comical. Every pair of eyes in the room, barring my father's and brother's, were bulging out of their sockets. Not wanting any more interruptions, I began again. "It is the truth, and when I got back to town, Nicholas and I continued a relationship on the phone and e-mail, and then one night when I had Jen over to hang out and have a few drinks, he showed up at my door. That is when all hell broke loose."

"Because she liked him too?" Mom asked.

"Oh, well, I guess I skipped a pertinent point. This is going to sound so dumb, but for some dumbass reason I didn't tell Nick that I knew who he was. I pretended like I had never seen the movies or read about him. I don't know why I did it, except that I guess I thought he wouldn't give me the time of day if he thought I was just another psychotic fan."

Adam busted out in a cynical laugh. "But you *are* a psychotic fan!"

"Okay, dummy, I know that, but I just, well…" I trailed off, and then, regaining steam, I said, "You know what? I am just telling you what happened. Judge me all you want, but it will never be as much as I have been judging myself. I don't expect your support, Adam, and you are free to leave when I am finished, but what has happened has the propensity to affect all of your lives, and so I owe it to you to explain."

Mom jerked back, confused. "What does that mean, affect all of our lives?"

"Damn it, you guys, let me *finish!*" I couldn't take it anymore.

Once everyone conceded, I gave one final roll of my eyes and said, "I never intended any of this. I just didn't want to be one of those starstruck girls. I never thought it would amount to anything. I mean, I thought a little lie was harmless." The tears came in abundance, blurring my vision from the people who loved me more than anyone in the world. "I didn't know we would actually start dating. I didn't know we would communicate beyond Omaha. I didn't know we would fall in love." The collective gasp in the room caused me to pause.

"Fall in *love?*" Christy's eyes were bulging from their sockets, her tone louder than I had heard her since we went to a New Kids on the Block reunion concert together. Being such a soft-spoken person who typically lets our crazy family be nuts while she just shakes her head and quietly chuckles, no one expected such a spat of an answer from her.

I, however, was thankful for the attention to shift, if only for a second, to my sweet sister-in-law behaving uncharacteristically. I looked out the sliding glass doors onto the backyard patio my father had built when I was a sophomore in high school. It was a beautifully gigantic slab of white concrete created in a perfect *L* shape. One tiny square was cut out where my dad had imbedded the concrete square from our previous patio that held four tiny handprints from when I was one year old. The patio was surrounded with beautiful annuals and perennials my mom kept up with year after year. She has always been quite the gardener, and aside from describing the sheer beauty of each individual color and texture, I, myself, am unable to label more than one rosebush for you, dear reader.

In the split second that the room shifted uneasily at Christy's outburst and Adam blatantly laughed at his wife, I managed to size up that it would take around eight full-length steps for me to make it to the patio door and escape. My eyes were focused on the last stretch of carpet I would traverse before I hit the door when Maggie's big blue eyes were three inches from my brown orbs and her arms were wrapped around my neck.

"Oh, sissy!" she let out and disengaged the full weight of her head onto my shoulder.

"Okay," I creaked as I pushed Maggie away from me and turned toward the others. "I haven't even gotten to the good part."

My dearest brother rolled his eyes and asked, "Can you speed this along before the second coming?"

Continuing to ignore Mr. Snarky, I finished, "He showed up at my house and Jen was there and I had to quickly and secretly tell Jen that I had been seeing him and that he didn't know that I actually knew who he was and so Jen spilled the beans and they both walked out on me!" I caught my breath and then added, "And apparently Nick has fallen off the face of the earth, and

Jen is going to cash in on God-only-knows what…probably her pride…maybe her marriage…and definitely my friggin' friendship, and do an interview with *Entertainment Tonight* about it and splatter my name across every TV screen, newspaper and magazine in the world!" I was heaving, literally heaving, like I had just finished a marathon. Oh, who am I kidding? I was heaving like I just had to get off the couch and answer the phone. Marathon shmarathon. I have never been able to even run to the mailbox at the end of my driveway.

Maggie, who was still standing next to me annoyingly rubbing my back, began making a shushing sound like I was about to melt down, which surprisingly I wasn't. It was actually a relief, an unexpected relief. Just being able to tell someone other than my therapist, who has to be unbiased, felt like a mountain of guilt and shame were being lifted off my shoulders by a hot-air balloon.

As my breathing actually steadied to the ridiculous shushing back rub, I glanced around the silent room and let my eyes land on my father's. Looking into his brown eyes was precisely like looking into mine. As if knowing *exactly* the words I needed to hear, he clapped his catcher's mitt hands together and spoke loudly, "Welp, his loss, Allie Belle. And screw Jen. I never liked her anyway." With that, he rocked forward, pushing in the footrest in one swift move, and stood up to his feet. Walking toward me, my daddy bent down and kissed the top of my head, whispering, "Don't sweat it, kiddo. Just ride the wave." He then walked into the kitchen and started loading the dishwasher. I have never loved that man more.

Paul was the next to speak, reassuring me. "AB, we got your back. If he knew the real you, he would realize walking away from you was a big mistake. We are behind you, sister!" I loved that my brother-in-law always called me by my initials. It was a privilege only unspokenly granted to him. As he arose and joined my dad in the kitchen, he poked Maggie in the ribs, exclaiming, "Let her breathe, babe."

As if on cue, Adam and Mark both got up simultaneously, Mark giving me a side hug as he said, "This is unchartered territory, Al, but whatever we need to do, we will do."

Adam, punching me in the shoulder, added, "Well, you are a jackass for lying, he is a jackass for leaving, and Jen is a jackass for just living. You're probably gonna need me or Dad to come stay with you if all hell breaks loose with the media. Just let me know what day the hag is gonna be on TV. I'll be there." That was as much as I could ask of my dear brother, a product of my emotionally uncomfortable father.

With the men of the family leaving us alone, I sat next to Lisa on the loveseat while Mom slinked into Dad's chair and Maggie returned to her post. Christy plopped on the floor, shaking her head in disbelief. The five of us hashed out the rest of the details, me answering the questions I would only feel comfortable sharing with the women of the family. The nervousness over the entire situation was coupled with intrigue as each woman in the room had burning questions to divulge in reference to my relationship with the untouchable Nicholas Price. Christy and Maggie were definitely living vicariously through my love experience, while Lisa was more interested in the fame and notoriety that was to come. Mom was just wringing her hands, worried about my safety and the well-being of my son.

The culmination of the evening brought forth a plan of action, including a general family response in the event that paparazzi were to begin hounding (a resounding "No comment!") and yet another schedule of overnight visitors for me and Sam. After my beautiful Chris died, my family took turns staying with me for a month to ensure that I wouldn't have to grieve alone. This was going to be different. This was to ensure that I *would* be left alone. Oh, how I love my family.

As it turns out, the media attention was more intense than I could have ever imagined. They were outside my house every morning when I arose and were still clicking pictures at night when I shut off my porch light. Sam found it rather exciting in the beginning, as did the female members of my family.

When *The Sun* broke the story, it took a good twenty-four hours for the first of the paparazzi to arrive in front of my school. My principal had been kind enough to (*a*) not fire me and (*b*) call a mandatory staff meeting the day I gave her the lowdown on what was to come and had me explain the situation to my colleagues. I, of course, did not get as specific as I had with my family, but for the most part, they were all very supportive and receptive to my needs. Of course, working in a building full of women, I suddenly had a dozen new "friends" who not only wanted every last detail about Nick, but were also suddenly interested in being within my presence, whereas previously they couldn't have cared less about me. Funny what the idea of fame does to people. Without using exact words, I think I made it pretty clear that I was not interested in, nor did I need any new friends. In fact, during the staff meeting, I specifically ended my story with, "Guys, I know this is all different and weird and to some, maybe even exciting. But here's the thing. I have a son to protect, and that is my only focus right now. Before anyone asks, I cannot introduce you to Nicholas Price nor do I have any pull in Hollywood. Or anywhere else for that matter, so please don't ask. This is a very difficult situation right now, and so, while I will be happy to answer what questions I can, I am begging you all to be very discreet when talking about this with anyone. And I have recently been in touch with a lawyer, so I can assure you that my only response to the media will be "No comment," and I hope that will be yours as well."

With that, my principal interrupted, "Oh, let's just say this, folks. If you would like to keep your job here, your response will be 'No comment!'" Of course, that was a bunch of bull and we all knew it, given the tenure state of 80 percent of the teachers at my school, but it was a sweet thought. Everyone nodded in agreement, but looking around the room, I could almost guarantee whose mouths would be flappin' to the media at the earliest available opportunity.

My first glimpse of the press was on a Thursday afternoon. The good ole Internet kept me informed about the article in *The Sun* on Wednesday night, and I had been pleasantly surprised that no one had greeted me on my doorstep that Thursday morning on my way to work. Adam had spent the night, and after an uneventful and surprisingly peaceful night's sleep and no sign of the press in the morning, I told him he probably didn't need to come stay another night, figuring the fact that *The Sun* was a British tabloid, it apparently kept smart, upstanding American paparazzi at bay. Heck, who knows if anyone on this side of the big pond even read that ridiculous magazine, let alone bought into it. Mercy me was I ever wrong.

I walked my students to the front doors of the school building upon dismissal, and as I was giving high fives, I noticed a lot of noise and hubbub surrounding the school nurse, who delightfully directs the crazy pickup line traffic. Her face was not the sweet, happy one I had grown so accustomed to seeing; rather, it was a panicked one with a mouth that kept barking into a walkie-talkie. I figured either a kid had gotten sick or they couldn't find someone, or something equally as ordinary during dismissal time, but I decided I really didn't want to be involved and needed to head back to my classroom to collect Sam and my things and bug out to his Tae Kwon Do class.

Just as I turned to walk back down the hall toward my classroom, I heard the stern voice of my principal boom, "Mrs. Holly!" (I still went by "Mrs." even though I was widowed.) She clonked her chunky schoolmarm heels on the tile floor as she approached and grabbed my arm, leading me directly through the school office and into her private office, where she closed the door behind us.

It hit me before she even said anything that this had something to do with the whole Nicholas Price ordeal. I didn't know if maybe a group of parents had found out and were making a stink or if it was the paparazzi, but by the look on her face and her mouth opened wide, I knew I was about to find out.

"Well, apparently the story has broken, and this place is swarming with press!" She was shaking, looking at me expectantly as if I somehow knew what to do, as if I had done this before and could guide her as to what the correct protocol might be. When I didn't respond, her already elevated eyebrows shot up at least another inch in frustration and prodding.

Finally, I shook my head, shrugged my shoulders, and said, "Well, what do you want me to do?"

Her eyes rolled back into her head, and her shoulders dropped as she exhaled a pissed-off sigh and raised her hands in surrender. "How should I know?" she yelled.

My mind whirled around possibilities, but all I could focus on was Sam and the protection of him. Finally I said, "Listen, call the police, first of all. Tell them what is going on. I am going to see if Terri can take Sam home so that they won't get a shot of him with me. Then I will just go out the teacher exit to my car, and hopefully, the attention will be pulled away from the front of the building and onto me. I have a hard time believing anyone will recognize me, but let's just see." I spoke so surprisingly calmly, and I remember actually feeling somewhat calm. Maybe a gift from my beloved Chris?

My principal nodded, and I left her office and exited toward my room through the teacher's lounge. When I approached the pod area where my classroom shared a wall with Terri's, I saw Sam on my computer playing a game. I hollered into the room, "Hey, buddy. I will be right there, okay?"

Not even looking up from the screen, he nodded. At this, I was thankful for technology. The same form of communication that was about to destroy my life was also keeping my son distracted and entertained while my existence was unraveling around me. Is that irony?

Remember that song "Ironic" by Alanis Morissette? I remember loving that song when I was younger and then feeling like a dingbat when someone made the comment that it really is a foolish song because the scenarios she describes are not true "irony." To this day, I feel insecure using the term in the event that I may be using it incorrectly.

And we're back! I found Terri sitting at her desk grading papers and filled her in on the drama and my plan. She agreed without hesitation to helping me and stood to give me a hug, an embrace that brought back the peace I had felt in the office. Terri always carried such grace and peace with her and poured it on all who cared to receive it.

Walking back into my classroom, I approached the desk. "Hey, buddy, you need to shut that down, okay?"

My sweet first-grade boy looked up at me and, surprisingly, didn't fight me for once. Instead, his dimples made a grand entrance at his smile, and he said, "Tae Kwon Do time, Mama?" He stood and grabbed his backpack.

"Oh, sweetie, actually, probably not today. Remember the story I told you about that guy I met in Omaha? The one who brought me the flowers, who is actually famous?"

"Yeah?" Sam urged.

"Well, buddy, apparently the people who work for magazines and newspapers and television found out about it and are curious to know more about me. Sammy, bud, they are all outside this building wanting to take pictures of me and interview me," I explained.

"Cool! Let's go!" he retorted, and headed for the doorway.

"Whoa, buddy, not yet. Listen, remember I told you some of the things they have to say are not necessarily going to be nice, so I actually don't want you going out there with me the first time, okay?"

"Um, so what, I'm just gonna sleep here tonight?" my sweet boy teased in the same sarcastic tone his dad had used so many times.

"Ha! Yep. I brought your sleeping bag and pillow. You can just stretch out on the floor." I loved it that I had the kind of kid who understood adult humor.

"So then what, Mom?" he impatiently pried.

"Terri is going to take you to her house, and I am going to assess the situation. And then when I feel like the coast is clear, I will come pick you up. Does that sound okay?" Not that it mattered.

"No, Mom," he began to whine. "I want to go to Tae Kwon Do. Today is my last class before testing!" Sam was testing the following Saturday for his green belt.

"Oh, Sam, I know, honey. And maybe we can make it up tomorrow or I will practice with you at home"—yeah right—"but right now we just need to deal with this, okay?"

He grumbled and shuffled his feet toward Terri's room as I called out, "I love you!"

I gathered my purse and a little grading I had to do and blew Sam a kiss as I passed by Terri's room, reiterating that I would call her cell phone as soon as I knew what to expect. Terri was going to wait a fair amount of time before leaving with Sam, just to be safe.

As I walked through the hallways and toward the furnace room, which also happens to house the "teacher's exit," I encountered several teachers who were standing outside their classrooms gossiping about the latest development. Most of them seemed giddy with excitement at the prospect of their face possibly appearing in a magazine. The two kindergarten teachers did not appear as happy with the whole situation as, when I rounded the corner before they spotted me, I heard one complain, "This is freaking ridiculous! She is a nobody, and now I can't even get into my car without people snapping pictures of me?"

The other concurred, adding, "If I was a parent, I would be so pissed that my kids were being subjected to this. She seriously should take a leave of absence for the sake of all of us."

They must have heard or seen me coming because the first teacher made a quiet shushing sound as I approached. My blood was boiling. I was pissed, but I truly don't know if I was mad that they were talking nasty about me behind my back, or if I was just mad at myself for the exact reasons they were describing. Nevertheless, I was definitely in a self-preservation mode at that particular moment, and without looking at either of them or missing a step, I quipped, "Screw you guys!"

2

I felt the heat rising in my cheeks the moment I pushed the bar on the big steel door and stepped one foot out onto the parking lot concrete. *What the hell was I thinking?* The whole thing was still so surreal, and the looming presence of paparazzi made it even more so. I had managed only two Payless-ShoeSource-cowboy-boot steps out the door before I heard the first voice yelling my name from across the playground. Thank the Lord they were not allowed on the actual school property. Within seconds, there were at least twenty more shouts from differing voice tones and volumes. Some called me "Ms. Holly," others simply "Allison." Not one voice from the crowd used the name I entrusted to those closest to me. This little detail gave me a small bit of satisfaction. Jen may have been on a quest to make my life a living hell, but she had not allowed these leaches in on a very pertinent detail to my existence: I was Allie.

The vultures scurried down the street to the opening of the parking lot, the threshold over which I would inevitably have to cross. They were still screaming as I got into my car and slammed the door. I counted to ten as I tried to steady my breathing. For vanity's sake, I was thankful I had been prepared for them earlier that morning when I dressed and primped. I'm not gonna lie when I say a small part of me was a touch disappointed that I had gone through all the work to look my very best when stepping out on my front porch only to be met by the sound of the nearby highway traffic and little else that morning. Being a mother to a first grader who wakes up on the wrong side of the bed every morning does not afford me the luxury of really caring much how I look. It is enough that I just can get him to "fake" brush his teeth and put on shoes. I remember saying aloud as I traversed the porch steps and into my car, "What a waste!" Unfortunately, eight hours with twenty-three fourth graders has a way of making even the most put-together supermodel look worn down and disheveled. And I, my friends, am no supermodel.

Instead of risking the chance of being caught on camera checking myself out in the vanity mirror, I plugged the shaking keys into the ignition and turned over the engine. A few more deep breaths and a glance at the frantic crowd mixed with not only media personnel, but by then also neighborhood residents and passersby, I pulled out of my parking space and toward the mayhem that awaited me. As my car inched closer and the swarm of people began to appear life-size and clear, I started freaking out. I could hear myself mumbling prayers and curse words all in a cluster of nonsense that only I understood while barely moving my lips so as to not give away my neurosis to these perfectly horrible strangers.

Not wanting to appear nervous or rude (Don't ask. I have no idea *what* I was thinking to actually be concerned about that, but I was), I looked into a few of the faces, smiled, and nodded, as if we were neighbors. Apparently, they didn't have the same concern for my opinion of them because after my brief stop at the stop sign and emergence into the street, they literally started banging on my car and shouting questions at me. Someone even tried to open my door! Thank goodness for automatic locks, something I hadn't even thought of when I had climbed into the car.

As I tried to turn right, I realized it was a real possibility that I was going to run over someone. They didn't seem to care; rather, they stood in front of the car almost "challenging" me. I panicked and raised my hand in surrender, beginning to grasp that I was probably going to have to get out of the car or else I would die a slow death in the unmoving car. Or I could spend eternity in prison for homicide. Both options seemed unacceptable so I placed the gear in "park" and had my index finger on the "unlock" button, ready to admit defeat, just as I spotted the flashing lights quickly descending down the street, almost as if coming straight from heaven.

A wave of intense gratitude swept over me and, with my finger still steady on the "unlock" trigger, I watched intently as the first, and then second, third, and fourth police car parked abruptly in the middle of the street and the doors flew open, delivering my personal saviors one by one. With hands placed firmly on the guns resting in their belts, seven police officers rebuked the crowd with just enough force to create a path for me to continue on my route. As they abruptly waved me on, I quickly stuck it in "drive" and pulled slowly into the open road. As soon as I was a block away, I checked my rearview mirror only to notice the cameramen and news personnel scurrying like ants to their respective cars. *Crap!* I didn't have much time.

Checking my speedometer, I pressed the accelerator until I was cruising at forty miles per hour. Surely the cops would be too busy controlling the crowds to worry about me speeding in a school zone. I rolled to a California pause at the end of the school street and, quickly checking to make sure I was not in imminent danger of being clipped, turned right onto a street called Black Bob, named after the chief of a band of Shawnee Indians. Most of the streets in that part of Olathe were named after prominent Native Americans as well as Christian settlers who served as missions in the area.

There was a teacher in my school who was fanatical about all things Olathe Kansas history. Quite honestly, she was socially unkempt and despised by most teachers and parents. She taught first grade, so I am not sure that her students were old enough to know what constituted a good teacher from a poor teacher at that point. Nevertheless, I had the unfortunate pleasure of being paired with her class as our "buddy class," and so I tried to be friendly the first year we worked together.

I was quickly made privy to her antics, however, when I invited her to a candle party I was having at my apartment and found my invitation returned to me in my mailbox in the teacher's lounge. At the bottom of the standard home party invite were the following words scrawled in red: "If you EXPECT me to come to your party, I suggest you learn the appropriate spelling of Black Bob! It is TWO words…not ONE as you wrote Blackbob!"

I stared at the card for quite some time in disbelief. And then, deciding there was no way she could possibly be serious, I headed straight to her classroom, invite in hand. "Hey," I chuckled as I rounded the corner and spotted her at her desk, while I held up the card. I was definitely giving her an out, fully aware that even a joke like this was not something I would ever be on the receiving end of from someone I truly enjoyed.

She held up her hand and smiled, putting me at ease if even for a split second. "Sorry," she began, "that is just a *really* big pet peeve of mine."

My eyes bulged from their sockets as I responded, "So you are actually *serious* with this note? I thought for sure it was a joke!"

"As a heart attack," she curtly barked and then turned back to grading papers at her desk.

I audibly sighed, a sound dripping with disgust as I approached her desk, ripped the invitation in half once and then again, and let the pieces fall out of my hand. Turning on my heels, shaking my head, I walked out of her room—the last nonschool-related conversation we have had.

I sped south on Black Bob Road to the stoplight on 151st street, made a hard right that felt like my driver's side wheels were coming off the ground, and hurried to the next street on the left, an entrance to one of the more affluent neighborhoods in Olathe, with sprawling all-brick homes and one-to-two-acre lots. Chris and I had dreamt about one day owning a house in the prestigious Arbor Farms neighborhood, and we would drive through it on lazy Sunday afternoons, fantasizing about what our future held in the estates. It was the first time I had driven through since he passed, and I had the pang of regret as soon as I drove past a two-story mansion with a full-size basketball court in the back.

Shattered dreams. Guilt so thick it had to be cut with a steak knife. Where did it all go so wrong? One day I was perusing beautiful lots with the first love of my life, and the next I was running away from paparazzi on the prowl sent by my horrific behavior with the last love of my life. Somewhere in between those quick two days, I had managed to give birth to the second—the young one who was by then being driven around town by a dear older friend because he was not safe returning to his childhood home with his mother. What in the hell had I done? What in the hell was I doing?

Before I had turned into Arbor Farms I had been obsessively checking the rearview mirrors for cars turning from Black Bob onto 151st, and when not one had surfaced, I decided it was the prime time to make another turn, thus my quick entry down memory lane. I continued to check my mirrors as I careened down the windy roads, and when it was clear I had made a clean break, I slowed in front of the parking lot to the community pool and playground.

Even though it was a mild Kansas winter's day, no one was out playing, a fact I was sure was short-lived given the timing of elementary school dismissal. Nevertheless I needed some air and a few moments to think, and so I backed into a parking space, for easy exit and to help conceal my license plate, and walked the short sidewalk distance to the swing set. There was a chill in the air despite the sun beating down on the hottest part of the day. I wrapped my very "teachery" sweater around me and sat facing the lot on the higher of the two swings.

The swing creaked as if it hadn't been sat upon in months, which could have possibly been the case since this was the first nice day in Kansas all winter. The pool chairs were all stacked under an awning, the chlorinated water dirty and low in the Olympic-size pool. Beyond the pool fence, I eyed the brown grassy hill that Chris and I had gone sledding down a time or two, the last time with Jen and Greg. Another pang of regret.

And anger. And regret again. How dare she? How dare I?

I stayed seated in the swing, unmoving, until the black rubber had squeezed the feeling out of my butt and my right thigh was throbbing. Certainly it had been long enough for the vultures to have moved away from the school's neighborhood and onto my home. I slowly stood up, the popping mimicking my age, and traipsed over to my car, unaware of exactly where I would go.

I hadn't even realized I didn't bring my cell phone with me until I unlocked the door and heard it violently vibrating in the bottom of my purse. I jumped in, fished through gum wrappers, squirt guns, Matchbox cars, and tampons until I saw the beacon of light at the bottom. As soon as I gripped it, the ringer stopped. *Damn it!*

I quickly flicked it on to discover I had nine missed calls. *Holy crap! Nine?* Every single one of them bore the same number: Terri Canter!

Have you ever had that dream in which you are trying desperately to dial someone's phone number but your fat fingers just won't cooperate and keep hitting the wrong damn buttons? That dream (or nightmare, rather) has multiplied in frequency and intensity for me ever since I took possession of a "smart phone." Truth is, it isn't actually just a dream, as shaking, freaking-out hands bring forth reality from the dream. Three times I tried to dial Terri, failing miserably each time until finally, my phone began blaring back at me. "Incoming Call. Terri Canter," the screen read.

I quickly answered a panicked, "Hello? What happened?"

"Oh, Allie, this is bad. Really bad," Terri's calm voice began. She was always calm. Always. Without exception. She once had a student bite her upper arm, drawing a tremendous amount of blood, and she still stayed calm. I, on the other hand, freaked out, screamed at the kid, and hollered so loudly for another student to go get the nurse and principal that the nurse and principal actually heard me from their respective offices.

"What's going on, Terri? What is it?" I was shaking, hysterical.

"They waited for me. I don't know how they knew, but they waited for me."

I racked my brain, trying to process why they would have waited for Terri, and then it hit me that if they had done the research to know at which school I taught, they had probably not exhausted their inquiry before noticing that I had a child that attended said school. What was I thinking, leaving without my kid in tow? These vultures, they were nothing if not crafty and skilled. Once they lost sight of me, they probably hovered behind bushes until the last car in the parking lot was spoken for, knowing that Samuel Christopher Holly had yet to make an appearance.

"Oh God, Terri. I'm so sorry!" I began.

"No reason to blame Him," she chided, reminding me once again of why I loved her. The woman loved the Lord with all of her heart, soul, mind, and strength and literally took Jesus's words and teachings to heart and into practice. Hence why she never freaked out!

"I have been driving around for nearly an hour, but I don't dare go home or back to your house, so I need to know what you think I should do?" It was one of the few times Terri had to ask me for guidance or advice. I am sure she already had an idea of a course of action, but I owed her this one as I had gotten her into this mess.

"Okay," I began, "I'm going to call the police and see if there is any way we can head to the station, just until we get this thing figured out. Does that sound okay?" I needed reassurance.

"I've already called, sweetie, and yes, that sounds like a good plan. They told me that they can't let us stay there long, as thus far no one has threatened us in any way…well, aside from our privacy, but that they may be able to get us an escort in an unmarked car to a destination of our choice."

Our choice, I thought, as I looked around at the sprawling brick homes encircling me. That would be *my* choice. To be delivered to one of these beautiful properties, Chris standing in the entryway, welcoming me with open arms, reassuring me that I was okay and that what I had done was not the end of the world. That it would get better. That he forgave me.

Maybe that was what was truly at the heart of all this. Beyond the guilt I felt for lying to Nicholas Price and putting my family and my own reputation at stake, hung the heaviest of all weights dangling from my neck like the clock around Flavor Flav's. I betrayed Chris, my husband. Against all odds and everything I had ever thought or felt about the prospect of ever meeting someone I could possibly love, I went and did just that.

3

The trip to the police station was incredibly uneventful for me until I approached the intersection directly to the south of the building. I spotted Terri's car already in the parking lot, thankfully empty. I knew Sam was safe. There were cars parked in lots on two sides of the station with cameramen and news personnel lingering about. As soon as I got a green light and entered the intersection, the focus quickly shifted from the entrance to the station to my approaching vehicle. Immediately, I was once again swarmed by hounds as I eased left into the station parking lot, thanking Jesus for the officer standing guard at the entrance. He stopped me, and as I unrolled my window to give identification, he immediately recognized me and waved me in. Apparently, bad news really does travel fast.

I could hear their shouts as I was escorted out of my car and into the station. "What were you thinking, Ms. Holly?" "Why did you abandon your son at school?" "Did you and Mr. Price ever have sexual intercourse?" "How would your dead husband feel about all of this?" The last one stung the worst. I kept my head down and shivered my way into the foyer. As soon as the warm blast of furnace pummeled my face I saw my precious son sitting in an armchair, tears streaming down his cheeks. What had I done?

I ran to Sam as fast as I could and knelt down so that we were at eye level. He threw his arms around my neck as I whispered "Shhh, it's okay, baby. It's okay."

Through broken sobs, he cried, "I...just...didn't...know—(sniff)—when...I...would...see...you...again!"

My heart broken, I just squeezed him as tight as I could without making him puke and stifled my own sobs into his neck.

Not wanting to involve sweet Terri anymore in my shenanigans, I told her to just let the police take her to her own house and I would go to mine. I mean, I couldn't avoid my home forever, so why start then? Before leaving the station, I phoned my brother and my dad, and they both agreed to come to my house immediately so that Sam and I would not have to be alone with a wild bunch of crazies looming about outside.

Then, instead of leaving my car and being chauffeured home (the police had already cased my house and the rats were already milling about, so no reason to try and protect the anonymity of my address), Sam and I buckled up in our car and were followed by a squad car all the way home, a trail of cars resembling a funeral procession tagging along. Same story, different location. The questions were shouted at the glass windows separating Sam and me from the evil ones. Thank God we had a garage to pull into so I would not have to witness the clarity of the words they spoke, the windows acting as a muffler.

I closed the garage door before we unlocked the car doors and exited. I knew they were not allowed to linger on my property, and the police officer had blocked the bottom of my driveway with his car. But still, I was not willing to take any chances with such precious cargo in my presence. Once the garage was fully closed, Sam and I made our way inside, me giving him strict instructions to stay in the kitchen while I traversed the house scouring for blinds and curtains that needed to be closed. Out of every window I peeked, I saw someone lurking with a video camera, notepad, and a microphone but most often a dirty, slimy camera whose only function was to ruin people's lives.

When I got to the living room windows, I spied a familiar black Dodge Ram creeping in front of the house, and for the first time since school was dismissed, I felt the tension that had slowly pulled as tightly as bungee cords holding a chest of drawers release; the immense immediate relief knocked me to my knees. My daddy had come to save me!

I ran to the garage and pushed the door opener so my dad could run right in, and then I kept the door cracked as I peeked through to make sure he made it in all right. Both the driver's side and passenger's side doors opened, and I spotted my brother exit as well as my dad. He was wearing a "cat who caught the canary" grin as he hurried into the garage alongside my father. As soon as they cleared the opening, I clicked the button to let down the door.

"Wow, sis," my brother began, "you sure know how to get attention!"

I punched him in the arm, the levity in his voice a welcome relief. "Yeah, I do, don't I? Thank you, guys, for coming."

My dad looped his arm around my neck and kissed the top of my head. "Of course, kiddo. You've gotten yourself into quite a pickle, haven't you? Now, where's my grandson?" He walked past me to the kitchen table where Sam was seated, staring off into space. "Hey, champ," he said as he gave him a noogie on the head.

"Hey, Pops," Sam replied in a sullen voice.

"What's wrong, my main man?"

Sam just shrugged.

"Hey, kiddo, so this is all pretty crazy, huh? All these people thinking you guys are pretty hot stuff?"

Sam shrugged again.

Curious, I approached and laid my hand on his shoulder. In response, he jerked away and stood, folding his arms across his chest, his eyes meeting the floor.

"Buddy, what's going on?" I pried.

Silence.

"Sam, what is it? Is this scary for you honey?"

Still nothing.

Adam shuffled over and, with his long arms, wrapped Sam in a full-out bro embrace. "Hey, little dude, all I could think about on the way here was whipping your butt in Mario Kart. You game?"

At that Sam cracked a smile and, looking up at Adam, whispered, "You said the *b* word."

Adam rolled his eyes and announced, "Your mom is too strict. Come on!" He led a pepped-up Sam into the living room while I took his place at the table, next to my dad.

"So, kiddo," my dad began, "I heard some things on the radio on the way here. Whew-wee that Jen is a vicious one. How the hell did you get tangled up with a girl like that?"

For some reason, I felt a little protective of my former best friend and defended her. "Dad, she wasn't always that bad. I mean, she has had a really rough go of it lately. I think she just needed to lash out, and I happened to be the one she chose to lash out at."

Snickering, my dad shook his head and retorted, "You always have been a merciful, forgiving person, haven't you? I mean, a person could beat the shit out of you, and you would still find a way to defend them."

"I learned from the best!" I winked.

"Well, according to your mom, I taught you all wrong."

I giggled, knowing that based on every other conversation in our entire lives, this one was about to be coming to a close. My dad was very short on words.

As if on cue, he rose, grabbed his duffel bag, and said, "I'm going to go check on the knuckleheads."

I nodded, suddenly wishing I had asked my mom to come along as well. I really needed to talk this one out. There were so many thoughts swirling about inside my head, the least of which was not my concern for Sam and his obvious anger toward me.

Staring at a sink full of dishes, I decided to avoid the inevitable and got online to see the damage that had been done. It didn't take long to find as my name was the top billed name trending on Yahoo! I clicked on it.

I could have scrolled nonstop all night and wouldn't have come to the end of the articles, websites, and message boards dedicated to yours truly. I even had a Wikipedia page. *A freaking Wikipedia page!* Of course it was only like two sentences long.

> An American mother and teacher from Olathe, Kansas, who is best known for her role in the sudden departure of actor Nicholas Price (of the *Exemption* franchise) from the United States. Born May 10, 1978, in Topeka, Kansas.

Underneath, where typically multiple sources lay italicized, was just one measly source: the stupid tabloid article in *The Sun*. They were in such a hurry to get information out about me that they hadn't even done any additional research, a fact that would become less true as the days and weeks progressed, and my freaking Wikipedia page was long enough to actually have a scroll bar added on the right hand side. I mean, everything about me—from elementary school to college to a doctor injecting sperm into my uterus nine months prior to Sam's birth. Oh yes, they left nothing out. My life—at least the factual logistics— were eventually laid out on a website for the world to gawk at.

Of course, the articles (some spot-on, some only half truth, and some completely false) did not go unanswered, as my story was surprisingly pushed along speedily once Jen's story broke. And within two weeks of that first crazy paparazzi ordeal, my side of the story was in the hands and homes of every American who had taken on the story as some vicarious extension of their own mundane life. That is when the shouts from paparazzi and the calls for interviews shifted in focus. No longer was I grilled (unsuccessfully, I might add) about why or how I could have done such a horrible thing. It turned into questions about my relationship with the great Nicholas Price, if I had spoken to him, had we had sex, if I was still in a feud with Jen. The content had changed, but the annoyance remained; and still, my response was always "No comment."

Sam and I somehow managed to get back into a weird, forced routine, and I found out very quickly that his anger had less to do with the people stalking us and more to do with the fact that he no longer had me to himself. It broke my heart when my brother Adam had managed to suck the information out of Sam while they played Mario Kart that night, and I cried myself to sleep, my entire body wrapped around my precious boy that night, as the flashes continued through the blinds into the first break of dawn.

The attention had started to recede just a bit before my own publication hit the surface, and I was half tempted to pull it altogether, truly believing that it all may just fade into the distance and that me bringing it back into focus would just stir a boiling pot that was just beginning to simmer. But when I made the suggestion to my publisher, I was not only met with dissonance but also a stern reminder about my contract and the large sum of cash I had already been paid. The money I would have given back in a heartbeat, but the breach of contract and legality jargon frightened me into submission.

The stream of attention waxed and waned for about a month as interviews were conducted and articles were written. As soon as my street had completely cleared of unwanted predators, some jackass who knew me from high school or one of Nick's childhood playmates would get their fifteen seconds of fame and destroy my next few days. I was always way too curious when anyone from Nick's camp responded, as I so desperately wanted to know how he was, what he was thinking. Unfortunately though, aside from his mother's words, which cut like a big fat Cutco butcher's knife, no one from down under had any current, real connection with Nick and were thus merely self-serving.

In the quiet moments, in between bouts of hubbub, when I was alone in my bed in the dark, I would think about him mercilessly, obsessively. Where was he? What was he doing? Did he think of me? Did he miss me?

My sister Maggie liked to remind me that I must have had some sort of lasting impact if it caused him to leave the profession he loved and the country he had come to call home. While it did feel somewhat good to think I could have had this sort of impact on someone so big and famous, especially as the long duration of time since I had seen him skewed my recollection of the past and what was real, there was still a big part of me that remembered how real it all was. He wasn't just some crazy fantasy. At least he wasn't in the end. I had truly grown fond of who he was, outside of *who he was*. I tried to explain this to Maggie who just brushed it aside, citing my rationale as euphoric recall.

"Oh, come on, Allie. There is no way it could have been anything but a fantasy. I mean Nicholas freaking Price, Allie!" she would remind me.

To which I would counter, "But, Mags, you are proving your own point. Why, on God's green earth, would something that is just a fantasy in *my* head cause someone *that famous* to leave the country unless it was real for him too?"

Maggie contemplated that for a while, and the ultimate optimist and hopeless romantic eventually came full force to my side of the argument. In fact, I believe *she* was more on my side than I was. With two months gone by and no word from Nick, despite my soul-baring tell-all, I was beginning to believe that maybe he had another reason for disappearing. I mean he did, after all, tell me under no uncertain terms that the Hollywood lifestyle was not really his cup of tea. Maybe he was going to leave anyway. In these moments, Maggie would try and reign me back in to my former way of thinking, an effort that was becoming increasingly more futile with every passing day.

4

By mid-April I was sluggishly moving through what could only be deemed the "hell months" of teaching. My students were acting like jackasses as spring fever had set in full bore, and a handful of them had parents who didn't just act like jackasses but were, in fact, jackasses. They found every way imaginable to try and sabotage my teaching career, going as far as holding drunken PTA-style meetings in homes to discuss how my "personal" life was affecting their children. The truth was that I had maintained the same level of professionalism I had always maintained; and my behavior, barring a few rocky days early on, had not changed in the least. I had sixteen other students and their respective parental units to attest to that fact.

These particular parents (mainly the mothers) were always encased in drama. They bitched about everything, every year. As a teacher you learn the different types of parents (once again, mainly mothers) very early on. There are the laid-back, support-you-no-matter-what moms. I love this kind. I fancy *myself* in this category. Then there are the helicopter moms. They are the ones who never leave the freaking school building, always keeping an eye on their beloved and including the teacher in every conversation regarding their child, down to the frequency of their bowel movements. I really don't mind these moms either. I learned early on that a mother's love sometimes knows no limits.

Similar to the helicopter mom, there is the worrier. This is the mom who sits across from the teacher at the table during the child's conference—the teacher thankful to have a conference that is probably going to be a breeze because the child is good and smart and on task and possesses all the other traits a teacher loves about a student—and once the mom is asked if she has any questions or concerns, she busts out a week's worth of math homework and declares, "I just don't understand why she keeps getting Bs on these papers. What is she doing wrong? What can I do at home? Why aren't you sending progress reports home every week so I can see exactly how she is doing on every single paper she does? I think you should be sending out a newsletter weekly instead of monthly. I need to know what is going on! Also, there is a boy in the class who is picking on her. Do you think she is being bullied? Should I have her start talking to the counselor? I've already gone to the principal with all of these concerns!" Oh, that B-scratch. Chill the hell out, sister! Nothing ruffles my feathers more than *that* mom. Well, not true. But we'll get to her in a minute.

There's the mom who could give a shit less about what happens at school, and the teacher finds herself wishing she could either shake the parent or adopt the child. Homework is never completed, phone calls are never returned and conferences are never attended. Basically, the teacher is 100 percent responsible for the success or failure of the student. It isn't fair, but it is an all-too-common reality. I do not like these parents either, but they are certainly not the bane of my existence.

Like this one: the mom who probably would fall into the "give a shit less" category given the fact that she spends most of her afternoons hitting the bottle and smoking cigarettes in her backyard while her children are at school. She has been *privileged* enough to be able to stay at home, maybe has a four-year degree, maybe just an associate's, but she is bored. Too bored to mind her own damn business, but never too bored to get a j.o.b.! So this chick makes it her full-time, alcoholic job to congregate with other yapping hens and destroy the lives of teachers at her child's school whom she deems unworthy of her affection. She is the mom who never figured out that the "popularity" game of high school was supposed to end upon graduation, and so she tries to carry it with her into adulthood—the elementary school being her playground and the staff, her targets. She has somehow gained enough street cred to usually be an esteemed member of the PTA, although it is unclear if she is truly liked or if, as back in high school, feared into positions of high rank.

This B-scratch usually gets her intoxicated, basc cake-faced friends together and, over margaritas, decides which teacher is "in" and which teacher is "out." Some of the outcast educators have earned their status by truly being incompetent or genuine douche bags. Others, like myself, get kicked out of the club for asinine, superficial reasons. And every year, the group of "cool kid" moms decides the fate of their child's teacher, so aside from the incompetent and the douche bags, it really is anyone's guess how their fate is to be determined. Most years, the bitches determine they want me on their "side". They have all requested me as their child's teacher and butter me up with praises and gifts, trying to outdo each other so that I will favor their little darling. I think because of my tragic history and the fact that I really am kind of a kick-ass teacher (It is my passion and it shows. I can't help it. I am not trying to brag, as I hate braggers, but my therapist encourages me to own my positive attributes, and I deem my job as a teacher one of those attributes! Stepping off soapbox.), most moms feel a touch of reverence for me.

Here is the catch though. Come to find out (from other teachers and parents, not from my own sense of self-worth, as my bragging ends when I describe the way I look or my physique. My mom tells me often, "You really don't know your own beauty,

Allie!"), a few moms don't like me because, in a nutshell, they think I am too pretty. Being one of the only single teachers in the school, and being relatively young, I have garnered attention from single, and sometimes married, dads. It seems every third year or so, the mommy bitch club wants me to pay for this fact, and they try to pick on me.

This year I gave an already volatile group an arsenal of ammunition. Damn it.

A few in the pack wanted a piece of the Nicholas Price action, and so they literally had to abandon their group in their attempt to gain access. I may not be worth getting voted onto the "cool kid" island, but apparently Nicholas Price was. Ha. They wished. The handful of Bs, however, used my little indiscretion as opportunity to try and sabotage me completely. I would love to say their efforts were fruitless, but there were several times during that last quarter of school in which I contemplated quitting and just living off of the hundreds of thousands I had already made off this whole ordeal. But alas, I would not let anyone—not paparazzi, not the bitchy parents, not Nick's mom, not Jen, not anyone—force me to sell out like some Kate Gosselin ho-bag who cared more about ugly fame and fortune than her own self worth and that of her children. I stuck the year out and even smiled wider, my cheesy grin reaching my eyes, every time I saw these bully women. They could have their chatter and their gossip. They could even make up lies and try to get me in trouble with my principal and, at the beginning of May, even with the superintendent of the Olathe public school system. But I was tenured. Bwahaha. The joke was on them!

I managed to pull my students along to the end of the school year, a crazy feat given the circumstances. Poor kids. After the press shenanigans for what seemed like days on end, security beefed up significantly, and there were certain sections of the playground in which children were no longer allowed to play because of the ease of access from those milling about. Three school resource officers were assigned to our school every day, but by late May, they really were no longer needed. Occasional gawkers with unprofessional cameras would swing by the school to snap a few pictures, but they really were no threat.

Not only did May bring the end of the exhausting school year, but it also brought the sticky humidity that promised a hot summer. The warmer it got, the more I was brought into sensory memory of my time with Nick and how much I truly missed him. Not a word had been spoken from him, and he had still not returned from Australia.

Despite my pleas online and through media outlets and the handful of letters I sent him (the one time I was actually thankful for nosy paparazzi was when his home address was leaked), he never contacted me. I knew I had done all I could do, and truthfully, I was a mother of a wonderful seven-year-old boy. Yes, I had screwed up royally, but I had apologized countless times and had tried to wrong my right. I needed to move on. A woman who can never manage to forgive herself is truly incapable of being forgiven. I had to forgive myself because I owed it to my son to show him what mercy and grace really looked like. I made a big mistake, and I did everything in my power to make it right. Once that was done, I needed to let myself off the hook in order to move forward. As a mother, we have no choice but to move forward if we want our children to grow up into mature, kind, genuine adults.

I do not wish to rehash Nick's mom's letter verbatim as it ran like a hamster on a wheel in my head for weeks after its printing, and I only recently found the courage to beat the hamster over the head with a mallet and bury him in the backyard. But the gist of it was that her young son had been taken advantage of and abused by a woman old enough to know better and that the identity of said woman really didn't matter. That she was just like every other money-grubbing, trashy American housewife with too much time on her hands and always expecting a handout.

Her main regret was that she hadn't appropriately taught her son how to spy someone so manipulative and conniving, what with his rise to stardom so sudden and unexpected. The letter was very generalized, placing me in the center of a pool of women "just like me" who do this type of thing to nice, unsuspecting people. Her words stung like a million bees, but being lumped into a group of, well, groupies stung even more. Apparently, Nick hadn't even managed to share any of my redeeming qualities with her. I suppose there were none to him. She never mentioned me by name, age, or location; and after that one article, the Price camp remained mum, in print, voice, and body. I wondered why it took her so long to say anything, as until Jen's story and my subsequent story hit the stands, no one from Nick's family made a peep. Apparently, they were just hoping to allow him to fall off the face of the earth and be rid of Hollywood and America forever. I guess Jen and I struck a chord in our revealing, and they felt like they had no choice but to counter with their own words.

My letter in response to Mrs. Price was full of guilt and pleading for forgiveness, but, like the letters I sent to Nick, I am fairly positive it was never opened. I truly feel that had it been opened, it would have made a difference in the level of communication I received, or lack thereof. Immediately following the big stories breaking, I obsessively checked Facebook and e-mail like some crazy lunatic, certain I would hear something. But as time wore on, I surrendered to the fact that while I may read about Nick's return to the States or to acting someday, I was most assuredly never going to hear from him personally again.

5

Sam and I maintained our typical Memorial Day routine with my family, a welcome getaway from the few months of always having to look over our shoulder to make sure no one was lurking around with a camera. It had become almost second nature to check my surroundings when I went anywhere: the grocery store, the bank, the library. Other than real-life daily living necessities, I never did anything social without Sam. The fact that my only real friend was no longer in my life had something to do with this sad existence, but honestly, I just didn't trust that anyone, barring close family and Terri, had my best interest at heart and so why would I wish to entertain them on an evening out, especially when my paranoia never truly dissipated when it came to leaving Sam unattended by me or my parents?

After our picnic at Chris's grave, Sam and I headed home from our relaxing weekend at the lake only to find a car parked in our driveway. At first I panicked, the details of the automobile not registering familiarity. I almost drove straight past the driveway until it clicked that the black Honda Pilot belonged to Greg. My stomach lurched into my chest.

When the shit hit the fan with Jen the previous summer, I was not surprised that I never heard a word from Greg. I figured he was pissed off enough at Jen for a bit of it to overflow onto me. It bummed me out a little, just because I was sure he didn't know my side of the story and also because he was Chris's best friend. We had grown close over the years, the previous few the opposite, as the single Allie seemed better suited to hang with just Jen, instead of both Jen and Greg together. For some reason when it was just Chris, Greg, and me, before Jen came into the picture, a three-person team worked effortlessly. And for a while after Chris's death, it seemed to work with Jen, Greg, and me; but once Jen started to turn a little freaky about the Nicholas Price thing, that seemed to end. For a while, when Greg stopped joining us, I concluded that it was probably just because he wasn't interested in our stupid girly talks about *Exemption* and the Hollywood stars accompanying the franchise thereof. After all, most of our interactions did exclusively begin to revolve around those very topics. But reflecting back, I almost wonder if it was Jen who put the kibosh on Greg tagging along with us.

As I cautiously pulled into the drive, cranking my neck to each side to make sure no paparazzi were around (habit and necessity, as how bad would it look to have *my* face and that of my betrayer's *husband* in the same shot?), I realized I was not going to be able to pull into the garage. Greg's SUV sat just enough to the left of the center line that for me to try and maneuver would likely end in a scraped side panel. I parked behind the truck, my back bumper barely clearing the driveway curb.

"Whose car is that, Mommy?" Sam asked from the back seat. He had been quiet since the drive home from the cemetery.

Each year, Sam had written his daddy a letter and laid it on his headstone during our Memorial Day picnic. What began as just scribbles slowly turned into picture drawings and, finally, well thought-out letters. This was the first year Sam did not want me to read the letter he had written to his daddy, and a part of me was saddened by his wishes for privacy. Sam was clearly growing up, and unlike the first six years of his life, his seventh had manifested itself in a slightly varied version of the first six. He was still my sweet, stubborn, manipulative, funny guy, sure. But he had also begun to pull back a little emotionally, not needing to talk to me quite as much, not caring when I couldn't play the Wii with him, actually preferring me to bow out of a game, proclaiming, "Mom, you are just too easy to beat, and I don't love Mario Kart anyway." While many of his friends' parents had allowed such things as Call of Duty to enter their homes, I was sticking to my guns (pun intended) and actually adhering to the video game ratings. Of course I was the most "uncool parent ever," but I didn't care. Because of this, Sam spent more time on my laptop, playing Minecraft and other games that encouraged interaction with friends. He even had his own headset so he could do whatever it is boys do when they play these games with each other. Had he been ten years older, he would have no doubt been pegged a "dweeb," but seven-year-olds can get away with computer games and headsets.

After Sam tore through his Mighty Kids Meal (a step up from the previous year's Happy Meal), he ran to a nearby trash can—throwing away the bag, the toy included (sigh)—and hollered that he wanted to check out the other "dead people" in the cemetery. I immediately corrected his word choice as I cringed, thinking, *Your dad is one to whom you are referring, Samuel! Have some respect*. But I just said, "Headstones, Sam. You are going to look at the other headstones."

Without acknowledging my correction, he skipped around the cemetery, at first pretending like he was in a maze or a race or something, dodging between headstones in a random pattern, making sure not to step where the casket may lie underneath (something I had taught early and reinforced yearly). Luckily and surprisingly, there were no other patrons visiting the cemetery at that time, though floral and patriotic evidence suggested they had been there recently.

As I watched Sam run around haphazardly, with no apparent rhyme or reason, I was struck by how much he had grown over the previous year. His legs, which I used to squeeze like raw pizza dough, showed no trace of baby fat and were long and stick-skinny. *When did he get so big?* When he was due for a haircut in May, he informed me that short hair was no longer cool and that he wanted to grow it out. I watched it flop into his eyes as he skipped past headstone after headstone. He was wearing a tank top—the only time I let him wear tank tops was at the lake, as I always thought they looked white-trashy—that revealed well-defined biceps and triceps, a product of Tae Kwon Do. I was admiring this little person, no longer my baby but always my baby, as he slowed to a walk and then stopped in front of a headstone.

It took a few seconds of him focusing on what he was apparently reading before he looked up and said, "Hey Mom, this says 5/1/05–5/1/05. I don't get it. What does that mean?"

I squinted at him through the sun, looking around to double-check our privacy and hollered back, "Sweetie, it means the baby died the same day he was born." I watched to see how my sweet boy would respond, and with a final glimpse back at the stone, he walked the few steps it took to reach the next one, stopping and reading. He continued in this manner for five more headstones, and when it was obvious he was going to probably finish the row, I decided it probably wouldn't hurt for me to take a peek at the letter he had written to Chris.

I scooted my way behind the big vase filled with flowers so that even if Sam looked up and saw me, if the distance between us alone wasn't enough to keep him from seeing what I was doing, the flowers would do the trick. I kept my eyes in constant shift mode, like I did when I was driving, transferring looks from the road that lay ahead to the road that lay behind through the rearview mirror. As I unfolded the torn out notebook paper, I was surprised by how short were the contents of the letter —just one paragraph reading,

DEAR DAD,

Its time to go to your grav agin. We come evry year. It is weerd write ing to a person I have not met. but mom sas its inportint so here you go. I gess I miss you. I wish I had a dad. Papa fishes with me but I think it wood be beter with a dad. I think I all most had a dad but then the guy got mad at mom and left and now all of these peepel hownd us and take pichers of us all the time. We are kind of famis. its weerd becase it is not a good famis. peopel at school tees me abowt it and tell me mom just wants to be famis. I dont beleev them but I dont no.ok so I hope it is good in hevin.

by

love sam

Obviously, I bawled like a baby after reading that. Man, these damn letters did it to me every time, but this time it was a different type of cry. This was nothing but a guilty cry. I quickly folded the paper back up just in time, as Sam turned from his perusing and headed back toward me. As soon as he reached me, he proclaimed, "I wanna leave now."

Had I been surer that my voice wouldn't quiver, revealing the shaky cry that I was thankful my big Jackie-O sunglasses were masking, I would have dug a little to find out about the sudden urgency to leave. But alas, I just nodded and collected my trash. He hadn't spoken since—until the foreign car appeared in the driveway.

"Uh, Sam, I think that is Mr. Greg's car. Do you remember Gre—"

"Oh yeah!" Sam beamed. He jumped out of the car and ran to the driver's side of the Pilot just as Greg swung the door open.

I cautiously got out of my car, gathering anything of value since the car would have to wait to be safely stowed away in the garage. I heard the familiar voice of my long-ago friend proclaim, "Hey, Sam, buddy!" and what sounded like a big squeeze as he said, "Oh my gosh, have you grown!"

I locked the doors, closed mine, and headed up the drive toward Greg and Sam, wearing a smile that could only be described as guilt-ridden caution. Had he come to yell at me? His demeanor toward Sam revealed nothing of the sort, but maybe he was pretending for Sam's sake.

As he looked down at Sam and ruffled his mop of hair, I took in the sight of him while I traversed the last few cautious steps. Greg looked good. Better than ever actually. He was, dare I say, buff? He was wearing baggy khaki cargo shorts and a white Nike Dri-FIT T-shirt that hugged his muscular arms. His calves had defined muscles that one might find on a runner or, better yet, an avid cyclist. His head was shaved close, but instead of looking like he was balding, it just looked like maybe he chose the style.

Unable to deny my presence within his personal space bubble, Greg forced himself to look up at me from Sam. He tilted his head, his kind eyes betraying any anger he may have felt toward me. My heart thumped hard in my chest as he spoke, barely above a whisper, "Hey, stranger," and turned his body from Sam, closing the gap between us and wrapping his muscular arms around me, pulling me close to his chest.

All the guilt and shame I had felt about the whole situation washed over me, and I remembered all the things I had done—from being a willing party to Jen's Nicholas Price obsession to lying to her and betraying her, to writing my side of the whole sordid story, which, of course, played out the marital struggles of Jen and Greg for all the world to read. (As we hugged, I wondered if he had read my book. I silently prayed he had not.) I felt like this act of mercy, this bear hug I had been given was a gift I never thought I would receive, never thought I deserved. I caved under the weight of it, becoming little more useful than a rag doll, as my body began to convulse in pent-up sobs.

Greg immediately pulled me back to look at my face, and through my tears I witnessed his puzzled features. "What's wrong?" he asked, with a sense of urgency. "What is it?" He looked panicked.

I was confused because it was obvious to me what was wrong. I had ruined his marriage! This fact was surprisingly not revealed to me by the media but rather through the ruthless gossipy teachers with whom I worked. I swear the school district network was almost as alive with gossip as was the *National Inquirer*.

Finally, I managed to say, "Are you kidding? I thought you'd never speak to me again for what I've done!"

Greg's eyebrows rose, his bare forehead unable to hide the inevitable signs of aging as it displayed a few wrinkles. "Allie, what are you talking about? You've done nothing wrong!"

Was he kidding me? Before I could respond, he pulled me back into an embrace, covering my mouth with his shoulder so that I was unable to respond. We stood there for a few seconds until Sam finally interrupted, "Um, hello? Can we go in, Mom?"

Shoot. I had forgotten to hit the garage door opener before I locked the car. I pulled away from Greg and fished my keys out of my purse, nodding toward the front door. "We'll go in that way."

Sam bounded ahead, his demeanor the polar opposite of what it had been as he'd sauntered to the car following his afternoon with death in the cemetery. Greg followed me down the front path and up the steps as I fumbled with the keys, trying to locate the correct one. No one used house keys any more.

A sweet memory came to my consciousness as I found the correct key and unlocked the door. When I was a kid, in sixth grade I believe, before garage door codes, I had received a bright pink *A* keychain in my stocking for Christmas with a key to our house attached. Oh, I felt so grown up and responsible. I had received a ton of presents that year, as I did every year; but that little key, the whole ensemble costing probably little more than five dollars, was my favorite gift. It was just such a sweet gesture from Mom, er, Santa, as being the youngest child I was *never* home alone. My mom was a stay-at-home mom who was always there when I got home from school, and if by chance there was some rare event that occurred (although I never remember it happening), I had three siblings who would be home before I was, waiting to take care of me. In other words, there was absolutely no reason why I needed my own key to the house, but I got one anyway, and it was the *best* gift I could have ever received—an invitation to a little independence.

The three of us entered the living room, and Sam immediately ran to the kitchen and opened the fridge. I swear that kid was growing at an unreasonable rate with how hungry he was all the time. My stomach was uneasy as I knew there was no way to have an idle conversation with Greg given the number of days that had passed since we had spoken in such a casual way. As I closed the door behind him, I took a beat to pray that he would let me off the hook soon in terms of his reasoning for making such an appearance at my abode.

I turned around and Greg was standing in the living room glancing around, possibly taking an informal inventory of any changes since he last graced my home with his presence. I asked, "Can I get you something to drink, Greg?"

He quickly turned to me and spoke, "Oh no, no. I don't want to intrude, truly. I just wanted to chat with you for a few minutes, if that's okay?" It was definitely a question, and I definitely had to answer, given the tilt of his head and the eyebrows raised expectantly.

As if it wasn't just a given that we could chat since I had directed him into my home, I coughed, "Well, yeah, I figured. Let's go into the kitchen. I'm sure Sam will be coming back in here to play a game or watch TV."

Like he was responding to my hunch, Sam came around the corner and plopped his butt down on the couch with two Ho Hos and a bag of Doritos. Greg and I went into the kitchen where I pulled out a chair for him and went to the fridge myself for a Diet Coke. "Are you sure you don't want anything?" I asked.

"Got a beer?" Greg responded.

Of course I happened to have just that, an entire twelve-pack actually, and decided his idea was a brilliant way for me to calm my nerves as well, so I replaced the Diet Coke with two Miller Lite bottles and brought them to the table, setting Greg's in front of him and my own in front of my place at the table before I pulled out my chair.

Almost as an instinct, Greg reached over and grabbed my beer, swiftly twisting the top off. I chuckled and thanked him. He responded, "I just know how much it hurts your hands to open these things."

Aw. How sweet. I took a long swig, allowing the crisp liquid to quietly burn my throat as it traveled down, promising impending warmth.

"Okay, so I guess I will just go ahead and start. Does that work?" Greg began.

I nodded and took another swig. My beer was half gone.

He cleared his throat and, as he looked down at his beer, I could sense frail nerves. "So… Allie… I'm sorry." As he finished his staggered comment, he looked up at me, his eyes filled with the salty liquid I had become so accustomed to shedding.

My first instinct was to reach over and hug this sweet man who was breaking down in front of my eyes, but my confusion as to why on earth he could possibly be sorry glued me to my place at the table where my eyes circled and fluttered open and close in an attempt to scour my brain for the possible meaning of such a declaration. What on God's green earth did Greg have to be sorry for? When it became obvious that he was tentative to speak again until he was let off the hook, I merely shook my head and responded, "I don't understand. For what?"

Greg's shaky voice let out an unfamiliar laugh as he said, "Allie, I let you down. I let Sam down. I basically abandoned the two of you when I promised Chris I would never, ever let that happen!"

The weight of his words and the mention of my beloved husband socked me in the gut. "Wait, what?"

"I said I let you dow—"

"No, not that, which you didn't do by the way, but I mean about Chris." I was trying to recompose myself.

"That I promised him that?" Greg asked, still not quite understanding that I obviously had no idea about this conversation he had with Chris, and I was becoming a little impatient at his lack of explanation about something that should be so obvious!

Slowing my heart rate by taking another, my last, swig of beer, I merely nodded.

He began again. "Of course I promised him that. I mean, what best friend wouldn't? It doesn't make me a saint."

My frustration got the better of me, and I stood up and walked toward the fridge to fetch another beer while I spoke, with as much composure as I could muster, "Greg, *when* did you have this conversation? I'm not concerned with what *you* said. I am concerned with what my husband said. I had no idea he had talked to you about this, and now I am just really interested to hear about a conversation my husband had that I never knew about. I want the details." I was exhausted.

"Oh." Greg raised his hands in understanding. If his face didn't betray him, he seemed a little hurt by my immense concern for my husband. I suppose it was just that this part of the conversation was probably not what he had planned on focusing on when he was playing out the scenario, and I obviously couldn't move on until it was dissected. "Okay, so when it was bad, like really bad, I think Chris knew he was going to die, he—"

I interrupted yet again. "Nope. Nope. Chris never knew he was going to die. It was a shock to all of us. He was supposed to have more treatment. He was in for the long haul. We had so many more procedures to do. He had no idea he wouldn't make it to those."

Greg tilted his head, giving me a kind smile, his eyes squinted. He stayed that way, wordless for what felt like a minute.

Not enjoying being stared at or scrutinized and, quite honestly, not understanding his hesitation at that moment, I picked up my second beer (that he had apparently opened for me without my noticing) and just shook my head, looking down at the table. When I set it back on the table and Greg had still not spoken, I merely quipped, "Nope" one last time for effect.

"Okay, so anyway"—he sat back in the chair and stared out the back window (was he avoiding my eyes?)—"I guess he was just thinking *if* something terrible did happen to him, he—"

"Like when he left the sperm." It was a statement, matter-of-fact, spoken just to solidify my point.

Hesitating and continuing to draw his eyebrows together, Greg spoke, "Yes, like with the sperm. But anyway, he and I had a conversation in the hospital about when—"

My eyes grew accusingly, threateningly, as if to say, *You claim he knew he was going to die one more time, I'm gonna punch you in the throat.*

Clearing his throat, he corrected, "*If* he were to pass away that he wanted to make sure I took care of you. He told me about an issue you all had been having with your hot water heater that the landlord wouldn't fix and…"

I thought back to those early years of marriage and the issues we had with our landlord never fixing anything. I hadn't thought about the hot water heater in years, a major source of tension for Chris.

Greg had continued talking, and I refocused as he finished, "…your car's oil change schedule and how he really wasn't comfortable with you driving back to Topeka any more in that car, that you should take his car or I should lend you mine. He also told me that your windshield wiper fluid needed to be refilled. I came up to the hospital and took care of that one immediately when you were staying up here one night. I don't know if you ever even knew that, did you? And by the way, you should really lock your car, Allie. Anyone could have gotten in there and stolen God knows what. I can't even tell you all the times one of my patients has had their car broken into. And you didn't even give a burglar a fight. I mean that night, of course, I was thankful *I* could get in, but still. Anyway, *did* you know I had done that?"

Note taken. I could not shake the image of my dying husband giving orders to make sure I was well taken care of. I started to cry, unaware that I was leaving a question hanging in the air between us unanswered.

"Oh, Allie, I am so sorry!" Greg was up on his feet, leaning over to hug me before I even quite understood why. "I didn't mean to make you cry."

As comprehension set in, I shook my head and pleaded, "Oh no, no. It isn't you, and I'm not sad at all."

Greg retreated back to his chair, his eyes never leaving my face, patient, waiting for more of an explanation.

"I just...I can't believe he thought of all of that stuff and thought enough to make sure I was taken care of and—"

"I tried, Allie. I really tried."

"Oh, no, no." I quickly shook my head. "Oh, Greg, I know you did. I remember now. You really *did* take good care of me. I am not saying you didn't, and I *will* be more conscientious about locking my car. I just can't believe he went through all of that for...well, for *me*. I'm hardly worth it." I looked down at my hands, realizing instantly how pathetic and martyr-ish I sounded. I hadn't meant to come across that way, but I *didn't* feel worthy of such affection.

"Oh, Allie, of *course* you're worth it! Chris knew that, and that's why I am here, I guess. Because in the beginning, after he died, I really was trying to take care of you, but then…well, how do I say this?"

My mind instantly grasped the shift in tone and impending conversation and snapped to high alert. I looked at Greg's eyes. He was looking at his beer. His hesitation made my gut clench.

"Um"—he looked into my eyes—"after a few weeks of me checking in on you every day, Jen started to get mad." He exhaled with force, as if a weight were being lifted off of his shoulders.

"Oh," I began, relieved that this thing he seemed so distraught over was really not a big deal at all. "Okay, I think that makes sense. I mean, that probably would get old having your husband always helping out someone else's wife."

Greg didn't look relieved or let off the hook. He continued, "Allie, here's the thing." He began squirming in his seat. "I have so much guilt over all of this." Greg ran his hand over his head, his eyes rolling up to the ceiling. He was obviously very uncomfortable.

"Greg, am I missing something here?" I asked, not enjoying the discomfort he was now bringing onto me.

After a long exhale and allowing his eyes to slowly fall back into my line of sight, he gave a kind, apologetic grin and continued, "Allie, this is all my fault." He instantly put his hand up to keep me from interjecting. "I should have warned you about Jen. Listen, I should have done this a hell of a long time ago, and I am so pissed at myself for letting this all happen and even more pissed for not manning up and making things right long ago. I guess the longer time went by, the more uncomfortable it became."

I was a statue—a clueless statue.

"I know it is no surprise to you that Jen and I had some problems, but I am not sure you know all of it, and I am not going to rehash all of my marital woes with you. But I will say this: Jen was incredibly, I mean *insanely* jealous of you. I didn't know all of this at first when we first got together and got married. I mean, things were great for a while. Sure, I was a little weirded out by the fact that she had dated Chris in the past. But Chris seemed to be completely over it, and honestly, so did Jen. We talked about it at length in the beginning, and she truly seemed to have such a healthy attitude about it all. And then you guys became friends, and everything was just…well, just perfect. Well, at least I thought it was."

Dun dun dun. I waited for the bomb I had yet to identify to drop.

"I think things didn't actually start to get weird until right after Chris died, when I was coming by quite a bit to check on you. One day, she just freaked out on me about it, accusing me of preferring spending time with you instead of her. It was completely ridiculous, of course, and I knew a lot of it was hormonal. Annabelle was little, and Jen had been kind of postpartum-y ever since she was born. I didn't think it was completely unrealistic for her to feel the way she felt, so I stopped coming by to help out. I don't know if you even remember that."

I didn't. In fact, I barely remember Greg at all during that time. I had been so self-absorbed. I remembered my family and Jen being there for me but had completely spaced off—or maybe taken for granted the fact that Greg was a constant presence during that time. I just nodded.

"Well, good. I mean, it doesn't seem like it affected you as much as it could have." He seemed a little hurt. This I did not understand. "Anyway, me stopping coming over seemed to make Jen happy, and so I didn't think much about it until a few months after, when the whole thing came up with Chris leaving you the…" Greg produced a nervous laugh. "Well, the 'sample' if you will. Jen came back from that night when you told her about it, and she was hot. I mean, *hot*…livid."

I racked my brain to recall the conversation Jen and I had about the urologist and the note and the sperm that Chris left for me to create our angel-baby Sam. Hot? Livid? That didn't make sense. That didn't match the way I remembered that conversation at all. Jen had been nothing short of ecstatic for me, elated! A little drunk, yes, but elated nonetheless.

I shook my head and began to explain that his rendition of that night was incorrect when Greg interrupted, "I know, I know. That isn't how she acted at all to you, was it?"

How did he know? I only managed, "Right."

"That's what she told me too. When I asked her how she had responded to you, praying that she hadn't made you feel bad about it, she called me something like a jackass and told me that she wasn't an idiot and that of course she didn't let you know how ridiculous she thought this whole idea was. She went on and on about how stupid it was that you would even consider such a thing and how your child wouldn't have a dad and on and on."

The weight of this confession almost knocked me back in my chair. I barely managed to hear the rest.

"Once I calmed her down and convinced her, or thought I had convinced her, that it actually was a really cool thing Chris had done and that you would make a phenomenal mom and that this was going to be a great thing, she broke down in hysterics and confessed a whole buttload of crap that I had no idea about."

Brace yourself, Allie.

Greg looked into my eyes. "Can I have another beer?"

I couldn't speak and just merely nodded, a little pissed that he was going to stretch this thing out. While he went to fetch his beer, I tried to mentally place myself back in that time period, the time when basically my entire world was like something out of a dream and I was still unclear as to what was reality and what was perceived reality. Losing the love of your life so tragically and so young means that for a good solid year everything in existence becomes a bit of a blur. Some days, like the day of Chris's funeral, the colors of the earth were more vibrant, vivid, and beautiful than anything I had ever seen, a color scheme I likened to that in heaven. On most other days, however, the earth took on more of a dull tint. Flowers were not as bright nor as fragrant. The grass was not the luscious green that I had grown accustomed to in my lifetime living in the midwest. It was muted and thin. The physical dimensions of the people and familiar objects in my life became shallow, almost in two-dimensions. Flat. My world, my senses—every single one of them were flat. What had I missed when I looked at Jen and Greg? What had my shortsightedness and my flat, two-dimensional angle on life allowed me to overlook about my very best friend on earth?

Greg sat back down, took a drawn-out pull from the beer, and began again. I sat back in my chair, sure I was about to embark on a long, strange ride. "It turns out that Jen had issues that went beyond postpartum. And most of her issues at that time revolved around you and Chris."

I swallowed hard, audibly. *What on earth?*

Politely noting my shock with a slight nod, he continued, "You see, Jen had never really gotten over Chris. Well, she had started to get over him, and then he walked back into her life that day at the bar. Remember? The night we met her?"

I didn't need to say anything. Of course I remembered. I stared at him, unwilling to blink, for fear I might not hear something of what he was saying.

"I didn't find out any of this until the whole thing with you having Chris's baby came up. For the most part, our relationship was good, and our marriage was good until that point. She never really let on that she wasn't over Chris. In fact, if anything she seemed the opposite. Kind of…what's the word? Apathetic? Yeah, apathetic toward him. I mean, really, she always acted like she couldn't care less about what Chris was doing. And then when you and she finally became friends, she was all about just hanging out with you. It was great! For a long time, it was really great, remember? We would all go out, and since she had become friends with you, I could hang out with Chris more. I mean it was awesome, wasn't it?"

He was looking for affirmation of his euphoric recall of that time in our lives. Of course, I remembered it the same way, so I nodded vehemently and finally spoke, "Yes, it was awesome! And no, I never noticed her pay any attention to Chris. I mean they teased each other a little, and she and I talked about it one or two times in the beginning, but it was about as normal a situation as could be. I thought."

"Right." Greg smiled. "That is exactly how I remember it. That's why it was so weird when she was breaking down about all of it after he died and you went in to that doctor. I still think some of it was her hormones, but basically, she told me that you had stolen the life she was supposed to have and that Chris had been the love of her life and the fact that he had died and you were getting all of the attention when really she had known him longer than any of us and had really been his first true love and… and…"

I felt like I was going to puke. Literally, like right there at the table, throw up the two beers I had inhaled and the nasty McDonald's I had ingested earlier. Barf all that crap up right there on the table in between us, which would have been specifically directed at my so-called friend Jen and our fake friendship.

Greg apparently sensed my queasiness as he reached over and grabbed my hand. "Oh my gosh, are you okay? I know this is a lot to take in."

I just sat there, willing the vomit back down my esophagus into my stomach where it should stay put and be digested just like everything else.

"Take your time processing this, Allie. Let me know if or when you want me to continue," he sweetly spoke, "or if you want me to leave." Greg laughed a nervous laugh.

I waited a few seconds until I was sure the vomit had listened to my command, and then I decided it was best to just get it all over with and out of the way. "Go ahead, Greg. I'm fine" was all I could get out in an effort to make sure I could breathe.

After asking me at least two times if I was sure I wanted him to continue, he did begin again. "So I don't remember where I was, but basically, Jen confessed a ton of stuff that first night and actually several days in a row afterward. A few conversations were in person, but a lot of it was over e-mail and some of it was brought up in counseling. I had to sort through a ton of Chris's stuff she had saved and letters he had written her back when they were dating. She kept *everything*, and apparently, I found out through counseling, she looked through it all often. Here is the hard part though, and the part that I have played over and over again, because really it would seem that all that stuff was enough reason for me to leave her. The problem was that she *wanted* to feel differently. She knew she was wrong to keep harboring these feelings for Chris, and deep down she really *did* love being your best friend. I mean, I truly believe that she loved you dearly, but she struggled with it because she wanted to hate you so much because of Chris. She was caught between a rock and a hard place."

I tried to absorb his words.

"Of course what we discovered in counseling was that this was about way more than Chris or you or me or Annabelle or anyone other than Jen. Jen's issues were with Jen. Sure, they manifested themselves in ways that affected all of us, but the root of it was that she basically hated herself. Well, still does, I imagine."

I felt the vomit again, only this time it wasn't being pushed up to the surface by shock, but by the sadness and regret with which it was laced.

"Anyway, that was the beginning of our issues as a couple. That was also when Jen started seeing a counselor by herself. And things got better for awhile, or at least they seemed to. She seemed to get over the fact that you were going to have Chris's baby and even seemed genuinely happy for you at times. I think the fact that she was your best friend, the one you always called, made her feel good about herself, and it became easier for her to overlook the fact that you had married the love of her life." Greg looked down as he finished this thought. I felt so sorry for him as I watched the embarrassment dance across his shadowed face. What a reality to face. Your wife admits she is in love with another man—your best friend, no less.

This time I reached across and grabbed Greg's hand. I could feel my eyes dampen as I said, "Greg, I am so sorry you have had to hear all of these things. I had no idea."

His head continued to hang, and then I saw it. One little drop of liquid fell from his cheekbone onto the table. My heart broke for this sweet man. I rose from my chair, still holding his hand, and knelt on my knees, wrapping my arms around his neck and pulling him close. "Oh, Greg, I am so sorry." And I was. Oh, was I ever sorry for what Jen had put him through. I was sorry for my part in the whole Nicholas Price fiasco. As if going through the letdown of your wife being in love with someone else one time wasn't enough. Then he obviously went through it again when she became infatuated with Nicholas Price. And then this sweet broken man didn't even have his best friend to talk to about all these slights, all these acts of emasculation.

Greg shook a little as a few sobs escaped; and then, wiping his eyes with the back of his hand, he lifted his head so our heads were two inches apart. Through unshed tears, he whispered, "No, Allie. I'm sorry. I let you down." With that, his head dropped again, and the sobbing commenced.

After a good ten minutes of tears shed on my kitchen table from both Greg and myself, and an interruption from Sam asking what we were having for dinner, only to be turned away at the sight of two crying grown-ups, the rest of the story came out.

Over the previous years Jen battled constantly with jealousy and envy toward me, and her marriage to Greg was a never-ending battle as well. What she had told me about their fertility issues was indeed part of their struggle, but it hadn't gone down exactly as she had portrayed. Apparently, she had been put on antidepressants after being diagnosed with anxiety and depression, and she had quit taking her medication at various times, which always sent her into a tailspin. Her ups and downs took such a toll on their marriage and their efforts to become pregnant. In addition, Greg's pride had taken a major hit, and in one of their heated battles, it came out that one of Jen's major motivations for adding to their family was so that she could have one more child than I had. With that, Greg decided that bringing another life into such a tumultuous home was not a good idea and called it quits on their efforts to try and conceive. Of course, this led to even more of Psycho Jen.

Everything else about Nicholas Price was the same as I already knew. Surprisingly (although not really, considering the nasty graphic details Jen had already revealed to me), her story matched with what Greg told me about that time period. There were a few tidbits I didn't know, like how when I was in Omaha she basically stayed awake the whole weekend, freaking out about why I hadn't called her and wondering aloud if I had seen Nicholas Price. I guess after I told her that I had met him she basically went apeshit and told Greg that I was probably screwing him and that I was such a slut that I would do just that. She built up a story so big in her head about it (which was crazy considering the fact that the truth was actually a lot more damaging to her ego than her own story in which I was a horrible, skanky, groupie slut) that it was during that weekend that Greg decided he was going to leave her.

They had a huge blowup that weekend in which he basically told her it was over. He told her that she was completely crazy for thinking the things she was thinking and obsessing about the whole thing with Nicholas Price and that he was done being the only man alive, it seemed, with whom she wasn't completely head over heels in love (a sock-in-the-gut irony). I guess by the time the proverbial "shit hit the fan" that night at my house, when Nick appeared, Greg had already contacted a lawyer and was in the process of filing for divorce, a little detail that Jen, in her blind oblivion, had no clue was coming.

She had come home from my house an absolute wreck and expected Greg to sit down with her while she dealt out every single detail of the night. Greg said that he was sure Jen thought he would be on her side and gang up on me too, especially since he had such ill will toward her behavior regarding Nicholas Price, but what she got instead was an announcement that he had filed for divorce. Apparently her breakdown was just yet another confirmation of what needed to happen.

Greg concluded, "I'm just sorry, Allie. Now that I know what I know about Jen, I never should have let her talk me out of being there for you. I should have stuck up for you. I should have warned you or told you about her feelings toward Chris. I knew she wasn't a true friend, and I failed to tell you that. And now all of this has happened, and I wish so much that I could have done something to prevent her from going forward with all this stuff to the media, but I was just so done with her that I didn't really care at that point. And I should have cared. I at least should have cared long enough to talk her out of doing anything to further hurt you, but honestly, she had been all talk up until that point, and I didn't think she would actually go through with contacting the press about you. And then Annabelle told me that she did and that she was just going crazy about the whole thing. Then when it came out and you wrote what you did, Anna told me about that as well. Great job, by the way! Who knew you were such a writer?" Greg gave me a halfhearted grin. "Anyway, I wanted to come talk to you several times, but the longer I went silent, the more scared I became. So I stayed silent and allowed our lives to just drift apart, and I am sorry, Allie. I am sorry I didn't fulfill my promise to Chris. I am sorry I didn't take care of you…back when he died, and every day since. I'm sorry." He began sobbing again.

I went to him, embracing him as before, shushing his tears, and whispering, "Greg, it's okay. You did nothing wrong. This is not on you. This is not. It's on me. Shhh. You are fine, Greg."

This time, when he wiped the tears away and looked up at me, something was different. It was the same pair of glossy eyes, the same smooth skin, the same thin lips, not smiling yet not frowning. But something was different. Something inside *me* was different, and it was just for a split second, like an electric current that instantly ran down my body from my head to my toes. Its shock was so abrupt that I literally jerked backward just a bit.

Greg must have also sensed this shift in something as his glistening eyes widened while remaining locked on mine. My eyes remained locked on his. Why were my eyes locked on his? Why didn't I just turn away?

6

It was a second, two or maybe more, before the cylinders in my brain made the connection about what was happening. By the time they connected, it was almost too late as my eyes began to close and I felt Greg's lips brush against mine. Just as quickly as the connection was made, the dorsal medial frontal cortex part of my brain kicked into gear, and I yanked my head back. At that exact nanosecond, Greg did the same, his eyes wild with panic.

"Oh my gosh!" I blurted, probably too loudly but thankfully not loud enough to rouse Sam in the other room.

"Oh man. Um...I...um...I'm sorry?" Gregg responded. A question, for sure. *A question? Why did he inflect at the end?*

I sat back in my chair, stunned, unsure. Neither of us spoke for an eternity. Like literally, Adam and Eve were planted in the garden, all the stuff happened in Egypt (whatever actually happened in Egypt—I never was too keen on the Old Testament), and John the Baptist showed up and ate his bugs. Jesus came and went, the early churches started, the world spun out of control, the second coming, Armageddon, gnashing of teeth, etc. All of it happened in the span of time that Greg and I sat motionless looking at each other and then looking down. Looking at each other, looking down again. *But it was a question.*

Finally, I spoke, "So you are sorry?"

Greg cleared his throat and paused, obviously wanting to get whatever he said next right. "Well, I don't know."

"You don't know?" *So it was a question. Ha!*

"No. I don't."

"Why not?" I didn't dare say more than a few words, for fear that my shaky voice might betray the stance I obviously had to take on this whole thing.

"Well, I mean, I should be sorry, I think. Shouldn't I?"

Oh no, buddy. You are not turning this around on me! I stayed still, unwilling to give him an inch, lest he take a mile. A mile of what, I was unsure.

When I didn't waver, Greg fidgeted in his seat and said, "Look, I better go."

Crap! What? Now? But I didn't say anything. I didn't know what to say. Should I have told him not to go? Should I have walked him to the door, telling him to not let the door hit him where the good Lord split him? What was the correct thing to do when your dead husband's best friend just tried to kiss you and you weren't sure if you actually tried to kiss him back, if not physically than mentally?

The look on my face must have screamed something at him because he seemed prompted to explain himself. "I don't know what to do here, Allie." My name on his lips, the lips that just brushed mine, the lips I had never looked at seductively in my life—until now. "I mean, I suppose I should be sorry for kissing… well, almost kissing you, but the truth is…oh God!" He ran his hand over his head again, like someone would do who had hair, only it didn't make much sense given the fact that his head was shaved so close. He squirmed in his chair, and his eyes darted all around the room looking everywhere—everywhere except at me.

Finally, he caught enough courage and, looking just over the top of my head, blurted, "Allie, the truth is that I want to kiss you, and I have wanted to for a long time. I would feel guilty about this fact since Chris was my very best friend, except for the fact that I think he would bless it." And it was out.

I choked on my own spit, coughing a laugh that was filled with cynicism. "Oh really?" I patronized. "Chris would bless that? Ha!" I was kind of being a bitch, but I had no idea what else to be.

Then, with what appeared to be anger flurrying into his eyes, he gazed directly at me and through gritted teeth said, "Yes, Allie, really. I know he would because when we were talking in the hospital about me taking care of you, he told me that he wished you had picked *me* that night at the bar instead of *him!*"

Mind blown. Spinning. Vomit arising again. *What the fu—*

"Now, just wait a second before you jump to any conclusions. He just said that because he knew he was going to die and he hated seeing what it was doing to you. He hated the fact that you had to endure his death, and he loved you so much that he wished he could have saved you the pain and heartbreak you were going to go through. And I guess he thought I was a pretty good guy and would be a good catch for you."

I was hot. Burning red, steaming mad. "Stop saying that, Greg! Stop saying he knew he was going to die because he didn't. That's a lie! He had no—"

"Damn it, Allie, *Yes. He. Did.* He *did* know. He *did!*" Greg was shouting at me. Why was he shouting?

My head shook violently. Chris didn't know. He didn't because I didn't know, and I knew everything about his health and treatment and cancer and…wait, did I? Was there something he didn't tell me?

I felt a hand on my right arm and then another on my left, but my vision was too blurred to see the person in front of me. *Who is at my house again? What day is it? Where am I?* Then what I assumed were those same arms encircled my neck and pulled me close to a warm muscular chest where I heard the wild beating of a heart.

Greg whispered, "Allie, I'm so sorry to yell. I'm so sorry. Chris did know though. He did know he was going to die. The doctors had told him very early on that he didn't have long and the treatment he had was only done to bring you peace of mind so that you would know he had tried everything he could, but he knew he wasn't going to make it. His death was not a shock to the doctors, sweetie. It wasn't."

Thump. Thump. Thump. The heartbeat slowed over the next five or ten minutes as I just leaned against it, my mind replaying those last few months of Chris's life once, twice, three times. He had known. He had known all along and pretended not to know, right along with me. He pretended to fight as I was fighting. He talked about the future just as I did and shared in my dreams for our "tomorrows," and yet he knew he wouldn't be here for our tomorrows. He knew. He knew and I didn't. How come I hadn't seen it?

"Mom, I'm hungry…er, um, never mind." Sam was standing at the entryway to the kitchen, and as soon as I heard his familiar voice, I jolted upright.

He was just turning around to walk back into the living room, obviously uncomfortable with what he was seeing when I composed myself enough to say, "Sam, it's okay. Come here, baby. What do you want to eat?"

He didn't turn around, only kept walking to his room, slamming his door. *Crap!*

As I stood to follow, Greg announced, "I should leave."

Without giving him another glance, I merely replied, "Yes, you should" and headed toward my sweet boy's room.

As I knocked quietly, I whispered, "Sam? Can I come in?" I heard the front door open and close and knew Greg was gone. What was the pang of regret I felt in that instance? Why was it there? I didn't know, but I did know that whatever it was, it was secondary to the pang of regret for what Sam saw, or thought he saw. It was secondary to the pang of regret encompassing the realization that while I was selfishly clinging to my husband's recovery, I had failed to see his reality.

I knocked again, and this time, when the response was again silence, I let myself in. Sam was lying on his bed, the covers pulled up over his head. I went to him immediately. "Sweetheart? What is it?" *I* knew what it was, but I was unclear about what *he* actually thought it was.

A little more prodding and he finally looked at me with the same tearstained cheeks that I had caressed so many times and spoke, "Mr. Greg, Mom? Really? There are a million guys in the world and you choose Daddy's best friend?"

"Oh, sweetie," I shushed. "No, it isn't like that at all. In fact, he was only hugging me because he had reminded me of when Daddy was sick. And I don't know. It hit me all over again, and I started crying. I think he felt bad."

Sam looked up at his ceiling, pondering. Then, after wiping his cheeks with his comforter, he finally said, "Okay. Sorry. I just...I just..."

"Shhh," I consoled again. "No need to apologize."

"Let me finish!" he blurted with a hint of anger.

"Whoa, buddy. No, sir. You do not talk to me that way. I know you are upset, but you do not need to be disrespectful."

"No, I mean, please let me finish what I was saying."

I nodded.

"I just don't know if it is Mr. Greg that bothers me or really if it's you dating anyone that bothers me. I thought I would like it, I mean, when you finally decided to get a boyfriend. Actually, for a long time, I wanted another daddy. But now, I don't know."

He was still searching the ceiling, and while everything in me wanted to push for further information, I knew he needed to come up with the words himself—when he was ready.

"I don't know. Maybe Mr. Greg would be a good choice. I mean he's always been so nice to me..."

I began to shake my head, which Sam did not notice until he peeled his eyes off of the ceiling and onto my face.

"What? Why not?"

"Nope, Sammy. Not Mr. Greg. He is just our friend."

"Why? Do you not find him handsome?" Sam asked.

With my head still shaking away the impossibility, I replied, "Nope. He is plenty handsome, just not gonna happen."

"Why not? What's wrong with him? I think he is pretty awesome!" He was getting heated again. What was with this kid? First he was pissed that I was hugging Greg, and then he was pissed that I wasn't interested in him.

"Nothing, Sam. He is awesome. Just not for me."

"Well, I think he would make a pretty good dad."

"Sam, I am so confused. Just a second ago, you were freaking out that I was going to make him my boyfriend, and now you are freaking out that I'm not."

Sam released a long, heavy, fatigued sigh, rolling his eyes and responding, "Mom, I didn't say he has to be your boyfriend. I am just saying that it wouldn't be the worst thing, I guess."

I knew this rollercoaster was never-ending, so finally, I just kissed the top of his head and said, "All right, buddy. If something ever comes up, I will let you know. But in the meantime, I'm going to go make you some mac and cheese. You just sit tight here, and I will come get you when it is ready."

As I made my way to the kitchen, I stopped in the living room to see if Greg had actually left, which he had. I cooked up some mac and cheese, and when I went in to get Sam, he was sound asleep. Poor sweetie. If I was a better mom, I may have put the mac and cheese in the fridge for Sam to enjoy later; but alas, I am not a better mom, and I ate the whole stinkin' thing myself, right out of the pan.

Instead of retreating to my own room for bed that night, I scooted my baby boy over to one side of the bed and slid in next to him, wrapping him into my body. Oh, how I adored that little man, growing up too fast. I was just dozing off at around 10:00 p.m. when I heard a strange buzzing sound coming from the direction of the kitchen.

Startled, I climbed out of bed and made my way toward the foreign noise, only to realize as I approached that it was my cell phone buzzing. Apparently, I had switched it to vibrate. *Who on earth is calling at this hour?* Long gone were the days of drunken residents calling in the middle of the night for a sober ride home.

I didn't recognize the number and thought about just dismissing it when something inside told me to answer. Attempting to sound irritated, I whispered, "Hello?"

"Allie, hey. It's Greg. I'm sorry. Did I wake you?"

I contemplated exaggerating my state of slumber but decided to spare him. "No, I just laid down actually." My volume resumed to a normal level.

There was silence for a split second. I thought maybe he had hung up. Then he said, "Look, Allie, I am so sorry. Truly sorry—"

"No, it's okay, Greg," I interrupted. "Truly. It is all fine."

More hesitation and then, "Okay. Well, how is Sam? I feel terrible."

"Ha. Actually he is fine. He was confused a little, but then… funny story…he went from freaking out that I was going to date you to wanting me to date you. So weird." I chuckled.

"Really?" he sounded surprised.

"Yeah, well, he is young…and confused. But I assured him nothing like that was going to happen."

"Oh," Greg mustered. I could tell I had hurt him. "Well, listen, I'm glad things are okay with Sam. I will let you go. Just do me a favor, okay?"

"Okay? What's up?"

"Will you call me when you need something? Anything? I mean, I know you are pretty self-sufficient and you have your family, but I am close. And so if there is something you can't do, will you call me? Please?"

"Of course. Thanks, Greg. Truly."

We hung up the phone, and I went back to bed in my own bed, unable to sleep. Had I hurt Greg's feelings? Obviously, I had hurt his feelings, but was it irreparable? Was I as convinced of my convictions to never date him as I had alluded to on the phone? Sometime in the night or early morning, I finally dozed off, thinking of Greg…and me…naked in my bed. My dreams followed my thoughts. I awoke with panic and guilt, yet I longed to climb back into my dream.

7

The guilt continued into my morning routine of making coffee and plunking down Eggo waffles for Sam. It encircled me as I hopped online to read the recent news on Yahoo! and as I munched on a granola bar. As I put on my swimsuit, gathered towels, and lathered Sam up with sunscreen, it gnawed at my psyche.

When we were ready to go to the local pool (a feat that is exhausting before we even leave the house what with all the lotion and toys and towels and ID cards to locate and tote), I opened the door into the garage and pushed the opener. Nothing happened, so I pushed it again. Still nothing. After five or six more hits of the button and sweat dripping down my brow, my mind immediately went to calling my dad, and then *his* face flashed in my mind. I could literally tell I was blushing at the thought of Greg.

After calming a sulking little boy with promises of heading to the pool as soon as the garage door was fixed, I sat on my bed, staring at my cell phone. Was this a sign? A God thing? I mean, I totally could call my dad and ask for guidance or even run over to the neighbor's for assistance. And of course, there were always garage door people who would come fix it for a fee, but this seemed like an omen. I mean it happened merely a few hours after Greg had made me promise that I would contact him if I needed anything.

I quit stalling and looked at the most recent number in my call log and pushed it, my heart racing. After three rings, I was sure it would go to voicemail, and so I breathed a sigh of relief. But just then, the phone was picked up, revealing Greg's very alive voice. "Hello?" He sounded a little surprised, maybe skeptical.

"Um, hey. Uh, Greg, this is Allie."

"I know. What's up, Allie?"

"Well, funny thing actually. You may try being careful what you ask for. Ha." I was clearly nervous. I wanted to hear him chuckle or something to put my nerves at ease, but when he just waited silently, I continued. "So, um, I am so sorry to bother you, but you told me to call you. And as it turns out, my stupid garage door isn't working."

"What do you mean isn't working?" was all he asked.

"Well, I keep hitting the button, and it won't lift up," I explained.

"Okay, well I am at the office until noon. Wait, didn't you park outside last night? Are you able to at least get out if you need to?"

I was, of course. But I am the type of person who, when something is amiss or broken or lost, I cannot move on with life until it is rectified, fixed, or found. I think even Sam knows this about me, which is why he hadn't demanded that we go to the pool anyway, broken garage door and all, because he knew I would just be stewing about it until it was fixed. "Well, yeah. I mean, Sam and I were going to go to the pool, but since the door is broken…" My voice trailed off.

"Well, heck, go to the pool, and then I will be by around twelve thirty. Does that work?"

I hesitated, but I knew it was silly to wait around until it was fixed. "Okay, sounds great. I'm sorry, Greg. Really, I hate to bother y—"

"Hey, stop. I really truly *want* to help you. I am so glad you called. Don't think another thing about it, Allie. Okay?"

"Okay," I said with a roll of my eyes. "Thanks so much. Really."

"Of course. I'll see you soon, okay?'

We hung up.

The trip to the pool consisted of "Hey, Mom, watch this!" and me ruminating about my afternoon with Greg. Why was I so weirded out about this whole thing? Yesterday I hadn't had a thought of the man, a fact that had been consistent for several months. But within twenty-four hours, I couldn't get him off my mind. I was for sure losing it. In fact, in all the years I had known Greg, never once had I ever thought of him as anything but Chris's best friend, Jen's husband, and my own friend. Nuts.

Of course, I was a drowned rat after a couple of hours at the pool, so I convinced Sam to head home an hour before noon so I could freshen up a little. (Of course, I didn't tell Sam that was the reason!) Back at the homestead, I instinctively pressed the garage door button on my sun visor as we pulled into the drive; and as the door went up and I crept forward, it hit me. *Oh crap! It isn't broken!*

I slammed on the breaks, my mind racing with a prospective plan. Had Sam been paying attention that the door went up? I flashed my eyes to the rearview mirror to see if he was even paying attention. He wasn't. He was looking out his window at the neighbor's kids. I quickly pushed the button again to close the door when the peanut gallery chirped up, "Why are you shutting it?" and then a half beat later, "Hey, I thought the garage door was broken!" *Crap! Busted.*

"Oh my gosh! You're right, Sam. Look, I don't think it is broken anymore!" I hit the button again, secretly hoping it would not rise up again, to no avail. The damn thing made a fool of me. "Huh" was all I mustered as I sat staring in disbelief.

As we pulled into the garage and unloaded the car, I knew I had no choice but to call Greg and tell him the (not-so) good news. A sense of dread filled my heart as I realized I had been holding onto some subconscious fantasy of our reunion for the previous few hours. I finally had something to be excited about, and the entire thing was foiled. I dialed his number, somewhat hoping to get a voice mail, but he picked up on the third ring.

"Hey, Greg, it's Allie."

"Hey, Allie!" He sounded every bit as excited as I had felt earlier in the day.

"Hey, um, so get *this*. My garage door is working!" I tried to sound chipper—maybe a little too chipper.

Silence followed. It was uncomfortable silence, so I continued with "So I guess you don't have to fix it."

Greg cleared his throat, obviously contemplating his own course of action, and then replied, "Well, huh. That's weird. Well, obviously there is something wrong with it for it to have quit working and then started working again. I probably should still take a look at it. I mean, if you want…if that would help…" He trailed off.

Hooray!

"Yeah, um, that would be great actually. I would hate to wake up tomorrow and have it not work again. But only if you are sure." I was relieved.

"Oh, of course! I'll be there in a little over an hour."

The date, er, appointment was back on. I quickly cleaned up, fed both Sam and myself (what little I could eat), and sat waiting on the couch with a painstaking forty minutes to spare. As the clock ticked nearer to twelve thirty, I became an anxious mess at every car I heard chug down the street. And then finally, at twelve thirty on the dot, I heard a car slow down in front of the house, a car door open and then close. Greg had arrived.

In an attempt to appear breezy, I remained on the couch pretending to watch something on television when the knock at the door ensued, in the off chance that Greg could or would spy me through the window. After waiting a beat, I casually got off the couch and shuffled to the door. When I opened it, there he was, still in his scrubs. Damn, he looked good in scrubs.

"Hey," I greeted as casually as my shaking voice would allow.

"Hey yourself, Allie. How's it going? Where's the little man?"

"Oh, he is in the backyard. A neighbor got him a backstop thing for baseball because he thinks he wants to start playing. Of course, the season is already underway, but he may try to pick up fall ball." We were standing in the living room, looking everywhere but at each other.

Greg headed to the back window. "Really? I *loved* baseball as a kid! In fact, I had a scholarship to play for KU, but then pre-med stuff took up too much time and energy, so I only played for a semester."

"Really?" I sounded as shocked as I was. "I mean, what? Had no idea. How cool." I really couldn't picture it, but it was totally sexy.

"Yeah, man. In fact, I was so hoping Annabelle would get into softball. Remember she used to be such a tomboy? But after half a season of her playing in the dirt, she proclaimed, 'Daddy, this sport is too dirty. I wanna quit.' Of course, I informed her that it wouldn't be as dirty if she kept her ass out of the dirt—well I didn't say that exactly—but she was bound and determined to quit. I told her she had to finish out the season, but then Jen went behind my back and pulled her off the team. So much for teaching the kid commitment. Hmm, what a shocker."

I held up my hand to stop him. "Um, Greg, listen. I can't, um, I can't bash Jen, and I *really* don't want to hear you bash her either. As much pain as she put me through...and you through...I still have a tiny place in my heart for her—"

"Really?" He looked totally dumbfounded.

"I know. It seems crazy, but Jen and I had a lot of good in our friendship, and no matter how hurt I am or how many times I have wanted to make her pay, I finally decided it just hurt me to hold so much anger toward her. And honestly, I kind of feel sorry for her. What a lonely existence."

"Wow, Allie. I don't know what to say. That is so incredibly big of you. But that shouldn't be a surprise. You have always taken the high road." His eyes burned into mine for the first time since he had arrived. I wanted to look away. Like a train wreck or a drunk girl twerking on a dance floor, I couldn't look away.

Greg inched closer. Instinct told me to step back, but my feet were simply glued to the living room floor. Closer. His face a foot from my face. Closer. Six inches. Closer. Three inches. Closer. Eyes closed. Lips ready.

Bam! Something slammed into the sliding glass back door. Holy hell. Eyes open, lips agape, faces two feet apart, I turned toward the kitchen. Had Sam hit the door on purpose? Crap. When I reached the door, Sam's concerned face was staring back at me. I slid open the door. "Sam, what happened?"

Tears filled his eyes. *He knew! He saw!* "Um, I'm so sorry, Mommy! I didn't mean to hit the door. I was just practicing my hitting, and I hit it really hard. I'm sorry!" He broke down into a full-out sob just as I was silently praising Jesus he had seen nothing. I went to him, wrapping my arms around his sweet little sweaty neck.

"Baby boy, you are fine. Nothing broke. It is fine, just maybe scoot out toward the fence a little, okay?" He shook in my arms as he nodded. "Oh sweet pea, I love you. You're not in trouble. I know it was an accident." He was still shaking.

A throat cleared behind our embrace, and Sam withdrew, looking to see who had come. He quickly wiped his eyes when he saw Greg and smiled.

Greg said, "Hey, champ, man alive that was a hard hit! I had no idea you were such a ball player."

Sam's smile widened, revealing his latest hole that had once housed a baby tooth. I let him go so he could welcome Greg with a hug.

They chatted for a moment before Greg asked if Sam would mind playing a little baseball in the back with him. Of course, Sam was on cloud nine, as was I. Greg looked at me with a hint of mischief and adoration. There was no embarrassment or anxiety for what almost happened the moment before. In fact, at the moment he seemed like the most self-assured man on earth. "Hey, Al, do you mind if I get to the garage door in just a little bit and play with Sam for a while?"

I shook my head, grinning like a dumb schoolgirl. "Of course not."

"But Mom, you can't play with us," Sam said and then turned to Greg. "She really doesn't have any idea how to play baseball and she throws like a girl."

Greg chuckled and retorted, "No, no girls allowed! She has to watch. Or maybe she can be our cheerleader." Greg looked over at me with a sly, seductive smile.

The heat rose to my face as my eyes widened and I looked down at the ground. "Uh, nope. I'll go inside and make some lemonade." I scurried to the house without taking my eyes off of the grass in front of my feet.

Greg spent the entire day at our house. After playing with Sam for over an hour in the back yard, he checked out the garage door situation, coming up empty-handed. We then took turns racing Sam in Mario Kart until dinner time, during which we ordered a pizza. The longer he stayed, the calmer I became. It felt nice, comfortable even, to have him there. It was as if he already belonged, an observation that left me both giddy and alarmed.

After dinner, Sam retired to his room to play Legos, an activity that would have included Greg had I not put the kibosh on it. Selfishly, I wanted some adult time and maybe a few alcoholic beverages to ease any tense nerves that remained. When Sam sulked back to his room to play alone, I grabbed a couple of Miller Lites (my staple) and invited Greg onto the back patio to enjoy the nice, if not somewhat sticky, evening.

Once we settled into some small talk and had a couple of beers, the inevitable became invited. With a sexy smirk, Greg said, "So, um, that was pretty intense earlier, huh?"

I felt good, and the idea of flirting felt good. As I grinned with tight lips, I looked down at my beer and circled the bottle opening with my finger. With my chin still tilted downward, I looked up into Greg's eyes and responded, "Yeah, well, I have no idea what you were trying to do."

"Ha! Oh really? So you just normally close your eyes and purse your lips when someone moves closer?"

"I did not!" I shouted as I chucked my bottle cap at him, hitting him square in the chest.

"You did too!" he laughed, scooting his chair around the corner so we were side by side.

"How would you know? Why weren't your eyes closed?" I looked back down at my beer, unable to reach his gaze for fear that something might happen—something that I wanted to happen but of which I was still afraid, despite my loose muscles.

"Because I had no idea why your eyes were closed! I was just coming closer to get an eyelash off your eyelid."

He sounded so serious for a split second that I blushed, wondering if I had totally misjudged his intention. When my eyes widened and met his, I knew immediately he was toying with me. I punched him in the shoulder, which was extremely hard and buff. Resisting the urge to squeeze it, I looked back down at my beer. In the same instant, I felt his warm fingers underneath my chin, tugging upward.

"Oh no, wait, it's still there," he whispered and began moving his face toward mine, holding my chin steady so I couldn't pull away. As he got so close that I could feel his hot breath and his eyes had to visibly move side to side to look into each of mine, he moved his thumb from my chin to the soft part beneath my eye, where he swiped. "Got it," he said.

"You are full of it!" I accused.

"Am I?"

My throat closed, so all I could do was nod. Was this really going to happen this time? Was it okay? Was it wrong? I didn't know, and I really don't think that at that moment I cared. I just continued to look from his eyes to his mouth, willing his lips to reach mine. As slowly as he could, he inched his face closer, his eyes never leaving mine. Just as slowly, he wrapped his hand around the back of my neck.

Greg then quietly commanded, "Close your eyes, Allie."

I did as I was told.

8

It was nice. I didn't see fireworks, but I wasn't grossed out either. His lips were soft, if not a little on the dry side, and his tongue was completely appropriate, entering and exiting at all the respectable times. My heart did skip a few beats, but nothing like when I kissed Chris for the first time—or Nick. Nevertheless, it felt good to be desired. It felt good to feel worthy of intimacy. It felt good to actually be held by someone over the age of seven who wasn't my mom. It was nice. Nothing more, nothing less. Just plain nice.

When we parted, I immediately sat back in my chair, nonverbally indicating that I was going to take a kissing break. I mean, let's face it. If it isn't the love of your life or a hot movie star kissing you, it's just kind of "eh." No reason to carry on for hours and hours. This move to distance myself had me thinking that maybe all the hype from the dream the night before and the day's anticipation had set me up for a slight letdown.

As if aware of my subtle detachment, Greg sat back in his seat as well. "So," he began, "can I ask you a personal question?"

Intrigued, I nodded. I mean, I had nothing to hide.

"Okay, so not that it matters, but I'm just curious. Have you heard from him?"

I'm sure my scrunched eyebrows did not hide my confusion, but I decided to respond with "Who?" I genuinely had no idea what he was asking. In fact, before he responded, I wondered if he was actually asking me if my dead husband had revealed himself to me in the form of a ghost.

"That actor dude, duh." Oh, to hear grown men say "duh" is comical and childish.

"Oh." It was a violent recognition, complete with cocking my head all the way back, quite possibly in an attempt to buy some time to formulate a response. Well, not really a response, but more of a tone to coordinate with the response so that my tone would defy my real feelings on the issue. If I replied solemnly, I was afraid I might hurt his feelings. But nonchalance was not authentic either, and I was afraid that would translate into solemnity. I was kind of screwed. "Sorry, it's been a while since I thought of him. For a second I thought you were talking about Chris," I joked, stalling. "I mean, wouldn't that be weird? You wondering if I had seen my dead husband?"

Greg flinched at my nonchalance. Epic fail. So much for playing it cool.

After I released a few nervous chuckles, I regained my composure and shook my head, admitting, "No, I haven't heard from Nick. Huh-uh. Not since, well, since Jen kind of put the kibosh on that relationship." I grabbed my beer and bore into it as I gulped several mouthfuls, hopeful that he would change the subject.

But, you know what they say about wishes? Well, I don't really either. I think it is something about if wishes were a-holes, but I'm not quite sure. "Well, um"—Greg looked down at his beer, suddenly bashful himself—"do you, I mean, are you still upset?"

"About?" I prodded.

"About him not contacting you?"

"Well, I mean, yeah, I guess." His eager eyes that had finally refocused on mine suddenly dropped again, defeated. *Lord have mercy. What have I started here?* "I just feel bad for the way things...ya know...went down, ended. I feel like a big jerk, so yeah, I mean, I wish he would forgive me, for sure."

Apparently not too eager to let me off the hook that easily, he retorted, "Well, I know you feel bad and all, but I mean, well..." He hesitated, obviously trying to compose his thoughts. "Okay, so let's say he called you tomorrow...wait, don't answer that. I'm not sure I want to know the answer about tomorrow. Let's say he called two days ago and forgave you and missed you and all of that..."

Don't say it. Don't say it. Don't say it.

"Would you want him back?"

You said it!

I knew the answer. It was the same answer it had always been. My feelings had never waxed or waned. While I sometimes got my panties in a wad and momentarily convinced myself that I should be mad at him, my answer was still the same. If Nicholas Price would ever give me a chance again, I would jump at it. Not because he was hot and famous and blah blah blah, but because I had fallen in love with him and he had done nothing wrong. Sure, during those times I convinced myself to be pissed off, I concocted weak offenses he possibly committed. I mean, not forgiving someone is not nice at all, right? Well it temporarily made me feel better during my worst moments.

I could not, however, spill all of this to a man who was not Nicholas Price and who had incidentally just kissed me, the day after he had professed his true love for yours truly. I mean, that would just be cruel. So instead of chucking my hand through his chest and ripping out his heart, I went for a kinder, more sensitive response. "Hmm, well I guess I don't know exactly. I mean, I might give him another chance. It's hard to say. I guess I've kind of gotten past it."

"Boy, lots of guessing going on," he spat, snarky.

Not acknowledging his rudeness, I said, "Well, I mean, come on, Greg. I don't really know. It would depend on a lot of factors. I mean, it would depend on what he said, if he really *wanted* me back, if he had truly forgiven me. I just am not quite sure."

Humbled, Greg whispered, "And now? Tomorrow?"

I feigned ignorance. "Tomorrow what?

He rolled his eyes, obviously aware of his vulnerability. My heart softened as he spelled it out: "If he came tomorrow, would you want him back?"

Letting him off the hook as quickly as possible, I grinned and said, "Well, now *that* would be a hard thing to do." It was the best I could give. It would have to do because I don't think I could lie straight to his face if he kept pushing.

Apparently, it was just flirty enough to appease him. Not that it mattered anyway; Nick was history. Even if he came back to the States and back to acting, he was never coming back to me. Never. So it was really a moot point.

Greg leaned in closer and put his hand on my hand that was firmly gripping my beer bottle. "Well, if he *did* come back tomorrow, he'd get one hell of a fight." And he kissed me tenderly at first, and then with a sense of urgency. The spark flickered a little brighter this time around, and I don't know if it was more ignited for Greg per se, or in the name of long-awaited lust. Nevertheless, I kissed back. And hard. I felt the longing in my clenched stomach and my rapidly beating heart. Had Sam not have been home, I probably would have taken Greg's hand and led him into my bedroom. Now, I'm not saying I would have had sex with him, but I certainly would have rounded a couple of seventh-grade bases.

Instead, we finished our beers, and figuring it was around eight o'clock, I suggested it was time to call it a night so that I could get Sam in bed. Greg didn't put up a fight, but instead, he cupped my face in his hands and said, "I had such a great time today, Allie. In fact, I don't know when the last time was that I have felt so alive. Sam is…oh man, Sam is so great. You have done such an amazing job with him, Allie. Truly. And you, ugh, Allie, you drive me crazy…in an intense, amazing way. I mean, being with you today, kissing you, looking at you, it's like what I have dreamed about for so long is coming true, and it is. Oh, Allie, it just feels really good." He suddenly became guarded and removed his hands from my face, retreating back into his chair. "Anyway, I mean, I'm not saying I have any expectations or anything. It just feels good, that's all. So thank you. Thank you for today."

I had a pang of tenderness for this sweet man who was once again professing his adoration. This time, I moved forward in my chair and grabbed his hand. Then, deciding that wasn't quite enough of a thoughtful gesture, I arose from my seat and sat down gently on his lap, grabbing his face in my hands as I brought him firmly to my lips. I spared no indulgence and let my lips and tongue do the talking as they smacked and slurped my almost believable mutual affection and adoration.

Our evening commenced with plans to reconvene the following evening at his apartment for Chinese takeout. Luckily, Sam had expanded his palate over the span of his short little life to include such cuisine. Although the giddy feeling from before our time together had dissipated, I was still thankful to have a companion—another adult with whom to engage in conversation and activity. The world seemed a little less lonely with promises of tomorrow as I watched Greg Manis drive off into the night.

9

The following night, Sam and I arrived at Greg's apartment with store-bought brownies and a bottle of wine. Greg's apartment most assuredly cost more than my house, with state-of-the-art everything and the finest furniture and accessories money could buy. I had wondered why a doctor would end up in an apartment, but then figured it was probably because Kansas is a no-fault state when it comes to divorce; and so, quite typically, the wife gets half the money. Well, apparently half of a physician's salary is all that is needed to score a sweet apartment.

Greg spared no expense when ordering P. F. Chang's, and we had a delectable feast. The conversation was comfortable, and the wine brought forth warmth. We transferred to the beautiful leather sofa, switching between *SpongeBob SquarePants* and *Wheel of Fortune* on the boob tube. Consequently, I kicked ass at *Wheel of Fortune* and guessed every clue long before the contestants, as well as my fellow couch dwellers.

The bonus round was just beginning and the stupid lady couldn't figure out the word "limelight" despite being handed the letters *L*, *E*, and *T*. I got it in two seconds. I was so proud of myself that I started doing a touchdown dance around the living room, rubbing in my mad *Wheel* skills. That's when the knock on the door came, interrupting my celebration. I instinctively covered my mouth, thinking that I was probably the cause of a noise complaint.

Greg started chuckling. "Your gloating wasn't *that* loud, Smuggy Smuggerson," he responded as he pushed off the couch and headed for the door. Sam's eyes were wide, afraid I may get in trouble. I slunk down into the couch beside him.

Greg unlatched and opened the door, and that's when I heard the formerly all-too-familiar voice. "Hey, so I'm in a bind and she puked on the way to my mom's and you know how Mom is about vomit, so I need you to take her for the night." And then more quietly, obviously turning toward her daughter, she said, "Sweetie, come on. Pick up your bag." And then more loudly, directing her passive aggression at Greg, she said, "Daddy is just speechless because he is so excited to have you. Right, Daddy?" She spat her words between gritted teeth. Jen. *Oh crap!*

Then I heard Greg. "Um, well, actually—" He didn't get any further before I saw above the top of the couch a blonde push her way past him into the foyer. I immediately turned my face toward the TV before I saw her face, hoping that would keep her from seeing mine. "What, do you have a date?" She scoffed, obviously making fun of him—until she spied me on the couch. I watched her out of the corner of my eye. I could tell it took her a few moments to register who she was looking at. And even when it registered, she remained stunned.

I had apparently stopped breathing because my light head made me suddenly feel as though I may pass out. This. Is. Not. Happening. I had no clue what to do or say. It was like I was staring at a lion, too terrified to move or blink, yet too terrified to stay and be eaten alive.

By the grace of God, Greg came to my rescue, commanding Jen's attention. "Hey, Jen, Belle, can I talk with you guys in the hall?" Luckily, I don't think Annabelle had spied us.

Without saying a word, a stunned Jen turned and followed Greg out into the hall, followed by their sweet, sick daughter. As soon as the door closed, I heard her voice, full of…well, what was it? Anger? Hurt? Hate? Maybe a mixture of all three. I could only make out a few words, but piecing them together, I located a gist and the gist was what in the hell was I doing there? Was I crazy? Was he crazy? What kind of scheme was he up to? Something about being hurt or hurting someone.

Greg's calm, cool collected responses were harder to decipher, but I know I heard him say something about being friends and that he was helping me out with a few things. Then there was more back and forth, and I looked at Sam whose eyes were still wide, but for a very different reason. He still was hanging onto the noise complaint idea. He then asked, "Um, so is this bad?"

I shrugged my shoulders, giving him the only answer I knew. Was it bad? It was bad. This was very bad. As if I didn't do enough damage "stealing" Jen's Hollywood crush, now I was taking her husband too? Oh my word. What was I doing? What had I done? My mind started reeling, as if coming into focus for the first time in two days. The woman who was so incredibly distraught by my actions one year ago that she literally destroyed my public and private life was standing outside the door of her ex-husband's apartment in which I was nonchalantly dancing around the living room like a skanky flake. I was a horrible person. This was bad. I was bad.

With a few more shouts about being a terrible father, Jen stomped down the hallway with, I assumed, a sick little girl in tow. I sank into the leather cushions, wearing my dread like a funeral veil. As Greg opened the door, I turned to Sam and said, "Hey, buddy, we're gonna go soon, okay? But first I need to talk to Mr. Greg in private, so we will just be in the kitchen."

As he nodded, my sweet son asked, "Mom, what's a homewrecker?" Yes, he had caught that one last jab from Jen.

"Buddy, I will tell you later." I quickly got up so that Greg wouldn't have to be awkward and begin to explain the situation in front of Sam. I walked right toward him, grabbed his arm, and led him into the kitchen, complete with granite countertops and stainless steel appliances.

I turned to begin my good-bye speech, but before I could, Greg grabbed me and pulled me to him, kissing me firmly on the mouth. I kissed back for a split second and then quickly pushed him away. "No!" I firmly whispered. "No, this is wrong. We can't do this. I have to go. I'm sorry, but I never should have started this mess!"

"Whoa, whoa, whoa, Crazy. Calm down just a second, okay? Listen, you have done nothing wrong here. *You* didn't sabotage Jen's marriage by falling for a famous movie star who *she*, a married woman, had no business lusting after. *You* were the single one. *You* didn't sabotage *her* life by destroying *her* new relationship out of spite, like *she* did to *you*. *You* didn't become psycho and destroy your marriage. *Jen* did, Allie. Jen did all of those things, and I will be damned if I will let *you* or *me* feel guilty about trying to be happy. We have done nothing wrong, and yet we have been shit on." He took a well-needed breath.

I just stood there. What he said made sense, but I couldn't help but feel what Jen must have been feeling. I mean, this would suck royally. Did she deserve it? I don't know. Does anyone deserve anything really? Did she earn it? Most definitely. But that doesn't mean that her heart wasn't breaking, and for that I felt terrible. I never wanted to be the cause of a breaking heart, especially one that resides in someone's chest whom I used to care so much about. Sticky. That's it. This situation was sticky. Yuck.

Deciding to grab some perspective, we said our good-byes, and Sam and I headed home. I told Greg to give me a couple days to think things through and that I would be in touch. I'd like to say that I spent those few days "thinking" about the situation, but in reality, I spend those days obsessively checking my e-mail to see if Jen would send me some sort of hate letter. It never came nor did the pile-of-dog-crap-on-fire I was expecting to find on my front porch. Yes, I'm weird, but I have seen this prank too many times in the movies and was just certain I was going to be getting a delivery. Paranoid much?

Finally, when I knew if I continued to stall I'd be called out, I called Greg during the time that I knew he would be working. I was convinced there was no way he would pick up. Once again, I was wrong. On the first ring, no less. Without boring you with the deets, I basically told Greg that it just wasn't a good idea that we continue on with this nonsense, and he panicked and begged to come over that evening to discuss. Being a sensitive sucker, I caved and agreed. I mean, I kissed the guy. I owed him that much.

Sam had plans to have an overnight with my parents, so my dad came to pick him up in the late afternoon. I was so incredibly thankful that Sam hadn't mentioned that we had been spending time with Mr. Greg Manis. I really didn't have much mental room left to analyze the situation, let alone words to formulate in regards to the like. I went through the McDonald's drive-thru for dinner. (Yes, I am the only grown person on earth who will choose to have McDonald's even without children in tow. Their Diet Coke is to die for, dahling!) As I scarfed down my double cheeseburger meal, I decided it was time to formulate my side of the conversation that was to come. It was, after all, just ten minutes until Greg would arrive.

So, I'm just gonna say it. I was, well, weak maybe? Greg arrived, and I started in on my whole rationale. And then he, being so incredibly sweet, said he understood and validated my thoughts and then made a desperate attempt to reassure me that we could take things slower or do whatever I needed to be comfortable but that he wanted to be there for Sam and me and that he wasn't willing to give up yet. So naturally I took him to my bed.

Okay, okay, bear with me here. I'm not the slut that I play on TV. Oh wait, I'm not on TV. So I took him to my bedroom because, quite frankly, I was so damn horny. That and the fact that I had two beers and we were alone in my house. Alone! Do you know how often I am alone with a good-looking man in my house? Well, of course you don't, but I'll tell you, not often!

Now I don't know if I was committed to going through with it when I led him into my room by the hand with my seductive eyes, but I knew I was at least going to fool around a bit. That was for certain. Yes, I know that I was probably sending mixed signals. My mouth was saying, "It isn't going to work" while my body was saying, "Oh, have your way with me!" And of course, I used this little act to berate myself for weeks. I must love shaming myself and riddling myself with guilt because I am so flippin' good at it! I'm not only a self-shame member; I'm the president—which I guess also makes me the president of martyrdom.

So, let's get back on track. There we were, smooching on my bed, and I heard my cell phone ringing in the other room. Of course, being the first time I had been anywhere near intimate with a man in over a year, my initial response was to just ignore it. But then the shame and guilt sirens started going off in my head, blaring, "You have a child! What if something happened to him?" I immediately jumped up, apologizing, but reassuring Greg that I just needed to make sure it wasn't Sam.

I looked at the caller ID, and it was some random number I didn't recognize. Weird area codes are always indicative of telemarketers. Setting the phone back down, I ran back to my room. I had just settled back in, my mind beginning to gnaw at me that what I was doing was not right, but I decided to tell those thoughts to shut up and kiss Greg once again.

Then I heard a chiming sound coming from the living room and knew that whoever had just called had left a voice mail. *Hmm, that's weird. Telemarketers don't leave voice mails on cell phones.* Kiss. Kiss. Slurp. Kiss. *So then, who could it have been?* Smooch. Suck face. *What if it really is Sam, and he is calling from somewhere weird?* Muah. Nibble. *Kidnapped? The hospital?* "Crap,

I'm sorry," I pleaded as I backed away from Greg. "Someone has left a message, and I just need to make sure it isn't Sam."

"Didn't you check it already?"

"Well, yeah, but I didn't recognize the number, so I didn't answer it."

"So then it wasn't your parents' number, right?"

Oh, I didn't have time for this…or patience. "Right, Greg, but I don't know. Just chill out for a second." I was a little snarky, and I heard him huff and throw himself back on the bed as I hustled back to the living room. His eye-rolling was audible.

I grabbed the phone and clicked the voice mail icon, certain I would end up eating my words and hear a dumb computer rambling on about who I should vote for or lowering my credit card interest rate or something ridiculous like that. But I didn't.

The voice was hard to make out at first as it began as a long sigh followed by a throat clearing, and just as I was ready to count it as a wrong number and hang up, I heard my name spoken from a voice I had yet to recognize. "Um, Allie? This is, um, this is Nick." My heart stopped.

10

Oh how tempting it is to just end the story right here. I heard after my retelling of the events that led up to Nick's dismissal from America that people were ticked off! They viewed my story as a work of fiction and felt like I just cut off the story before it was over. Believe me, I felt that way too! I wished like hell that there was more to the story at that point, but unfortunately, that was it. Now that I realize I have a sense of control over people's emotions, I am sadistically tempted to stop right here and keep the story for myself.

But I'm typically not an ass, so I will continue. Of course, as soon as I heard him say his name, my ear picked up nothing else that he was saying, only hearing the thumping of my heart. I had to listen to the message twice before I comprehended all that was packed into the forty-six-second message.

After his introduction, the rest of the message went like this: "Um, Nick Price. Wow, it is so weird hearing your voice on your voicemail. So, I'm thinking we may have to set up a meeting with my PR guys to hash some things out, as I am coming back to the US to film *Resignation*. Um, I will be back in LA late Saturday night and can arrange a flight for you to be here by Monday morning. That's when my team can all come together to meet. I know it's short notice, but, um, well, it has to be done. We have to put all of this behind us so I can move forward with my career. Please call me back at…" Yeah right, like I'd tell you, dear reader, his phone number. How 'bout this "555——?" Or, even better, "867-5309."

Needless to say, that was not the message I had played over and over in my mind since the evening he left. In fact, it was nowhere close. It began a little tender and unsure, kind of sweet. Then it turned bold and bitter and, well, kind of bossy. My heart was still pounding with thoughts of his voice, his lips moving, seeing him again. But it was also pounding with the same familiar regret of Nicholas Price never looking at me the way he once did. Instead, I would forever be a completely crazy fan who stalked him. I was shamed and completely embarrassed all over again.

And I was pissed off. I mean, he knew I had a kid. Who does he think he is calling me and telling me he will get me a flight to be in L-freaking-A in three days? *Three days*, for crying out loud! Oh, yeah, let me just make arrangements for my kid and my life so I can appease *your* schedule so *you* can get on with *your* career! Jerk!

Okay, I know he wasn't the jerk in all of this, but damn, this sucked big time. How long was I to go on being embarrassed and hating myself? How many times would I need to publicly apologize in some ridiculous magazine for hurting Mr. Perfect? No, I wasn't going to go! I moved on. My life had finally begun to resume some semblance of normal. I was not going to let this bring me back down. No way. No how.

Except…I mean, I would get a chance to see him again; it was probably my only chance. Oh mercy, what was I going to do? Obviously, I had to call him back, but fear seized my heart and set my mind in perpetual motion. The hamster wheel was spinning away when I heard a familiar male voice say, "Um, Allie? Is something wrong?" *Oh crap! Greg!*

I quickly spun around, hiding my phone behind my back guiltily. How ridiculous. He knew I was going out to check my phone, but in my shocked state of mind, I had completely forgotten Greg even existed, let alone that he was waiting in my bedroom, on my bed, for me to return with some sort of explanation as to who was on the phone.

Obviously, despite the dim lighting, I looked like the ghost I felt and Greg rushed to me at once. "Oh my gosh, Allie, what is it? Is it Sam?"

Brain racked. Head shaking back and forth back and forth, buying time. Time for what? The inevitable? Yes. Truth. I needed to speak the truth. Oh man, what a buzzkill that would be for poor Greg. Why did I allow any of this to happen anyway? No matter how much I hoped to get flung away by the hamster wheel in my brain, my body stayed put, and I was left with no other option than to account for my behavior.

I looked up into Greg's eyes and simply said, "Greg, let's sit down." I led him to the couch and turned on the lamp on the table to the side. Turning to Greg, I just blurted out, "That was Nicholas Price." I decided to be formal with his name coming off of my lips so as to minimize the significance of the situation.

Greg's eyebrows raised in apparent confusion and disbelief. I think for a second he thought I was going to tell him I was joking and continue on with our make-out session. When I said nothing to indicate such a sick joke, he belted a nervous chuckle and asked, "Are you serious?"

I nodded and then added, as irritatingly as I could, "Yeah, apparently he wants me to come to LA on Monday so that I can meet with him and his stupid publicity people"—yes, I realize I was speaking like a child—"so we can, I don't know, corroborate our story or something so he can get on with his career." I turned to face the TV, which wasn't on, hoping he would buy my lack of enthusiasm.

"Wait, what? Are you serious?"

I couldn't keep up the calm charade for long, and so I was growing very impatient. "Yes, Greg. I'm serious. Anyway, listen, you better go. I need to figure this all out."

"Figure *what* out? Wait, are you wanting to get back together with him?" he accused.

"What?" I couldn't hide my irritation. "No, I just need to figure out if I'm going to go or what I'm going to do with Sam if I do go. I mean, this is all very sudden for me, and I only have a couple of days to figure it out, so..." I hoped that would be enough.

"Well, I'm going with you," he said matter-of-factly.

I choked on my spit. "Um, no, you're not. I mean, no, Greg. You don't have to do that."

"No, no. I know I don't, but I won't take 'no' for an answer. Listen, it makes sense. You and I have a lot to work out, and what a better way than to take a little trip, just the two of us. I will pay for the whole thing. It can be a little mini-vacation. Besides the nuisance of meeting with that guy and his people, we can actually have a good time. Let's face it, Allie. We both have had a pretty shitty year and could use a vacation." He was beaming, proud of himself.

I was fuming. My subtlety hadn't worked. In fact, every time I tried to let Greg down easy, he made it more difficult for me. I knew I had to set it straight right then and there. "Greg, no. Listen, this is something I have to do alone. I don't want a vacation. I really just want to go one day and come home the next—"

"Then I'll stay with Sam, and we can—"

"No!" I shouted; literally *shouted!* Oh, I am such a bad person. "Greg, listen," I said, softer and more gently, "this isn't going to work." I pointed back and forth between him and myself. "I have been so conflicted over this whole thing with you, and honestly, I just don't feel like it is right. I just don't. I'm sorry."

"Whoa, whoa. Wait a second. You were just about to maul me on your bed and then you get a phone call from this...this *infant* and *now* you don't feel like it's right? Give me a freaking break, Allie! You aren't over him. You're *not!* Just admit it, damn it!" Greg was shouting.

I scooted backward, actually a little fearful. Finally, I calmly spoke, "Greg, I seriously don't like to be talked to like that. I understand you are upset, but I don't deserve to be yelled at and cussed at. Seriously."

He was still fuming mad.

I continued. "Listen, I was already having doubts about this whole thing. You know that. That's why you came over here in the first place. And I'm sorry I took advantage of the situation and kissed you again. That wasn't what I intended to do, but I just kind of lost control. And I really do like you, Greg. I really do. I just don't think this is right. And no, Nick has nothing to do with it. All that phone call did was give me time to cool my raging hormones and take a second to think about what was going on between me and you. And I'm glad it did because it isn't fair to you if I make out with you or have sex with you or whatever and then tomorrow tell you we can't do this anymore. I'm not that type of person anyway."

Greg covered his face with both hands. Then he began shaking his head, easy at first and then more violently. "No, Allie. No. You don't get off this easy. I *know* you feel something for me! I *know* it. I will not let you go this easily."

Closing my eyes, willing this entire situation away, I shook my head in protest. It was a flimsy protest. Honestly, I just wanted him out of my house; and at that point, I was willing to do whatever it took to make him leave. If that meant providing maybe a glimmer of hope, so be it. "Listen, Greg, I've got to figure some stuff out. I'm tired. I'm going to California. I don't want you to watch Sam. Thanks, that's sweet of you, but then I will feel like I owe you something. I will call you when I get back from California. I promise. And then we can discuss this further. Everything is just so…so…I don't know, weird maybe? Out of control? I'm not sure what it is, but I feel like I am losing my bearings here, and it doesn't feel right. Just give me some time, okay?"

Greg hemmed and hawed until he hesitantly agreed. It was another ten minutes before he finally found his way out of my house. My nerves were frazzled, and the one thing that had not left my mind, even through my dissertation with Greg, was talking to Nick again.

Of course, I had to down a beer before I could make the phone call. It was 8:00 p.m. in Kansas, but I had no clue what time it was in Australia. I had to bank on the fact that since he had just called within the half hour, it would probably be an acceptable time to call. Man alive, was I nervous though. The beer did little to help my jitters. I didn't even know exactly what I was going to say. I mean, hadn't I said enough in my full admission? Certainly if he hadn't read it, he at least knew the gist of it and could hopefully sense my sincerity.

But then there was his message. It was laced with contempt. I was conflicted beyond belief. Should I play the victim? Should I beg for forgiveness? What did I hope to gain from that? What did I actually *want*? Not that it mattered much. I mean, pretty much the only thing that mattered to Nick was Nick at that point. He was moving on with his life and needed to take care of this one little annoyance so that he could continue on his ponies-and-rainbows life of fame, on a road that only goes up. Ugh.

Choosing to put on my big-girl pants and just call, I picked up my cell phone, went back to his phone number, and hit "send." Shaking my head and rolling my eyes, as if I had an audience to prove that I really was totally calm and cool with this whole situation, my insides defied me and vomit snuck up into my throat. Swallowing hard and then coughing, I nearly hung up the phone, but then…but then Nicholas Price picked up the receiver.

"Hello, Allie."

11

"Um, [*cough*] Nick? [*choke*]." Oh, I was an idiot.

"Yes." He didn't sound amused or worried about my hacking, which continued for a few minutes before I finally regained composure. I was so thankful it wasn't one of those attacks in which you feel like you are literally dying and the only thing that will help is to vomit.

Finally, trying to sound as cool as I had pretended to look just seconds earlier, I asked, "So, how are you?" Oh, I wanted desperately to know. This man who walked out of my life a year ago and who I had not heard from since was speaking to me on the phone. I felt so privileged yet suddenly very aware that I was the original reason he left.

"I'm fine. Listen, are you able to come or not?" Oh, he was pissed. Even when he was pissed, his accent was as sexy as ever.

How do I play this? I decided to go with the logical, adult, single-mom thing—you know, the actual reality of my situation. I said, "Yeah, um, about that. I just don't know that I am going to be able to swing that. I mean, I have Sam and everything. Plus, I really don't see the point." *Please don't take no for an answer!*

"Hmm, you don't see the point. Well, let me spell it out for you, Allie, if that is even your name. I am coming back to finish what I started with the franchise, and because of the havoc you have wreaked, my director is insisting that this whole thing be put to rest once and for all. In order to do that, they want to bring you in and have you sign some papers and formulate a statement. Do. You. Understand. The. Point. Now?"

Wow! What an a-hole! I sat speechless. Any hope or fantasy I had originally allowed myself to play out came crashing down on me with a bitter, foul smell. Maybe having Greg come with me wasn't such a bad idea after all. "Okay, so what are these papers I am supposed to sign?" I was trying to match him venom for venom, apathy for apathy. "I'm not going to sign away my rights for you, Nick, no matter how famous you are!"

"Don't call me that!" he spat.

"Famous? Puh-lease!" I laughed

"No! Don't call me Nick! Nick is reserved for people I care about and people who care about me!" he shouted.

Ouch. That stung. It stung so bad in fact that my resolve, my courage, the walls I had built up to protect myself, the ones that served as a daily reminder that I was fine and that it was all no big deal, came crumbling down around me. The tears followed suit. They weren't the silent pretty tears that beautiful actresses get to cry in movies either. They were the uncontrollable, stop-your-vocal-chords, heaving-chest, scrunched-eyes, snot-running-down-to-your-chin, hideous tears. Thank God the audience was pretend—at least visually. Unfortunately, my audience on the other end of the phone knew exactly what was happening and sighed in irritation as I wailed—yes, literally *wailed* into the phone. Like a damn baby.

"I'm so sorry. I'm sorry. I'm sorry. I'm sorry for crying. I'm sorry for everything. I'm sorry. I'm sorry..." My voice trailed off.

When his voice penetrated the air again, it was noticeably softer, in volume and heart. "Listen, Allie, I really don't want to do this right now, and I don't want you to be this upset. I accept your apology, okay? Let's just say it is water under the bridge.

But I really need to move on and come back and start fresh, and so we need to put this to rest publicly. The papers are just for my protection and yours. Confidentiality stuff. So will you please come?"

Okay, so now is the part when y'all are gonna want to hit me over the head with a bat! Like, "You dumb fool, don't you learn your lessons?" Trust me, I know. I react before I think sometimes. There, I said it. I am a major reactor and, as we have already established, a selfish youngest child. Remember the characteristics? Immature, manipulative, fun-loving, free-spirited…am I losing you? Okay, fine, I will get on with it. But please keep in mind that I know I am a moron for this next jerk-move.

My response to the man who had no business accepting my apology, but who kindly did anyway, was, "Well, can I bring someone with me?"

Given his hesitation, Nick was apparently thrown for a little loop. "O-Okay. Who, Sam?"

"Oh mercy, no. Um, a friend."

"Well, I guess. I mean, it will depend on when you want to fly out and home—if there are enough seats or any on standby. It's kind of last-minute so who knows. I've looked online though, and you could fly out on Sunday from KCI to LAX and fly back Monday evening. Would that work?"

"Well, crap. I mean, yeah, I guess. I need to see if my folks can keep Sam, or maybe Chris's folks." I was merely thinking out loud.

"Okay, well then, let me go ahead and try and book you and your friend before I head to the airport. What's her name?"

Oh, crap. This was it. "Um, well, actually, *his* name is Greg. Greg Manis." I wondered if the last name would ring a bell, what with Jen's name being smeared all over the Internet.

Silence.

Good. Maybe he does still care! "Hello?"

"Um, yeah. Okay. Greg Manis. I will see what I can do and call you back in a bit." There was a click, and then he was gone.

Well, that went well. Although it didn't. What was I doing? Trying to make him jealous? I didn't even want Greg to go, did I? Oh, what an idiot I am. I contemplated calling him right back and telling him that Greg couldn't go after all. I had the phone in my hand, ready to dial, and then it began ringing. Startled, I jumped three feet in the air. Oh, I get so pissed off when I get scared.

I am the ultimate hypocrite. I absolutely *love* hiding behind corners and scaring people. It gives me a sense of thrill and exhilaration. It is like when I was a kid and would be playing hide-and-seek. I would have to hide in the bathroom because I would get so excited that I always, without fail, had to pee. This is how I always felt when I hid around a corner to scare Sam. I got so giddy with excitement that I would almost start giggling.

Anyway, my childhood home was always full of scares and pranks, and so naturally, I set that stage in my own home. The only problem is that I can dish out the scares but absolutely cannot take them. I am the worst sport ever. And of course Sam, at the age of three, mastered the art of scaring the pants off of his mother. Anytime I would go to the bathroom, he would stand right outside the door, waiting to hear the flush; and as soon as the door opened, he would scream "Ra!" as loud as he could. I would jump a mile in the air and then simultaneously be pissed and embarrassed. Or maybe I was pissed because I was embarrassed. Or the other way around? Who knows.

So when I jumped out of my skin as the phone rang, my first instinct was to be pissed, but the instinct quickly quieted at the idea that it was probably Nick. When I noticed the number was Greg's, however, the irritation returned; I hastily answered, "Hello?" almost shouting into the phone.

"Uh, uh, Allie?" Greg was pensive.

"Yeah?" I was way too rude.

"Um, what's wrong?"

"Nothing. Whatcha need?"

"Wow. Um, okay, so I guess I'll get on with it. I was wondering if you could talk for a few minutes."

My irritated sigh couldn't be dismissed, and when I started to speak, Greg interrupted, "Never mind. Geez. Goodbye, Allie!"

"No, wait, Greg!" But it was too late. He was gone. Of course, a nice person would have immediately phoned him back and apologized…

I dialed the phone and waited three rings before my dad picked up.

"Hey-a, kiddo."

"Hey, Dad. How's Sam?"

"Who?" Oh, my dad thought he was hysterical.

"You're a dork! How is he?"

"I'm sorry, who are we talking about?"

"You know, your beloved grandson?"

"Oh, Sam! Yeah, how is he doing, Al? I haven't seen him in forever. He really should have an overnight soon."

"Oh, you're irritating. Let me talk to him, and then I need to talk back with you or Mom."

He was defeated. "Hang on." I could hear him holler for Sam.

"Hey, Dad," I shouted into the phone.

"Yes?" He sounded skeptical.

"I'm sure hoping you are calling Sam from the bed that he should have been in a half-hour ago."

He just laughed and called Sam's name again. My parents always let him stay up too long, and they thought I was a Nazi for being a stickler for bedtime. I often remind them that they gave me a bedtime until I was a senior in high school, and not only that but my mom would irritatingly holler out the front door (when it was still daylight!), "Beds Neds!" as we were playing with our friends. Oh, my brother would get so ticked off that she would embarrass us like that in front of our oh-so-lucky friends who at least got to stay up until it was dark. Now, of course, with grandkids, all bets are off!

"Hey, Mom." Sam was out of breath.

"Hey, sweets. Whatcha doin'?"

"Just beating Grandma at Pong, as usual." My parents had a vintage Atari that Sam *loved* to play.

"Are you in your jammies?" It was a loaded question.

He called my bluff. "Okay, love you, Mom. Bye!"

"No, sir!" I shouted. "Don't you dare! You tell me the truth. Are you?"

Sam sighed long and hard. "No, Mom, I'm not in my jammies."

I heard my dad in the background say, "Oh, for Pete's sake, Allie. Get a grip!"

"Um, you tell Papa that I'm the mom."

"Papa, she says she's the mom…as if you didn't know that."

My dad laughed. When did my son turn into such a smart-ass?

I had other battles I needed to fight. This one wasn't that important, and I knew I was crazy obsessive about it; but if you had to deal with my child after he hadn't received enough sleep, you would feel the same way I do. "Okay, tell Papa that he gets to keep you for a week. Then he'll see."

"Yes! Papa, you get to keep me for a week!"

"No. No. I'm just kidding. Oh, you silly goof. I love you, and please don't stay up late, okay?"

"Okay. Bye."

"Wait. I said 'I love you,'" I pleaded.

"Ugh, I love you too," he replied halfheartedly.

"Let me talk to Pops."

When my dad returned to the phone, after I gave him one of my all-too-familiar lectures on the importance of a good night's sleep for adolescents, I explained the situation at hand concerning LA. His idea was just to keep Sam until I returned, but the thought of not seeing my son for the following three days bummed me out, so I suggested that I come and stay with them the next night and then drive to the airport on Sunday. Yes, Topeka is much further from KCI than Olathe, but I hated to make my dad drive Sam home for one night and then come get him again, and I didn't want to drive to Topeka and back twice within a twenty-four-hour time frame.

As I was about to tell my dad good-bye, my other line beeped. Hurriedly, I bid my father adieu and retrieved the call before it went to voicemail. My heart leapt yet again at the sound of Nick's voice. Would I ever get over him?

"Hey, Allie, it's Nicholas Price." Duh. And what was with the formality?

I decided to play along. "Hello, Nicholas Price. How may I help you?"

"Ha, uh, so I booked the flight." I could hear a hint of amusement in his voice in response to my playful antics. Did he know he was being kind of pompous? Maybe. He continued, "But unfortunately, the flight out was completely full except for one seat, so I was only able to book you. I hope that's okay. Will your *friend* be all right if he doesn't get to come?"

A-ha! Busted. I didn't know if I should let him off the hook and pretend like Greg being unable to come would be no big deal, or if I should correct him and say Greg was my boyfriend. Yes, I am (was) a brat. But let's face it. Sometimes we girls play games to get what we want. I don't care if you are the youngest child or the oldest, the female species has learned how to play the system. And you know what? As well we should. After all, the media and advertising do their best to paint a portrait of the "ultimate" female that none of us can live up to yet try so desperately hard to. In my opinion, society has pushed us into playing games just to keep the playing field fair. If we didn't feel such pressure to be thin and perky and beautiful and fun, and felt desirable just for being "us," we would have an easier time just being "us"!

Rant over. That's my story, and I'm sticking to it. But in this instance, I decided to take the higher road and not lie. I mean, hadn't lying gotten me in enough trouble with this man? Not that claiming Greg was my boyfriend would be a flat-out lie. I mean, we had seen each other a few times; and if I just said the word, Greg would jump at the chance to be my boyfriend. But that still didn't make it truth.

"Okay. No big deal," I said.

He didn't push further for information on this topic, a fact that admittedly left me disappointed. Instead, he just gave me the details of my flight and told me he would have a car ready for me at the airport. He had booked a room for me at the Beverly Hills Hotel. As I never had been to LA, it sounded kind of shady, like a generic name for a hotel. Not that I was a hotel expert, but I usually tried to stay in hotels I had heard of, chains if you will—Holiday Inn, Courtyard, Hampton Inn, Marriot (if I was lucky). I was picturing the Bates Motel in my mind. Maybe he was trying to get back at me by putting me up in a piece of crap hotel.

Being completely unfamiliar with California at large, I asked, "So, I thought I was flying to LA. Why would you book a hotel in Beverly Hills?"

After a condescending chuckle, he responded, "LA is huge, and Beverly Hills is basically a part of LA. On a Sunday, morning traffic won't be too terrible, maybe an hour or so drive. But the hotel you'll be staying at is a short distance from Melrose, which is where the PR firm is. I'll have a car pick you up at ten on Monday morning."

"Okay, so you keep saying you will have a car pick me up. How will I know which car is picking me up?"

Another snort, and then he said, "You'll know. Hey, listen, I have to go. I'll e-mail you all the info." And then *click*; he was gone again. There was no good-bye or anything. Oh, I was irritated.

Of course I couldn't sleep a wink; but contrary to every sleep expert's advice, I didn't get out of bed and busy myself. I just lay there and suffered. My mind was swimming with ideas and possibilities. Quite frankly, I could not even believe I was going to be seeing Nick in two days. After a year of nothing, I was going to be able to look into his eyes once again. Sure, it wasn't how I had imagined or fantasized, but it was something nonetheless.

After a two-hour fitful night's sleep, I awoke at 7:00 a.m. Despite my fatigue, I was giddy with excitement. I quickly checked my e-mail, printed off all the info (no, there was absolutely nothing personal in the e-mail—a fact that saddened me), and began packing. Of course I packed the cutest outfits I could find in my limited wardrobe; and then I locked up, grabbed my bags, and headed out into the garage. Pushing the garage door button, I was met with a bunch of crap as the stupid thing refused to open yet again.

No, no, no! Not today! Pushing it several times and willing it to budge, I finally pounded it with my fist, dropped my bags, and went back into the house. I retrieved my phone from my purse. How on earth I was going to explain this one to Greg without sounding like a total user, I knew not, but it was the best shot I had. So I dialed his number.

"Yep," he barked after the third ring.

"Um, hi, Greg. How are you?"

"Fine." That was it.

"Hey, sorry I didn't call you back last night. Things are just kind of crazy, but you'll never believe this."

I waited for him to inquire about what I was referencing. Nothing.

Continuing, I said in a chipper voice, "So my freaking garage door won't go up again. Ha. Can you believe it?"

"Yeah?" was his response.

Oh, he was gonna make me work for it.

"Well, I was wondering…I don't know. Do you think you could come help me?"

There was silence on the other end for ten seconds, and it was followed by a long, drawn-out exhale. "Allie, you only want me when you need something."

I sat on that for a while, stunned frankly. And then it hit me. I didn't ask for this. He was the one who insisted upon me calling him for help, in the name of Chris. Knowing now was probably not the best time to call him out on it, but deciding to anyway, I barked, "Never mind, Greg. See, it is crap like this that reinforces to me that nothing in this life is free or selfless. You made me promise that I would reach out to you if I needed you, no strings attached, and now it is oh so obvious that there are strings. There always was. You didn't want to help me for me or for Chris. You wanted to help me for *you!*" I hung up the phone but not before pushing the 8, pound sign, and star in a hasty attempt to reach "end."

I was fuming hot. Tossing the phone back into my purse, I marched my steaming butt out into the garage, tried the button one more time, and then walked directly to the metal door. I remembered when I was a kid, before garage door openers (or maybe not before, but my parents were the last to get everything—call waiting, answering machines, VCRs, cable, for crying out loud), my folks would always turn the handle and lift up the door manually. I tried this. Um, it didn't work.

Huffing back to my purse, I retrieved my phone and dialed my dad, the shrill in my voice leaving my words unable to be deciphered. Finally, after he all but hung up on me for being so incoherent, I calmed down enough to explain the situation. Of course my dad, being the jokester that he is, couldn't stop laughing at my dilemma. When I reprimanded him through my sudden tears, he said, "Oh, for God's sake, Allie, you need to know how to do this crap if you're gonna live alone." Yet another time my dad could not handle my tears.

I reminded him in my childish fit that it was not my fault that my husband was dead and told him not to yell at me. This, of course, began a whole bit on how he was not yelling and I was being too sensitive and if I wanted to hear him yell, he would, but he had not actually yelled. Blah, blah, blah. Visions of him pointing his finger and hollering, "Stop crying or I'll give you something to cry about" came flooding into my consciousness. Oh, I really *was* a child.

Finally, we got past the nonsense, and he proceeded to tell me where the pull thingy was on the garage door opener that would release the motor or whatever. Of course my freaking car was in the way; so instead of being able to just climb on a ladder like a normal civilized homeowner, I had to climb to the top of my car to reach the damn thing. A dent on the hood and one on the roof served as a gentle reminder that maybe I needed to lay off the McDonalds.

Y'all (yes, I pretend to be southern sometimes; my accent is spot-on), I don't know how on earth I managed to actually follow his directions without screwing something up or falling off the car to my death, but I did it! I really did. I pulled the thing, unhooked whatever it was attached to, and then shimmied off the car, leaving one more "tiny" butt-print dent in the hood. When I got to the garage door, lo and behold, with a turn of the lever, the damned thing disengaged and with a little elbow grease was able to be lifted. Greg Shmeg. I didn't need no stinkin' Greg.

Having no clue where I might find the key to the dang door, I locked the door from the garage to the house and left the garage door unlocked. Hey, if someone wanted to steal my crappy, fifteen-year-old lawn mower, or the ancient weed eater that only saw use when my dad came over once a month, they could have them both. If my yard was any indication, they would see that the mower I had to push around every week didn't cut the grass evenly (that's what I tell myself at least. It couldn't possibly be user error), and since Dad hadn't been over to weed eat in a month, the areas around my trees and up against the house told the story that the weed eater wasn't even functioning. Just between you and me (and my dad who makes fun of me for it), the tall grassy outline of my home is two feet wide all the way around. I am so deathly afraid of snakes, and I know they like tight spaces, that I won't even come within a couple feet of the house with the lawn mower—even with pants on, long socks, and duck boots. Yes, my fear of snakes propels me to wear 1980s duck boots in the blazing hot summer!

So I pulled out of the drive, silently praying that the thief wouldn't steal my trash or recycling bins. How would I explain *that* one to Deffenbaugh? With one last glance at the house to make sure no lights were glaringly turned on, I pulled onto the street and headed toward the stop sign. As I turned right to traverse my way through downtown Olathe toward the highway, a familiar black Honda Pilot passed by. The driver (Greg, of course) was checking himself out in the vanity mirror. My heart sank. I knew where he was heading. I slowed down as I approached one of the million roundabouts with which the city of Olathe has damned us and looked in my rearview mirror to spy if my hunch was correct. Indeed, Greg turned down my street. *Crapola!*

The tug-of-war began in my head once again. Should I turn around or just pretend like I hadn't seen a thing? Once again, the bitch won out, and I continued toward I-35. It wasn't five minutes later when my cell phone rang. Knowing exactly who it was, I took a few deep breaths before answering as chipperly as I could. (Chipperly is officially a word because I said so!)

"Allie? Hey, um, so I'm at your house. Will you please let me in?"

Aww, man, I was a jerkface. "Oh, hey, Greg. You know what? I actually am not home. I just left like literally ten minutes ago. I can't believe I missed you."

"What? How? I mean, how did you get out, with the garage door and all?"

"Ha. Well, it turns out that I don't need a man!" I meant it as a total joke, but considering the circumstances, which I obviously hadn't at all before opening my big mouth, it probably wasn't the best response.

Apparently Greg didn't think so either because with laughter nowhere to be found in his demeanor, he simply quipped, "How did you fix it?"

"Greg, I was just kidding about the not-needing-a-man thing. I wasn't thinking, but I actually did need a man. I needed my dad to tell me how to unhook the box thingy so that I could just lift the door manually."

He sat on that for a second before returning with "Well, why is the handle turned on the garage door?"

"Oh, well, I don't know where the key is, if I even have it, so I just left it unlocked so I could get back in. Don't worry though. The door to the house is locked."

"Well, are you coming right back because you know someone could easily see that this is unlocked and come in and steal whatever is in your garage right?"

"Ugh, I know that. And no, I'm not coming right back, but I already counted my garage assets and truthfully, besides my lawn bags, nothing else would be that great of a loss."

"O-okay. So where are you headed off to this morning?" Greg was trying desperately to sound aloof. He wasn't fooling anyone.

"Well, I'm heading to my folks' house." I was being vague, yet truthful.

"Oh, to pick up Sam? Well, what time will you be back tonight?"

"Well, I won't actually. I'm spending the night." *Oh, please let it go at that, Greg!*

No such luck. "Okay. Well, what time will you be back tomorrow? I'll just meet you here and try and fix the door then."

"Well, um, actually, I won't be home until late Monday night."

"Really?" He was genuinely surprised. Clueless even. And then, as if in a split second, recognition set in. "Oh. Oh. You're going, aren't you?"

"To my parents'? Yes."

"No, you know what I mean, to California."

I paused long enough that I didn't have to continue.

"All right, Allie. I gotta go. Have fun with your *boyfriend.*"

There was no need to respond. It no longer mattered what I said. He was already closed off, and quite honestly, I didn't have the patience to console Greg at that moment as I merged from I-35 onto 435 heading west. "Bye, Greg" was all I said, as breezy as I could be.

Once again, there was no good-bye on the other end, just a quiet click. What was it with me and men hanging up on me? Refusing to ponder the thought, I focused my attention on the merging traffic and the road ahead. My therapist once told me that when I found myself getting anxious or worrying about the past or present, I needed to become hyper-aware of where my hands were, to stay in the moment. The notion behind this is that if you tell yourself, "Stay where your hands are," you will force yourself to focus on the current moment and every sensation present thereof. In this case, my hands were on my steering wheel, and instead of thinking of Greg whom I was leaving behind and Nick who lay ahead, I brought my attention to my car. The smell of my car's interior (a combination of French fries and pine tree from the car freshener), the sounds of the cars outside my windows, the feel of the leather steering wheel, the taste of the gum I had just begun chewing, the colors of the cars passing by, and the patches of grass lining the highway—becoming cognizant of these things kept me in the moment, at least *for* a moment. By the time I reached I-70 West, my hands were in California, seeing Nick and touching his face and kissing his lips. I no longer could taste my gum, but only his sweet kiss. I couldn't hear the cars outside, only his words reassuring me that he did indeed love me. And his smell, oh his masculine smell of cologne mixed with aftershave, quickly replaced the stink that was the inside of my "mom" car. Hmm. I think I needed to practice this exercise more.

The rest of the drive to Topeka flew by in this state of bliss. When I arrived at my parent's house, it was almost like waking up from a ridiculously amazing dream from which you never wanted to awaken. Reality sunk in that not only was I exhausted, but I also had to be "Mom" for the day and then hop on an airplane bright and early to fly halfway across the country only to have a formal "meeting" with the man who hated my guts.

When my little sprite came bolting out the front door with his arms wide open, I was reminded once again that in all actuality, my life *was* a dream. This little man, despite his recent "too cool for you" attitude, loved me more than anything on earth. How blessed I was. How blessed I am.

12

The afternoon was spent swinging in the backyard with my little man, going on a hot and humid bike ride with my dad, helping my mom cook my favorite meal for dinner (Granddaddies Chicken), and playing with my precious niece, Maya, whom Christy and Adam had brought home from China in March. Though she was a "newborn" (a term the agency used loosely as she was already five months old when they found out about her) when the adoption process began, she was a tiny fifteen-month-old when they held her in their arms for the first time in March. To tell you how incredibly precious this little munchkin was to our family would take up a whole new book. Like many children, especially girls, given up for adoption in China, she was born with a cleft pallet, something for which Adam and Christy had already sought consultation and scheduled her first surgery to take place later that summer. Some scars, however, are environmental, and sweet little Maya Rae had continuous nightmares. She was also extremely attached to both Christy and Adam—a product of severe separation anxiety.

When my precious niece arrived, I assumed the usual position required for her comfort and sat cross-legged on the living room floor. Adam set her on the floor at his feet across the room from me, and I held out my arms with a smile on my face. Sam and my parents were in the back room waiting. When Maya heard loud noises or too many people were gathered in a room, she would immediately begin rocking back and forth, holding her ears. The perceived "chaos" she was experiencing was indicative of the discord she experienced in the overcrowded orphanage. With adequate therapy and due diligence on the part of us, her family, she was expected to overcome this hurdle. In the meantime, however, reintroductions took patience and perseverance.

Apparently, my parents and the rest of my family, including Sam, had already conquered Maya's reluctance for contact. In the short three months she had been a part of our family, they had gained her trust, being able to spend time with her on a regular basis. I, on the other hand, only got the opportunity to see her once, maybe twice, a month, so I still had some work to do. As I sat there with my arms open, Maya looked up at me, and for the first time upon reintroduction to me, she smiled! Oh, my heart leapt with joy! Once again I was reminded, who needs a stinkin' Hollywood hunk when I had this amazing family?

It took a few minutes (Christy strategically placing herself next to me and my brother verbally and enthusiastically encouraging her); but then, in less time than ever before, my sweet niece began crawling to me! Oh, for the love of Pete, I was excited! I wanted to shriek with delight (but knew better of it because she would have freaked out). As she reached me, she hesitantly touched one of my outstretched arms with a finger. It took everything I could to not just scoop her up in my arms, but this routine is kind of like that with an unfamiliar dog, or a feral cat. One always reached out the back of the hand for the dog to sniff before petting it.

After another couple of minutes with me whispering words of praise and love and Maya touching me several times, making darn sure I would not hurt her, she climbed onto my lap! I wrapped my arms around her and rocked her slowly back in forth, the tears silently escaping. The look on Adam's face was one of pride and unconditional daddy love, with maybe just the slightest hint of affection for his younger sister.

Once everything was calm and Maya climbed off my lap to play with a toy in the corner of the room that was deemed "Maya's Corner," my mom and dad came out together, only to be welcomed with a smile and a wave. They crouched down for a hug, but Maya was too busy playing to be bothered with pleasantries. Since Sam was not as familiar to her as my parents, he stayed back until Adam had a chance to explain who else was in the house. Sam was used to this whole routine; and so quietly, he came out of the back room, crouched down several feet away from her, and outstretched his arms, saying in his singsong voice, "Hi, My-My." It was so cute that my baby boy had made up the nickname for her that everyone had latched onto. She turned from her toy and absolutely beamed when she saw him. Crawling quickly (her motor skills being delayed due to her environment in China that she had only just begun crawling and was months away from walking), Maya reached Sam within no time, offering him a small toy she had managed to clutch in her tiny hand as she crawled.

The two of them settled into a rousing game of "throw the toy and crawl after it" while Aaron, Christy, Mom, Dad, and I went into the kitchen and enjoyed a good half hour of uninterrupted conversation. My brother and his bride beamed with pride as they told of the strides sweet Maya was making. They had been able to leave her with Mom and Dad on one occasion for an hour, which was huge progress. She had also begun saying "Dada," a little morsel that left my brother grinning from ear to ear. Oh, I was so incredibly thankful for their little bundle of happiness! Christy was able to stay home with Maya and work with her nonstop on her motor skills, both fine and gross, as well as her verbal skills. Aside from her social issues, which were indeed improving, and her upcoming surgery (the first in a line of many), the only other glaring problem were the nightmares. Maya slept in a crib next to their bed, but most nights she would end up nestled between them, latching onto one of them for dear life as she was soothed back to sleep following a nightmare. They had also started noticing her violently trying to smother her baby doll with pillows on more than one occasion. As Christy researched the possible reason behind this, she was afraid that Maya had probably bore witness to babies being suffocated at the orphanage. This, of course, would take a lifetime of therapy to get past.

The evening commenced with a rerun of *America's Funniest Home Videos*—jammie style, and a bowl of popcorn. After complaining to my mom about how nervous I was and about my lack of sleep the night before, she hooked me up with one of her Xanax pills. My sweet mama had always suffered with depression and anxiety, so her medicine cabinet was for sure a sight to see. I was thankful for the medicine as it knocked me out within an hour, and I stayed asleep until the alarm went off at 5:30 a.m.

Sam had quickly snuggled into his summer sleeping schedule as soon as school got out, so I knew he wouldn't awaken for at least another two hours. I tiptoed into his room and kissed his sweet cheeks several times (I had already said my "good-byes" the night before), grabbed my to-go cup of coffee my dad had made me and headed out the door. Per my momma's norm, she wouldn't rise until ten or after, and so I wasn't surprised at the scarce send-off party. Dad was enough with his coffee handout and sound advice: "Don't bow down, kid. You've said all the sorrys you need to say on this one. And listen, parts of LA are super rough. Please, please be careful. I stuck some pepper spray in your purse. Don't be afraid to use it. And here is some extra cash for you to park in the garage lot at the airport. I don't want you out in economy having to wait on a damn bus." I love my daddy!

It took a little over an hour to get to the airport. I have to admit, it was mighty nice being able to pull into the garage right out front. I had preprinted my boarding pass and was only taking a carry-on, so all I had to do was grab another coffee—Starbucks this time—and wait at the terminal for my 8:20 flight. Praise the Lord, it was a direct flight. Props to Nick for that one.

I hadn't even bothered to look at my ticket to see what my seat number was. Quite honestly, I usually flew Southwest, and they have open seating and boarding groups. So when the lady started to announce boarding, I finally glanced down at my ticket to check which boarding group I was in. Of course, with American Airlines, there is no A, B, or C boarding group, so it took me a second to figure out I was in *first class*! The few times I have been on an airplane that has first class, I always feel like a total dork walking past the people who were already nestled in their extrawide seats, cocktail in hand and legs stretched all the way out. But that day it was *my* turn, and I felt completely smug. With my nose in the air, I walked past all of the "second-class" flyers, bounced down the Jetway onto the plane, and found my seat. I couldn't wait to look up into the faces of all the "lesser" people boarding the plane in the moments that followed. Yes, I am being a snob on purpose. Being a meager, single-parent teacher in Kansas, I don't get many opportunities to enjoy the finer things in life.

The flight was a delightful, spoiled-rotten three hours of quiet bliss. I think I had one stewardess all to myself. It was bizarre really. There were two ladies working our section, and I swear I never saw the one who served me serving anyone else. I mean, I saw her help out the other stewardess, delivering drinks and food, but she never personally "waited" on anyone other than me. I never once had an empty glass or a plate that sat for even five seconds after I had swallowed the final morsel. To top it off, I was given a bottomless supply of warm blankets and a pillow. I mean to tell ya, as soon as the blanket cooled off even a little bit, a new one was brought. Now *that* I know was just a perk of being me, as everyone else had to ask for a warm blanket refresher. I was sure it was all just a fluke. I mean, Nick hated me. In no way did he arrange for me to be spoiled rotten…unless…unless he wanted me to get a taste of what I would be missing out on. The thought crossed my mind that this trip would be the only time I would be treated in such a fashion during travel, and maybe that was the point. Maybe he was just trying to rub the whole thing in my face, like "Ha-ha, look what you could have had, Allie, but not now, even though *I* get it every day!" What a jerk!

I glanced at the empty aisle seat to my right. Initially, I was overjoyed that the seat lay empty. I could spread out and do my thing; I didn't need anyone bothering me on this my maiden first-class voyage. But then, when I was becoming agitated at the fact that this had all been done as a reminder of the treatment a woman more deserving of Nick's affection would receive daily, I longed for conversation, companionship. I mean, no way would I tell the whole story. I was just getting past my most infamous, desperate-woman status, but at least I could channel some of these thoughts. I thought of the movie *Bridesmaids* and suddenly wished any one of those women were on this flight with me. I peeked back at the curtain separating the elite from the average, secretly hoping Kristen Wiig would come barreling through wasted on alcohol and sleeping pills. "There is a colonial woman on the wing," she would shout. "There is something they're not telling us. She was out there churning butter. She was churning butter!" Gosh I needed a little Kristen Wiig hilarity to ease my angst.

I was imagining her saddling up next to me—the actress, not the character—and carrying on a hysterical conversation, when it hit me. I sat up straighter and pushed my butt off the seat so I could turn around and see the rest of the cabin. There were three empty first-class seats. A rather large man, not Kristen Wiig unfortunately, was coming through the curtain from coach. As he pulled it to the side, I quickly glanced around the rest of the airplane. If a lack of heads was any indication, it would seem that there were at least a handful of empty seats back there as well. *Hmm. Interesting.*

You see where I'm going with this? Nick had told me it was a completely full flight and that he couldn't get Greg on the flight. But then, gasp, what was that right next to me? *An empty freakin' seat!!* And there were several more just like it all over the airplane. He *lied!* Wait, *he lied?* My mind began to swarm around the possibility that Nick was, in fact, a little jealous and, quite frankly, a little controlling. Had he made up the whole full-flight story just so I wouldn't bring a man with me? I pondered this on the rest of the flight to LA, and like the shoulder-angel-and-devil phenomena, the battle in my head raged on. If it were given a voice, it would sound like this:

"He hates you!"

"But he's jealous of another man!"

"He just wants you to see what you're missing out on."

"But maybe all of this special treatment was because he cares."

"No. He is flaunting, bragging. He is throwing your mistake in your face, ya dummy!"

"But what about the seats? They're empty."

"The airline was mistaken. Maybe people cancelled."

"But he did hesitate when I told him it was a guy. Maybe he didn't want him to come."

"Maybe he didn't even try to get him on the flight because he didn't want to waste any more money on you than he already had!"

Yeah, that last one stuck. I mean sure, he may have been a little jealous or actually probably just pissed that I would have the nerve to bring a guy out to LA on his dime after I had completely broken his heart. In fact, as the plane's wheels touched down and we skidded to a crawl, it hit me how ridiculously selfish I had been, yet again. I had lied to him, made him believe I was someone I wasn't, and had broken his heart. Then, when he finally was stable enough to return to his life, I drop the stupid bomb on him that not only am I possibly seeing someone but also that I expect him to fly that person out with me and put him up on *his* dime. Who the hell did I think I was? As we taxied to the terminal, I was gutted with the sudden realization that I did not, under any circumstance, deserve Nicholas Price.

13

Once the captain approved the release of seat belts, my flight attendant was right at my side with a bottle of some expensive, cold water and a Ghirardelli mint. She inquired about my satisfaction with the service I received, much like a puppy sits at one's feet after pooping in the yard, awaiting his affection and a treat. I, of course, commended her on her superior service, after which she graciously nodded her flushed-faced head, grabbed my bags overhead, and asked if I would like her to carry them out of the terminal for me. Okay, folks, I have never been in first class before, but for real with this? This was excessive!

I literally laughed at her. I couldn't help it, and I stifled it as soon as the first chuckle escaped. *But come on, lady! I am a fully capable woman and guess what? I'm not that special! At all, in fact.* Once I composed my amusement, I gingerly smiled and said, "No thanks, that won't be necessary." I wanted to sound all professional, what with how I was being treated. I retrieved my two bags from her hand and exited the plane.

When I made it to the end of the long Jetway, I rummaged through my purse to find the instructions Nick had sent about navigating my way out of the airport. Luckily, it was a short jaunt to the doors that opened to the bright California sun. I headed toward a set of doors and was intercepted by a man in a black suit, holding a sign that I hadn't bothered to read. He said, "Ms. Holly?"

I was confused. How did someone know me here? Stay with me, guys. I'm not gonna lie; it took me a second to piece it together. I literally thought someone from back home recognized me. And by the way he used my formal name, I assumed it was a parent from the school at which I taught. Only kids and their parents called me Ms. Holly. Well, and telemarketers.

I cocked my head and squinted at the man, who was hard to identify given the way the sun was cascading a halo around his entire body, like he was a Greek god. "Yes?" As he outstretched his hand, I awaited the mention of a familiar name.

"I'm James Stafford. Pleasure." And he shook my hand.

I still didn't get it, guys. I really didn't, so I just responded with a casual "Um, hi?" A question, not a statement.

"Right this way, ma'am." And then he reached out for my bags.

Ha! Oh, duh. I'm an idiot. "Oh, yes, yes!" I exclaimed. "I'm so sorry. I'm just not used to having someone meet me to pick me up at the airport. Please forgive me for being a doofus." Oh Lord, I said "doofus." I really did, you guys. I mean, who says that still? It's like people who still say "Not!" after they make an exclamation. Or "Psych!" I liken my doofus comment to someone who says they had a "brain fart." Can I just tell you how much I hate the word "fart?" It is such an ugly-sounding word, which evokes images involving all five senses. First, and most obviously, a certain smell always comes to mind. Then you hear it and see the ugly face of the person squinting their eyes and grunting one out. Then you can literally "feel" the air pass through their pants into the outside world, polluting the earth. And finally, the taste. I'm sorry, but imagining someone's "fart" actually tastes! Okay, maybe I am going too far; but in my family, once my sister had kids, we started calling them "fluffs." And it just sounds so much sweeter, doesn't it? Like a little squeak with no smell, coming from a tiny toddler. Is that a stretch?

I followed Mr...Oh crap! I had already forgotten his name. "I'm sorry, sir. I was so out of it back there. What's your name again?"

He gave me the sweetest pity smile and reminded me, "James Stafford."

"Oh, that's right!" I hit my forehead with the palm of my right hand. "I'm Allie Holly."

Mr. Stafford (I have to call him that because he seemed too formally dressed to be called by his first name) nodded in silence, still grinning as I remembered him addressing me by my last name just seconds earlier. Continuing to feel like an idiot, I spotted my full name typed out on his sign. Mercy's sake.

So I followed Mr. Stafford out to what happened to be a gorgeous, freshly washed, black stretch limo. And it wasn't just any stretch limo. It was obviously one of those expensive brands of car, like a Cadillac or a Mercedes or something. I never took the time to notice. With his keychain, he unlocked the doors and jogged in front of me to open my door for me. I climbed in the backseat, trying my damndest not to stick my butt in his face. I had on shorts that were definitely too short for a woman my age to be wearing, but I just need to tell y'all that when your legs are the only part of your body that haven't gone to hell in a handbasket, you try and accentuate them. After all, I was going to LA, for Pete's sake. You know, LA? The land of the leggy, pencil-thin blonde bombshells! I had to appear to fit in. At that moment, however, I was second-guessing my decision, hoping I wasn't giving Mr. Stafford a peep show of my granny panties, err, G-string. I meant G-string! Yeah right.

As soon as I was planted safely on the leather backseat, Mr. Stafford shut my door; and by the motion and sound at the back of the limo, I could tell he was securing my bags in the trunk. It took my eyes a second to adjust to the darkness, all the windows being tinted the darkest color one could tint windows. When Mr. Stafford climbed into the front seat and engaged the ignition, the running lamps came on, and I could see every beautiful thing in the car. Now this wasn't one of those cheesy, disco-like limos. This baby was plush and modern with sophisticated features. There would be no horny high school boys affording this bad boy for the senior prom. No sirree. One had to have some bank to afford the price tag of this thing.

As I visually scoured the place, Mr. Stafford unrolled the window separating himself from me and spoke tenderly, "Ms. Holly, there are beverages in the console on your left, a bottle of red wine and chilled white to your right. If you will notice that refrigerator to your left, there are all sorts of fruit and cheeses for your pleasure and crackers and snacks in the cupboard beside. Please help yourself. Also, Mr. Price has provided an advanced screening of *Liberation* for your viewing pleasure, if you would like. I have it all set up and the remote control is right next to where you are sitting. Simply turn it on and push 'play.' If that does not interest you, press the button on your left to buzz me, and I will give you step-by-step instructions to watch the television or other movies. Does this suit you at this time?"

Uh, what? I was still stuck on the part during which he mentioned Mr. Price's name. I mean, I knew Nick had sent this man to pick me up, but I figured he probably just called some company, gave them his credit card information, and directions. I didn't think it was like a personalized thing in which he actually met with the guy and brought him a DVD for crying out loud! Of course, I would later find that it wasn't a DVD at all, but a digital stream from some electronic device. Nevertheless, Nick had a major hand in all of this.

Mr. Stafford cleared his throat, patiently awaiting the reply I had forgotten to give.

"Um, hey, that sounds great. Thanks so much Mr...." *For the love of God, do not forget his name again!* "Stafford. You are too kind." Nailed it!

"Don't mention it. And please, call me James."

I nodded, although I already knew I would never call him James.

"Our drive today should be around one hour, depending upon traffic. Would you like me to stop anywhere? Are you hungry for more than the snacks you can find back there? I would be happy to stop somewhere to get you takeout."

"Oh no, no. That won't be necessary. I am great. Thank you so much!" And with that, he rolled up the window and off we went, merging into the hellafied LAX traffic.

I eased back into the seat and continued to take in the sights both inside and outside the car. Soft music played on the speakers and I reached for the remote control. There was a button for the music station (XM radio) and then the buttons for the television. I decided to take a peek at *Liberation*, although I knew I wouldn't have enough time to finish it. Nevertheless, I wanted to see the Omaha set once again and view the scene to which I had bore witness that summer day, which seemed like ten years before.

Once I turned on the television and hit "play," I crawled up to the console, which was basically a large leather-encased cooler, and opened the hinged lid. Nestled into the ice lay a six-pack of Miller Lite bottles and two sixteen-ounce bottles of Diet Coke. This could not possibly be a coincidence, could it? In the short time I had spent with Nick, I drank my weight in Miller Lite, and I am sure I relayed my love of Diet Coke to him at some point. Had he really made sure my favorite beverages would be waiting for me in the limo?

I convinced myself that this was probably just another fluke, like the special treatment on the plane ride, or maybe yet another attempt to make me regret what I had done. I didn't dare allow myself to consider the possibility that he still held on to some sort of compassionate feelings for me. To assume so would only set me up for further disappointment. After all, he had been pretty clear on the phone that my visit to LA was strictly business to ensure his vocational success.

To calm my thoughts, I grabbed a Miller Lite, used the built-in bottle opener to twist off the cap, and settled back into my comfy seat. I could not even stomach the thought of eating anything as my anxiety had kicked up a notch since the final descent of the plane. The opening credits were appearing on the screen as the camera took the viewer on a long, twisty ride down a two-lane road through hills, the plains, and a forest before finally slowing on a long driveway up to a farmhouse (*the* farmhouse!) and the final name, Nicholas Price, appeared on the screen as the music silenced. I swallowed hard. His name, in bold, on the television. I would never get used to that.

I began gulping—yes, *gulping*—my beer. I was going to need all the relaxation I could get to make it through this movie. I briefly thought of Jen and how the other two movies in the series I had seen for the first time had been with her. I ached for her now. If only she wasn't so psycho, she could possibly be sitting next to me watching this special screening in a fancy limo in LA on our way to meet up with my boyfriend. Oh, if things had only worked out differently.

The first twenty minutes strictly consisted of stupid Sarah Alton and the other actors (I forgot their names) who played her captors. The longer I watched that nasty girl, who, by the way, looked gorgeous even when she was made up to look hideous, the more jealous I felt. I'll be damned if I ever looked as good fully made *up* as she looked fully made *down!* And despite my natural inclination to pick apart her acting skills, she was as brilliant as always!

About thirty minutes in, Nick made his debut. Had I been sitting in a theater, all the women and teenagers would have been whooping and whistling at this point. But in this highly expensive ride, there was just me, myself, and I having trouble taking my eyes off the lips I had once tenderly, and then more passionately kissed. Oh, he was so damn hot. The way he walked and spoke, even accent-free, was the sexiest thing I had ever witnessed. It made me long to touch him. Even while I was fully engrossed in the movie, my mind would frequently click to the realization that on the following day, I would be seeing him again. I grabbed another beer.

Traffic was slow. I was totally fine with it. In fact, sitting in the limousine, I felt safe, as moments attached to moments brought me a sense of comfort. It was just me, the nice man who was driving, and Nicholas Price. I didn't want to move forward. I didn't want to exit the car. Knowing that the time would soon come, however, I chugged my beer and grabbed yet another, just as the scene I had the privilege of witnessing with my own eyes came upon the screen. I scooted to the edge of my seat, as if inching closer would bring me right there; back to where I was on that glorious day, sitting in the chair with my headphones on, listening to Nick call me beautiful for all within earshot, or headset-shot, to hear.

It is crazy what they can do with technology. The raw footage I had watched on that screen on set was great, but set to music and added lighting, it was phenomenal! I felt so proud sitting there watching the man with whom I had fallen head-over-heels in love. I had shared some of the most precious moments of my life with him during those few days; and in a few weeks, millions of people would be watching this same thing on the big screen, having no idea that during this particular scene, a smitten thirty-something Midwestern mom was on set in the background falling in love.

The car, which had been holding a pretty steady pace as we traversed the highway to the outskirts of town, was now slowing on an exit ramp. My heart rate quickened as I peeked out the window. I saw buildings and houses, but nothing too impressive. Certainly this wasn't Beverly Hills. I grabbed another beer and continued watching the movie as Mr. Stafford navigated the stoplight-filled streets.

Every time the car came to a stop, I would glance out at my surroundings, just to make sure I wasn't at my destination yet. I wasn't ready—or maybe I was. I was becoming keenly aware that I was a little tipsy; and with every stop, start, and turn, my tummy began feeling a little queasy. I realized that watching the movie in the car, along with the booze was probably not the best combination, and so I scooted over to the left window and unrolled it.

We were at a stoplight and the warm air did not feel the least bit refreshing, but at least the open window brought in some light. A car pulled up next to us in the left-turn lane, and all eyes were on me. Panicking, I quickly rolled up the window and sat back. The thought hit me that what if people in LA would recognize me from the news and magazines? Surely they weren't so incredibly used to seeing limousines that they stopped looking at them, trying to get a glance at the passengers in the back. I mean in California, of all places, you have the best chance of actually seeing a celebrity in a limo; unlike Kansas City where the prime limo inhabitants are teens dressed in formals, or bridal parties. Of course they would check out the limo in LA; and if they scrutinized too hard, they would surely recognize me, wouldn't they?

Maybe I was just having beer paranoia, but nevertheless, I turned off the film and opened the sunroof to let in some fresh air. As we continued down more streets that were not quite suburban yet not quite urban either, I realized that most vehicles that passed contained at least one individual who would gawk at our car.

Finally, we began to slow, although I did not see a stoplight nor any cars slowing in front of us. *We must be getting close. Crap.* I looked out the passenger side windows and saw a sign proudly displaying Beverly Hills. We were there! Mr. Stafford turned right and up we crept a treelined road. The scenery was beautiful with the hills, valleys, and the trees. It was amazing, but not half as amazing as the first home we came across. Holy cajoles! I am telling you, if you haven't been to Beverly Hills, drop this book right now and hop on a plane! It is spectacular and immodest and, quite plainly, overindulgent.

The houses that I could actually see (the ones that weren't tucked behind a grove of trees or an enormous privacy fence) were a sight to behold. The pictures you see on TV of houses belonging to the rich and famous do not do the sheer size of these mammoth mansions justice. The infinity pools, tennis courts, hot tubs, and landscaping-encased homes that were at least ten thousand square feet were beyond breathtaking. Most, if not all, had at least one guest house larger than double the size of my home. Oh, and the views! Each of these properties overlooked the most amazing views of rolling hills, vineyards, and the city. No wonder so many celebrities live in Beverly Hills. It was phenomenal!

I was contemplating how this area, set atop a cluster of foothills, could be full of such luscious wealth while just down the hill sat some of the most crappy houses I had ever seen. It reminded me of New York in a strange, twisted way. In both places, all of these rich and famous people choose to live in the filthiest cities on earth. Sure, their penthouse apartments are beautiful and spacious in lower Manhattan, but then they exit the building and are hit square in the face with stank and pollution. They walk past homeless men taking craps on the sidewalk. Interesting phenomenon. I decided right then and there that if I ever became famous (ha-ha) I would never leave the crisp, clean Kansas air.

We passed a sign that read "The Beverly Hills Hotel" and literally looked like it was scrawled in the sixties. I couldn't imagine how on earth such a crappy hotel could sit in the middle of this Beverly Hills beauty until Mr. Stafford stopped at an iron gate to speak to an attendant and I got my first glimpse of the hotel. My heart leapt with joy as I realized I was going to be staying in a beautiful, rich, prestigious five-star hotel that night.

As the gatekeeper opened up the large electric wrought iron gate, the limo slowly pulled through, stopping under the awning at the entrance. Two men greeted me at my car door and called me by name. "Good morning, Ms. Holly." One of them offered a hand to help me out of the seat. Instantly, I panicked, wondering if I had any cash with which to leave a tip. I rummaged through my purse as Mr. Stafford appeared from behind the car with my bags. He very slyly shook hands with one of the gentleman, exchanging cash with his right hand while pushing my hand that had retrieved a measly five dollars, back into my purse.

"Not necessary," Mr. Stafford whispered out of the side of his mouth. "It has been taken care of."

Feeling suddenly shy and unworthy, I simply said, "Uh, thank you."

"I will tell Mr. Price you said so," Stafford replied.

Another punch in the gut at the mention of his name. The two gentlemen had already shouldered my bags when Mr. Stafford turned to face me with a pleasant smile. "It has been a privilege, Ms. Holly, and here's my card. I will be here at ten tomorrow morning to get you, but in the meantime, I have strict orders that you are to notify me, and only me, when you would like to go somewhere, and I will return to take you wherever you would like to go."

I scrunched my eyebrows. Was he serious? Could Nick really care that much about my well-being, or was he merely only looking out for his own hide so that I would remain incognito, traveling via a blacked-out limousine, everywhere I went? I contemplated fighting this issue right then and there and informing Mr. Stafford that should I need to go anywhere, I would be calling a cab, but it seemed pointless. He would counter and then probably call Nick and get Nick all fired up. The bottom line was, if I wanted to go somewhere, I would go wherever I wanted, whenever I wanted, and *however* I wanted. I answered to *no one!* So in the end, I just smiled and nodded, as if in agreement.

The two men asked me to follow them, and I did as I was told, nodding one last time at Mr. Stafford before I walked empty-handed toward the revolving brass-lined doors. As we entered the lobby, I was stunned speechless with the magnificent beauty of the place. Glass and rose gold and chandeliers and the scent of heaven—it was all present in this large, marble-floored room. I was severely underdressed, by the way.

The two gentlemen were apparently not interested in me taking my sweet time admiring every little thing in the lobby as they were halfway across the floor and approaching a hallway when one of them noticed I was no longer following. They were so far away from me that I couldn't even hear the one tell the other to hold up. I could just read his lips. I nodded and hurried my step toward them.

When I was within earshot, the one who had spotted my lag asked, "Ma'am, is everything all right?" apparently assuming I had a problem with the hotel or something.

"No, no. Everything is great! I have just never been here before, that's all." And with that explanation, I swear I saw the silent one look me up and down with the slightest eye movements, as if saying, "Well, duh! Look at you!" I glared at him, my facial expression betraying the rosy cheeks of embarrassment. I nodded toward the hallway, encouraging them to continue their lead.

We arrived in front of room 121, and the nice man handed me a key and nodded toward the keycard slot. I pushed in the card, and the door clicked unlocked. Before I had a chance to reach the handle, the same man grabbed it and opened up the door, holding it back for me to enter. This whole pomp and circumstance was a little too much for my quiet Kansas lifestyle.

As I walked to the end of the foyer, my eyes adjusted to the breathtaking beauty of the space in front of me. There was a living room with a Victorian-looking sofa and love seat nestled around a stone fireplace. A kitchenette to the side employed only stainless steel appli—*Wait a second! That smell! I know that smell!*

I instantly took off on a brisk walk through the living room, following my nose like Toucan Sam. Where was it coming from? I pushed open the first door I came to: the bathroom (though I'm sure they called it the "powder room"). Nope, not coming from in there. Ahead of me was a double door leading to what I assumed was the bedroom. A quick four steps and I was at the threshold, pushing both doors open with crazed urgency. The aroma overtook me as I saw it. There, floating in a gigantic lavender vase, was a beautiful bouquet of tuberose!

14

Okay, this was too weird. Tuberose was my all-time favorite flower, and when Nick had gotten in the habit of sending me flowers every day after we met, the final bouquet I received was the tuberose. I had only received roses from him up until then and never, I was sure of it, mentioned to him that the tuberose was my very favorite. When he sent them I went crazy, mentally trying to figure out how he could possibly know. I mean, the tuberose is not a flower that people usually think to send. Heck, most people don't even know what it is. I was going to get to the bottom of it when all hell broke loose and I ended up crushing his faith in me and he disappeared. Needless to say, I never asked how he knew I loved them.

I heard one of the gentlemen in the other room clear his throat in the foyer and realized I hadn't "dismissed" them as I was certain was customary. I may not be high class, but I had seen enough movies to know that in a situation such as this, you dismiss the bellboy and tip him. Once again, scrounging around my purse, I retrieved the five-dollar bill and scurried into the other room, the smell of tuberose still blessing my nostrils.

"So sorry, you guys," I said as I reached for my bags.

"No, ma'am. Where would you like us to set them?"

"Oh…um," I said, looking around, "over there on the sofa would be fine." I never called it a sofa. It was always a couch to me, but sofa sounded more highbrow.

They carefully placed my bags on the *couch* and retreated toward the door. I intercepted and held out the money, confessing, "I am so sorry. This is the only cash I have."

"No, no." The nice one shook his head. "This isn't necessary. It has already been taken care of." Of course it had.

"You know what, I insist!" *Come on, dude. This is the least I can do. Let me feel like a second-class citizen at least. Even a second-class citizen tips a bellboy.*

The nice one looked at the jerky one and shrugged his shoulders, as if asking what he should do. In return, the jerk just shrugged his shoulders back.

Letting them both off the hook, I exclaimed, "Look, you take it or you will make me very unhappy!"

The nice one gave me a big grin, realizing my desperation, and gingerly accepted the money before bowing and stating, "Thank you kindly, ma'am."

I closed the door after them as they left. I'm sure the jerk was probably making wise cracks about my cheap tip and my cheap clothing, but I was over it. He was a bellboy after all. Screw him. I wandered around the suite, opening every cupboard and drawer, until I finally pulled back the sheer curtains covering the French doors opening to the private patio. Unlocking the doors, I let myself out and was stunned by the beautiful garden view. Every type of tropical flower and plant was present among the luscious green grass. There were palm trees and a stream, the water source somewhere nearby as I heard the heavenly cascading waterfall. *Man, I could get used to this!*

It was late morning in California, and I had a full day of no plans. I had no intentions of calling James Stafford for a ride anywhere, so all my fun would have to be had on hotel property. Clearly, I would need to get cleaned up and wear the only halfway appropriate thing I brought to wear—the same sundress I had worn in Omaha the night I met Nick. I had planned on wearing it the next day in some sort of half attempt to rekindle old feelings and bring a little nostalgia to the meeting, so I would need to fight my natural ability to spill something on myself.

I opened the refrigerator and found bottles of water, more Miller Lite, and Diet Coke. Of course. Either it was the sweetest gesture ever or the most cruel. I was still undecided. The fridge was also stocked with every food imaginable. Fruits, veggies, dips, sweets—you name it, it was all there. Mercy, how long did they think I was staying? They would have to roll me out if I indulged myself in all they had to offer.

I grabbed a cold water bottle and headed into the master bath. The Jacuzzi was huge, with a fireplace already lit, at one end. There were single roses nestled in bud vases all around the rim. I started the bath and returned to the living room to make sure all the doors were locked. Safe and secure, I returned to the bathroom, opened up the closet, and found the softest robe in the world draping from a hanger. I pulled it off the hanger, folded it on the side of the tube, undressed, and sank into the heavenly Jacuzzi waters.

I have no idea how long I soaked there in those raging bubbles, but if my prune-like fingers were any indication, I would guess at least an hour. I even think I dozed off a couple of times, the scent of tuberose still faintly present, despite my acclimation to it. When I finally emerged from the water and wrapped myself in the soft-as-clouds robe, I scampered into the living room, forgoing the sundress altogether. There would be no going anywhere that day. No getting dressed. No doing hair. No makeup applied. I had everything I needed right there in that suite. The actual name of the suite, I learned as I read the hotel literature, was the Grand Deluxe, with a hefty price tag of around four thousand dollars a *night!* And to think I was convinced Nick was putting me up in the Bates Motel!

In between my reading about the hotel history and surrounding area, I caught a few movies, ordered room service (yes, still in my robe), and called Sam a couple of times. More than once, I felt pangs of regret as I wished I could call Jen and tell her all about my experience. I missed having a best friend. Sometimes even more than I missed having a husband, I missed having a best friend. I mean, sure, I had friends from school and church whom I adored, but not one of them would be someone I would call to gossip about my crazy experience in LA. Jen would be that person. Jen *was* that person.

I shook her out of my thoughts and called my sister Maggie instead. She and Lisa would totally indulge my retelling of the days' events, even if they did have other stuff going on in the background. They may not understand its magnitude the way Jen would have, but they loved me unconditionally and could get into petty high school drama if I insisted. I must admit, I was kind of surprised and quite bummed that I had not heard from Nick at all that day. The fact that we were in the same city and then the personal touches I sensed were from him (Miller Lite, tuberose, etc.), I guess I thought maybe I would hear from him. Even more shocking, yet not disappointing at all, was that I had not heard from Greg.

I knew my time in LA was way too short, so after I talked to both of my sisters and my sister-in-law, I lived vicariously through the guide books and brochures and decided that was enough for this trip. In the morning, I would awaken, make myself look halfway decent, meet Nick (Oh my gosh, I was meeting Nick!), and fly home that evening. As for what I was going to do from the time the meeting was over until my return flight, I had no idea, but I halfway sensed I would just be spending it in paradise, err, my hotel suite or the airport, what with being a fish *completely* out of water in this town.

A round midnight, I turned off the TV and the fireplace and, exhausted, I managed to put on my T-shirt (one of Chris's

T-shirts in which I slept), and climbed into the massive, pillow-topped four-poster king-size bed. Adjusting the nine—yes, nine—pillows, I laid my head down, and miraculously that was the last thing I remembered. It is amazing the sleep that can be had on a mountain of cold, fluffy, feather-stuffed bedding.

The next morning, forgoing a wake-up call, certain I would be up at dawn, I awakened to read 8:45 on the alarm clock. Wow, I was impressed with my mad sleeping ability, yet I shouldn't have been surprised given the serious lack of any sort of effective slumber throughout the previous few days. I showered, dressed, and then headed to the cafe for a complimentary breakfast. Of course, at the Beverly Hills Hotel, a complimentary breakfast consisted of the most gourmet foods I have ever tasted, most of them French.

With a few minutes to spare, I went back to my room, touched up my makeup, grabbed my purse, and headed to the lobby where, surprisingly, James Stafford was already waiting in the lobby, leaning against a two-story pillar with sunglasses on. Ooh, incognito. He thought he was pretty cool apparently. As he saw me approach, he straightened up and met me halfway across the lobby, nodding and simply acknowledging, "Ms. Holly."

"Hey, Mr. Stafford."

"Please, call me James."

"Then call me Allie," I teased.

I saw the smallest of grins as he said, "I can't promise anything, but I'll see if I can get away with it."

"Man alive, your boss must be a real stickler."

He chuckled. "Mr. Price is very kind." And he pointed toward the door for me to lead the way.

A-ha! Freakin' *Nick* was his boss! I decided to say nothing, although it confirmed my suspicions that the refreshments in the limo were not a random coincidence. We walked toward the revolving doors, and I kid you not, my mind was so incredibly preoccupied with this newfound knowledge that I completely forgot to get out of the damn thing when it opened to the outside! Once I realized, I was already back around to the lobby. Oh my gosh, you guys, my cheeks burned with fire. I was humiliated! Quickly, I got my bearings and looked out to see if James flippin' Stafford had seen me. What, was I crazy? He had to see me; he was behind me in the stupid glass stall behind me.

There he stood, head tilted with a silly grin on his face. I could tell from the top rim of his sunglasses that his eyebrows were scrunched together. He was confused and amused. I couldn't help it; I burst out laughing. It was either that or start crying. I think my nervous energy from the morning, mixed with my humiliation, created a perfect storm of intense emotions inside of me that could no longer be contained; and everything just burst out of me in the form of hysterics—first laughter, then tears. It was all just too much.

I had been holding it together so well since I received Nick's voice mail three days before, convincing myself that none of this was that big of a deal, nothing to get too excited about. But that was just me lying to myself, much like the way I lied to myself when Chris was sick; deep down, I believe I knew he was dying. But as long as I refused the magnitude of it, it didn't exist. The same was true about this visit; and there, in the revolving door at the Beverly Hills Hotel, on my second time around, I absolutely *lost* it!

As I finally came sauntering out like an idiot I was smiling, bowed head shaking from side to side with tears streaming down my cheeks. I reached Stafford and lifted my chin, not giving a crap if he saw the internal struggle magnified on my face. "You okay, kiddo?" he asked. Aww, what a sweet man.

"Um, yeah. You know, I don't know. That was funny. I mean, that was so me, but today it just feels like too much, ya know?" I'm sure he had no clue what I meant, but he nodded and put one arm around me, squeezing me tight.

"You're okay, hun. It's gonna be okay."

Well, thank you, Mr. James Stafford, because showing me affection when I am already down is the fastest way to enhance my meltdown, 100 percent of the time. Like a damn fool, I turned into his big chest and sobbed. It took him a second to know what to do, but he finally encased me with both of his arms. In hindsight, I now know why it took him a few seconds to respond; but at the time, I thought he was just uncomfortable with the random freak-out from a total stranger.

In that moment, I wanted no one but my daddy. Only he could give me the biggest teddy bear hug and actually make me believe everything would be all right. I mean, Stafford did the best he could; but with me being a total outsider in a foreign land, on the brink of entering an intensely uncomfortable situation... I don't know. Maybe even Dad couldn't have convinced me that everything would be okay at that point.

Finally, feeling silly, I wiped my face with the back of my hand this time, instead of Stafford's button-down breast pocket, straightened myself up, and shakily commanded, "Okay, let's hit it. Sorry, Mr. Staff—Fine, I've snotted on your shirt. I'll call you James." That got a huge heartfelt laugh from Stafford and tickled me quite a bit as well. We headed toward the gorgeous limo, Stafford leading the way and opening the door.

I tucked my purse behind my back as I tried my hardest to not look like a buffoon and stick my butt in Stafford's face again, while I "gracefully" climbed onto the seat. I made sure the hem of my sundress was tucked under my butt so it didn't get stuck in the door and nodded at Stafford that he could close the door. Sweet, poor man, having to deal with me. He was still amused as he shut the door, and I watched him travel up the passenger side of the car toward the front. And that's when something caught the corner of my left eye, and I jumped. I was not alone in the back of the limousine.

15

My head shot to the left and my eyes widened as I grabbed the door handle. I don't know what I was assuming, but I'm pretty sure it had something to do with a knife-yielding serial killer. Picture Freddy Kruger, if you will. As my eyes adjusted to the mass murderer sitting beside me, I realized that my life was actually not in danger—my pride maybe—but not my life, as Nicholas Price was stifling a smile, his eyes burning holes into mine. Holy crap!

You know how people who have survived near-death experiences always describe the moment right before they almost "die" as being one filled with their entire life flashing before their eyes? Well, this wasn't my entire life flashing before my eyes. It was just the past three minutes, consisting of me getting wrapped up in the revolving door and then hysterically crying on Nick's limo driver. The words "Look kids, Big Ben, Parliament" served as the background music to the scene being played in my mind as I sat there in shock.

The smirk that never took on full effect faded, and Nick said, "Hello, Allie" in his stupid, sexy accent.

Still unable to find my voice or my pride, I turned and stared ahead. This was going to take me a minute. What was he doing in this car? Wait…what? Was I crazy? It was *his* limo. He had every right to be in it. But why *then?* Finally, deciding to consciously inhale and exhale a few times, I said, "Um, so what are you doing here?" still looking straight ahead.

"Excuse me?" he asked, not like he hadn't actually heard me, but more like "Who the hell do you think you are asking me such a dumb question without even saying 'hello'?"

I forced myself to look in his direction, avoiding his eyes. Backpedaling, I said, "No, I mean, it's fine. I'm just surprised to see you here, that's all."

"In my limousine?" He paused between each word and heavily exaggerated the inflection at the end.

"Right. No, I mean, I just thought, I don't know, that you would already be there or something. I'm just surprised to see you, that's all. I didn't think you would come pick me up." I knew as I was saying the last part that I shouldn't have. It sounded like I was making the assumption that he *wanted* to come pick me up. That isn't what I meant, but it was too late for me to rewind the words. And so I just sat, frowning through gritted teeth, hoping he would let it go.

"Um, I didn't come pick you up, Allie. James did. And since James is my driver, well, he picked me up too. We are, after all, going to the same place."

"I know. I know. Gosh, never mind." I felt defeated. He was being mean. All these months I had visions of what our first re-encounter would look like, and this…well, this was the exact *opposite* of what I had envisioned. This was a disaster.

We traveled in silence for a moment, and then I saw Nick start shaking, or bouncing or something, out of the corner of my eye. I turned to him, and his lips were pursed, clearly stifling an expression he didn't want me to witness. But the shaking/bouncing got the better of him, and finally, he burst into crazy laughter.

Stunned, I pulled my head back, certainly revealing a bewildered expression. Finally, he looked at me and, still laughing, he said, "Oh my gosh, Allie, seriously, the look—" He cracked himself up again before resuming. "Oh gosh, the look on your face—" There was more laughter. This was weird. What was he doing? His laughter was so contagious, however, that I realized I was grinning from ear to ear. To see the man I loved so tickled to death about something he was actually going to share with *me,* the woman who ruined his life, well, that made this first encounter seem not quite as bad.

"What?" I finally shouted over his laughter "What is so funny?"

About twenty seconds later, he finally composed himself to quickly spit the whole thing out. "When you went round and round in that door and the look on your face at James—" There was more laughter, but at least this time I knew what was so funny, and my face lit up pink all over again.

Damn it! I had momentarily placed that event in the back of my mind as soon as the whole "Why are you in the limo with me, Nick?" debacle occurred. And oh my word, he just wouldn't stop laughing *at* me! You know that BS statement "I'm not laughing *at* you. I'm laughing *with* you?" Yeah, well that is such horse manure when *you're* not laughing *at all!*

Now let me tell you something here, I am usually a chick who can laugh at herself, except for when someone scares me, which we have already covered. In fact, it takes a lot to totally humiliate me. But let's face the facts here, peeps, how often does one make a complete and total jackass out of themselves in front of the most famous and smokin' hot Hollywood star? Let's put some perspective on this, okay? I mean, sure, I had grown a little accustomed to him when we had our brief "relationship" the previous year, to where I was just *beginning* to possibly become the slightest bit desensitized to his celebrity status. Okay? But now here are the facts: I had only *seen* the man in person that weekend in Omaha and the one evening at my home for a very, *very* short time. So then, yes, the pomp and circumstance that happened earlier in the year with the media frenzy and his mom's interview and Nick's noted silence, that also helped me to become a little, I mean, the tiniest bit desensitized to the hubbub surrounding all things Nicholas Price. But then, crapola! Here I was staring at him in a limousine in Los stinkin' Angeles, California, and he was laughing at one of the more embarrassing moments of my *entire life*, immediately following my crazy-girl meltdown with his limo driver and the intense emotions I had been feeling leading up to this moment—emotions that had been intense, mind you, for a good solid year! Indeed, for the previous insane year, my emotions of fear, sadness, anger, brief moments of happiness, embarrassment, regret, and loneliness had all been sitting in a pot, bubbling, ruminating, waiting…waiting…waiting for…for what? For *this*? For sitting next to a man who hated my guts and yet found it in his heart to forego his hate for a second and laugh his head off at me? Perfect. Just what I had been waiting for.

So, no. No, I didn't initially laugh at this catastrophe. So I sat at an impasse, with my mouth agape no less and my burning eyes struggling to decide if they were going to actually produce tears. I stared at the laughing hyena for a good solid minute, my conscious mind conflicted about how to proceed, as my subconscious longed to weep but my gut kept leaning toward laughter. "If you can't beat 'em, join 'em," it whispered. Finally, something clicked deep inside that allowed me but a glimpse of the situation from an outsider's perspective; and in a single, passing instant, I gained clarity about the ridiculousness of this whole situation. My bottom lip closed and began to twitch.

My chin quivered as my lip twitched, and I bit the inside of my cheeks, unsure if my body's response was the appropriate one. But emotion took over, and the harder I bit, the more my lip twitched and the corners of my mouth began to curl upwards. Deciding to just let it go, I smiled a toothy grin and started chuckling myself. When I finally broke loose a bit, Nick's laughter was brought to a new dimension; and he just busted a gut and started retelling the whole scene, complete with actions, as if I hadn't just lived it.

Feigning irritation, I shook my head as I smiled and listened, occasionally allowing myself to physically respond to his hilarious laughter. I couldn't help it. It was funny. It was contagious, even if I was the stupid reason for it. I indulged him for a good five minutes, allowing him to beat the dead horse in retelling the story five, six, maybe seven more times. By the final time, I was done laughing, and quite honestly, my cheeks hurt and I was ready to move on to something else.

Every time the car would finally become silent, I would feel the seat begin to shake again, and Nick would absolutely lose it. I had a flashback during one of his outbursts to when Chris and I were first married. Oh my gosh, still to this day, it is the funniest darn thing ever. Let me set it up for you.

So it is no secret amongst those close to me that I am an absolute mess. Literally, I am one of the messiest, least organized people I know. When I was a child, my room would get so incredibly messy that when my mom would tell me to clean it up, I would sit in the middle of the pile of toys and cry, having no clue where to start. This followed me through college and into adulthood. My dorm room was disgusting. Now don't get me wrong. I never ever leave dirty dishes or food lying around; but clothes, empty water bottles, magazines, papers, and every other nonperishable you can think of clutter my world. Of course, when Chris and I finally got a place of our own, I took some pride in the space; and so I reserved most of my mess for my car and our closet, though sometimes it would spill out into the master bedroom.

One night, maybe a week or so after we had returned from a trip to Colorado, we were lying in bed with the lights off, having just finished, well, you know. (This isn't *Fifty Shades of Grey*, folks. There are no graphic details in this story!) Chris got out of bed to hit the bathroom because, well, that's what he is instructed to do following…you know. Anyway, as he navigated his way to the bathroom, a pretty easy task when you know your apartment like the back of your hand, I heard the loudest scratch sound and then a heavy, hard thud that made the room shake. Well, and then, of course, a few choice words.

I shot up in bed and asked, "What happened, babe?"

A few more choice words as he barked, "You've left this (choice word) suitcase here for (choice word) ever, and I tripped over the (choice word) thing!"

Oh man, was he hot! I squinted to adjust my eyes into focus in the darkened room; and there, against the wall, I could make out the silhouette of the suitcase I hadn't put away yet and the shape of my dear husband's bare butt sticking up in the air. And then the full visual filled my imagination, and I burst out in laughter. I couldn't help it, and I honestly thought he might find the humor in it as well. He didn't. In fact, my laughter made him even angrier. "What's so damn funny, Allison?" he huffed as he struggled to his feet, falling back once again before finally climbing out of the suitcase.

So I tried to explain what was so funny; but the problem was, like Nick and the revolving door explanation, I couldn't get a full thought out in the midst of all the laughter. Finally, when I belted out the jest, being that my mental reenactment of his naked body falling into a suitcase left me tickled pink, he spat, "Oh, I'm glad you can find humor in me hurting myself!" and then slammed the bathroom door behind him.

I sat there embarrassingly berated yet still unable to control my giggles. My mind always plays this trick on me at the most inopportune and inappropriate times. In church, when it is time for silent prayer, I always start laughing. I can't help it, even though absolutely *nothing* is funny! The more I know I am not supposed to laugh, the more the pressure builds into full-out hysterical combustion. My shrink once tried hypnotherapy on me for my anxiety and sleep issues and I couldn't stop giggling, even though it just plain *wasn't funny*!

Chris stayed in the bathroom long enough for me to get back in my T-shirt and underwear, not worrying about the other "stuff," and roll over, pretending to be asleep. He hastily came back to bed eventually, huffing and puffing and flopping as loudly as he could. Finally, when he settled into his pillow with a final irritating sigh, the room sat still. Oh, dear Lord, no! The pressure was on. Silence.

I tried, I really tried, for a good three or four minutes to just breathe and lie as motionless as possible. But the pressure got to me, and I was unable to shake the vision of the naked suitcase man with his butt up in the air; and, softy at first, the bed began to rumble. It came in spurts. Three quick rumbles and then stillness. I seriously was even praying that I could stop the laughter. Three more rumbles and then stillness. *Oh, sweet Jesus, don't make this bad for me. Please help me control myself.* Then the rumbles turned into shakes. Four, maybe five shakes in a row and then stillness. At this point, Chris adjusted his pillow again, obviously sensing something was amiss. Another round of shakes until a full out 25-cent vibrating bed engaged and could not be turned off, accompanied by my high-pitched squealing at the top of my voice box, trying to escape through the tightest sealed lips I could manage. My chest heaved up and down as the pressure was too much to contain, but the dam finally broke and the undeniable syllabic pattern of my all too-familiar cackle broke free.

Now you know how laughter can be very contagious? Yeah, well, apparently mine was not that night. No matter how hard I willed Chris to give it all up and find even a hint of humor in the situation or, at the very least, be unable to control his stoic disposition due to my uncontrollable cackle and just offer a tiny smile, he didn't. In fact, he slept on the couch that night. Boo.

Luckily, I had a better sense of humor than Chris and was way more apt to laugh at myself, so every time Nick busted up, I couldn't help but let out a short giggle myself. I had never seen him like this, and it made him so…so…human? He reminded me of myself, and it was so endearing that I almost shared with him the story of Chris in the suitcase. As was to be my new norm with Nick, I found myself thinking through every potential thought or conversation before I actually opened my mouth. It was just too risky.

After playing through the entire conversation about Chris and the suitcase in my head, I decided to forego mentioning it, as I was fairly certain the conversation would turn more serious at that point. In fact, I imagined Nick trying hard to listen intently without interrupting with his own giggles at my revolving door plight. The more he tried to stifle it, the more it would actually stifle. And then I would finish the story about my funny, naked, dead husband, and Nick would not find it half as funny as it actually was. (How could he? It was definitely a "had to be there" moment.) And then he would feel sorry for me and my dead husband, and finally, he would be brought back to the reality of our current situation, remember why he was so mad at me in the first place, and I would no longer hear his giggles. No, there would be no stifling. There would be no storytelling.

Instead, the rest of the drive to the public relations firm was spent in quiet stillness; the only sounds were our patterned breaths and the thumping of my heart in my ears. We both looked out our respective windows, and as my mind whirred, I wondered if his was doing the same. The giggles had fizzled out, and each time I would catch a glimpse of Nick out of the corner of my eye, he looked deep in thought. Of course I hoped he was thinking about me, but he was an actor. He could have been thinking about anything, and I would have no clue. His world was something I knew virtually nothing about, aside from what he had shown me on the set many moons ago in Omaha and what he had disclosed on the telephone. On any given day, my mind consisted of thoughts about Sam, school, my family, and Chris, always laced with thoughts of Nick. Of course more recently, the thoughts had made room for Greg and the whole ordeal with him, as well as the new nervous thoughts of Nick and this meeting.

Even with the weight of those thoughts, I was sure my brain was not nearly as cluttered as the ever-elusive, intricate brain of the famous Nicholas Price. How could it be? Hollywood stars kept unreasonable hours, were in front of cameras all day long, had to get naked in front of an audience, kiss perfect strangers, avoid paparazzi (okay, I guess I did understand what that was like a little) and try to maintain a sane "home life" in some gigantic mansion with cooks and maids and bodyguards. Yeah, not only was Nick definitely not thinking about me, he had probably forgotten I was even in the car.

My heart sank as we slowed on Melrose at N. Gower Street and turned left. We quickly turned right into a parking garage, and I knew that we had arrived at our destination. I didn't even need a stupid GPS to inform me. The changing scenery was so strange on the fifteen-minute jaunt from Beverly Hills to Melrose Avenue. *Eclectic* might be a word some would use. I just found it outright strange. How could you go from such a sinfully rich part of a city and then pass by a run-down building exclaiming, "Girls! Girls! Girls!" in bright neon lights in less than twenty minutes? And there were homeless people everywhere. I couldn't get past it. Here were these gluttonous, filthy rich celebrities tucked away into the hills with more money than they knew what to do with; and at the bottom of the hill, people were suffering, just wishing they could eat a meal. If these stars just each gave one thousandth of their monthly income to fight the war on poverty, we could eradicate it all together in the United States. The thought sickened me. Now I know they all have charities they support and blah, blah, blah, but come on. Let's face it; if they really wanted to make a difference, they would live modestly and spend a large percent of their income on practical, tangible resources that could serve thousands, if not millions, of homeless folks. Crap, they could grab a dozen of their disposable assistants and put them on the job. They could erect homeless shelters all around Los Angeles within a matter of days. There are so many abandoned, dilapidated buildings in that town that they could even get a cheap price and use their savings on another pair of Louboutins. In fact, screw the Louboutins. The oversized closet is already stuffed full of shoes they wear once. Donate half of the heels and convert the closet (which I am sure is larger than my modest home) into a domestic violence refuge or a place for pregnant teens to stay.

Okay, maybe I am naïve; but with the resources these people have, they could figure out a way. With lawyers and agents and assistants, they would certainly find a way, if only they could let go of the unused tennis court, Olympic-size infinity pool, and twelve bedrooms when they live alone. Gluttony. Ugly, ugly gluttony.

Whew-weee, that got my blood pressure going. Okay, so back to the parking lot on Melrose. Stafford pulled directly in front of a set of glass doors to let us out. I started to tug on the door handle when Nick reached over and gently grabbed my arm. The electricity that ran through my body could have lit all of Los Angeles. For less than a nanosecond, I thought he was going to say something important before we went inside, like maybe profess his love again? And then when the first thing he spoke was "Don't open the door," my heart leapt into my throat. This seemed important. Maybe he *had* been thinking about me the whole ride over. Eyes wide, burning into his, I just waited for what he was going to say next. And then it came: "James insists on opening doors for my guests and will be irritated if you don't let him." *Bum, bum, bum.*

As I felt the blood once again rise to my cheeks, I said nothing and immediately turned my attention to my window, awaiting the arrival of Stafford. I had a quick thought of an article I had read on how to tame migraine headaches by soaking your hands and feet in hot water with an ice pack on the nape of your neck. The theory is that the blood will flow away from the cold part and into the warm one. This makes perfect sense in terms of reducing swelling by adding cold packs to affected areas, but science be damned because the only thing this tactic ever did for me was give me a cramped back and a stiff neck, thus perpetuating said migraine. My flushed cheeks, burning with heat, reminded me that maybe I was doing the migraine trick wrong because the blood was certainly clambering to take up residence in my face. Nick got out of his side of the car, and before he could even close the door, Stafford was opening mine. I nodded in appreciation and, with a scowl, glanced at Nick for direction. "This way" was all he said as he led me toward the glass doors.

No word was spoken as we approached an elevator, stepped inside, and headed up to the fourth floor. In the same follow-the-leader manner, I exited the elevator, one step behind Nick, as we rounded two corners, people greeting him all the way. Everyone in this office was particularly put together, and I felt a little like a disheveled homeless girl who was about to be chastised.

We entered a corner office where two men were obviously awaiting our arrival. One was behind a desk, and the other relaxed comfortably in one of two leather chairs across the desk, his back facing us. As we entered, they both stood up, all broad smiles and outstretched arms, as they greeted Nick and introduced themselves to me. I instantly forgot their names, my brain involved in an entire dramatic play, enacting the possible conversation that was about to take place.

I'm sure I introduced myself and possibly even smiled, but I can't guarantee. The lesser man (only lesser because it was obviously not his corner office) motioned for me to take a seat in the chair he had just been inhabiting. I obliged and quickly noticed how warm the seat cushion was. Man, he had obviously been there awhile. Were we late? I checked my watch, just to be sure, and we were right on time. Nothing could make me look more careless than I already did like being late to this appointment.

"So, Ms. Holly," Mr. Corner Office began, "tell me about yourself."

I was caught a little off guard, unprepared to divulge too much about my identity. I sat for a second, a deer in headlights, and then responded, "Um...well...I...uh...Well, what do you want to know?"

I heard Nick stifle a chuckle as Corner Office explained with a hint of impatience, "You know, tell me about yourself. Who are you? Where are you from? What do you do?"

I quickly looked at Nick, who had resumed his stone-faced persona, his eyes glued on Corner Office. Squirming in my chair a bit, I released my handbag and felt myself sink a little into the leather, like a child who was afraid to talk with a stranger, even though the "stranger" was someone at church who their parents insisted was a friend. Ashamed of my intimidation or, more accurately, pissed at their obvious attempt to intimidate me, I had half a notion to say, "Read the book, jackass! Or any other piece of media circulating the earth over the past year." But I refrained.

Instead, I gave them what they asked and nothing more. "I'm Allison Holly, a widow and a mom who is from Topeka, Kansas, but currently resides in Olathe. I'm a teacher." That was it. That was all I was giving.

Corner Office glanced at Mr. Less Important and raised his eyebrows. My chin pulled downward, begging to reveal my shame; but I fought it and continued looking straight into Corner Office's eyes with my own eyebrows raised, as if to say, "What now, beeyotch?" Oh yeah, I was feigning badassness.

After a condescending chuckle, he continued. "Okay, well, let's just get right down to it." He shuffled some folders on his desk, pulled out papers, and laid them in front of me with a black Montblanc pen. "I have some things for you to sign. This one states that any and all events or conversations shared between Mr. Price and yourself will remain completely confidential from this moment forward. Do you understand what that means?"

Man, I felt like the biggest tool. Number one, what did they take me for, some idiot? And number two, the weight of this document made me feel like a leper or, worse yet, a nasty prostitute who, in an effort to legally protect herself, had to sign away her rights. Or maybe even a stalker. That was it. I felt like a freaking crazy teenage stalker who had to promise to stay the hell away from the great and powerful Nicholas Price.

My humiliation arose in the form of anger, and I snapped, "Do I know what the word *confidential* means? No, please enlighten me, oh wise one."

An unexpected burst of split-second laughter erupted from Less Important as a mocking, almost evil smile played on Corner Office's lips. It truly reminded me of the president in *Hunger Games*. At any moment, I was expecting to see him pull out a rose and tuck it behind his ear. Evil. Evil. Evil. He turned his attention to Nick, who was in the chair next to me, a few feet away. "Man, you really got stuck with a live one here, didn't you, Nicky boy?"

Ouch. *Got stuck with?* That stung. That was shamed stalker woman. I wanted to scream, "You dummy! He did not get stuck with me. He *chose* me! And I am not some psycho witch or, as you put it, a 'live one.' I am a pretty upstanding professional woman with a sad history and loving heart. I am worthy. I am worthy. I am worthy."

The tears threatened my ducts, and so I blinked tightly twice. They would *not* present themselves in here. They would *not!* I refused to give that to this man. He was the one who was not worthy of witnessing my sad, ashamed, pissed-off tears. I cleared my throat and heard Nick reproach, "Come on. Get to the point, T."

Against my will, I turned to him. His jaw was clenched, and one single vein was constricting in his neck. He was burning a hole into T a.k.a. Corner Office.

Corner Office cleared his throat, and rolled his eyes; and then, looking at the paper set before me and not at *me*, he breathed, "I mean, do you understand that you may not talk to anyone, not your mom, not your dad, not your sister, not your brother, not your grandma, not your grandpa, not your kids, not your BFF, not your aunt, not your uncle, not your husband, not your—"

"Shut the f—— up!" Nick yelled so loud that I jumped up off the chair a good six inches. Frightened, I sank back down and stared at him. He was now standing, ready to pounce, his hands balled into fists. Less Important had advanced in front of my chair, separating Nick from Corner Office with his hand up a few centimeters away from Nick's chest.

"Okay, okay, calm down, Nick. Just calm down," Less Important cooed. "Let's all just take a few breaths, have a seat, and get this over with. This isn't fun for anyone."

To that, I couldn't help it. I let a croak of amusement escape my throat. Corner Office was the only one to look my way, with his head tilted as if awaiting an explanation. Against all better judgment and the seconds-before reprimand of Less Important, I decided to give one more teeny-weeny jab, always being one to have the last word.

"By the looks and actions of this *gentleman*"—I gestured to Corner Office, my eyes not leaving his—"one would be led to believe that this were a big ole celebration."

Less Important let out an exhausted sigh and returned to his previous post. With my eyes burning holes into Corner Office, I could see a faint smile dance across Nick's lips. Mine turned up as well.

"Now, where were we?" I asked in my most upbeat, partygoer voice. "What's next?" I leaned forward and scooted the form to the side without signing.

Corner Office looked from my hand to my eyes and then over to Less Important before rolling his eyes and retrieving another form from the stack. I had gotten to him. Ha! He shoved the paper in front of me and gruffly barked, "This one ensures that you will refrain from having any contact with Mr. Price. This includes phone calls, e-mails, social media sites, in person, postal mail"—he paused—"telegram, pony express…"

Oh, I get it. Poking fun at my advanced age, are we? I didn't flinch. Instead, I slowly and carefully slid the paper over to the other one, gently stacking it on top. Then I looked up at Corner Office over my probably clumpy mascaraed lashes. "Are we done here?" I grinned.

Shaking his head, Corner Office stated, "Hardly" as he rummaged around for yet another form to be signed. He turned it to face me. "This one—or should I just stick it over there in your smug little stack?"

Cheeks. Heat. Bright red. When the pressure is not quite at full combustion, I can generally think of something witty and clever to say in my defense. But when the pressure gets too great, I have what I like to call the "hindsight disorder." I absolutely freeze, and my mind goes blank. I say nothing, look like an idiot, and usually tear up; and then twenty minutes after the event when the perpetrator is nowhere in sight, I come up with the greatest response known to man. I mean, I come up with some doozies that would go viral if I had actually used them in the moment and uploaded them to YouTube. I would be like that witty girl who held up the signs and quit her job, telling her boss off, except mine wouldn't be fake and only for publicity's sake. Mine would be real and raw and genius. In fact, people would start using my retorts, and instead of saying "You've been burned!" (which yes, I know, is so yesterday), they would say, "Ooh, you just got Allied!"

Okay, okay, maybe I am getting ahead of myself here, but you get my point. Like a jackass, I had absolutely no response to the jerk at the time. Later, I came up with a million responses. Even sitting here now, I have a handful of new ones I wish I could tell you I actually said, but I'm just not that cool or dishonest. So I said nothing.

Instead, Nick chimed up again, "I'm outta here. You are a child, T!"

As he stood up, I stood as well and whispered, "Thank you" while glancing his way.

Instead of looking at me with expected sympathy, however, he scowled at me and said, "Oh, Allie, you are no better!" and stormed out the door.

16

The room was spinning quietly. Having no clue what I was supposed to do, I sat back down in the chair like a child sitting in the principal's office. I looked down at my hands in my lap, shame filling my heart and my eyes. This time, the shame couldn't be contained behind the surface and flowed down my bright red cheeks. I sat this way for what seemed like minutes.

When Corner Office spoke, I looked up, only to notice that we were alone. Apparently, Less Important had followed Nick out the door without my awareness. Corner Office cleared his throat, his eyes softening presumably at the presence of my tears. When he spoke, his voice was much less coarse than before.

"Allie," he began, obviously as uncomfortable as I was, "listen, I apologize for acting like such an ass. In this business, it's…well, it's easy to become harsh and treat people as if they are not quite human. Truly, I'm sorry. I can see by your reaction that you are, indeed human."

This small act of grace and humor caused me to not only cry a little harder but also to crack a smile. Was Corner Office not such a bad guy after all? I grabbed at a tissue on his desk just before the snot started dripping from my nose. Oh, I was a child.

He continued. "I can also tell by your reaction that you really did have a thing for Nick, and I'm sorry for that too. I'm sure this whole thing is probably difficult for you."

I wanted to interject that I was actually getting along just fine, thank you very much, before Nick walked back into my life. For some ridiculous reason, as if I owed this guy anything or as if he mattered even one ounce in the grand scheme of my life, I wanted him to know that I wasn't just some dumb, awestruck, silly stalker girl, contrary to the mountable evidence set before him. I wanted to tell him how Nick really *did* like me too at one point. But there was no use. Certainly he had read my story, which was the complete truth, and still decided to see me as a thorn in his side. I just needed to get on with the meeting and find out if I even had a ride back to the hotel. I was sure Nick was already on his way to who-knows-where he needed to be in his fancy limousine. I imagined he probably called and paid for a cab for me.

Lost in thoughts of self-preservation, I almost missed when Corner Office said, "Okay, so here is the final form for you to sign. This one states that you will not try and profit from any future stories concerning Nicholas Price nor will you speak to any media outlet from this point forward concerning anything or anyone who has ever had relations with Nicholas Price. Does this make sense?

It didn't. I mean, I didn't even know who all Nick had ever come in contact with, first of all. And second of all, was this inferring that I was only after media attention and money? I wanted so badly to clarify this information, but I decided to stick with my plan and just nodded my head, my tears finally drying on my streaked face. Instead, I grabbed the final form and, placing it on top of the others, gathered them in my hands, stood up, and reached for my purse. "Are we finally finished here?"

Corner Office squirmed in his seat. "Um, er, well, not exactly."

I raised my eyebrows and tapped my foot impatiently.

"Well, and honestly, I haven't even had legal look over this yet because it seems kind of silly to me, but I'm sure you are familiar with a Ms. Sarah Alton?"

Confused, I allowed a grossed-out look to dance across my face. The mere mention of that snot's name made my stomach churn. "Who isn't?" I managed. What on earth did I have to do with her?

Corner Office was obviously uncomfortable as he looked down at his lap and replied, "Well, apparently, Ms. Alton was not happy with the way you portrayed her to the media in your 'tell-all.'" (Yes, he literally did air quotes.) "And, despite our attorney's insistence that absolutely nothing you wrote was slanderous or attempted defamation of character based on Nick's corroboration of your accounts, she still thinks you should have to sign this." He handed me a piece of paper across his desk. But the room was spinning so I couldn't quite grip it and it slipped between my fingers.

Nick had *corroborated* my story? This was new information. Trying my hardest to maintain my composure and compartmentalize this newfound knowledge until a more apropos processing time, I bent down to pick up the form, not even realizing the weight of the contents contained in said form. When Corner Office mentioned Nick's participation in the discussion of my story, my brain quickly released any mention of Sarah Alton, let alone the fact that she had concocted a *form* for me to sign. That morsel of news wouldn't even return to my conscience until later that evening when I was left alone to read through the papers.

As I turned to leave, still unable to formulate words, Corner Office piped up, "So, um, Ms. Holly? Where are you going?"

I was taken aback. Confused, I turned back to him and questioned, "What do you mean? I guess I'm gonna head back to the hotel for a while before my flight." Had his tone been a little different, I may have assumed he was going to ask to take me to lunch. But I sensed his question implied that we weren't finished with business quite yet.

He chuckled and rubbed his forehead, fatigued or maybe stressed. "Well, you haven't signed the papers yet. And I don't know if Nick, er, Mr. Price told you or not, but we would like to get a statement from you. You know, for the media."

I didn't waste any time with my response, as I had been planning it since I slid the first form across the desk. "With all due respect, it can't possibly be a surprise to you that I would never sign anything without reading the fine print. In fact, I plan to have an attorney look over these documents. And as far as—"

His stupid laugh interrupted my smug resolve, leading into him stating, "Our attorneys have already looked over these documents Ms. Holly. Listen, I don't give a rip if you do anything with the one regarding Ms. Alton, but the other three are absolutely mandatory unless…"

"Unless what?"

"Ms. Holly, we don't want this to get ugly. You are here, which leads me to believe that you at least care enough about Mr. Price to want him to be able to resume his career in a respectable fashion. You knew why you were coming, so I don't know why this is all such a shock to you. But if you must know, this office, combined with Mr. Price's fame, could single-handedly smear your reputation in every town in America, making it very difficult for you to ever get a job, let alone be able to show your face in public. And—"

This time, I interrupted him. "With all due respect again, Mr. Corner Office, (yes! I totally called him that!) if your entire office teamed up with Nicholas Price to do *anything* to my reputation, it wouldn't be single-handed at all, now would it? It would be multiple-handed, and those multiple hands, sir, would each be slapped with a hefty, hefty lawsuit!" I turned on my heels, pretty damn proud of myself.

Just before I reached the door, however, he called back, "Tit for tat, Allie. The fact remains that we are in the entertainment industry. Trust me, we are used to dealing with a whole lot more than anything you *think* you could throw at us. Have your lawyers look over the papers. That's fine. And then I sincerely hope, for the sake of Nick's future in this business, that you highly consider signing those damn papers so he can get back to work. And before you cut me off, I was going to clue you in on the fact that our lawyers are damn good and have already been alerted to start digging for a bulletproof case against you in the event that you don't sign. I really don't…more importantly, Nick really doesn't want it to come to that. He's innocent here, Ms. Holly. Please remember that."

I couldn't respond or even turn all the way around to look him in the face as my throat seized, threatening to close off all together. Then the tears came. I bolted.

Hurrying down the hallway, I quickly realized I had no clue where I was going. I turned a few times, but it was like a labyrinth— or worse, a terrible maze. Imagine you're in *Children of the Corn*, running and running and never really knowing where you are going or worrying that at any moment, some crazy person will pop out of nowhere. There were definitely a couple of faces in that office that I had no desire of seeing ever again. After about seven obviously wrong turns, I decided it was time I sought assistance. I stopped in front of an office, and just as I was about to knock on the doorframe, I realized it was Corner Office's blasted office. *Oh, for the love of Pete!* I quickly backpedaled, praying to God that he hadn't seen me, when I bumped into someone.

I quickly turned around to extend my apologies when it became very clear that the person had not taken a step back to allow me room. I was standing face to chest with…with…Nick! You guys, I have never in my life been so happy to see that man. I mean, yes, he had abandoned me and insulted me; but he was the only person in the entire blasted state of California who I halfway knew, and certainly the only person in that stupid office who I wanted to show me the way out. I hated admitting defeat.

Since he refused to move, I stepped to the side of him, not wanting to back up too far and be spotted by Corner Office.

"Whatcha doing, Allie?" Nick looked a little amused.

"Oh, just leaving. You?" I whispered.

"Why are you whispering?" he asked in an exaggerated whisper that was actually louder than his speaking voice.

Panicking, I studied Corner Office's door to make sure he wasn't surfacing. "Um, let's walk out, okay?" I pleaded and started walking away from whence I came.

"Uh, wrong way, Allie." Nick corrected, pointing in the direction that would force me to cross in front of Corner Office's open doorway.

I was at a crossroads (or a crosshalls, ba-dum-dum). Either I could make up some lie about wanting to see the rest of the place or I could gun it past the deadly office. Lying to Nick had not resulted in favorable circumstances the first time, hence the reason for my visit to this stupid place, so I decided to say nothing and just hightail it. I sped past Nick and turned the corner, knowing full well that my backside was in Corner Office's line of sight until the next turn, which I still did not have a clue where the correct next turn was. I slowed to let Nick catch up so as to lead the way; and when he did, he was chuckling to himself, his head shaking.

I didn't even need to ask why. I knew. I knew I wasn't fooling him at all. Once again I had made an ass out of myself by getting lost, not even twenty minutes after I was so smug and condescending in the office. I always failed at being a true badass. I could never keep up with it. I always did something stupid to thwart my reputation as a strong, confident, witty, don't-mess-with-me, cocky woman.

When we finally escaped through the double doors, Nick stopped and turned to me. "So you didn't sign the papers, huh?"

Apparently, his amusement with the plight of my escape had ended. Now he was back to business.

"No, um, I didn't yet." I couldn't look at him. And so, with my eyes on the concrete, I awkwardly rocked from side to side, transferring my weight from one foot to the other.

"Do you have to go to the bathroom?" he accused.

Shocked and completely humiliated, I caught his eyes and shouted, "No! Why would you ask me that?"

He pointed toward my legs. "Well, you're dancing around like a little lad who has to go pee."

That was it. I couldn't take it anymore. I started walking toward the parking lot, fuming. It was LA, for heaven's sake. Certainly if I could make it to a main street, I could find a cab to hail. I've never been comfortable hailing cabs and have only had to one other time in my life, but that discomfort far outweighed the discomfort I would be feeling if I spent even one more second in the presence of Nicholas Price.

I was hightailing it, the breezeless air managing to whip the bottom of my dress around from the sheer speed at which I was walking. Nick hadn't even bothered to comment on the fact that I was wearing the very same dress he had so admired before. He probably didn't even notice it was the same. Well, as I flitted across the parking lot, the back of that dress was the last he would see of me!

The tears that were stinging my eyes were nothing more than tears of fury, and I welcomed them. As I approached Melrose, I spotted a bus stop and figured it was probably a safe spot to wait for a cab as well. There was an older African-American gentleman sitting under the plexiglass shelter. I nodded politely and dug my sunglasses out of my purse. Although I didn't mind the fact that I was sobbing with anger, a perfect stranger might not be very comfortable with it, so I decided to hide the evidence.

I sat down a few butt spaces away from the gentleman on the bench. I was getting ready to ask him how often taxicabs rolled by when a black limousine with tinted windows turned the corner onto Melrose and stopped before us. *Crap.* As the back window unrolled, I turned to the gentleman next to me and joked, "Your ride's here."

He chuckled and shook his head, answering in a low gravelly voice, "In my dreams."

Nick barely had to raise his typical conversational volume to reach my eardrums since the bus stop was so close to the curb. "Get in the car, Allie" was all he said.

The nerve of that man! I just ignored him.

"Allie!" he exclaimed. "Get in the bloody car!"

Oh, demanding much?

My cheeks were hot with fury and embarrassment. The gentleman next to me leaned forward and then voiced an expletive followed by, "That's that famous guy! Hey, that's that big movie star!" He was staring at me wide-eyed, waiting for me to freak out with him. When I didn't, he just continued to point at Nick and pant, waiting for some sort of recognition from me.

When Nick finally flung the door open and stepped out, the man was up on his feet with his hand extended, ready to meet this *amazing superstar.* I rolled my eyes at his admiration but secretly hoped Nick would indulge him and make pleasantries. Nick did not disappoint. He really could be very kind. I noticed him discreetly hand the gentleman a wad of money before he patted him on the shoulder and advanced toward me. I crossed my arms defiantly and turned my cheek to look down the street, willing a cab to speed toward me.

Nick stood above me. "Allie, seriously you have to get in the car. I'm responsible for you until your flight out, and so for the next few hours, I need you safe. Once you're on the plane, you can do whatever you want and ride around with whomever you want. Now get in the car!"

I looked up at him, the sun creating a halo effect around his whole head. Sheltering my sunglassed eyes with my hand, I spat out, "Don't worry. I won't sue you if I get mugged, Nick. Just go! Pretend I'm gone. I am not, under any circumstances, getting in that limo. I can find my own way back to the hotel. Go!"

Silence.

He could tell I was serious because after about ten seconds of just staring down at me, scrutinizing my sincerity, Nicholas Price turned on his heels and spoke, "Good-bye, Allie."

Something about those closing words socked me in the gut. It was all too familiar to hear those words from Nick and to watch him walk out of my life. This was it. I knew I would sign those dang papers and let Nick off the hook, and so there would never be any reason for us to come in contact again. The thought sickened me, and I turned a deaf ear to the man at the end of the bench who was rambling on and on about the craziness of his superstar encounter. The only thing that subdued my grief was the sight of a bright yellow taxi rolling down the street.

17

When I finally made it to my room after the cab driver decided to take the longest route to the hotel, I was so fatigued I could barely stand up. It was lunchtime but I wasn't hungry so I flopped on the bed fully clothed and dozed off to sleep. It couldn't have been more than ten minutes before the loud banging on the door awakened me. Seriously, I had just been out long enough to start drooling and encase myself in my own sweat. It took me a few seconds to get my bearings.

When I finally remembered where I was, I stumbled out of the bedroom and into the living room of the massive hotel suite. Completely unconcerned with who may be knocking on the door, assuming it was just housekeeping, I wiped the spittle spread across my face with the back of my bare arm. My breath was nasty; my hair a wreck. Sleepy-eyed, I opened the door with a yawn.

Holy crap, it was Nick! Instinct outperformed reason, and I immediately slammed the door shut, Nick's mouth agape, not even having a second to speak. It seriously was like in one of those movies when the girl slams the door and freaks out on the other side of it before opening it back up again, her hair readjusted and lip gloss applied. Well, without the lip gloss. I didn't have time to run back to the bedroom and primp. I just had a few seconds to slow my thumping heart and remember to breathe.

When I opened the door again, Nick was messing with his phone. "Oh, okay, I thought you weren't going to open back up so I was telephoning."

"Why are you here?" I asked, feigning irritation.

"Well, hello to you too, Allie." I couldn't help but continue to adore his accent as he pushed past me. "Quite a nice room you've got here, eh?"

"Seriously, Nick"—I closed the door behind me and turned back into the room—"why are you here?"

He continued to check out the living room and then helped himself to a seat on the couch, pushing the cushions as if he were contemplating purchasing the set. "Well, as it turns out, Allie, as pissed off as I am about you not heeding my advice and getting in the limo, I was equally as worried about you."

"I'm fine. There. That's settled. Bye now." I was bluffing big time. There is no part of me that wanted him to leave, despite the 101 reasons why I should. My heartbeat was completely out of control, and I had such a burning desire to excuse myself to the restroom so that I could put myself together. But then again, I didn't want him to know I actually cared what he thought of me.

"Nice dress by the way."

Wow. "Oh, this old thing?" I joked, blushing.

"Yeah, I'm sure it was not packed by accident."

"What is that supposed to mean?" I was allowing him to get to me again.

He laughed and looked me up and down three times, sending shivers through my entire body, before saying, "I'm pretty sure you know what that outfit does to me."

Okay, I totally wanted to play along. I needed this flirtation; I had craved it for a year! "I don't know what you're talking about. Have you seen this dress before, Nick?"

I was standing about five feet from where he was sitting. And as he stood up, eliminating the distance between us by four and a half feet, my heart literally stopped. Reaching out and tugging on the spaghetti strap of my dress, Nick whispered, "Yes, I've seen this dress before. And if I'm being honest, I much would have preferred seeing it on the floor."

Oh crapola! Are you kidding me with this? I had no idea what to say or do. I wanted to lunge at him and attack him, both with my lips and with my fists. I wanted to ravage him in a good way and a bad way. But I wouldn't dare. No way. Not after all I had been through. Plus, I had a sneaking suspicion that he was deliberately trying to get to me, that he was up to something no good. Was he trying to manipulate me into signing those papers? The thought weighed down my floating body.

"Listen, Nick, if you are just trying to win me over so I sign the papers, don't waste your time. I have every intention of signing them. I just need to take my time, okay?"

He stepped even closer, his breath warming my forehead. "Oh, Allie, I'm not trying to win you over," he continued to whisper. "By the way you're shaking, I would say I have already won. I was just being honest about where I would have liked to have seen that dress." He stepped back, cleared his throat, and then, in his speaking voice, proclaimed, "But that was before. Much has changed since then, and so I honestly don't really give a damn about the dress." And just like that, he was back to being cold and horrible.

He walked back to the couch and grabbed his phone and wallet. As he breezed past me, I could see he was completely flushed. I panicked. I didn't want him to leave.

"Wait!" I exclaimed, way too urgently.

Nick stopped and turned around, just short of the door handle. He raised his eyebrows, a nonverbal gesture for me to continue. When I stood there speechless, he said, his voice quivering, "Give me a reason to stay, Allie, or I need to leave now."

Oh my gosh, what was I supposed to say? There was no reason I could ever come up with. Hindsight disorder or not, I still can think of nothing that would have been appropriate to say at that moment. Nothing I could give him could be enticing enough for him to completely forget about the lies I had told. And I am not talking about sex because that was not even an option for me. I didn't care who he was. Sex was something I learned to take very seriously in my adult years; and no one, not even the ridiculously hot superstar Nicholas Price, would change that.

I guess Nick realized that nothing I could say would be reason enough to stay either because following my long pause, his next words to me were "Okay, well, do you need me to sign anything before I go?"

Confused, I asked, "What do you mean? I thought I was the only one who had to sign the papers."

"No, I mean my autograph. Do you want me to autograph anything for you? I mean, you are still a Wesley's girl, aren't you? That is the *only* reason you came to Omaha after all, wasn't it?" The veins were bulging from his neck.

I had no idea how to respond. I was so humiliated. Nick looked at me like I was some starstruck superfan stalker girl, which I had been, hadn't I? But why did he keep flip-flopping on me? I mean, he wanted me to give him a reason to stay and then he totally cut me down in the next breath. My cheeks were burning red, and it wasn't the result of the anger I had before or even the embarrassment I had felt numerous times that day. It was serious shame. I was full of shame. Oh, he must have looked at me with nausea and pity. To him, I was this completely pathetic, overage, undersexed loser mom with nothing better to do than stalk a young movie star—the apple of teenagers' eyes, for crying out loud!

Suddenly I had a violent urge to vomit. The events of the day were too much for me. I couldn't take it anymore. Not wanting to humiliate myself once again in front of Nick, I ran for the bathroom, and as I could feel the acidic puke pass my esophagus and reach my soft palate, I managed to choke out, "Good-bye!"

My knuckles white, I clung to that toilet bowl with every ounce of strength I had. The violence regurgitated over and over again as I watched each preconceived glimpse of hope I had held on to for all of those months swirl down the pipe, flush after flush, until burning yellow bile dripping with loss was all that was presented. I laid my head across my forearms on the toilet seat and sobbed. I had, of course, wet my pants. (It was a by-product of having a baby and not doing enough Kegels. Stop doing Kegels and continue reading!)

The wet reminder of my dear son and the way in which he came to be flooded my soul, and I couldn't stop the hysterics! What was I doing here? How did I get here? I had a perfectly wonderful life back home with my precious son, and here I was grasping at something ridiculous that was never going to be again. Why had I agreed to come?

Through my guttural wails, I cried out to Chris, something I hadn't done in years.

"Why Chris? Why? Why did you have to leave us? Chris, what have I done? I'm so sorry, babe. I'm so sorry!" My teeth were clenched so tightly I likely chipped a tooth. I lifted my head and stared up at the unknown heavens. "Chris, I miss you so much, and I have made a mess of our lives. I have made a mess of you and who you were. Why did you leave us? Why? Why? Why?" I pounded my fists against the toilet seat as I screamed out to him, missing him more than I had since the moment he passed.

And then a breeze of a whisper infiltrated my soul, exclaiming, "You are My daughter, with whom I am well pleased." I froze. Now I know the Bible pretty well and I know that this statement is one that God makes to Jesus in Mark's gospel when Jesus ascends from the water after being baptized by John. I knew it was probably just my imagination going crazy that God would actually say these very words to me. For one, certainly he would pick a more opportune time to "speak" to me than when I was screaming and puking into a random toilet in California after just having had inappropriate thoughts toward a young man I had lied to. I am not immune to the voice of God reaching out to me. In fact, when Chris passed, God's voice was the main thing that got me through. He had reassured me several times that Chris was in heaven with Him and that I would indeed be reunited with him again. But, come on, never in my life had He reached out to me on or anywhere near the can.

Secondly, I knew well and good that God would definitely *not* be well pleased with the choices I had been making. No way would He say something to me that He declared to His beloved Son—the Savior of the freakin' world—immediately following His baptism. How on earth could I, a stupid, lying, deceitful, moronic stalker who didn't even pray every day, receive the same message from God as the only sinless man in the history of time? Did I heal the sick? Did I welcome the poor? Did I die on a cross for anyone? No! In fact, in my current state, *I* was sick! I was befriending the filthy rich. And I didn't sacrifice anything for anyone! No, it was surely my own imagination selfishly trying to make myself feel better.

Folks, I apologize for the self-deprecation. I am sure it is exhausting, but living in a world in which one is absolutely positive that God chose the wrong person to take, given that person's amazing worth, one spends a lot of time in the emotional dunk tank, wishing he/she would have been the one taken. Certainly the world would be better. Call it survivor's guilt or whatever, but since Chris died, I had done an amazing job of literally kicking the crap out of myself for living. This day, enveloping the surely expensive toilet basin, was no exception to my continued habit of feeling worthless, hopeless, and lost in this world, constantly missing my dear husband and inevitably failing as a mother. Was I feeling sorry for myself? Most assuredly. I was entrenched in a full-blown Allie Holly Pity Party. Number of guests in attendance: one.

But then…then there was that ever-present sense; that still, small voice tugging at my subconscious, whispering in times like these that all really would be well; that maybe I was doing *something* right. Maybe I really *did* have a greater purpose here on earth. Usually I chalked it up to my own style of crazy, as I most certainly did that day in the barf-room (see what I did there?); but it didn't change the fact that every time I was at my lowest of lows, *something*—dare I say something greater than me—would always pull me up out of the sludge, and somehow I would end up carrying on the next day.

Bewildered by the possibility that God could have actually spoken those words to me and overcome with exhaustion at the realization that I would never live up to such words, I folded down onto the cool tiles and closed my eyes. I had no idea how I would scrape my body off that floor in the few short hours I had until the limo would arrive to take me to the airport. I truly didn't even care if Stafford had to come collect me himself, with my red eyes and blotchy face. I felt like I did the moment after I delivered Sam, unashamed of my appearance and frankly too exhausted and emotionally drained to care.

After a few more minutes of self-pity, I picked myself up off the floor and went into the bedroom. I flopped onto my back on the bed and dialed my mom's cell phone. There was no one I needed more than my mommy. She picked up on the third ring sounding haggard. I contemplated hanging up, but then knew it would be pointless as she could see my number on caller ID.

"Mom?" I cried.

"Allie, what is it?" I couldn't tell if she was worried or annoyed by my tone.

"Um, well, how is Sam?" I asked, stalling.

"He's fine. What is wrong with *you*?"

"So why do you sound so harassed?"

"Allie, for the love of God, forget about me. Everything is fine. Just tell me what's wrong!"

I was obviously making her even more frustrated, so I decided to just explain. "Well [*sniff, sniff*], it's just that…I don't know. I guess maybe I'm just feeling sorry for [*sniff, sniff*] myself." The quiver in my voice was undeniable, but I think it was more because of embarrassment at that point than sadness, as it was obvious I was catching her at a bad time. I mean, your fully grown daughter calls you from sunny California where she is having a meeting with a child superstar while you are watching *her* son, and she has the nerve to whine about her own problems? Oh, more shame. I was getting pretty good at this "shame" thing.

Mom let out an annoyed sigh but indulged me. "What happened?"

I wiped my eyes, trying to compose myself. I had half a notion to act pissed and just tell her it was no big deal and I would see her later. My passive aggression often came out in the form of manipulation when I was embarrassed for feeling sorry for myself. Instead, I said, "Well, it's kind of a long story, but—"

There was a knock at the door. "Ugh! Again?"

"What's again?"

"Nothing. Hey Mom, can I call you back?"

"Oh, for crying out loud, Allie! You can't just call me sobbing and then let me go. Tell me what's wrong!"

"Mom!" I was way too gruff. "Listen, I said I'll call you back! Someone's at the door. Bye!"

I hung up and wiped my eyes one last time, checking myself in the dresser mirror before heading toward the door. My suspicion that Nick had returned was thwarted when a woman looking to be around fifty stood on the other side of the door.

"Ms. Holly?" the woman asked as she was looking at a clipboard. There was a long black padded case at her side.

"Um, yeah?" I responded, looking up and down the hall to see if anyone else joined her.

"Are you ready for your massage?" she asked.

"Excuse me?"

"I have come to give Ms. Allison Holly a massage. Is that not you?"

"Um, wait. Are you with the hotel? Is this like a free service or something?"

"No, ma'am" was all she gave me.

"Okay, well, I actually didn't call for a massage. I mean, don't get me wrong. It sounds just about perfect right now, but I didn't do it. And I actually don't really have the money for it."

"No problem, Ms. Holly. It's been taken care of."

"By who?" I was shocked.

"Ma'am, the person who requested this chooses to remain anonymous, so I'm sorry that I can't disclose that information."

A-ha! "Okay, well, um, I'm kind of a mess." I ran my fingers through my oily tear-soaked hair. Then the thought hit me that maybe the whole thing was a big sham. What if she was part of some big crime ring and came to take my money or, worse yet, kill me? I know, I know. I'm a paranoid freak, but one can never be too careful. I mean, how easy would it be for someone to call the front desk and find out the names of people staying in the hotel and then go to their room pretending to be a massage therapist sent by an "anonymous" source? Although, this *was* the nicest hotel on earth, so the chances were slim that the hotel would give out any information on guests. But nevertheless, I asked to see some identification.

After showing me her license, she extended her hand and said, "Allison, I'm Charlotte. I completely understand being a little skeptical, so to put your mind at ease, let's just say that it is a really good thing the anonymous gentleman who requested the massage was an extremely handsome Australian, or else I may not have agreed to be so sneaky." Charlotte winked at me as she reached for her case and nodded toward the open living room. "Will the living area work?"

Smiling for the first time in over an hour, I led Charlotte into the living room, bolting the door behind me. She set down her black case and another shoulder tote I had failed to notice and got to work. I stood watching as she set up her table, pulled out oils and candles, and proceeded to strategically place and light them around the massage table. Then she went over to the fireplace, the backdrop for the placement of the table, and flipped it on. Charlotte then walked back to her tote, pulled out the softest white robe, and handed it to me. "Here, sweetie. Take your time getting changed in the powder room, and then when you are ready, come back out to the table."

I adored that she called me "sweetie." I needed to be "sweetie" to someone. I obviously wasn't very sweet to my mom. Crap. I needed to call her back. Instead, I silenced my phone, grabbed the robe with a nod, and headed toward the "powder room." Ha. Oh, my sweet grandma used to call it a powder room. I loved that. I was already feeling better, and the massage had yet to begin.

As I reached the doorway to my room on the way to the bathroom, someone knocked on the dang door again. I turned, wide-eyed and annoyed, to Charlotte and was about to tell her to just ignore it when she held up the palm of her hand.

"It's okay, sweetie. It's for me."

A sudden pang of the earlier fear I had about Charlotte being a serial killer returned; but, as if sensing my paranoia, she calmly said, "I asked the housekeeping staff to do me a favor with your sheets and blanket. Don't worry. It isn't another random old lady sent from a particularly sexy Hollywood actor." Another wink and she was off to the door. I was off to the bathroom.

18

The massage was exactly what I needed. Charlotte was amazing. Despite her small stature, homegirl had the strength of a bull! With the robe tied snug, I made my way out into the living room. There was a tall glass of ice water with strawberries, kiwi, cucumber, and lemon slices floating about. The lights were turned low, and my pulse slowed instantly at the sound of crashing waves coming from the speakers. Charlotte told me to drink a significant amount of the water to keep hydrated. She then turned around and had me disrobe and climb under the sheets face up. When I was all snug as a bug in a rug (those sheets were *heated*!), I signaled that I was ready.

Charlotte began by removing my makeup with an oil that smelled heavenly. She then began massaging my temples, moving to my scalp and then my face. Who knew having your face massaged could be so incredibly relaxing? I guess we have no idea how tense the muscles in our face tend to be. She then massaged the base of my head, the tissue surrounding the cerebellum. This is the tensest part of my head and, I'm convinced, is the source of the majority of my headaches. Since I had developed a postweeping/barfing stress headache following my little fit on the bathroom floor, the acute attention to that part of my scalp and neck was eerily intuitive. Charlotte missed nothing.

From my neck and shoulders, which she massaged while supporting the full weight of my floppy head, Charlotte moved onto my arms, hands, fingers, legs, feet and toes. I then got to roll over onto my stomach while she held up the top sheet and blanket for easier transition and had an angelic back massage. Once again, she worked my arms and legs as I dozed in and out of consciousness. Oh, I didn't care what my source of despair had been in the bathroom. It was taken all away and set sail on the crashing waves of the sea while I lay on a cushy beach towel spread across the warm sand, the slightest breeze caressing my cheeks as the smell of—what was that? Tuberose?

My body jolted awake, much like the unpleasant experience one sometimes has when they are on the brink of REM sleep and a semiunconscious dream begins in which they start falling. As they hit the ground, or maybe just before, their body physically jolts at the impact. Oh man, does that ever piss me off. It is the most uncomfortable feeling. My breathing and heart rate will be syncing into a much slower pace, my mind is at peace, and I'm fully relaxed. But then my body doesn't quite get the memo that it is asleep and should just mind its own business if my mind decides it wants to fall from a twelve-story building. Stupid body.

Charlotte sensed the flinch (hard not to when I jumped a couple inches off the table) and said, "Oh, honey, I'm so sorry. Did I hurt you?"

Still a little foggy, I croaked, "No, no. I'm sorry. I had just dozed off."

She chuckled. "Okay, hon. That's probably exactly what you needed. Our bodies have a way of taking care of us, even when our minds won't."

Well, the big jolt awake wasn't very helpful of my body, but I was still incredibly thankful for the opportunity to get entranced in total relaxation prior to my rude awakening. Certainly this couldn't be Nick's doing, could it? Now I have never been very good at that baby shower game in which the hostess passes around various baby food jars and the guests smell them and try to guess which nasty pureed vegetable resides within. They all smell the same to me—like the vomit that had protruded from my body that day in the hotel. I always would get the answer wrong while my goody-two-shoes supermom friends would not only know the vegetable but could also tell you what brand it was, how much it cost at the grocery, and why their own homemade batch was "so much better for the baby!" Dude, Sam was onto the desserts before we even conquered the green veggies. Two days of him spitting that disgusting mush in my face was all it took for me to forego everything I had read in *What to Expect the First Year*.

Departing from my rant, I'm just saying that I don't have the keenest sense of smell, unless we are talking about approaching rain, automobile air conditioning (my second favorite smell on earth), and, indeed, tuberose! Now, of course, the actual fragrance that permeates from the petal oils of tuberose is my very favorite scent, but lotions, candles, bubble baths, and perfumes all tie for a close second. Tuberose, my dear friends, is the aroma that was penetrating the air in room 121 at the Beverly Hills Hotel.

I evened my respirations as Charlotte finished the massage, determined to not let her know anything was amiss. She tucked my leg back under the sheets and pulled her fingertips down the entire length of my body to signal that the massage had come to an end. She then whispered, "Take some time to just relax. Your robe is right at the foot of the table, and your water's refreshed right here on the table. Make sure to drink plenty of fluids the rest of today and be careful when you rise because you may be a little dizzy. I'm going to give you some privacy and will just come back later to collect my equipment. It's been a real pleasure, Ms. Holly."

I offered the customary moan of pleasure and total relaxation one courteously displays following a great massage. It was not a rouse, but the far too recent lurch off the table may have taken my pleasure down a notch. Through an exaggerated yawn and stiffening of my arms and legs as I stretched them as far as they could reach, I expressed my gratitude. "That was so awesome, Charlotte. Thank you so much! If I wasn't so incredibly relaxed, I would get up and hug you right now, but I'm afraid my jelly legs would fail me."

Charlotte snickered and then patted my leg, still under the sheets. "Don't get up, sweetie. You need to rest."

As she reached down to grab her purse, I knew I had a limited amount of time to do what I needed to do. I could not let her escape without at least asking her something that had been nagging at me since she revealed the source of her requested service, and even more so since the tropical recognition stung my nostrils. "Um," I said, buying a few seconds while I unsuccessfully tried to flip onto my stomach discreetly. One of my boobs popped out, and sweet Charlotte just turned her back to me without embarrassment or acknowledgement.

I, of course, was mortified, and the heat rose to my cheeks for the seventy-ninth time that day. "I'm so sorry." I laughed nervously. "These things just have a mind of their own!"

Charlotte laughed reassuringly. "Trust me, Ms. Holly, I have seen a whole lot worse!"

A-ha! My opening. I pacified my embarrassment for the opportunity to segue into my inquiry. "So, speaking of what you have seen, and I hope I'm not overstepping my bounds, but just curious, have you had other requests for your services from Nick, er, Mr. Price?"

Without skipping a beat, Charlotte tilted her head confusedly and asked, "Mr. Price?"

My eyes widened in disbelief. Had I misinterpreted? Backpedaling, I said, "Um, well, uh, I thought. Oh my gosh!" I slapped my hand to my forehead, the sheet falling once again below my boob. *Crapola*!

As I quickly snatched the sheet back up, Charlotte's face broke out into the biggest, toothiest grin I had ever seen. Tickled pink, she placed her hand on her heart and soothed, "Oh, sweetie, I'm so sorry. I truly should not have done that. That was so incredibly naughty of me. I was just playing onto our conversation when I arrived. Please, Ms. Holly, please forgive me."

Ah hell, how could I be mad at such a genuinely lovely woman? I managed to embody her amused delight and took the opportunity to really laugh at myself and this whole absurd scenario. "Crap, maybe I should just prance around here naked. You've already seen my right boob twice."

Charlotte belted out the deepest guttural howl that made me lose myself yet again until the two of us were crying. It was a laugh-fest born out of embarrassment and pure amusement. We carried on that way for a good two minutes until Charlotte finally penetrated the air with actual syllables.

"Oh, Allison, I haven't laughed that hard in so long. Most of my clients are so boring and treat me like I am the hired help who they don't need to speak to unless they are barking orders. 'Rub harder!' 'Not so hard!' 'Ouch, that hurts!' 'Don't mess up my makeup!' I swear, some of them are so incredibly high-maintenance. And that doesn't even include the ones who think it is perfectly *fine* to prance around naked. I tell ya, these Hollywood divas think that their bodies are God's gift to the world and that anyone should feel so fortunate to get the opportunity to look at them. I literally had one gal, not naming any names, who asked me to squeeze her newly enhanced breasts to make sure they felt real!"

"Oh my gosh! Did you do it?" I beseeched, entranced by her illustrious tales of woe.

"Well, yeah. I mean, when Pamela Anderson asks you to squeeze her jugs, you do it."

My mouth dropped. Holy crap! Pamela friggin' Anderson? Are you kidding me with this?

"Ha! Gotcha."

Oh, that stinker.

"Sweet girl, do you think I would really dole out the names of my clients and breach their confidentiality?"

And that's when my balloon deflated. What were the chances I was going to get any information out of her about Nick, no matter how hard I probed?

As if sensing my retreat into defeat, Charlotte tilted her head once again. But this time it wasn't a look of feigned perplexity; it was more a maternal look of compassion. "Now I think you were asking me a question?"

My stomach knotted, and for an instant, I almost told her to forget about it, that it was no big deal. But then I realized that this was my last shot, so I put on my proverbial big-girl pants and asked, "Well, I was just curious if you have known him for long."

She contemplated before responding, "Well, I'm not sure exactly to whom you are referring, but I do have this one hunky Australian gentleman who is my client who I have known for, oh, about two years."

"Really? So, and feel free to tell me it is none of my business, but has this gentleman had you give massages to other women?"

"Well, since you have no idea who this super hot Australian is, I would never tell you it was none of your business. I mean, it could be any number of Aussie clients of mine, right?"

I laughed and nodded.

"So, in answer to your question, no. This gentleman has only asked me to perform one massage that was not for his benefit."

"And that was for me."

"I can neither confirm nor deny." Charlotte winked again.

"So, did you know who I was before you came today?"

"Yes, ma'am, I did."

"Is it because of the article I had written?"

"No, that is not how I knew who you were."

I was befuddled. "So then, did Ni—er, your client mention me to you?"

"Yes, ma'am."

"Just like today? Or did you know about me before today?"

"Before today."

"How long have you known about me?"

"Since my client knew about you."

I was shocked. I didn't know how to proceed, but knew I must. "So why would your client have told you about me?"

"My client was out of town on business and had met a woman with whom he was quite taken. He asked if I would be willing to fly to his location to perform my services for this woman." Charlotte then burst out laughing. "Oh my gosh, I sound like I'm a prostitute!"

I couldn't contain my thrill with this newfound information as well as how tickled Charlotte became. I laughed nervously then continued. "So you didn't come though, did you?" The thought crossed my mind that maybe she did come and that quite possibly I wasn't the woman to whom she was referring.

"No, I couldn't make it. Despite the generous offer and the amenities included, I had a full schedule of appointments, some with clients I had known a lot longer than Ni—um, Mr. Australia, although none as likeable. So I had to turn down the offer."

"So what were these amenities and what was the offer?"

"Well, my client was going to fly me first class to his location, put me up in a much nicer hotel than even he himself were staying, and then pay me a hefty sum of money."

I wanted to know the amount but didn't dare ask. I wasn't that uncouth. "So, well, what exactly did he say about me?"

"Well, the woman that my client had met was, in his words, unlike any other woman he had ever met. She was smart and sophisticated and funny, and, once again his words, sexy as hell!"

I blushed something fierce. "Really?" I was way too excited.

Charlotte shifted her weight from one foot to the other, suddenly looking uncomfortable. "Yes." There was an awkward pause. "And then…"

I waited. *And then what?*

"Well, anyway, I guess the rest is history. So, Allison, it has been so great meeting you. Like I said, drink lots of water and take it easy for a while, okay?" Charlotte turned to leave.

Despite my urgent need to hear the rest of the story, I knew I was lucky to get what I had, and so I sheepishly smiled and softly said, "It was so nice to meet you too, Charlotte. And thank you so much for taking such good care of me today."

Charlotte halted and turned around to face me. She then strode back across the room and gave me a tight hug, whispering in my ear, "For what it's worth, he'd never been happier than when he met that girl." And with a wet blink of my eyes, Charlotte was gone.

19

I sat for a few more minutes on the table, followed Charlotte's order, drank down the delicious glass of water, and went into the bathroom to shower. It was shortly after two, and I decided that after my shower I would pack up and head to the airport, even though my flight didn't leave until 6:15. I would grab a bite to eat there if I could manage to regain some semblance of an appetite and maybe buy a book that looked like a good escape. I wasn't prepared, however, for the fatigue that would settle in my bones from the heat of the shower.

Forgoing my original plan to sit like a loser at the airport, I grabbed a snack from the minibar and, wearing only the super soft terry cloth robe I shimmied under the sheets.

The banging on the door yet again woke me with a start, and when I looked at the clock, it read 5:03. *No! No! Oh crap!* I sprang out of bed and ran to the door. Stafford stood looking somewhere between highly irritated and highly concerned. "Oh my gosh, I know, I know! I'm so sorry. Just give me a sec. Come in."

I didn't even wait for him to respond. I flung the door, hoping he would catch it, and ran into the bedroom, stripping out of the robe and into a pair of shorts and a T-shirt. I threw all my crap in my bag and when I dashed back into the living room, the numbers 5:06 flashed by my line of sight. Not bad, I must say.

Stafford was smiling and shaking his head when I barreled past him, twisting my unbrushed hair into a bun. "Man, I've never see a woman get ready that fast in my life!"

Out of breath and holding the door open impatiently as if I were waiting on *him*, I teased, "If this is me ready, you must have a really low opinion of me."

We sped as fast as the limo would go to the airport, and when Stafford pulled up in front of the doors, I didn't wait for him to open my door, much to his obvious dismay when he grunted as he rounded the back of the limo.

"Thanks for everything," I said as I reached up to give him a hug, a gesture that surprised myself possibly more than it surprised Stafford. I guess I just felt like he had taken such good care of me that I needed to show him my appreciation.

"Ms. Holly, I have someone waiting right in front of that door to take your bags and walk you to security. You will be able to go to the front of the security line and then another man will walk you to your gate. You should be on time, but if not, don't worry. They are holding the plane for you."

"Aww, you are so sweet. Thanks so much! I really wish you the best, Mr. Stafford." He nodded, and I hustled away.

A large African-American man with a headset on was waiting for me as planned and hurried me to the front of the security line. I began to breathe easier, knowing we still had ten minutes to spare. I really, really didn't want to be that jerk who walked onto a plane late, the one who thought she was better than everyone and important enough to have an entire 747 waiting on her. Unfortunately though, my underwire had other plans and when I kept setting off the security alarm, without a reasonable explanation as to why, the clock quickly ticked away. Finally, when the woman asked me for the fifth time, after frisking me five times, if I had any metal on my person (and my shoes, socks, hair tie, and jewelry were all removed), I huffed all too loudly, "I don't know, ma'am, you have me down to my underwear, bra, shirt, and short. Are any of those typically made of metal?" *Ooh, burn.*

But the joke was actually on me as she started laughing as loud as she could and retorted, "Girl, have you ever heard of underwire?" *Oh, screw her.*

So rushing to put all my accessories back on, my earrings of course giving me fits, I spied my next chaperone and took off through the terminal toward my gate. The woman waiting to take my ticket looked highly irritated with me. I had stuck the ticket in between my teeth when I was jacking with my earrings, and when I pulled it out to hand to her, it was indented with teeth marks and stained with spittle. She grabbed it with just the tips of her thumb and pointer finger like it was traced with anthrax and quipped, "You're seven minutes late!"

Not in the mood to be embarrassed or intimidated by anyone, I glared into her steel gray eyes, smiled, and patronized, "Oh, good for you. You can tell time!" I headed down the Jetway; and when I heard the perturbed woman badmouthing me to one of her colleagues, I turned around, still smiling, and flapped a robust wave. In response, she stomped to the heavy-duty steel door at the top of the Jetway and attempted to slam it shut so as to have the last word. Unfortunately for her, however, the door was spring-loaded and only jerked halfway shut before suspending and slowly continuing its closure. Ha! I wasn't the only one who was red-faced that day. I began to rotate forward again as I knew I must be getting close to the bend in the Jetway and, as if in cinematic slow motion, a figure appeared through what little space was still exposed from the slowly closing door. In the time it took for my brain to register what had pierced my eyes, I was face to face with the impatient flight attendant listening to the heavy door latch behind me, leaving Nicholas Price on the other side.

I can't tell you anything that happened on the flight home. I was in first class again, but I don't remember what I said, what I ate or drank, or what the person next to me looked like. My mind was in a foreign world in which Nicholas Price would show up to the airport to see me off. It didn't make sense. I was so conflicted, and it was taking its toll. Life seemed to be easier when he was out of the country and hating me. At least then I knew where I stood and could get on with my life. The confusion surrounding the events beginning with the phone call and culminating in the airport left my brain reeling. For real, you guys, it is like being a clichéd little girl and pulling petals off a flower, saying, "He loves me. He loves me not." It was too darn much!

I walked myself through the entire weekend several times, trying to analyze and pick apart each moment to gain some clarification on Nick's thoughts and intentions. The whole thing was made even more complicated by the forms that I finally scoured through. That Sarah Alton had quite the nerve! The wording on the form was indicative of her young age and lack of a quality education. Obviously, she had written the thing herself and had gotten one of her many assistants to type it up. I knew it held no legal weight whatsoever as there were no attorney signatures on it while there were several on the other documents.

To summarize her highness's wishes, she wanted me to give my Joan Hancock that I would not continue to defame her character and slander her name to any media outlet and that, despite the failure of the restraining order motion passing, she would like me to stay at least one hundred yards away from her, although "five miles would be ideal." The document contained more dialogue than an artsy Sundance Film Festival film. Completely inappropriate for a legal document. I wondered if Charlotte ever had the unfortunate displeasure of massaging stupid Sarah Alton. If I wasn't so sidetracked with my scrutiny of Nick's erratic behavior, I would have found humor in the document. I may even have called my mom to crack jokes. As it was, I balled it up and stuck it in my carry-on to prepare for landing.

As I deplaned, I realized I had completely forgotten where I had parked my car just one day prior. Trying my best to settle my reeling thoughts, I stopped just inside the airport to get my bearings. The mental image of my vehicle clicked into focus, and I proceeded through the gate and out the glass doorway. Swiveling my head to find the closest exit, I spied a woman who looked disheveled barreling toward me with purpose. It was my mother!

Trying his best to keep up with her, Sam was trailing behind by my dad. Boy, were they a sight for sore eyes. And apparently, so was I (at least for my mom) as she grabbed me into a firm embrace and whispered, "Don't you ever scare me like that again!" *Oh crap! I didn't call her back.*

"Oh my gosh, Mom, I'm so sorry!"

"Yeah, well, you should be, Allison. I didn't know if you were dead or alive, and I called the airport in LA to make sure you were getting on your flight since your damn phone just kept going to voice mail and they told me that you were not on board your flight. What on earth, Allie?"

I squeezed Sam, who was hanging on to my leg, and said, "But you are here, so you must have known I boarded."

"No," my dad chimed in, "actually your mom was having a cow and demanded that we come anyway and that if you didn't get off the plane she was heading to the ticket booth to catch the next flight to California and, in her words, 'hunt that SOB Nicholas down!'"

"Oh, for the love Mom. Seriously?"

"Don't 'for the love' me, Allison Belle. You do *not* do to your mother what you did to me. Do you hear me, Samuel Christopher? Don't *ever* do to your mom what she did to me," she commanded, adding under her breath, "not that she doesn't deserve it."

Dad grabbed my bag and nodded toward the exit. "Okay, Allie Belle, did you learn your lesson, missy?"

I couldn't help but laugh at my dad's levity and sarcasm. "Wait, my car is here, guys. I can't go home with you."

"Oh, Allie, we were going to come anyway," my mom said. "Sam was missing you so much that we thought it would be nice for you two to drive home together and for you to not have to come back out to Topeka."

"Yeah, Mama. I wanted to surprise you! Are you surprised?" Oh, my precious boy.

"Well, yeah, sweetie." I bent down to scoop him into my arms. "There is nothing better in the world than seeing you right now." I kissed his sweet cheeks, which he promptly wiped off. Man alive, was this child ever heavy. I walked about ten steps before I had to release him.

"So your dad will drive your car home, and you can ride with me and Sammy," Mom commanded.

"Hmm, let's see, ride with you who is going to nag and guilt me the whole way home or ride with Dad who will probably just let me sit in silence? Hmm. That's a tough one," I teased.

"Oh, smarty-pants, you really want to go there after I single-handedly took care of your son all weekend?" she rebutted.

"Ahem? *Excuse me*? Single-handedly huh?" my dad defended. "Hey, Sam, my man, who played with you all weekend long?"

"You, Pops," Sam answered.

"Yeah, and what was Grandma doing the whole weekend?" *Oh, Dad, why must you antagonize her?*

"Playing on her Facebook."

"Aha! Busted, Grandma!" I chided.

"Oh, I *was* not! I was cleaning house and cooking for these two yayhoos and toting Sam Man all over the place. I can't believe you would even *think* about trying to make her believe I did nothing, Joe! I'm the one who does…" Mom rambled on for a good three minutes while Dad and I each grabbed one of Sam's hands and began swinging him in the air, obviously finished listening.

When we reached their car, Mom was steaming something fierce, her mouth set in a straight line and her arms crossing her chest. Dad knew he had no choice but to acknowledge her hard work, so he closed in beside her, put his arm around her and, as tenderly as a callous man can actually be, he cooed, "Oh, Sharon, come on now. You know we were just teasing. You do everything for your grandkids."

"Don't patronize me!" she barked as she climbed into the driver's seat, slamming the door.

"Ouch," I said. "You know what, Dad? Why don't you guys just drive on back to Topeka together? That way you don't have to go all the way to my house before heading all the way home. I mean, Sam and I will be fine driving home alone, and besides, I'm beat."

"Um, okay. Are you sure?" Dad seemed conflicted.

"Yes, I'm positive. It seems like you guys have some making up to do anyway, and quite frankly, I don't want to hear about it all the way home. I just need some peace." It felt so good to be able to just be honest. I was too emotionally drained to put on airs.

"Okay, Allie Belle, whatever you need, honey. At least let us drive you to your car though."

"Actually, I'm right around the corner. We got this, right, Sammy?"

Sam was yawning, not even paying attention to our conversation. "What?"

"Nothing. Thanks, Dad, so much for everything." I reached up and hugged him and then knocked on Mom's window and waved.

She scrunched her eyebrows, obviously confused, and began frantically searching for a way to unroll the window. Oh, dear sweet mother who never has been one to embrace technological changes. She hadn't owned a car with manual windows in over fifteen years yet she never could get used to the electric ones. I took the opportunity to grab Sam and hurry away from the car, knowing that as soon as she realized the keys needed to be in the ignition to unroll the windows, she would fling open the door and holler after me.

She didn't disappoint. Mothers are nothing if not consistent. But by the time she got out to question me, we were already turning down another aisle in the parking lot and I pretended to not understand what she had said, replying, "I love you too, Mom! Bye!" She hollered something after me, but I was already pulling Sam to the car.

The drive home was uneventful with the exception of the call from Mom. Oh, was she hot. Apparently, they were planning on staying the night at my house to help out with Sam, assuming I would be exhausted, have laundry to do, and want to get in bed early. Had I known that, I would have jumped at the opportunity, but my dad hadn't revealed their plans to me. When I mentioned they could still come and that I would welcome it, she passive aggressively informed me that they were already heading toward the toll road and so there was no point. Oh, the guilt that woman was capable of piling on. She then let me know how incredibly rude it was of me to peel her grandson away without letting her say good-bye, not to mention the fact that I didn't properly thank her for all she had done for me.

She was right, and I was an evil manipulator who used that reminder as a chance to launch into the spiel about why I had called her earlier crying. I know, I know. I'm a horrible person who is completely uncomfortable with guilt, especially when it is founded, and I try unabashedly to make myself out as a victim. It's ugly. I did it with Chris when I wanted to try and get pregnant, despite the fact that he was clearly not feeling well, and then I did it again with my mom, who had every right to be pissed at me. Growing up the youngest of four, I learned the repulsive way how to get what I wanted, no matter the cost. Unlike pooping my pants and picking my nose, which thank the Lord I grew out of, manipulating those I love to get my way never went away.

By the time I finished the California saga, my folks were getting off at their Topeka exit, and my mom was finally able to crumble the chip on her shoulder toward me. We said our good-byes, and I apologized once again. All was better with my mom, and so a few ounces of my gallon of guilt evaporated.

When I pulled into the garage and exited the car, I noticed a piece of paper taped to the door going into the house. It was then that I remembered the garage door fiasco from when I left and wondered how on earth had I just opened and closed the garage door with the opener, a complete habit that I would not have even remembered and shouldn't have worked had I not seen the paper.

It was a note from Greg.

> Allie, I fixed the door. Sorry but I couldn't stand the thought of someone being able to get into your garage and steal something while you were away. I really hope you had a good trip and that you got what you were looking for. I really would like to talk to you, and I am so incredibly sorry for being such a douche! Please forgive me? I don't want to lose your friendship, Allie. You and Chris are too important to me for that to happen. Call me at your leisure.—Greg

Feeling a tad bit guilty for not having even thought of him once from the moment I laid eyes on Nick in LA, I folded the paper nicely and made a commitment to myself to phone him in the morning. After all, Nick wasn't *here*, was he? Greg *was*. Even though I didn't ever think I could look at Greg as more than a friend, I knew I could trust him and count on him. After my whirlwind weekend in a pretentious world where rich people spent more money on lip gloss than I spent on my car, I realized the life I longed for was right here in humdrum Kansas, where the people weren't plastic and the poor were cared for. Yes, Greg was a constant who should continue to be in my life, no matter what the capacity.

Sam and I went to the park the next morning and just played. I did whatever he wanted to do. If he wanted to swing, we would swing. Go down the spiral slide? Sure, Sam. Teeter-totter? You bet. Play shark on the jungle gym? Not too busy for this today, son! It was only when we were walking home and he was in his own little world counting the trees we passed that I decided a phone call to Greg wouldn't make Sam feel as though I was being inattentive.

Greg picked up on the second ring and sounded relieved to hear my voice. "Allie, wow. I didn't expect you to actually call me."

I was taken aback. "Uh, well, um, I mean you asked me to."

"No, no. It's great! I'm glad you called. I guess I just didn't know if you would, you know, given the way things were left."

"Oh yeah, I mean, it's fine, Greg. Let's just leave all that in the past. And hey, thanks for fixing my garage door. That was so nice. You didn't have to do that."

"Oh, I know, but I figured that since I was already over there, I might as well make myself useful." Greg released a nervous laugh. This was awkward.

Silence ensued for a good three seconds, which felt like much longer. Finally, I cleared my throat and asked, "So what's been going on?" Such a standard question reserved for a casual conversation with someone from whom you really don't care to hear the answer.

"Well, let's see." It sounded like he was stretching, possibly leaning back in his office chair or something. "I went fishing this weekend at Shawnee Mission Park. That was cool."

More silence as I thought he would elaborate. When he didn't, I jumped in, as if I had missed my cue. "Cool! Did you catch anything?"

"Oh, a few bites and a couple of small ones, but no keepers."

Ticktock. Ticktock. *Crap. What should I ask next?* "Well, that's a bummer. Did Annabelle go with you? She loves to fish with you."

"No. She was with that witch she calls a mom."

Ticktock. "Oh, I see." No matter how mad I was at Jen, it still hurt to hear him speak of her in that manner. It just didn't seem like the Greg I had once known. "So, busy day at work today?"

"Naw, I mean, no more than usual."

Ticktock. Ticktock. Okay, so I was getting quite annoyed with the fact that *I* was the one asking all the questions. That is one of my biggest pet peeves. It is even worse when the person who is being so rude is the one who requested the communication to begin with. Not to mention the fact that they were kind of a jackass and should be trying extra hard if they really want to maintain some semblance of a relationship. So, to relay my feelings on the issue, I decided to just give a one-word response and wait. "Oh" was all I said.

"Hey, Mom, check this out!" Sam beckoned from half a block ahead of me.

Thankful for the distraction since Greg didn't seem to take my silent hint, I hollered, "Hang on, sweetie" and used my allegiance to my son as a reason to get out of the painful conversation with Greg.

"Hey, Greg, I gotta go. Good talking to you though." I couldn't fake it. I just couldn't. It was so obvious by my tone of voice that I was irritated with his terrible telephone etiquette, and I was okay with it being obvious, damn it. Don't apologize and ask me to freaking call you and then act like you are completely bored with my conversation. Jerk.

Of course, my inability to disguise my disgust did not serve me well as Greg panicked. "Wait, what's wrong, Allie? What did I say?"

Oh, for the love of God. I was not up for another "Greg drama," which had somehow become the norm with our recent conversations. I bluffed. "Oh, nothing. I'm just walking home with Sam from the park, and he wants to show me something."

"Mom!" Sam huffed impatiently. "Are you watching?"

I held up my finger as I stopped walking, unable to talk, walk, and watch at the same time. I used to be the master at patting my head and rubbing my tummy, a skill that my dear grandpa used to give me nickels for. But since becoming a widowed mother, I had lost all ability to multitask. Man, I would give anything to go back to the days when practicing the head-tummy task was the only thing occupying my time and brainpower for thirty minutes straight. For that matter, I would give anything to go back to the time when five cents was worth something.

"Oh, okay. Well, hey, I would love to see you and Sam sometime soon. Do you have any time?"

Ugh. I really didn't want to have time for that. See how inconsistent I am? I flipped from wanting to have all the time in the world to just pat my head and rub my tummy, but then when it came to having time to interact with a man who had once been such a dear friend, I suddenly wished I was too busy. I'm such a hypocrite. "Well, yeah. I mean, we probably have some time this week."

"*Motherrrrr!*" Sam was not letting up.

Completely ignoring the fact that my son was screaming at me in the background, even though there was no way in h-e-double hockey sticks he couldn't hear him, Greg suggested, "How 'bout tonight?"

I used Sam's rude behavior to pretend I didn't hear what Greg had said and shouted back at Sam, "Young man, that is *not* acceptable behavior!" and then, quickly returning my attention to the phone, I said, "Hey, Greg, I've gotta go deal with this naughty little boy. I'll call ya sometime, okay?"

There was no way he could ignore my impatience, and so he just sulked. "Okay. Talk to you later." Oh, I hate men who pout.

Not dignifying his reaction, I cheerfully closed with "Okay, talk to you later, Greg" and immediately hung up the phone. Phew, I averted that discomfort.

Sam and I returned home, made some lunch, and settled in to watch *Wreck-It Ralph* for the ten thousandth time. Yes, folks, that was about as violent a movie as I allowed my son to watch. I was so *lame*. One can only take so much "gl-gl-glitching" before she decides to tune out the movie and use the duration to take a much-needed nap. Sam didn't mind, as he took the opportunity to bust out his *Wreck-It Ralph* figures and reenact the movie scenes on the living room rug. He had begun to detest it when I would listen to him play and usually just went to his room when he wanted to play make-believe. I could totally relate because I remembered my own playtime at that age and how embarrassed I would get when my brother would stand at my door listening to me play Barbie, and just about the time things were starting to get heated between Barbie and Ken, he would show his ugly mug and start making smooching sounds, teasing, "Oh, Barbie, I so want to make out with you. Muah, muah, muah." Oh, how I would get fired up and scream "Mom!" at the top of my lungs. Adam would retreat to his room and act like he had been playing by himself the whole time.

During these moments of reminiscence, I was thankful that Sam didn't have to contend with an annoying sibling, but then it also reminded me of the fact that he would grow up and not have the love and support upon which I had come to depend on with my sisters and brother. It was yet another reminder that I was completely alone in this parenting world and would never again reproduce to provide that same sense of comfort and stability for my sweet Sam.

I listened to him for a spell, pretending to be asleep, as he brought to life every scene verbatim, and then I finally drifted off with visions of lemon drops and lollipops dancing in my psyche. I didn't even stir when the movie was over, and Sam began it yet again. In fact, I wasn't even sure what the repeat count was up to when I was startled awake by the home telephone ringing.

Sam was still on the floor playing, but the *Wreck-It Ralph* characters had been replaced with Legos; and I'll be darned if my little man hadn't created an exact replica of the race car used by Vanellope Von Schweetz and the actual structure of the Fix-It Felix Jr. apartment complex, complete with Ralph's dumpster abode. Oh, he was such a little genius. I rolled off the couch and strode into the kitchen, uncaring about whether I would reach it in time. I really had no desire to talk to anyone.

The caller ID said "blocked," and I almost walked away; but then it registered in my mind that if it were yet another dumb telemarketer, it would say "unavailable" or something to that effect. Someone had to purposefully block their number from being picked up on Caller ID, so I decided to see who it was. Had I been awake enough to guess, I would have speculated it was some paparazzi nut or one of the stupid PR geeks from Nick Price's camp

"Hello?" I answered, ready to be annoyed at whoever was calling me from a blocked number.

There was silence on the other end.

"Helloo?" I said again, obviously perturbed. "I can hear you breathing, whoever this is."

Click. What a moron!

I hung up the phone and went back into the living room to give Sam the bad news that TV time was over. I had already let him watch far longer than any parenting magazine would ever suggest. "Time to do something else, buddy. Why don't you go outside?"

"But it's so hot," he whined.

"Oh, for Pete's sake, it is not. And guess what? Tomorrow is supposed to be *really* hot so you better get your outdoor time in today, little dude."

"Don't call me that!" he barked.

"What? Dude?" *Please, Lord, don't let him know what "dude" actually means.* Certainly I had at least a year or two left before the outside influences supplied him with an arsenal of inappropriate knowledge.

"No, Mom, not 'dude.' I'm talking about calling me 'little.' I'm not little, and I don't want you calling me that anymore, understand?"

Whoa, I don't think so Mr. Smarty-Pants. "Excuse me, Samuel Christopher? Did you seriously just talk to me that way?"

"You say that all the time to me, Mom," my big-britches boy defended.

"Yeah, Sam, because I am the *mother*! Do you understand what that means? It means that I'm allowed to speak to you like that. You, however, are *not*!"

Sam just shrugged and rolled his eyes, which set me on fire even more. See, now this would have been an opportune time to play the wait-until-your-dad-gets-home card; but alas, that wasn't an option for me. So instead, I grabbed the remote, flipped off the TV, and spoke three firm words that sent chills down my spine as I realized my voice had transformed into that of my own mother: "To. Your. Room."

My bulging eyes must have done the trick because Sam instantly arose and stomped to his room. When he felt he was at a safe enough distance away, he wailed, "You are the meanest mom *ever!*" and then slammed his bedroom door. Job well done. Images of dusting my hands off played in my head.

I was just getting to my feet when the blasted phone rang again. "Oh, for the love," I muttered under my breath. I mean, nobody called home phones anymore. It had to be the same dummy from before.

Being the Curious George that I am, I couldn't just let it ring without checking who it was. I believe it was at this point that the name Nick began tugging at my psyche. I was greeted with the same "Blocked" salutation on the Caller ID and, like a fool, decided to pick it up anyway again. Unearthing my badass alter ego, I hissed, "Hello?"

Silence ensued, but this time I wasn't going to let them off the hook. "Ha. It doesn't really matter that you blocked your number because the FBI has tapped my phone and know *exactly* who this is and have just been dispatched to come to your location and—"

The person on the other end cleared their voice and then asked, "Is this Allie?"

But it wasn't Nick. It was worse—much, much worse. It was Jen.

20

So you know how I claim my heart stops beating anytime something significant happens? I mean, let's be real. If my heart really stopped beating all those times, I would have been in cardiac arrest like fifty times. Hearing Jen's voice, however, seriously *did* stop my heart. I mean I had to actually check my wrist for a pulse. Well, maybe not that bad, but I did about pass out. No exaggeration! I just wasn't expecting it. In fact, Jen was probably the last person I expected to hear on the end of that receiver. It's so interesting because technically Jen is the root cause for everything I had been going through—the drama with Nick; having to go to California to sign papers; the paparazzi and the media infesting my life; and then, more recently at the time, the awkward relationship I had found myself in with Greg. None of those things would have existed in my life had Jen not single-handedly tried to *destroy* my life. Yet she was the *last* person I was thinking about when she spoke for the first time.

I knew Jen's voice instantly although I pretended I didn't. "Yes?" was all I answered.

It took her a second, and had I not known it was Jen, I would have deduced that it was a telemarketer caught off guard by someone actually answering the phone and that she had to organize herself to prepare her speech. "Allie, this is Jen."

I so wanted to ask "Jen who?" as if I was totally over her, but I figured that would be a jerk thing to do. So I just said, "Uh-huh?" Kind of jerky in and of itself, but what can she really expect?

She took a big deep breath and then said, "How are you?"

Aaackkk! *Are you freaking kidding me with this?* Oh, guys, the should'ves, would'ves, and could'ves have run rampant in my idiotic brain since that conversation. In fact, they were already running rampant just three back-and-forths later, but the timing was off to pursue any of them.

So instead I said, "Um…fine?" Why did everything I said commence with an inflection at the end so as to sound like a question?

I used to get so mad at Chris when he would do that to me. I'd call him at work and he'd answer the phone, knowing it was me calling, and say, "Hello?" like *Why are you calling me, Allie?* And then I'd say, "Hey babe," and he'd respond, "Hey?" as if he still were completely unclear as to who I was or why I was calling him. Just hear these words being spoken to you with a long, drawn out inflection at the end, and then you'll get my gist. Oh, I'd get so flippin' mad. He sounded so skeptical, like I was going to ask him for money or a favor. And then—oh, my blood's boiling now—if I didn't have anything noteworthy to talk about, you know, 'cause I'm a girl and sometimes we just call to say "hi," I'd feel like a total donkey who just interrupted my husband's day for no particular reason.

On more than one occasion, I got my panties in such a wad that I let him have it. Following his "Hello?" and "Hey?" and "Fine?" I would scream into the phone, "Whatever! I get it. You don't want to talk to me, and I am such nosy, clingy wife who had the *nerve* to actually want to talk to her husband while he is at work!" Chris was either completely caught off guard or being the biggest smart-ass in the world when, as I was one second shy of hanging up, he would say, "Okayyy?" Gosh, how I miss that man.

Had Chris been physically present in the house at the time of Jen's phone call (I have good reason to believe he is often present spiritually/supernaturally), I guarantee he would have stopped dead in his tracks (terrible use of a pun), mouth agape, eyebrows raised, shaking his head. He would whisper the word "hypocrite" as I tried to stifle a laugh. Man alive (another bad pun), I would give anything to have that beautifully flawed man standing in front of me and calling me names!

But alas, it was just me, myself, and I to contend with my hypocrisy toward an ex-best friend who sabotaged my relationship with the most famous young movie star on the planet and added insult to injury by splattering my indiscretion around the globe for all the world to see. Oh my word, do you see the Jerry Springer episode in the making here? I would feel silly even writing these words had they not been so painfully true!

So back to the phone call we go. Jen hesitates yet again before responding, "Good. I'm so glad to hear that, Allie." And then there was more awkward silence. I swear to you I spent more time in awkward silence during that three-day stretch than I had in all of my life years put together.

I don't know what Jen expected in those silent seconds, but if she had thought that her absence of words would lead to my asking of her the same question, she had another thing coming! While I absolutely *did* care how she was, I really shouldn't have, and I sure as hell was not going to let on to her that I did! So I matched her mute for mute.

Finally she began again. "Listen, Allie, I know this is a lot to ask, but do you think there is any way we could maybe get together and talk?" Oh, the nerve of that woman!

I didn't know what to say. My nerves were so shot that I really didn't think I could take the stress of seeing Jen face to face. To stall until I could wrap my brain around the prospect, I asked, "Why?"

This took Jen aback. "Well, um, because there are some things I would like to say to you."

I puffed up my chest to boost my courage, saying, "Oh, Jen, don't you think you've said enough to me? I mean, really, your words used to have such an effect on me. But now…Well, now, Jen, I really don't care what you have to say." Ooh, I was brave. This was the one time in my entire life that I didn't have hindsight syndrome.

The phone went silent, and I thought Jen had hung up. Ooh, I hate that when I just make a really snazzy point and then the person on the other end of the receiver goes so silent that I have to break my sense of superiority to ask "Hello?" But I had to do just that, and that's when I heard the shaky sniff. Jen was crying. *Oh brother, where art thou?*

After Jen snotted into the phone several times, I finally sighed loudly and caved in. "Fine, Jen. When and where?"

It still took her a beat before she could control her shaky voice enough to respond. "Um, I don't care. Are you available tomorrow? Like in the morning?"

I thought about my Wednesday and couldn't come up with anything pertinent, try as I might, so I was left with no choice but to concur. "Um, yeah. Okay. So where?" I was being very curt.

Jen was still trying to steady her voice and responded, "Your call."

I hate it when people can't make decisions, especially since Jen was never shy about telling me what our plans were going to be. But I didn't have a sitter for Sam and really didn't feel like getting one. I seriously could not see Jen and I having an intimate conversation at Starbucks, or anywhere else where there are other people. Plus, while the paparazzi had been at bay as far as I was concerned, I had no clue if Jen was constantly being followed. I finally suggested, "My house?"

Without even pausing to decide, Jen blurted "Yes!"

"Okay?"

"Sorry, I just really don't want to go out in public anywhere, ya know?"

I didn't know exactly why, but I didn't want to act interested in why she wasn't too keen on it, so I just said, "Uh-huh. Hey listen, I'll probably sleep in a little so how about ten?"

"That sounds great. I assume you still live in the same house?" Jen laughed.

If homegirl thought there was going to be some sort of camaraderie here, she had another thing coming. I exhaled. "Yes, I'll see you tomorrow, Jen," and then I hung up the phone.

Sure, I had acted all aloof, calm, and collected on the phone; but, guys, inside I was *dying*! I had literally spent almost a full year scrambling to keep my life together at the hands of Jen Manis, and now I had to face her in the flesh and listen to whatever it was she had to say. Oh gosh, what did she want to say?

My heart started racing, and the soles of my feet began to sweat. I went to the freezer and grabbed one of Sam's booboo bags and pressed it against my forehead, sitting down at the kitchen table. As I sat, my legs began to shake. Oh no, what was happening to me? Was I having a heart attack? I became violently dizzy. Clutching my cell phone, I dropped my head between my quivering knees. I tried to call out to Sam, but my own voice was muffled in my ears. I started to press 911 but then quickly hit "end" and dialed my mom. Thank the Lord she answered on the first ring.

"Mom," I cried. "I...I...um, I think..."

"Allie, honey, what is it? I can't understand you. Where are you, in a cave?" She chuckled at herself.

"Mom, no! Something's *wrong*!" I shouted into the phone.

"Is it Sam?" She panicked.

"No, it's *me*!"

"Oh, thank God." My dear mother exhaled a sigh of relief.

"Thanks, Mom!" I was scared to death. Why wasn't she more concerned? I didn't have time for this. I had two, maybe three minutes until I was sure I would be lying dead on the floor.

"Oh, Allie, I'm just saying. Well, you know, he's my grandbaby and—"

"Mom, shut up, damn it!"

"Whoa there, Allison. Don't you dare curse at me."

"I'm gonna hang up, Mom. Seriously, I think I'm having a heart attack."

"Whoa, whoa. Okay, slow down, Allie Bear." *Now* she wanted to be consoling? "No one is having a heart attack. You are only thirty…well, thirty…Wait, how old are you?"

For the love of all things holy, this woman! And then I couldn't remember. I couldn't recall how old I was. Oh my gosh, how old am I? I was dying for sure, and the oxygen must have been slowly depleting in my brain cells. Oh no. This was it. And then it hit me. "Thirty-five! I'm thirty-five!"

"Okay, yes, sweetie. You are thirty-five. No need to shout. You know, I *did* have four of you! And you and your brother are so damn close in age. Now wait, how old is Adam if you're thirty-five? Are you sure you're thirty-five?"

Guys, I couldn't take it. I was sitting on the phone with my head between my knees while my mother decided it was an opportune time to sort out the ages of her children. I burst out in laughter. "Are you freaking kidding me with this, Mom? I tell you I'm dying and first you're relieved that it is me and not Sam. Then you can't remember how freaking old I am, and so then you decide *now* is the appropriate time to contemplate the ages of your children while on the phone with your dying daughter. Are you for real?"

"Well, it's as good a time as any I guess." She was completely impassive.

It took me a second, but then I burst out in amusement. "You are so full of crap, aren't you?"

"I don't know what you're talking about." I could hear the chink in her deadpan armor.

"Uh-huh. Yeah, sure ya don't. I see what you're doing, missy."

She finally let out a little chuckle, and it was then that I realized I was sitting up in a normal, if not relaxed, slouch.

"You're unbelievable, you know that, Mom?"

"Is your panic attack over yet, sweetie?"

Then it hit me. She knew all along. She knew before I knew. My smarty-pants mother knew what ailed me before I even did, and she was only hearing my voice through a telephone receiver.

"Oh, Mom," I cried. "How did you know?"

"Allie, you're my daughter. I know you like the back of my hand. I know the way your voice muffles and shakes when you are panicking. I know that you instantly turn angry and desperate when someone doesn't respond immediately to the feelings you are having. And I know what it really means when you say that you are dying or having a heart attack or a brain tumor or an aneurysm or—"

"Okay, okay, I get it. Sheesh. You don't have to remind me of *all* my crazy in one setting."

Laughing again, my intuitive mother asked, "So, crazy daughter of mine, what's got your panties in a bunch?"

Feeling the blood back in my limbs and head, I stood up to delve into the Jen saga. I have always been one to pace when I dispense drama over the phone. I said, "Well, you're not gonna believe who just called me."

"The pope?"

"No, dork."

"The president?"

"Nope."

"Well, then…" I was expecting her to extend silence, thus giving up. But instead, she finished her thought with "Jen?"

Stunned. Just. Simply. Stunned. How in the he——? Wait, was my mom tracing my calls? Oh, the absurdity. "Mom, how did you know that? I mean, seriously, how on earth could you possibly have known that? You went from the pope to the president to Jen? Are you kidding me with this?"

She giggled, clearly proud of herself. "Well, ya know, it's a natural order. I mean, short of Chris calling from heaven, who else would you get that worked up about hearing from? I would say Nicholas Price, but you've gotten worked up about him calling so many times, I would doubt you would have a flippin' heart attack over it. And then the president, well, that would make anyone crap their drawers. The pope…Well, I don't actually know why I started with that. I mean, it would be a pretty bizarre phone conversation, but we're not Catholic and so you probably wouldn't be within seconds of dying if he called. So the next logical conclusion was Jen."

"Wow, well, you're just full of this psychic stuff, aren't you?"

"I just know you well, Allie. It's no different than how well you know Sam and how much more you will get to know him as he changes and grows. So, back to Jen, what did she want?"

"To meet and talk."

"Whoa, that's a doozy. How do you feel about that?"

"Oh, you know, no big dealio. I'm just chill about it," I teased.

"Ha. Well, I know you had a heart attack over it. But now that you have had your triple bypass, how do you feel?"

"I don't know. I mean, it just doesn't make sense. Why on earth would she want to talk to me, unless she is feeling really sorry for herself because she has lost everything and so now she's like 'Huh, maybe I oughtta make up with Allie so I have at least *one* friend. She's stupid enough to take me back.' Ya know?"

"Yeah, I suppose that's one way of looking at it. Certainly, hindsight is twenty-twenty, and no doubt Jen is feeling the pangs from the choices she made. But what if she genuinely feels bad and realizes that what she did was so wrong? I mean, could you forgive her?"

"Oh, Mom, I just don't know. I mean, is there any way to truly know if someone is sorry for their actions or if they are just sorry for the consequences they have had to endure?"

"That's a very good question, Al. And unfortunately, no, I guess there is not a surefire way to tell. However, maybe that isn't necessarily the question you should be contemplating."

"Huh?" I asked, confused.

"Well maybe this isn't about whether Jen is truly sorry or not but rather about if you can forgive her even if she's not."

"Oh, Mom, I feel like since I've kind of let it go, I have forgiven her, ya know? I mean, I feel sorry for her really, and I guess feeling pity for someone makes it easier to forgive them. Plus, you know the saying 'Forgiveness isn't necessarily for the other person as much as it's for yourself'? Well, I think I have adopted that philosophy pretty well over the years."

"Oh, but, Allie, maybe forgiveness really *is* about the other person."

"About letting her off the hook?" I was aghast that my mother would even suggest such a thing. "I mean one can forgive but never forget, right?" I wondered if my mom deciphered my biting tone.

"Oh, poo with your sayings. That's all they are, just sayings. Of course, the heart has a hard time forgetting offenses, but it is what we make of those unpleasant memories that betters us or keeps us in the pit."

"Mom, have you been reading another self-help book?" I teased, the chip on my shoulder sliding to the ground.

"Ha. No, Allie, I haven't, but I mean that sometimes we look back on tough situations and are so incredibly thankful for them because we see the larger plan that was at work during the dark days. And that truly is a gift. The same thing with forgiveness, Al. Forgiveness is a gift you can give another person. Sure, selfishly you can forgive to make yourself feel better, to get the weight off or whatever. But forgiving for the sole purpose of extending grace and mercy. Well, that very well may be something Jesus would have done."

"Touché, Mom. Touché." God bless this woman and her wisdom.

"Now, do I need to come straight there and drive you to the hospital or can I just call an ambulance for you?"

"Oh, shut up!" We both laughed at the absurdity of it all.

"Okay then, tell me about my grandson. What has he been up to while you were in the midst of your heart attack? And can I talk to him?"

"Who knows? I've probably scarred him for life. Either that or he is willing me to kick the bucket since he didn't even come when I called for him."

"Well, he may be attuned to your little 'episodes' by now."

"Either that or he is seriously just like Dad and hears nothing when he is transfixed in front of the TV."

"Yeah, that's probably more like it. Do you know I have been standing here in the doorway between the kitchen and family room the entire time we've been talking and your dad is literally ten feet away watching TV and hasn't so much as even glanced my way? Crap, you could be dying, Allie, and he'd never even know it."

And then I heard a rumble that sounded an awful lot like my dad coming through the phone line. "What did he say?"

"Yeah right, Joe. Of course you hear me when I don't want you to. It's when I'm actually speaking directly *to* you that you all of a sudden go deaf and mute." A few seconds later, she said, "Yeah, well, just this morning I walked right in front of you when you were watching the damn TV and told you we were having dinner at the Grants' tonight and not an hour later when I mentioned it you had no clue what I was talking about."

The grumbling continued, so I decided it was time to interject for my dad's sake and shouted, "Mom! Do you want to talk to Sam or not?"

She whispered into the phone, "Oh yes, and your *dad*. Of *course* he heard me say his name, but do you think he ever listens to me when I want him to? No way! He just—"

I could actually decipher the singsong tone of my dad's voice as he teased, "Can still here you!" *Busted.*

"S*aaaam?*" I hollered. I didn't want another rehashing of my dad's uncanny ability to be, well, a *man*.

"Oh, hello?" my mom asked.

"Yeah, here's Sam." He wasn't actually there yet, but I set on foot to find him, holding the phone at my side.

When I found him, I gave him the phone and told him to just say good-bye when he was finished and hang up. Then I left him to chitchat with my mom. I was oh so thankful for my mom. She knew exactly what I needed when I called, despite her initial *fake* reaction. That stinker! Nevertheless, I felt quite a bit better about meeting with Jen. My mom was right, after all. Mercy was the perfect gift I could give Jen, or anyone for that matter.

Thinking of extending mercy and grace, I immediately thought of Greg and how blasé I had been with him on the phone earlier. My irritation with him from before my trip had inadvertently carried over to my arrival home. He didn't deserve that from me, no matter how maddening and irritating he had been prior to my departure. I decided that if I were going to agree to meet face-to-face with Jen, a woman who sabotaged not only my life but also that of Greg as well, I should certainly agree to get together with Greg.

Not knowing if I was going to mention the conversation with Jen or the impending reunion, when I dialed Greg's number, something inside me decided against it when he answered the phone. I don't know if I just reasoned that I really had nothing to tell until after Jen and I met and I figured out what she had to say, or if I just didn't want to hear him speak ill of her again and grill me about details, but something nagged at me. That something was enough for me to keep silent about the whole ordeal.

Greg was extremely glad to hear from me, a response that I fully expected. We only chatted for a few minutes, but I already felt as though the tension had melted and the ease of conversation had transitioned back to one of a friendship, not a potential courtship. It was refreshing. Truly, I desperately needed a good friend, especially one that was local. We made plans for him to come over the next evening for pizza and a movie. Sam had been invited to spend the night at a friend's house, so it would actually work out perfectly for Greg and I to just hang out casually alone, and Lord knows I would probably need the decompression and distraction from my impending time with Jen that morning. I felt good after Greg and I hung up, like things just might turn out all right.

21

You know that expression "I didn't sleep a wink"? Usually, when someone says that, I just assume they are exaggerating and probably got a measly five or six hours of shut-eye, so I don't typically feel sorry for them. The night before Jen's appearance, however, I fully understood what it meant to not sleep one solitary wink. I'm not exaggerating here, people, like those other fools who actually *do* sleep at least one stinkin' wink. Not. One. Wink. I had three brain tumors, one, aneurysm, and four heart attacks during that night with no winks. And oh was I hurting in the morning.

My first instinct was to cancel with Jen. Not only was I already so tummy-knotted about the whole thing before the winkless night, but adding extreme fatigue to an already volatile situation induced some sort of trancelike state of being in my psyche. I had to have only been a few nonexistent winks shy of full-out psychosis, complete with delusions and hallucinations. Luckily, a strong cup of Starbucks coffee (a mocha to be precise, but I like to sound cool by saying I drink "coffee" La-di-da) kept the schizophrenia at bay; and by the time ten o'clock rolled around, I could at least see straight. My jittery disposition due to a combination of fried nerves and caffeine overload, however, was a different story.

I had waited until morning to explain to Sam that Jen was going to be coming over, hoping to spare him a night of worry. My protection was all for naught though because Sam could barely even remember who Jen was nor the significance of her making an appearance at our house later that morning. It was only when I reminded him that she is his good friend Annabelle's mom that he showed any indication of recognition. "Oh yeah, Annabelle! Hey, I haven't seen her in a long time."

I giggled because Sam and Annabelle had been so close, and when she changed schools and disappeared out of his life, he had been pretty distraught. It just shows you how resilient kids are—and what video games do to the brain. Instead of reliving the horror of that life season again for Sam, I just gently reminded him that Jen and I had endured a big fight, and that was the reason he didn't see Annabelle anymore.

"Oh yeah. Duh!" Sam conked his head with the palm of his hand. "I remember now. You and Ms. Jen got in that big fight over the Pricey guy." Yes, my dear readers, I had managed to keep my beloved son in the dark about a few things. In fact, the paparazzi and media harassment was explained away to Sam as being a response to a story I had written. The names Nick and Jen were rarely brought up past the initial damn-breaking. Oh, how my forgetful son made me long to go back to childhood.

Nevertheless, I gave Sam pretty strict instructions about occupying his time away from me and Jen while she was at our home. Okay, so maybe I bribed him with a new DS game. Don't judge me! Without hesitation, he agreed; and to his surprise, I manufactured a new DS game right then and there. "Wait, you mean you already got it? But h-h-how did you know I would obey? How *do* you know I'll obey?"

"Oh, sweet Sam, Mom knows *everything*. And I know you will obey because you are a good boy. And let's just say I somehow knew I would need it for an occasion such as this." That was basically true. I figured a bribing opportunity would come soon enough when I bought it, and if not, there was always a birthday party he would be going to or his own stocking I would need to fill at Christmas time. The stinkin' game was on sale at Wal-Mart, and I have an impulse-buying problem, okay? So once again, judge me.

Sam ran to his room to begin his game while I downed another half cup of "coffee." This time I made my own wannabe Starbucks mocha in my Keurig. Not the same at all, but if I add enough chocolate syrup, it is hard to tell that it is as nasty as it really is. The clock was ticking faster and faster as ten o'clock approached, in rhythm with my heartbeat. I wondered if Jen was experiencing the same kind of debilitating nervousness. Was *she* having incessant panic attacks that convinced her she was dying? Did *she* get a wink of sleep the previous night? Did *she* wish that she just had an IV bag hung on a rolling pole filled with coffee so that she didn't have to stop to make a cup? See, these are all very good questions to which the answers, had they been yes, no, yes, would have made me feel just a slight bit at ease.

When the doorbell rang at quarter after ten (being "fashionably late" was not setting a very good precedent considering the volatile circumstances, by the way) I counted to five in my head before proceeding to the door. The last thing I wanted to seem was too eager, especially considering the fact that Jen didn't even have enough courtesy to show up on time. Yes, I am a bit of a time Nazi.

I plastered on the fakest smile I could muster as I turned the door handle. You guys, I am not even lying that I didn't recognize the woman standing on my front porch. I squinted my eyes for a second as if to ask, "May I help you?" assuming the solicitor had the wrong house. But then when my eyes met the striking blue eyes of the woman staring back at me, I knew.

Haggard. That is the only way to describe Jen's physical appearance. Of course, her image on the cover of *OK!* magazine should have prepared me, but that was a while ago and she was wearing sunglasses. Quite frankly, I just assumed they had photoshopped it to make her look disheveled and distraught. Those crappy magazines do that all the time. They take the worst possible look a person has ever documented on film and then skew it even further to get the exact image they want to tell a particular story. You know how people say that an image is worth a thousand words? Well, in my limited experience with the media, I can confidently report that they take this concept to heart. They want the image to not only draw people in to want to read the article, but they hope the image itself tells its own story. So naturally, I assumed they were merely trying to tell a sick story about an aggrieved psychotic best friend who had just ruined her own life. And no, I'm not referring to myself. Ha. My magazine pictures were rough, don't get me wrong, but nowhere near as hideous as Jen's. And unfortunately, the story her photos told was spot-on.

As I was opening my mouth to say hello and invite her in, I realized my artificial smile had ceased faking it. I tried once again, certain my previous expression was one of horror, as I softly said, "Hi, Jen. Come in."

Jen merely nodded before stepping into my home. When she was tucked inside a few feet, I closed the door. Jen just stood still, her head leading her eyes all around the room.

I didn't know what to say or do. I mean, come on, she was the one who wanted to talk; and here I lingered, wondering what in the hell I was supposed to say. I strode past her into the kitchen. "Come on into the kitchen. Can I get you something to drink?" I was trying with a soldier's might to keep my voice steady.

"It looks the same" was all she spoke, unmoving. Something was very different. Very *off.* Her demeanor was as unrecognizable as her appearance. Had the events of the previous year taken an even harder toll on her? It seemed impossible, but if any random passerby who had lived under a rock the previous year were to stumble upon us both, I am certain they would think I was the one who emotionally *destroyed* Jen. Not the other way around as it stood.

Cautiously, I walked back to where she was still standing, gazing—no, not gazing—*gawking* at every piece of furniture, framed photograph, and adornment preserved in my cozy living room. I stood beside her, allowing my own eyes to land on each item as she did, wondering what on earth could possibly be going through her mind. Finally she exhaled slowly and audibly and then, smiling, looked at me and said, "Um, can I just have ice water?" She took the first step toward the kitchen. I followed, thankful we were actually moving toward something.

"Have a seat." I nodded toward the kitchen chair as I strolled to the cabinet to fetch two glasses. As I carefully filled each glass with ice and tap water, despite my shaking hands, Jen sat stoically looking down at her hands. I *really* did not want to have to be the one to commence the conversation, but my wish looked bleak.

As soon as the glasses were full, I set Jen's on the table in front of her and, stalling, asked her if she would like something to eat. Man alive, the woman looked like she hadn't eaten in days. My original musing about Jen's Kate Gosselin appearance was not very far from reality. Her blonde hair hadn't been highlighted in what appeared to be months, and it was cut rather short and unkempt. Her makeupless face was pale, and the dark rings encircling her eyes made it appear as if she had been punched in both eyes. Her clothes hung off of her; and had she been naked, she might be able to pass as a white Ethiopian or, at best, Kate Moss in her skinny days.

Jen just shook her head, and so I decided the inevitable was upon me and it was time to cease resisting. I sat down at the head of the table, took a sip of water, and turned to her. Her head was still bowed. So, I did what any good person would do, and I cleared my throat. Ha. I'm a jerk. I wasn't ready, dang it. I didn't want to start talking first. If you could hear the voice in my head right now as I narrate those last two lines, you would hear how big of a whiny baby I can be.

Luckily, the throat hack was enough for Jen to look up and take a sip of water. When she finally looked in my directions, I raised my eyebrows, as if saying, "Yes? What do you want?"

With lips pursed and a slow nod, Jen looked back down at the table and then opened her lips to speak. "Um" came the unsure childlike whisper. Clearing her own throat, she began again. "Um, so I'm sure you're wondering why I wanted to talk to you." It was a statement, not a question, but her inability to look back up and into my eyes made me feel a pang of sadness for her.

I decided to let her off the hook. "Yeah, um, a little." I nervously chuckled.

She managed to raise her eyes to meet mine, or at least my chin. Baby steps, folks. And then she said, "Well, first, um, I want to tell you how incredibly sorry I am." Tears filled her eyes. I waited. "Um, I know it doesn't matter and no words will ever be enough or right, but I have to say that first and foremost. I am very, very sorry, Allie. Very."

I just nodded, my mind screaming, *"Mercy and grace! Mercy and grace!"* I started to offer her my forgiveness when she held up the palm of her hand as my mouth opened to speak.

"No," she sternly ordered. "No, don't forgive me, Allie. Please don't. I don't deserve it, and that is actually not why I am here."

Huh. That one threw me for a loop.

Noting my confusion, she explained, "I mean, of course, I would *love* your forgiveness, but that is not the reason for me coming to talk to you. I'm here because…well, because I have to warn you."

Whiplash head. If a neighbor had been peeking in the window, they would think I was either (*a*) headbanging to

Metallica or (*b*) just ate a lemon *whole*! "I'm c-c-confused. Wha-what do you mean?"

Jen took another sip of her water before continuing, "Allie, I know you were with him. I know. And I need to warn you."

I had no clue what on earth she thought she had to warn me about. Was she threatening me? "Jen, I don't know what exactly you are talking about, but yes, yes I was with Nick and it was only because—"

Jen was vehemently shaking her head as she swallowed another drink of water, obviously pissed that her throat didn't ingurgitate more speedily. I used the opportunity to get another word in edgewise. "Well, actually, the reason is not important, but I can assure you there is nothing going on there, and quite frankly, I don't appreciate the threat. You warning me…" I shook my head in disbelief.

The swallow finalized, and Jen's mouth hung open, ready to pounce. "No," she urged. She was frantic. "No, Allie, that's not what I mean. I'm not talking about stupid Nicholas Price." So there was *that* jab. "I'm talking about Greg, Allie."

Huh. Interesting. *Okay, I'll bite.* "What about Greg, Jen?" Not letting her answer, I said, "There is *nothing*, I mean absolutely *nothing* going on there. Seriously we are just frie—" There was the damn headshaking again. Exasperated, I finally spat, "What?!"

Jen jerked and then recoiled back into the chair, her eyes wide before immediately dropping back to the table. I had startled her. *Weird.*

I squinted my eyes in scrutiny as I watched a single tear fall from her face and hit my table. The weight of the situation created a mental auditory splash upon the landing of the salty fluid. What in the hell was going on? Nothing made sense. "Um, I'm sorry, Jen. I, uh, I didn't mean to sound so mean or scare you or whatever just happened. I guess I'm just really confused right now. I mean, you have to understand how I'm feeling a little, ya know? You wanted to come talk to me and then you apologized profusely and I *do* forgive you, Jen. I really do. But then you start throwing out threats or warnings or whatever, and it just seems like…I don't know…someone who is sorry usually doesn't turn around and threaten the person they are apologizing to, you know?" And then I waited patiently.

Finally, Jen managed to wipe her bloodshot eyes with the back of her hand and look up at me. She softly said, "Maybe I shouldn't have come. You are obviously on edge around me, and I don't blame you. Listen, I don't want to get into the whole thing about Nicholas Price and all of that. I was a sick, sick woman. In my head. And I know I told you part of it about trying to have another baby with Greg, but there was more…a lot more…"

Jen continued to talk, but I tuned out for a second, remembering what Greg had told me about Jen's burning flame for my deceased husband and her jealousy toward me. I had kind of forgotten about all of that, or at least put it in the back of my mind. Hearing her bring up the stuff with Greg and trying to have a baby brought it to the forefront of my consciousness, and I began debating whether I should call her out on it or not. But as I looked across the table, at the jabbering homely skeleton sitting across from me, I couldn't bring myself to thrust one more blow upon her.

I tuned back in and heard "So that's why I had to come to you. I don't want the same thing to happen to you. By 'warn,' I didn't mean threat. I guess I meant 'inform' or even 'protect.' I wanted to protect you, Allie."

Oh, crap! What did I miss? What a fine time to tune out of a conversation, you dummy! I nodded like an idiot before proving myself to be. "Um, okay. So, Jen, can you say that again, just so I get it all?"

Jen's furrowed eyebrows spoke of her skepticism. "Uh, okay?" Oh man, that was *my* line to make people feel stupid. Inflection at the end and all. "So, I said"—she was clearly patronizing me with her slow, drawn-out words—"I just wanted to inform you, or I guess protect you."

Crap. Not that part, dummy! I heard *that*! I need the meat, sister. The *meat*! I shook my head, disgusted with Jen...okay, okay, disgusted with myself. "No, before that. Just like, start over. I mean, after the baby part."

Jen's cocked head and distrusting eyes made me feel even like more of an idiot, but all facades of being a calm, cool, collected individual flew out the window when I saw her standing on my front porch. No matter how frazzled and disheveled I behaved, Jen surpassed me—by a long shot. I widened my eyelids to signal I was waiting for a response and would not further explain why I was such an idiot.

Jen took a deep breath and dare I say a little smirk played at the corners of her lips? *Comfort*. She then began again. "Um, well, I said that I wanted to caution you against Greg." My skeptical eyes did not sway her resolve to continue. "I don't remember exactly the words I said, which is funny because I had it all rehearsed and ready to go. It's kind of like taking a test I guess. As soon as you are finished with the exam, you forget everything you studied. So let me try this again, but forgive me if I mince my words. He really is dangerous, Allie. I know it is hard to believe what I say at this point, since I have obviously betrayed you and your trust, but as I said before, and this part I remember, Greg is not who he seems to be. He used to be...I think, but then something switched in him and now he's...well, he's dangerous. Like I said, at first it was just verbal stuff. Calling me names, getting mad at *me* for not being able to get pregnant again. Things like that. And then after the Nicholas Price thing... well, then it turned *really* ugly."

Oh my gosh. What was she implying? Certainly not...no, no way could she be claiming what I think she was. I wouldn't have it. I just wouldn't let her sit here in *my* home, at *my* kitchen table, drink *my* water, and bash *my* friend. No way! I was so mad

I could scream. I stood from my chair and shouted, "Get out! *Now*! I cannot believe after all you have done to me and to Greg that you have the nerve to come into my home and try to feed me these crazy-ass lies. You know what, Jen? I *know*!" I started nodding vehemently. "I know all about you and your scheme, Jen. Oh yeah, Greg told me *everything*. I know you were insanely jealous of me. I know you had the hots for Chris the entire time we were married and even after. I know that you sabotaged your marriage because you couldn't wrangle your stupid feelings for a man who didn't belong to you. He never belonged to you, Jen! *I* am the *only* one Chris ever loved. Do you hear me? *Do you hear me, Jen?* He *never* loved you! But do you know who did? Huh? Do you know, Jen?"

Jen's eyes were wide with terror. Oh, I was getting to her good. *Real* good. How dare she? She sat silent, a statue unable to even nod, let alone muster a verbal concurrence that yes, she did indeed know who loved her. She didn't have to. She knew, and I knew that she knew. That was enough.

"Yeah, the same man who caught you getting hot and sweaty all over pictures of Nicholas Price. Uh-huh. The same man who loved you through your constant crazy, even when he caught you rummaging through old love letters and pictures of *my* husband! Did you hear that, Jen? *My* husband!" I drove my finger into my chest multiple times as I drove home my point yet again that Christopher Holly was mine and only mine.

Okay, so I know some of you are probably giving me a standing ovation right now. You have been waiting for this, right? Me spewing everything that I should've, could've, would've hurled at her had I been given the chance? Oh yeah, folks. I let it all out.

I continued. "You have never stopped scheming and plotting my demise, have you? You make me believe that you came here to make things right, to clear the freakin' air. And then when I allow you, grrrr [*yes, I literally growled at her*], into my life again, you pounce at the opportunity to ensnare me with your wicked claws, you…you skanky whore!" My head continued shaking for a good ten seconds while I caught my breath, and then I finished with "Oh, Jen, you bring out the nasty, ugly in me, and I'm sorry sweetheart, but there is only one nasty, putrid, disgustingly ugly skank sitting at this table. And it isn't me. Now get out. I have a date tonight with your ex."

Whoa, okay, so maybe I was a little harsh. And of course, later I would regret being so. But come on! And there she sat, unblinking, just staring at me as if she was…What? Was she *challenging* me? Oh, surely not. Oh, hell no, homegirl, you don't know when to throw in the towel, do you?

So, like any good Christian girl, I proceeded to fib, once again. "And you know that night you came to Greg's house?" Of course, I didn't wait for a response, "Yeah, that night, right after you left, Greg and I climbed into your old bed and we had the most naugh—"

Easy, Allie.

Wait. What? What was that? Who was that? My eyes darted around the room a little. I mean, I knew it wasn't really someone outside of myself talking to me. I began again. "Oh, Jen, it was so nast—"

She is my beloved daughter too.

Umm, okayyy? Unlike the supernatural quip I thought I heard in the hotel bathroom, *this* one I didn't doubt. Of course, that left me in a bit of a pickle. I could either continue with my preposterous erotic tale and sink even lower into the pit of total bitchiness, or I could heed the warning and try to figure out a way to abate my rubbish, with what little dignity I still retained. I decided on the latter and said, "Never mind. It doesn't matter. Look, I think you should just go, Jen. I'm tired. I'm saying things I will probably regret. I just…I don't know."

Jen finally looked back down at her hands and reflected, "No, it's fine. I get it. I mean, I deserve your distrust. I do. But, Allie, I swear"—she looked up at me with pleading eyes—"I promise you that I am being completely honest here. I would never have said anything if I hadn't seen you at his apartment, but I felt like I owed it to you to let you know. Allie, please belie—"

I held up *my* palm this time and said, "It's over, Jen. Okay? It's over. I'm sorry I don't believe you, but the more you rattle on with this story, I'm afraid I am going to blow up on you again. To slander someone's name…Ha, I guess it's something you've gotten good at, but I just can't have you doing it to Greg. Seriously, haven't you done enough damage to that poor man?" I really didn't want her to respond. I needed her to leave, but before I could retract my question, she opened her mouth.

"Yes, I guess I have." She wilted. "Thanks for the water, Allie, and for meeting with me. I'll see myself out."

Geez, Louise. Who *says* that? *I'll see myself out.* Did she think she was in a soap opera? Never mind. Don't answer that. Of *course* she did. Homegirl lived in a crazy-ass fantasy land. Oy vey! Despite her obvious martyrdom, I decided to let her do just that. *See yourself out, Jen. See if I care!* I simply nodded and said, "Yeah, I think that's best" and then proceeded to take both of our glasses to the kitchen sink.

When Jen was at the doorway between the kitchen and the living room, she said, her voice resonating, "He's lying, Allie. It's all a lie. Please be careful." And out she went.

Oh, the nerve of that girl. As if I was going to believe a word she said after the facts that I had known before Greg and I ever spoke, the e-mails to Nick and the fights she and Greg had over it, had been corroborated in his rendition of their past. And Greg…poor, sweet Greg had suffered so much at her hands, and yet it was never enough for Jen. She *still* had to show up at my house and "warn" me to stay away from him. When would she ever stop? When would her jealousy and contempt for me ever find closure? I'm sure it stung seeing me with the husband who had left her, especially since I ended up marrying the love of her life and dating her celebrity crush. I mean, yeah, I couldn't blame her for being a little upset. Heck, I would have felt the same way had the situation been reversed, but it wasn't really my fault. I mean, I didn't even know anything about Jen when I met Chris. And crap, I was the one who encouraged the relationship with her and Greg, even *after* I found out that she was the girl whose heart Chris had broken. And the Nick Price deal? Well, okay, that one was kind of on me, but for the love of God! She was *married!* Can I really be blamed for pursuing a man on whom we both had major unrealistic crushes?

My coffee high had seeped out of my sweaty pores, and I was suddenly very fatigued. I needed to make lunch for Sam as the sweet boy hadn't even come out to ask for a snack the whole time Jen was at our home. I, on the other hand, had absolutely no appetite. The overload of coffee plus the lack of sleep and disgust with Jen made me feel completely nauseous. Knowing sleep would be difficult with the hamster in my brain running on his Jen Manis wheel, I decided to give my mom a call and fill her in.

We chitchatted about the mundane while I made Sam lunch, and by the time I had left the kitchen to begin my dissertation on the twilight zone meeting with Jen, I couldn't stop yawning.

"Sweetheart, maybe you should call me later. You are exhausted," Mom advised.

"Oh, Mom, I know, but there is no way I can fall asleep right now with all that is going through my brain." I sounded like a whiny child.

"Baby girl, don't you have any of the Xanax I gave you? Crap, you better! I sent you with enough to get you through the weekend in California."

Oh, Mother, you incredible genius! The Xanax! I had completely forgotten, and of course, I didn't take any in LA. Unlike my sweet momma, who was used to having these little pills on hand, even though she rarely took them, I was completely unaccustomed to having *anything* at my fingertips that could solve my problems—or at least make them seem not as significant.

Oh, no siree! I had to search high and low for a solution to any of my calamities, and when I *always* came up empty-handed, a phone call to my mother with the misfortunate news of my impending demise at the hands of heart failure, a brain tumor, or a stroke always ensued. Darn. If I just would have had the sense to get my hands on a prescription for those "happy" pills, maybe all of my woes would vanish. Ha. Wishful thinking, *but* taking one to actually clear my mind for a much-needed nap was a *magnificent* idea!

"Thanks, Mom, you genius you! Why didn't I think of that? And no, I totally even forgot I had them in LA."

"Well, good. Call me when you wake up, and you can give me the deets about your visit with Jen then, okay?" I loved it when my mom pretended to be hip with her lingo. "And I have a feeling after some good sleep you'll be able to view this whole situation in a refreshed way. You know, sleep is the number one ingredient to superb mental health."

"I know, I know. We have this conversation all the time. Look, when I call you back I'll be bright-eyed and bushy-tailed and not at all concerned about the crazy-ass accusations Jen made against Greg and how I literally stopped just short of physically mutilating her in my kitchen. Verbally, however, well that's a different story. Okay, good night, Mom!"

"Oh, you little rat! How dare you do that to me?"

"Oh, don't worry. Xanax can fix *everything*!" I chuckled at my brutality.

"Very funny, Allie. Seriously though, I'm a bit concerned that you verbally attacked her. That's not like you at all. Why would you do that to Jen?"

Too exhausted to even produce an audible laugh, I just let the amusement escape from nasal exhalation whispers. "Oh, Mom"—I unhinged my snakelike jaw for the biggest yawn and rudely continued speaking through it—"I'll let you later, okay?" My bed was calling my name.

"Yeah, okay. Well, please make sure you call me back *tonight*, got it? I don't want to have my own trouble sleeping tonight worrying about this whole thing."

Compassionate woman, huh? I assured her I would and hung up the phone. Within seven minutes, I had told Sam the plan, turned the TV on in my room for him to watch while I napped, taken a Xanax, slid under my delicious covers, laid my head on a heavenly cloud, and fallen fast asleep. Hell, I didn't even make it long enough for the stupid Xanax to kick in. What a waste.

22

A two-hour nap does a body good, and I woke up feeling refreshed indeed. The Xanax may not have been the catalyst for my drift into somnolence, but I tell ya, that stuff keeps the dreams under wraps. Nothing says amazing slumber like a total lack of dream recall. Luckily, Sam was right where I left him, snuggled up next to me in my bed. Oh, how I loved lazy afternoons like this! Unfortunately, the glorious nap only pushed the pause button on my life. I had so hoped the reset button would have been pressed instead. But ultimately, the images of the morning came oozing back into my consciousness. Boo, hiss.

It was a quarter 'til three in the afternoon, and I had to take Sam to his friend Garrett's house at four. I was thankful that he had apparently forgotten that Jen had come, or maybe he never even realized she had. We packed him up, and I hadn't even put the car in "park" when Garrett came rushing out of his house afflicted with elation. Goodness, I love the energy of little boys! Failing to bid me adieu, let alone sneak in a kiss, Sam hit the pavement running.

I got out of the car, retrieved the duffel bag he had forgotten to grab in his spastic haste, and walked up the sidewalk to Garrett's front porch.

Sam turned. "Mom, why are you out of the car?" Oh, the nerve of that little rascal.

So in my sarcastic nature, I turned around with his overnight bag still dangling over my shoulder and said, "Okay, bye, Sam. Bye, G [a pet name reserved for those adults close to Garrett]" as I walked back toward the car.

It wasn't until Garrett piped up, "Sam, your mom has your bag, dude!" that Sam realized what an imprudent mistake he had made.

"Moommm, wait." *Busted.*

I turned. "Yes, sweetheart?"

Sam's face tinged the slightest pink. His head hung, and he pointed at the bag. "My bag."

"Oh, this?" I whacked my forehead with my palm. "Silly me. I almost *forgot* to give it to you! Isn't that *silly*, G? I mean, *forgetting* his bag? That would have been *very* irresponsible of me, wouldn't it?"

Garrett chuckled nervously, conflicted on with whom his allegiance should lie. Sam, however, was used to my shenanigans and rolled his eyes as he approached me, his palm up as if expecting a handout without so much as a "please" or a "thank you."

"Yes, Sam? Can I help you?"

He grumbled, "Mom, just give me the bag."

"Whoa," I gnarred. "Have you forgotten your manners, Samuel Christopher?" Ooh, I knew that would tick him off. He got so embarrassed when I rebuked him using his full name in front of his friends. Luckily, Garrett and Sam had been friends since the first week of kindergarten, so Sam's allergy to my low-toned reprimands stayed at bay when G was around. G's mom, Katie, and I had become pretty close, and we often mutually "used" each other for babysitting and play dates. Our parenting styles were similarly lax and roguish, and I truly feel that those two traits are what helped shape our boys into the witty, good-natured confident boys they had become. Neither Garret nor

Sam ever took themselves too seriously and were able to laugh at their mistakes. I treasured that in Sam and was beyond grateful that he had found his counterpart in childhood and ultimately that I had found my parenting counterpart in Katie. She felt the same way about Sam that I felt about Garrett, even being one of the few people to feel comfortable calling Sam "Sammy" as I did. Jen used to be able to call him Sammy as well. Nostalgia set in.

"Puhlease, Mom? Can I *please* have my bag?"

And then I crossed over the line into total jerk-zone. "Of course, my dear sweet Sammy. All I need is a big ole smooch, and I'll be on my way."

Sam rolled his eyes, a character trait learned from yours truly, and grabbed my hand, planting the quickest peck on my palm before hastily ripping his bag off my shoulder and hustling back to his friend.

Wanting to have the last word, of course, I hollered back, "Aww, Sammy, I had totally forgotten about the kissing hand! Do you want me to give you *yours* too?" Oh, I was so pleased with myself and was in midrevolution to head back to my car when out of the corner of my eye, I spied Sam bounding down the porch steps toward me.

At first, I thought he was going to give me the riot act upon approach. But instead, he had his palm lifted, and he looked up at me with those incredible green eyes—Christopher Holly's green eyes. When I realized what was happening, my heart melted into a puddle; and I gently grabbed my son's hand, pulled it up to my face, and placed a tiny kiss in the center of his palm. Sam closed his palm around the invisible kiss and placed his fist above his heart. "Got it, Mom. Love you." And with that, he was gone. And boy, oh boy, so was I!

I waited until I was in the driver's seat and I could tell the front door was securely closed when I let loose the deepest wail. Mine were tears of joy, regret, pride, and longing all mixed into a pool of salty emotion. I loved that kid more than words could express, and the fact that he still loved me enough to swallow his pride and indulge me with a sign of affection made me more proud than if he was the starting pitcher on a winning World Series team. That kiss also brought back the past seven and a half years of my life and all I had done wrong—and right—and imported memories of Sam's precious babyhood, toddlerhood, and early adolescence. When he was three years old and in preschool, his teacher, Ms. Joy, read the students *and* the parents a book entitled *The Kissing Hand*, written by Audrey Penn. In this adorable book, Chester Raccoon is starting school and is afraid, not wanting his mother to leave him. She lets him in on the secret of the kissing hand, in which she kisses the palm of his hand and assures him that any time he feels alone at school, he can press his hand to his cheek and he will feel his mother's love. In turn, Chester does the same for his mother because—let's face it, kids starting school is usually harder on the parent than the child. It is such a precious story, and Ms. Joy had the kids in her class as well as us parents make a tracing of our hand, cut it out, and place a heart sticker in the palm. Then we kissed it and the kids kept theirs in their backpacks and we took ours home with us. Sam doesn't know this, but his tiny, outgrown paper kissing hand found its home in my bedside table drawer where I still, to this day, pull it out on occasion when I am missing him. It happened to travel all the way with me to LA, in fact. Boy, had my kid grown!

I cried like a baby all the way home and contemplated calling Katie to make sure she knew Sam was there. I mean, how could she not? But usually when I dropped off Sam for a playdate, I took the time to at least say hello to the parents before I flitted off. Thank goodness Katie wouldn't care either way because I was in no shape to have any sort of coherent discussion on the phone. Which reminded me—Greg would be at my house in less than an hour. *Crap!*

As I drove the rest of the way home, I had to remind myself that I had nothing to prove with Greg. Just because we had kissed a little didn't change the fact that at one point in my life, I was perfectly comfortable with him seeing me with no makeup on or my hair undone because he was just a friend. In fact, he was just Chris's friend, so I really couldn't have cared less what he thought of my appearance. And if a friend was all I wanted him to be, then there was no reason to go home, wash the tear streaks off my face, and primp. Okay, well maybe I would wash the streaks off, but I certainly was not going to primp. This was to be a casual *friendly* evening of pizza and a movie.

I had yet to decide if I would bring up my visit with Jen to Greg. Had her visit been one of olive branch extension and nothing more, I would definitely have brought it up. But considering the content of her message, I felt uncomfortable at the thought of tainting our perfectly "normal" friendly night of idle conversation and pizza with absurd calumny. I mean, what a downer. Maybe it was selfish, but my disdain for Jen had grown exponentially that morning (while I never thought such a prospect possible), and the idea of stirring up Greg's own hatred of her left a sick feeling in my gut. That was definitely *not* my opinion of a good time, no matter how good it would feel in the moment to have someone with whom to commiserate in my perceived victimization.

I'm sure the last thing Greg would want to hear about was how his psychotic ex-wife was defiling his name and accusing him of not only verbal abuse but apparently physical abuse as well. I never let her get so much out of her mouth, however, because what kind of friend would I be to Greg if I let someone slander his name? He was a great guy, a well-respected physician and, quite honestly, the only person from Chris's past who I actually cared to be around. Chris's mom was surely not a person I enjoyed nor trusted to have my best interest at heart. And John, Chris's dad? Well, they were kind of a package deal, so naturally avoiding Judy meant avoiding John, although that broke my heart a little as I had always really enjoyed John.

Don't get me wrong; I made darn certain that Sam was in their lives and that they were invited to every special occasion concerning him. But that particular May, when my birthday rolled around after the big blowup, was the first time since I had met Chris that my parents did not invite anyone from Chris's family to my birthday celebration. My mom was just not okay with the words I had heard Judy speak about me and how Chris should have ended up with Jen and so Mama Bear Sharon couldn't bring herself to include Judy in any celebration concerning me. I didn't blame her. I didn't want Judy there either.

Greg was different though. Chris actually *chose* Greg. He found something in him that he admired and cherished, and the two were stupendous friends who I never once saw fight or even argue. I mean, sure, they would banter back and forth about their favorite sports teams or which actress was the hottest, but they just kind of rolled with each other. They were obviously meant to be friends, and I was so thankful that Chris had such a great male supporter during his illness. Let's face it, me and his mom were nuts during that time. We were emotional wrecks! I remember Greg would just come up and be all calm and collected. They would banter and talk basketball and act like everything was exactly as it should be. No, Greg was not disposable to me. Jen on the other hand? I'm pretty sure Chris couldn't have cared less if I booted his ex-girlfriend out the door. Had she remained a loyal friend to me and come to me with the accounts she tried to imply that day, maybe it would be a different story. But the truth was that a crazy, mean, jealous friend who sabotaged my life did *not* trump the kind, gentle soul in whom my amazing husband had trusted and adored. I suddenly felt shame for ever even indulging in mean conversations about Greg when Jen and I *were* friends. How quickly I had turned my back on him when he was so unbending with the whole Nicholas Price thing. I thought he was too controlling, but the truth was that he was right! His wife shouldn't have been gallivanting around pining after a child celebrity. Chris would have behaved in the exact same manner. I'm sure of it.

The truth of the matter is that I played a part in fueling Jen's fire when she was upset with Greg, and it made me feel insanely guilty. Selfishly, I allowed Jen's disengagement from Greg to soothe my own case of loneliness. I don't remember ever consciously giving her advice that was only self-serving on my part, but I certainly didn't do enough to encourage her to patch up her marriage if it meant more time away from me. I can't even believe I am admitting this, but it was kind of nice for me when Greg and Jen had a falling out that lasted a few days. That meant I would have a companion with whom to talk on the phone and hang out. I can't believe I did that to Greg, especially knowing what I now know about Jen.

Well, that night I decided I would make it up to him, even if he didn't realize I carried guilt for this dastardly offense against him and his marriage. Greg and I were going to have a great night despite—or maybe *because* of—Jen. And I certainly wasn't going to say anything that could potentially hurt him or set him reeling with anger against Jen. It was settled: no talk of stupid Just Jen!

Greg was right on time with a Pizza Shoppe Butcher Block pizza in hand. I *had* managed to at least wash my face, brush my hair, and pull it up into a bun, so I wasn't a complete disaster when Greg arrived. I rented *Life of Pi*, which neither Greg nor I had seen. I had thought about a chick flick, my preference, but I decided to spare Greg the horror. I was so incredibly thankful when Greg walked in wearing cargo shorts and a T-shirt since I was just in my jammie pants and a T-shirt myself. I was equally thankful when I saw a case of Miller Lite swinging from his hand. Oh, this was going to be a great night!

We ate our pizza and each had two beers out on the patio as we made small talk. Greg had some of the funniest stories as well as painfully sad ones as a pediatric oncologist. My time spent at the hospital with Chris during his quick cancer diagnosis and ultimate demise had provided me with enough medical knowledge to hold my own when discussing certain procedures and scenarios with Greg. He seemed pleased that he could talk shop with someone outside of the office who had some sort of clue as to what he was referring.

There was a light breeze, and the conversation flowed right along with it. In no mood to stop talking to watch the movie, I suggested we have a few more beers on the patio before retreating inside. It was only six o'clock, and we had at least another two hours of daylight to enjoy. Greg was game and mentioned that he had almost suggested the same thing.

We cleaned up the pizza mess and brought out another round of brewskies. Oh, how nice it was to just enjoy someone's company without any stress or a child around who always seemed to need something. It was so comfortable, in fact, that I thought about bringing up the whole Jen thing several times. I mean, he was telling me about recent events in *his* life; shouldn't I do the same? I still wasn't sure I wanted to go there.

Instead, I decided to try a more sly approach. I asked, "So what's new on the parenting front?"

"Heh, oh you know, just toting Annabelle around everywhere. I swear that kid has more friends than I have collectively had in my whole life!"

I laughed, endeared by fatherly pride. "I hear ya. Sam has been asked to spend the night with like seven different boys already this summer. It's crazy! I need a full-time secretary just to keep up with his social schedule."

"Totally!"

"You know, we should have Sam and Annabelle get together again. They used to be so close, and I brought her up to him the other day when Jen was—" *Craptastic, you dummy!* I cleared my throat and took a pull of my beer to buy a few seconds. How the heck was I going to get out of this one?

Greg's chin jerked to the side, and his eyes squinted as he questioned, "Jen was what?" He sounded skeptical or annoyed.

"Oh nothing, just when Jen was on my mind." *Allie Hollie, you are a genius!* I looked down at my beer, still able to see him at the top of my periphery and hoping his face relaxed, indicating he bought my fib. He did. Phew. "Anyway, so he didn't remember Annabelle much until I helped him jog his memory. Man, Greg, they used to be so close." I looked up at him. ·

Greg shifted a little in his seat. "Yeah, well, Jen sure as hell went ahead and screwed all that up, didn't she? Why were you thinking about her by the way?"

So remember my "sly approach" plan? Yeah, not so sly. My big fat mouth pushed me off the high dive right into the stupid pool. I sure hoped I wouldn't drown. "I know it got screwed up, but that doesn't mean our kids have to suffer, does it? Especially because you and I are friends." I silently prayed he wouldn't second-guess my effort to keep the conversation *away* from Jen at that point, despite his efforts to take it right to her.

"Well, I don't know," Greg began. "I mean, maybe it is for the best that they don't see each other anymore, what with all the nasty history there."

Huh. That wasn't cool. "Really? I mean, yeah there is some weird history, but it hasn't been with Sam and Annabelle. Those two got along great! And Sam is really none the wiser about the whole thing. I tried really hard to protect him from the worst of it. Didn't you protect Annabelle?" It came out wrong, obviously. I was insinuating he didn't protect Annabelle; I just felt a little defensive of the fact that he didn't want his daughter to interact with my son.

Greg raised his brows and smirked. "Um, what the heck is that supposed to mean, Allie? Of *course* I protected my daughter. Why would you even suggest such a—"

I interrupted, not wanting to be misunderstood further. "No, no, no! That's not what I meant. That didn't come out right. I was simply saying that we both protected our kids from the really bad stuff, right, so why can't they play together again?"

Greg took a moment to recompose himself before regaining his relaxed composure and continuing. "Well, yeah, of course I protected her. But Jen didn't, and so Anna knows stuff about all of it. Plus, let's face it. Those two kids would end up having the hots for each other, and then we would have to monitor their interactions." He laughed a little too loudly and a little too forcefully for it to be authentic. *Curious.*

Not willing to leave well enough alone, I teased (with a chip on my shoulder by the way), "Oh, come on. Are you for real with this, Greg? Seriously you don't think they shouldn't get together because they might end up *liking* each other? Are you really that kind of crazy dad who has your shotgun ready for the first boy who steals a kiss?" Okay, it was a little biting, but puhlease! I wasn't buying his crap any more than I bought Jen's garbage about him being abusive!

"Let's talk about something else, Allie, okay?" Greg lifted his nearly full beer to his lips, tipped it toward the twilight sky, and downed it in two swallows. *Yikes.* Very controlled, he set it gently on the glass tabletop and released a drawn out "Ahhh," as if his body was thanking his mouth for the refreshment. Or maybe his mind was thanking his mouth for the buzz.

Either way, I decided it was best to shut my piehole and take another swig of my own beer. Trying to ease back into comfort mode, I looked around the backyard and up at the sky. "Isn't it a beautiful night?"

When I didn't get a response right away, I looked back down at Greg. I could see a vein pulsating in his neck. His jaw was clenched, and his eyes were burning holes into mine. Then a split-second later, his eyes relaxed and he smiled broadly. "Yes, it is so beautiful. I love nights like tonight." He began to look around as well.

A few more minutes and one more beer later and the ease with which we began the night was existent once again. I still wondered in the back of my mind why he wouldn't like for Annabelle to play with Sam and worried that he might think Sam was a bad influence, or maybe even me. But as the gold liquid pierced my blood with its hypnotic effect, the worries just seemed to fade into the background. I was feeling warm and fuzzy and refused to allow any insecurities I had about me, my son, Greg, or Jen get in the way of a much-needed night of relaxation.

23

When Greg and I arose to begin our movie a little after eight, the sun had lowered into dusk and my buzz presented itself with every step I took. Wobbling as I walked up the steps to the back door, Greg grabbed my upper arm to steady me. "You okay there, Miss Tipsy?"

"Ha! I don't know," I gurgled. "Crap, I'm a little more buzzed than I had thought."

Greg laughed and called behind, "Lightweight" as I entered the kitchen to throw away my bottle. I stood at the trash, contemplating having another beer to begin our movie. Apparently, Greg didn't need to mull it over as he headed right to the fridge and grabbed two more.

"Ya ready?" he asked.

"Oh, I was just thinking about that. Not sure if I should maybe drink a glass of water in between or not."

"No, not the beer. You are *definitely* ready for another beer. I meant the movie."

"Oh." I felt silly. "Yeah, um, let me grab a bottle of water at least."

Greg chuckled condescendingly. "You really *are* a lightweight. The Allie I knew could tie one on with the best of 'em back in the day."

"Ha," I bluffed. "Well *that* Allie is a mother now who never gets enough sleep nor who drinks half as much as she used to."

Our conversation carried over into the living room. "Oh my gosh, do you remember when we went to Westport that one weekend back before the ho came into the picture?"

"What ho?" I asked, trying to remember if I ever saw someone who could be described as a ho in Westport. Don't get me wrong, Westport is chock-full of scantily clad women, but I never saw an actual prostitute or anyone who could be mistaken for one. Or had I?

"Oh, Allie, come on darlin'. Stay with me now," Greg chided. "Are you really too drunk to identify the only ho in either of our lives?'

I still wasn't catching on, and his patronizing made me definitely want to *catch on*!

"Are you freaking kidding me, Allie? Um, Jen? Ring a bell?"

My eyes widened in comprehension. "Oh," I drawled. "I get it." But that was it. That was all I had to say. I mean Jen was a lot of things, but *ho* was not a word I would ever have used to denominate her.

Apparently, Greg wasn't happy with my unwillingness to indulge in berating his ex as he just rolled his eyes, exhaling perceptibly. I was okay with that. Tipsy or not, I refused to sit around all night bashing someone who wasn't there to defend herself, no matter how good it may have felt, especially given our recent interaction earlier that morning. I had more reason than anyone to yammer about Jen and all she had done to me, and believe you me, I had embraced every opportunity when the whole thing was first going down. But that was with family and this was…well, this was with her ex-husband who she used to love and who used to love her. This was with the man who had kissed me and whom I had kissed back. I felt as if it were morally wrong for me to get into a big gossip session about Jen with Greg when it felt so dangerously close to a man and his mistress talking smack about his unsuspecting wife. Of course, the situation was immensely incomparable, but it still felt the same to me.

Luckily, Greg acquiesced and moved on with the conversation. Phew, another bullet dodged. "Anyway, it was pre-Jen and we were in Westport at—Oh, what's the name of that Irish bar?" He snapped his fingers, trying to retrieve the name of the bar.

"Kelly's?" I asked.

"Yes, that's it! Kelly's. And remember we were so drunk. Man, how many did we have that night? Like twenty each?"

I vaguely remembered the night to which Greg was referring, but I knew if it was Kelly's we weren't just drinking regular mugs of beer. We had pewter tankards that held at least twenty ounces of beer. "I don't know, but they were those tankards, remember?"

"Yes!" Greg sounded so excited that I remembered that much. "And remember how we went out around the side to their pizza place that's right there? Remember it? What's it called? It's owned by Kelly's."

I knew what it was called but he just kept interrupting *himself* that I had to wait a couple of beats before I responded. When he finally inhaled, I blurted out, "Joe's!"

I guess my outburst startled Greg a little, but I was getting impatient. Apparently, he took notice because his alcohol-induced manic-like state settled down a bit when he said, "Yeah, Joe's. That's it."

I felt kind of bad for obviously embarrassing him, so I added with positive enthusiasm, as if I was having as much of a blast as he had been traveling down intoxicated memory lane, "Remember how the owner told us to try honey on our pizza and it was like the best thing ever?"

My matching enthusiasm sparked Greg up again a little, and he smiled. "Yeah, that's actually what I was going to say about the whole night. Remember you got so drunk—or *we* got so drunk and then had that pizza. Chris and I just put one little drop of honey on ours, but you…oh not little Miss I'll-Try-Anything Allie. Oh no, you doused the thing in honey and then you…you…" Greg started giggling so hard that he couldn't finish his thought.

I, of course, knew exactly where his thought led, and it was something I hadn't recollected in quite some time. "Yeah, yeah, yeah. I puked. I remember." I feigned boredom at the memory.

Greg couldn't stop laughing, which made me begin chuckling myself. I had forgotten what a contagious laugh he had. His face turned beet red, and his body convulsed. He had such a great smile and perfect teeth. It made me wonder, for a split second, why I had decided to call things quits with him romantically.

He regained a little composure. "Oh, Allie, you poor thing. I just remember you sitting on the curb with your head between your knees and that nasty slice of pizza was next to you half on the paper plate and half on the disgusting concrete."

I completely had forgotten that visual. It was disgusting for sure.

"And then"—Greg wiped his glistening joyous eyes—"Chris couldn't take it. He started gagging himself, and so I had to help you up and take you to the bathroom. Remember that?"

Another piece I had forgotten. One of the very few times Chris actually let me down a little. I nodded somberly, a smile still dancing on my lips so as to not reveal my miniscule sense of disappointment.

"You know what's crazy?" he asked, not waiting for a response. "When I was holding your hair as you puked in that nasty toilet that night, I remember thinking to myself, 'Man, Chris is a really lucky guy.'"

I cracked up at his sarcasm. "Yeah, I bet. Man alive!"

Greg's face relaxed, serious. "No, Allie, I'm dead serious."

I reached across the couch and hit his arm lightly. "You are a dork!"

But his face didn't change, and his smile was gone. "Allie, listen to me. I am dead serious."

I was taken aback, not so much by the fact that he thought Chris was a lucky guy while he stood there holding my puke-soaked hair but rather by the fact that he was dead set on me understanding how sincere he was being about the whole thing. It was strange. I knew better than to argue a third time, so I just said, "Huh" and turned my head toward my beer bottle, taking a final swig.

"What does 'huh' mean?" I could sense that he was still looking at me with that austere expression.

In no mood to get into an uncomfortable thoughtful conversation, I feigned yet another smile and in my most bubbly voice said, "I don't know. Hey, are you ready to start the movie?" I started to move off the couch.

"No, wait." Greg's voice was uneasy, almost panicky.

I sat back down and looked at him, masking my apprehension for the impending conversation. "What's up?" I chipped, like a schoolgirl.

Greg gave me a "You're an idiot" look and then asked, "What's *up*? Really? That's all you got?"

I tried to appear innocently confused, but based on his next comment, I'd be wise to assume I failed miserably.

"Um, okay, so why are you so uncomfortable talking about this?"

Oh, for the love! Really? We have to go there, Greg? I know now that my stupid, fake dimwit shtick was failing miserably, but I still held out a little hope then as I pierced (literally, like a shrill little girl, pierced), "What? What do you mean?" I seriously should have been twirling my hair around a finger and playing with my gum. That's how ridiculous I sounded.

Greg tilted his head, scrutinizing me. I'm sure he was thinking, *Who the f—— is this chick, and why am I sitting on her couch?* But luckily, he didn't say that. Instead, he just shook his head and quipped, "Let's just watch the movie, Allie!" Ouch.

Crossroads. Right then and there. I was at a crossroads. You all know exactly what I am talking about because it is the same crossroads that we women have brought a poor unsuspecting man to many, many times. It is the "Do I look fat in this?" crossroads. Or the "Do you think she is prettier than me?" crossroads. You know, the one in which you are asking him to choose who is prettier between you and your celebrity doppelganger? I mean, how on earth is he supposed to choose? If he says you are, which is ideally what you secretly hope he will say, then you want to know why exactly. So then when he says something like, "I don't know, her mouth is weird and she looks old," *bum, bum, bum.* Homeboy is in for an ass-whoopin' because let us not forget that *everyone* tells you that you look *exactly* like her! Oh, for the love of God. They can't win for trying.

Of course, this exact crossroads to which Greg so courteously brought me is the one of which we women are masters. It goes something like this: Your husband has been invited to a basketball game with two of his buddies on your coveted weekly date night. He calls (or probably texts because he is afraid of you) and mentions that he has been invited, not even asking if he can go or not, but more just providing information to feel you out. You, of course, already get your panties in a bunch and respond, "Well, do you want to go?" *Ding. Ding.* Crossroads number 1: check.

Your spouse either knows his goose has been cooked and chooses the correct path of "Heck no! It's date night!" or he stands clueless at the crossroads and truthfully answers, "Well, yeah, kind of," to which you respond, "Fine. Go." And then cease communication. *Ding. Ding.* Crossroads number 2: check.

He's damned if he goes. He's damned if he doesn't (albeit less damned if he doesn't—for any men who may be reading this).

If he goes, there will be hell to pay before, during, and after the event. If he doesn't, he misses out on fun with friends and there will still be hell to pay before, during, and after the event whilst he is with his *wife*! Oh yes, we women know how to make a man pay for a decision he never even made if he even remotely eludes to the fact that he would have liked to have made a different decision. *Ding. Ding.* Crossroads number 3: check.

And this is the crossroads at which I stood with Greg. I had already been busted for not wanting to talk about anything serious with him and acting like a seventh-grade donkey, and he had already responded in kind with his passive-aggressive pretend movie-watching desire. Now all that was left was me standing at the crossroads deciding if I would match him smug for smug or if I would kowtow to him and appease his wish to exhume every untold thought or feeling either of us had ever carried. To spare myself, and what was supposed to be my relaxing night, any discomfort, I chose the latter road and softly said, "Okay, so I just can't believe that you would have seriously thought that as you were watching me puke."

"I said let's just watch the movie." The vein throbbed in his neck once again.

I cleared my throat trying not to get strike two and said, "Why weren't you disgusted by me puking?"

The bulging vein slowed in rhythm, and he finally turned to me, exhaling as if he were at a crossroads himself. Should he let me off the hook that easy or continue to make me pay? For what, I really didn't know. Finally, he cracked the tiniest of smiles and spoke, "Allie, I'm a doctor, remember?"

I released the carbon dioxide that had been silently stored in my lungs with my held breath. I even managed to let out a little snicker. "Oh yeah, duh!"

"Plus, you were so sick and fragile. Do you remember I had to kick those two chicks out of the bathroom and lock us in so that you could have some privacy?"

Honestly, I didn't remember, and I wondered, why, if he was so gallant in his taking care of me, would he would sit there and boast about it. I mean chivalry and humility are both attractive qualities, but one without the other isn't as much so. Regardless, sticking to my decision to accommodate his need for this asinine conversation, I merely nodded in recollection.

"That night you were so much fun. I mean, that was the first time you *really* let loose in front of me and you were going to town dancing at that one club and then making friends everywhere we went. You toasted like, what, fifty times?"

I laughed at the memory I actually *did* recall. I really did used to be fun, darn it!

"Oh my gosh, *you* were the reason why we had so much fun that night. You just kept pushing us and pushing us until we were both out of our shells and cutting loose. It felt so good, especially after the stress and pressure of grad school for me. I really, *really* needed that night, Allie. And I got it—because of *you*." Greg extended his finger and poked my shoulder.

I have to admit, that little soliloquy served its intended purpose of tugging at my heartstrings. I really was a fun-loving person back in the day. I remember Chris and I once took a spiritual gifts assessment at our church, and although I scored highly in teaching, I was off the chart in hospitality. Oh, how I used to *love* to entertain and welcome people into my home, my circle, my *life*! Back then I didn't know a stranger, you guys. I had enough self-confidence to approach anyone and strike up a conversation. Chris used to just sit back and laugh, letting me do my thing. Never actually questioning how he felt about it, I took his teasing in stride and did not waiver from my ability to make anyone and everyone feel comfortable in my presence.

And apparently it didn't go unrecognized, because here was Greg telling me he noticed and appreciated that gift in me. It was strange thinking back to that woman. Where had she gone? These days I just kept mainly to myself and avoided eye contact with people out in public. Certainly I had good reason. I mean, who on earth could I trust after the Nicholas Price fiasco and the fishbowl world I lived in following? For all I knew, the woman in the produce aisle at the grocery store was a reporter for the *National Enquirer*. That man getting his hair cut at Great Clips next to Sam? He could be some sexual predator who was stalking me after seeing me in a magazine. One could never be too careful, sure, but did that really mean I had to be as antisocial, as I had become?

The long-forgotten memories of that night at Kelly's came flooding back. I *did* remember dancing at a bar called Westport Beach Club. We had huge fishbowls of margaritas. I also remembered going to the country bar, The Beaumont, and leading an entire group of people in a line dance that I had made up! I devised a plan to make up the most ridiculous moves I could think of and get total strangers to follow along. Chris and Greg had both thought it impossible and bet me that no one would follow along. Of course, their suggested wagers were a couple dollars. I upped the ante and insisted that the loser(s) had to ride the mechanical bull at the other end of the large wood-floor room. Of course, Chris, the practical man he was, tried to resist, but Greg called him a not-so-nice word that insinuates wimp and assured him that there was no *way* they would lose the bet. Chris finally obliged, and off I went onto the dance floor. It took half of an Alan Jackson song before twenty or so people, men and women alike, were lined up around me, mimicking my every move. After the song was over, I was approached by several of them, wanting to know the name of the dance. I answered, "The bull ride!"

Chris and Greg were absolutely dying when I made my way back to the table. I bowed a self-congratulatory curtsy and then waved my arm to present the bull at the other end of the room. "After you," I said, motioning the way. Chris tried to refuse, but a few more nasty names out of Greg's mouth was enough to give him the nudge. As it turned out, it looked like so much fun that I had to try it myself and stayed on longer than the two of them. Of course, I didn't let that go unmentioned every ten to twenty minutes for the duration of the night.

It was so strange to think back to those days. I truly didn't recognize the carefree woman I had once been. I *had* been the life of the party at one point, and honestly, I had those two men to thank: Chris *and* Greg. They made me feel safe, secure, and completely confident. They let me be me, no matter how annoying or overly daring I became. They were the types of guys who were confident enough in themselves to not feel threatened or intimidated by an inordinately confident woman, even if her self-assurance was but a ruse. Chris was so laid-back that he never even got jealous when another man would hit on me or dance with me. Greg, on the other hand, was a little more protective. I could remember more than once being in an uncomfortable situation with a handsy guy, and Greg had stepped up to tell him to back off. I knew Chris would have his back if one of the jerks had tried to start something, but luckily, it never came to that. For months, the three of us would go out, and I felt so incredibly safe and confident. That confidence propelled me to jump out of my shell and try new things. And I had an audience of two who thought I was pretty darn humorous and charming. Looking back, I realized that oftentimes, *I* was their entertainment for the night. *I* was the center of their worlds. Wait…

My mind started reeling back, chugging like an old VHS tape on rewind. Was I really the center of *both* of their worlds? I mean, Chris's certainly. I was *his* after all, but I didn't belong to Greg. Sometimes though, it felt like I belonged to both of them. I mean, Greg *was* the one who would stick up for me when other guys got too close, and he *was* the one who held back my hair as I puked. Could I have missed something all of these years? Did Greg have feelings for me way back then, and did he think of me as his as well as Chris's? I shook my head at the thought.

"Yoo-hoo? Allie? Where did you go?" Greg was waving his arms in front of my face. "What were you just thinking about?" He scooted closer to me on the couch, closing the middle-cushion gap between us.

I awoke from my reverie. "Um, I, uh, I don't know. Nothing really."

"Oh, puhlease. You can't pull that crap on me."

I contemplated just blurting out what I had been thinking, but I hadn't exactly organized my thoughts or my feelings thereof, so I didn't know exactly how to word it. But I tried. "That was so long ago, wasn't it? I mean it is so weird to think back about how crazy and carefree we were, ya know?"

"Heh. You're telling *me*. Although I'm not sure that I was quite as carefree as you, given the weight of my schooling. That was such a strain on me, and sometimes I wish I could have been more relaxed and actually *enjoyed* my twenties."

"Oh man, you seemed to enjoy that night! Remember the bull riding?"

"Oh my gosh, I had completely forgotten about that. Yes! Oh, and you made up that horrific dance that all those people starting following along with. Remember that?"

"Of course, I remember it. That's the reason why you guys had to ride the stupid bull!"

Greg burst out laughing. "That's *right*! Geez, you bet us that people would follow you, and Chris and I were like 'No way, man.' And then, off you go and lo and behold, those crazy people *followed* your stupid dance!"

I was giggling right along with him, despite my unease at my seconds-before realization. "Oh, that was so much fun, and then you and Chris couldn't even hang on as long as I did on the bull. Remember that part, Greg?" I poked his rib cage, and he flinched like a scared cat. We both continued cackling.

"Yeah, but I stayed on longer than Chris, remember that?"

I didn't. And I really didn't see why it mattered, but whatever. I didn't acknowledge his subtle dig at my deceased husband and instead reminded him, "And I beat *both* of you. Ha!"

This time Greg poked me in the ribcage, and I matched his scared-cat flinch. He cracked up even harder. "Oh, ticklish are we?" And then he proceeded to poke me several more times until I jumped off the couch.

"Sto-op," I whined.

"Fine, I'll stop. Come here"—he patted the couch cushion—"and sit back down. I promise I won't do it again."

I returned to my seat. Greg pretended for a second that he was going to poke me again, to which I flinched big time, and we both started our hysterics all over again.

"Geez, you untrustworthy man, you," I teased.

We both sat unspeaking as we continued to chuckle until I recovered. "Oh, those were the days, weren't they?"

"Yeah, BJ," Greg replied.

"Uh, excuse me?" That was not a very appropriate response.

"Oh, you dirty-minded little thing. You know, BJ? Before Jen?"

I caught on. "Aha, I see." It was a dumb acronym, in both cases.

"Yeah, as much as I was stressed and uptight back then with school and everything, it didn't even *begin* to compare to the burden of my marriage." He laughed again.

"Uh-huh," I nodded, disagreeably.

Greg was silent for a few seconds before questioning nonchalantly, "So, have you heard from her?"

Crap! Crap! Crap! "From who?" I feigned obliviousness.

"Really? From who?"

"What?" I faked, the high-pitched preteen returning.

"Uh, from Jen maybe?" His annoyance had returned.

Without even thinking through the potential repercussions of lying, I matched his nonchalance. "No, huh-uh," I said and looked down at the floor.

"Really?" He looked skeptical.

"Nope, really."

"Huh. That surprises me."

I didn't want to bite; I really didn't. But I knew that if I said nothing, he would be suspicious and think I was lying. So I feigned boredom, and I said the words he obviously expected me to say: "Why's that?"

He took a second to appear contemplative and then responded, "I don't know. I guess, you know, since she came to my house that night and all…I just assumed maybe she would try and contact you and I don't know…maybe talk smack about me or something."

Curious. Tempted to dig further but surrendering to my gut feeling, I just commented, "Nope. Not a word." Oh, how I wanted to see what he thought she might say to me. Was he used to Jen spreading horrible rumors about him? Had she let *him* have it after that night? Is *she* the reason why Annabelle can't be around Sam anymore? Oh, the nerve of that woman! Her jealousy had hit a brand new low if she was using her daughter against me now. I mean, how much lower could she possibly go? I shuddered at the thought.

"What are you thinking?" Greg interrupted my train of thought.

I seriously hated that question, and even more so coming from a man. We women are supposed to be the ones who are constantly concerned with what someone else is thinking. Men are supposed to be clueless and uncaring about that sort of crap. In fact, nothing would tick me off more than would I would ask Chris that very question and he would respond with "nothing." One time I called him an outright liar because there was no way a person could *not* be thinking something. He laughed at me and told me that I gave the male species way too much credit. He was probably right.

"I'm thinking…" I allowed my voice to tinge enthusiasm as I stood up, turned to him, and said, "Do you want to watch the movie?"

Greg scrutinized me for a few seconds before returning with "Oh, I don't know. It's been kind of fun taking a trip down memory lane. What do you say we have another drink and just chat? It's been so long since I've just been able to *talk* to someone, ya know?"

I did know. I knew very well. "Okay, that sounds good. I'll grab them. Do you want something else to eat? Are you hungry?"

"Nah, the pizza was enough for me."

I went and grabbed two more beers and chugged half of my water bottle on my way to and fro. I was hoping the conversation would steer itself away from Jen as the more I felt the need to avoid and lie, the worse I felt. I really had no reason to lie to Greg, but for some reason, I couldn't help omitting facts or skirting around the truth that evening with him. And then, of course, I flat out lied. I couldn't put my finger on why I did but speculated that it had something to do with the fact that we had been a little romantically involved and some guilt had seeped in and taken up residency in my mind. Plus, if I wanted things to return to "friendville," I needed to keep all conversations about his relationship with Jen off the table. One thing I had learned the hard way is that comforting someone of the opposite sex in their time of relationship woe usually led to confused, misplaced romantic feelings. I just didn't think I wanted to go there again. But alas, the alcohol in my blood some four beers later had different plans.

24

Greg and I talked about everything, from our children to our childhoods and everything in between. The longer we talked, the more intoxicated I became and the less I could remember the next day. I do remember at one point I was on the living room floor, proving to him that I *could* indeed still do the splits. Okay, so hindsight would tell me that I was completely set up on that one, but after the nostalgic conversation of crazy-Allie past, I was all about showing "I still got it." Now don't tell anyone, but the next morning I had no idea why my inner thighs were so sore and had I not been intoxicated when I slid down into those flippin' splits, I am 100 percent positive I would not have gotten back up. But when you are drunk, you get those "beer muscles," or at least that's what *I* call them. One time in early college I challenged a former marine to a wrestling match. What a dumb, dumb, dumb girl I was—am.

Shortly after the splits pageantry, I was back on the couch, and somehow we got back into our little poke/tickle match. This time I wasn't as reluctant and didn't hoist myself off the couch to get away. I was tipsy. I was lonely. I was kidless. I was tipsy. Did I mention that I was tipsy? So yeah, I probably let things get carried a little too far considering the fact that I was adamant our night be completely platonic. And the fact that I made darn sure that every topic of conversation steered clear of anything Jen-related or Greg/Allie-relationship-related would lead one to believe that there was no way *this* woman would let things get out of control! She was adamant, darn it! Yeah, well, here's the thing about Allison Belle Graham Hollie and resolve...

So yeah, we poked and prodded and tickled and teased and then *out of nowhere* (yeah, right), I ended up lying on my back and looking up at Greg, who had his hand held like a claw ready to attack my ribs. His other hand had my wrists secured together above my head. Man alive was the man strong. I had no idea. I was flopping around like a water-deprived catfish and squealing like a stuck pig.

It was complete torture as he was using the power he had over me to dangle his claw above me, lingering, as I was helpless to do nothing but anticipate. He was saying something like, "Should I do it *now*?" and he would force his hand toward my stomach and then jerk it back up. My eyes would clap shut every time as both of us laughed even harder. I tried everything: begging, pleading, demanding, fake crying. You name it, I tried it, because let us not forget what happens if I am tickled for too long. Luckily, I hadn't broken the proverbial "seal" at that point so I hadn't been rushing to the bathroom every ten minutes. Still, the thought *did* cross my mind. In fact, if my memory serves me, I just might have even threatened that I was going to pee my pants at one point. It didn't faze him.

Finally, when I believe Greg could sense I had taken about all I could handle, he forced his clawed hand down again. Yet this time, before his fingertips touched my ribs, he swooped his hand up and cupped my chin. Then, without even a second for me to comprehend what was happening, he pulled his face down to meet mine, which he had tilted up. His warm, moist lips pressed into mine, and once, twice, three times, they lightly pecked mine. I had yet to reciprocate any lip movement. Then on the fourth time, Greg used his tongue to flick my lips apart, and together, the two of us engaged in a very deep amorous kiss that lasted a good three or four minutes. Somewhere around minute 2 or so, a recognizable voice penetrated my thick skull and whispered the word "easy." It wasn't spoken like an adjective used to describe me (albeit deserved); it was more like an admonition or warning. I immediately shook away the thought and continued sucking face for the duration of the three or four minutes.

I was the first one who came up for air, although it was more like sinking down because I had to literally force my head back into the couch cushion and turn my face toward the open air of the living room before Greg stopped. He swiped the loose stands of hair off my forehead with his fingertips on one hand as he finally released his grip on my wrists from the other one. Once again, he cupped my chin; but this time it was to pull it back to the center so that I had no choice but to look into his eyes, a mere two or three inches away from mine.

When he spoke, I inhaled a whiff of his beer breath. "Allie," he whispered. "I have been waiting for this for a long time."

A little confused and feeling a bit exposed, I lightheartedly said, "It hasn't been *that* long Greg. What, not even a week?"

"Oh, you silly girl," he moaned. He brushed at my forehead again although I could tell there were no loose strands remaining so it was kind of senseless really, almost like he was trying to be all sensual like a scene in a movie. "That's not what I'm talking about, Allie, and I think you know it."

Did I? I mean, I was a little skeptical earlier in the evening when it hit me in some weird sense that long ago, in our bar-hopping days, he may have felt that I was equally *his* as much as I was Chris's. As I had recollected accounts of the past when we were discussing my Kelly's puking ordeal, it *did* occur to me that back then I very well might have been the center of Greg's world. But as the night wore on and the gold liquid burned *in*, I had completely abandoned the notion altogether. Once again, however, I needed to make a choice as to how to proceed. Man, this was getting old. Did I engage in yet another conversation in which I may find out something I really did not want to know, or did I just call it a night and see him to the door? There wasn't an option to avoid by simply changing the subject as I had just played tongue hockey with the man for four minutes and his face was close enough to smell barley and hops. Most assuredly, avoidance wasn't an option.

I tried to wiggle myself free a bit as sudden claustrophobia seized my chest; but the weight of Greg's body, now completely on top of mine, made it impossible. Finally, I took a deep breath and said in a strained voice, "No, actually"—I wiggled again—"I don't know what you're talking about."

"Oh, Allie"—and then that stupid hair swipe that was actually just a forehead swipe—"you have always been so naïve, haven't you?"

Okay, so that one pissed me off a little. Um, *excuse me*, dude? I decided to not just let this one go and said, "That's not very nice, Greg."

"I'm sorry. You're right. That was terrible. I guess what I meant to say was that you have always been so trusting and accepting of people."

"Well, what does me being so trusting and accepting of people have to do with what you are talking about?" Ha! I trapped him. No, he actually really did mean to say naïve. How was he going to weasel his way out of this one? For his sake, hopefully better than I had managed to weasel my way out from underneath him. I took some deep breaths to calm my anxious heart.

"Well, I mean, um…"

"Uh-huh, that's what I thought!" I managed to tease despite my discomfort. "You just meant what?"

Greg smiled and responded, "What I meant was that you always think the best of people. You always think they're on the up-and-up, that they're innocent."

"Uh-huh? Still waiting." I tapped my fingers on the couch cushion. I was half-tempted to hum the jeopardy theme song.

"Waiting for what? I just told you."

"Waiting to figure out how people being on the up and up and all innocent relates to whatever it is you are talking about. I mean, *who* hasn't been on the up-and-up?"

Greg sighed deeply and leaned his forehead against mine. "Oh, woman, why must you be so difficult?"

I laughed and then grabbed his cheeks in my hands, forcing his head back up so he could see my impatient, waiting eyes.

"Okay, so *me*, Allie! It's *me*!"

Confused, I asked, "*You*? What do you mean it's *you*? What's *you*?"

"I mean *I* wasn't on the up-and-up."

"You weren't?" I looked stunned, I'm sure, because I was.

"No, I mean, well, uh, I guess you wouldn't say not on the up-and-up per se. Because I was. But…arggh. You're killin' me smalls. Never mind. I totally meant 'naïve.' I did. I totally did!"

We both cracked up.

"Deserved" was all I said.

"But I don't know if that is actually the right word. 'Clueless' may be a better fit, but I thought you might hit me if I said that."

I did hit him. And then I kissed him. Oh, what was I doing? It was just that this bantering and teasing and the alcohol and… and…and…Okay, okay, I admit it. It felt darn good!

Until it didn't.

We continued to kiss and tickle and occasionally brush imaginary strands of hair off my forehead. The earlier conversation was just dropped, for which I was relieved. After several minutes of what some would consider foreplay (for me it was before, during, and after play because I had no intention of going further, no matter how intoxicated I felt), Greg came up for air and declared, "I've got to go to the bathroom. Don't move."

I nodded and watched him stand up and head to the bathroom. Whew. I was finally able to breathe again after being pinned under him for so long. Then I got an idea that made me giddy. I rolled off the couch and had to steady my light head as I stood. As I heard the bathroom door latch, I hurried to the kitchen to turn off the lights and then went back into the living room to turn off the television we had yet to watch and the table lamp. Then I hustled into my bedroom doorway, which was adjacent to the bathroom door, and I waited. Once again, the mind whisperer said, "Easy." And once again, I ignored it. Man alive, was I schizophrenic? I made a mental note to Google schizophrenia symptoms in the morning. For tonight though, I had bigger fish to fry—or scare the crap out of.

I swear the man had been hoarding liquid in his bladder for days because I could hear the stream continuously draining into the toilet water for at least a minute and a half, I kid you not. The longer it lasted, the more nervous I became that I would crack under the anticipation and start laughing, thus foiling my plan to scare the crap out of him when he opened the door and turned off the light.

Finally, the flush came, and my stomach knotted like it used to do when I would play hide-and-seek with my neighborhood friends. I was ready to pounce, and then I heard the sink. Of course, the stinkin' doctor had to wash his hands. Ugh. Finally, the sink was shut off and I heard the handle jiggle and the light switch depressed. As the door creaked open, I sprang like a leopard and shouted, "Raaaa!" at the top of my lungs.

Unable to see the features of his face but rather the dark silhouette of his body as it sprang up into the air and tumbled backwards, I beamed with pride. *I still got it.* The noise Greg made when he jumped was hysterically akin to a little girl, and the whole scene impelled me to squeal with delight. Through my amusement, I flicked on the bathroom light and managed to blurt out, "*That's* what you get for calling me naïve!"

Greg growled with mirth and came at me fast. I tried to turn and run, but he was far too fast and strong; and within seconds, he had managed to scoop me up like a cradled baby and stomp into my bedroom, tossing me onto the bed.

"Oh, girl, you're gonna get it," he teased. "I was going easy on you before, but oh no. Not now. All bets are off!" And then he pounced on the bed, straddling me and tickling me incessantly until I was sure I was going to pass out from hyperventilation, but luckily he stopped just short.

We were both panting hard, and Greg flipped onto his back to catch his breath. We lay in silence, save for our rapid respirations, until finally he turned toward me, propping himself up on his bent elbow, his head resting in his palm. I remained on my back but turned my face toward his and smiled.

"That was fun," I said, still a little breathless.

"It was," he agreed. "I'm so glad you invited me over tonight, Allie. I didn't know how things were gonna be, but I've gotta say, I have been pleasantly surprised."

Ugh. It was never my intention for him to be pleasantly surprised. In fact, I wanted the evening to be free from any sort of surprises whatsoever. But alas, I allowed things to take a turn once I'd had a little too much to drink and the lines had completely blurred. I was no longer sure of *what* exactly I wanted. It felt so good to be flirtatious and affectionate at the time, but I was wary of how I would feel in the morning, or even a few hours later, as I had stopped drinking quite some time before.

I turned my face back toward the ceiling and closed my eyes, taking in a deep supply of oxygen. I was starting to feel sleepy. I wondered what time it was and was about to ask when Greg whispered, "What are you thinking?"

For the love of God. I slowly inhaled through my nose and breathed out. "I'm thinking I'm getting a little sleepy."

Silence ensued. I was really hoping Greg wouldn't take offense to my statement, but I was too relaxed to open my eyes and check. For a few moments, I could only hear the sound of my breath slowing into a tranquil cadence and could only feel the weight of where Greg's body was positioned on the bed. I truly thought I might fall asleep and was too somnolent to care that Greg may very well fall asleep right next to me. But I was fairly certain that he hadn't moved and was still hoisted up on his arm; not a very good position for slumber, but who am I to judge?

I continued to steady my breathing and began to fade into disconnected thoughts that indicated the cerebral cortex of my brain was saying "Night, night" to the world. Just as I was in the middle of that glass Grand Canyon Skywalk, ready to parachute to the floor of the massive chasm, I felt something graze across my neck. I lightly regained consciousness enough to bring my hand up to my neck and scratch away the feeling. But soon it returned, and with it a sound I couldn't quite place. In my barely conscious state, I visualized some sort of insect sucking my blood. That jolted me completely awake, and I swatted at my neck, this time stopping short when I made contact with Greg's face.

"Oh my gosh!" I exclaimed. "I thought there was a bug on me or something. You scared me."

His bright, glazed eyes were burning holes into my groggy peepers as he whispered, "I'm not sleepy at all. I'm hungry." And then he proceeded to ram his lips into mine and replicate the same sound I had heard the insect making at my neck. This kiss was different than all the ones before. It was, as he had just admitted, hungry. His tongue took no time at all to force itself into my mouth, and within seconds, he was moaning in pleasure.

I, however, was still half asleep and not feeling so well. The short bit of dozing I had managed to attain was enough to metamorphose my dwindling buzz into the onset of nausea. Greg's mouth, dry and still tasting of beer, did nothing to settle my woozy stomach. Even though I was barely reciprocating his kiss, let alone the passion by which it was driven, Greg seemed either oblivious to or unfazed by it as he continued lashing his wanting tongue inside my mouth and then along my neck.

Conceding to the fact that I was going to have to actually voice my disinclination to make out with him, I pulled my head away from him. As I was about ready to delicately decline his efforts, Greg huffed, "Oh, Allie, I've been waiting for this for way too long!" He kissed and then licked my neck, his breathing rushed and shallow. "You have no idea how long I have imagined this with you." He continued kissing and licking and biting. *Ouch.*

I sobered up very quickly at his reference to the illusive "this" to which he was referring. I pushed against his chest with my one free hand that wasn't pinned beneath his warm body. "Wait, Greg. Wait." I barely got the words out before his mouth engulfed mine yet again. I tried to speak, but the words were muddled, much like trying to speak underwater. And he certainly had no intention of freeing my mouth to protest anytime soon.

I managed, however, to wriggle myself backward toward the edge of the bed to free my other arm before he hastily closed the gap once again. At least I could use both palms to push against his chest to allow myself some time to plead my case. "Wait, Greg. Wait. You know, I really *am* tired, and I don't know. This is all just a little fast and—"

Greg pressed his index finger against my lips and hushed me. "Let me finish, Allie. I've wanted to say this for a long time. I need you to know something, okay? Don't answer. Just nod your head."

Boy, he was sure being demanding for a man who was in *my* house and in *my* bed. My rebellious side took notice and refused to nod.

Apparently, Greg didn't need my permission to continue as he picked up right where he left off, failing to remove his finger from my lips. "Allie, I have been in love with you from the moment I met you. Remember that?" Once again, a question he had no intention of me answering. My wide eyes spoke volumes, however, because he responded in kind, "Yeah, that's right. You heard me right—*the moment I met you.*"

25

I swallowed audibly.

"When Chris ran to you in the bar that day in college and he carried you outside? Remember that?"

Expecting that my response didn't matter one way or the other, I just remained still.

Apparently, it did, however, because he continued. "Allie, if you remember, nod your head." There was something in his tone that told me I had better respond this time, so I conceded in a nod. "Good girl," he praised.

What the hell was going on?

"Well, I would have been the one to rescue you from that prick who was harassing you, but Chris got to you first. And I said 'dibs' as he was carrying you out of the bar. Apparently, Chris didn't quite *get* man code and claimed you for himself later that night at the hospital. Oh, I was so pissed at him, Allie. You have no idea. But in the end, look what happened, right?" He chuckled.

I lay motionless, my previously foggy brain beginning to comprehend the weight of his words.

"Don't you see how this all played out perfectly? Now you and I can *finally* be together. I've waited a very, very long time for this, Allie, and I'm here now, making up for lost time." Greg removed his finger from my lips and quickly moved his face toward mine. Looking into my eyes, he hesitated for a split second before licking his lips and proceeding to lick mine as well. "Mmm, you taste so good," he whispered, his hot breath against my chin.

Something was *very* wrong. I felt it in my gut before I acknowledged it in my mind.

He continued to lick, kiss, and suck on my neck while I steeled the distraction to lament over how to proceed. He would lick, kiss, suck, and then break to interject his thoughts. "I'm not…saying that…what happened…to Chris was…a good thing…but…it sure…worked out…in my favor…ya know?" I mean…some may call it luck…or to Bible beaters, a blessing…but I believe it's…" And then he stopped altogether and looked deep into my eyes before whispering, "Fate."

The vomit plunged up my esophagus and reached my soft palate before I managed to choke it back down in an aggressive swallow. My eyes stung with outraged, venomous tears. I needed to get off the bed. I needed to escape. The density of Greg's confession threatened to either bury me alive or consume me whole. I turned away from him toward the edge of the bed. There wasn't much room between the bed and the wall, but just enough for me to squeeze through and bid Greg farewell—for once and for all.

My feet never reached the floor. As soon as I turned on my opposing side, Greg reached his arm around my waist and pulled me toward him, so that my entire body was in alignment with his. "Where ya going, Allie?" Greg's voice was foreign to me.

I scrambled for an appropriate response, not exactly sure why I was feeling so afraid. I mean, I knew this man very well, didn't I? "I'm just not feeling good actually. I think I might puke." My voice shook.

"Oh, Allie," he soothed, "why are you shivering?" He pulled me into his body further and began stroking my back. My head rested on top of his so that we were cheek to cheek, the corner of his lips touching my ear. "Shhh, Allie. You're okay. You're not going to puke, sweetie. I'm gonna take good care of you, okay? You're just drunk, that's all."

I shook my head and tried to pull it back, but he used his back-rubbing hand to grab the back of my skull and pull it back to the same spot. "No, Greg, seriously," I whined. Why was I whining? I needed to be yelling at him, didn't I? This was wrong. This felt very wrong, but he wasn't behaving like he was doing something wrong, so it threw me off.

"Allie, listen to me," he whispered more gruffly into my ear, my head securely immobile thanks to his firm grip, "I told you that you were fine, okay? I'm going to take care of you. That's all I have ever wanted to do. It's all gonna be fine now. We are together finally. Chris is out of our lives permanently and Jen, ha, well, Jen took awhile for me to get rid of, but I think she finally gets the hint to stay away from me. God I tell you, I counted down the *minutes* until I could leave her after Chris died. If it weren't for Belle, her ass would have been dumped at his funeral."

Breathe, Allie. Breathe.

"And then of course I had to give you time to grieve. Blah blah blah. And of course you dummies *had* to go and get all horny for some punk kid in Hollywood. That took a toll on my plans. But then…oh, but then dear Jen played into my hand beautifully with that whole thing. I mean, who are we kidding, she was always a few cards shy of a full deck, if you get what I'm saying, but damn, she really *did* freak out hard-core over that crap with you and that loser. That bitch was crazy from the get-go."

Breathe, sweet girl. Breathe.

"And now…oh, Allie." I felt his tongue flicking around and inside of my ear. The sound was deafeningly soggy. "Now that you took care of business in California, now we can be together finally." He sucked and kissed my lobe and then…

"*Ouch!*" I screamed at the top of my lungs. He had bit my earlobe—hard. The pain jerked my head back, but Greg used it against me to flip the rest of my body onto my back. He straddled me, pinning my wrists just above my belly button.

"Wanna have some fun?" he questioned, his eyes alive with expectation, his mouth stretched into a cunning grin.

"Greg, listen." I found my voice as I began to try and wiggle free. "That really hurt me, and honestly, I'm a little concerned right now about what's happening. I'm not ready for all of this, Greg. Seriously. Please get off of me, Greg, and maybe we can talk about this tomorrow when we both aren't intoxicated." I was bluffing, of course, as I never wanted to look at the monster again, but it sounded like a very reasonable request to my ears and I don't know why I was so surprised when he failed to obey my wishes. He chuckled a very raw, almost throaty sound that I had never before heard come out of his mouth. I wiggled some more, thinking that if he was laughing then at least he was in good humor, no matter how bizarre the laugh sounded to me. Certainly a good-humored man would know when it was time to let someone get up from underneath them, even if the very words he had spoken to that person were enough to make them beat the crap out of him when they were freed.

When he didn't budge but merely continued to glower at me with squinted eyes and a smile that defied the rabidity in those eyes, I grunted, "Can you please get *up*, Greg? I feel like I'm suffocating." I twisted again in naïve anticipation of his obedience to my plea but was left unaltered.

"Tell ya what, Allie, I'll get up as soon as you get me up."

It took me a second to realize the vile insinuation behind his words, and when I squinted at him to double-check that I had indeed understood his suggestion, he raised his eyebrows and licked his nasty upper lip yet again.

I wanted to believe there was a chance, albeit a meager one, that Greg was just messing with me and that at any second he was going to swing his body off of me and tell me the whole thing was a joke. Of course, I would kick him out and never speak to him again regardless, but at least that scenario didn't leave me harmed or violated in any physical way. My desperation to have hope was so deep that I opened my mouth to suggest that he was just kidding with this whole thing. Before a word could escape my lips though, Greg *did* move one of his legs. But instead of swinging it off of me, he swiftly forced his knee in between my thighs to separate them and then jammed it hard into my crotch.

The pain coursed from my pubic bone up through my torso and rang into my ears. My back impulsively bowed as I cried out from the pit of my stomach. I had only felt that exact pain one other time in my life and that was when I was an adolescent and had kicked my brother Adam in the nuts. He retaliated with the same action against me, and I swore at that time that I would never be able to have children because of it.

My moan was low and loud, and through my tears, I asked, "What in the hell are you doing, Greg? What are you doing? This isn't you!"

"Oh, Allie, don't be so dense. You know you want it. You've wanted it for a long time and have just been teasing me. Well, I'm done with that, and now I'm going to take what's mine."

Still writhing in pain, I tried to reason with him through my tears. "Why, Greg? Why? If you really loved me like you say you do, why would you want to do something that I wasn't ready for?"

"Shut up!" he spat. "Just shut up, Allie!"

I tried to calm my voice as it was obvious my tears were irritating him. "But what have I done to you, Greg, to make you want to hurt me?"

"Shut up, you dumb lying whore! You act all innocent, but you're a *liar*!"

"What? I'm not a liar, Greg. What have I lied about?" I was trying so hard to buy myself some time, to say the right thing so that Greg would not do what I was so desperately afraid he was going to do to me. Unfortunately, it backfired.

"Are you kidding me? You wanna know what you lied about?" He repositioned my wrists above my head and then pressed his knee into my crotch yet again, this time moving slowly from side to side. His face was positioned about a foot directly above mine. "Where should we start?" he whispered seductively as he ground his knee against my pubic area over and over again. "First, how about the lies about your feelings for me? Huh? I know you feel something fierce for me, Allie, and yet, you want to continuously tease me, leading me on and then shooting me on. Why is that little girl? Huh? Why?"

I began to reason with him. "I didn't lie, I just—"

"Shut the hell up!" He positioned my wrists so that he only needed one hand to keep them clamped and squeezed my cheeks together with the other hand.

A distinct memory of my sister Lisa doing the same to me when I was a kid came flashing through my mind. Oh, how I longed for my family in that moment. My mind and emotions had been wavering all evening long about what I should think or say and how I should feel and act in response to Greg. The emotions had ranged from confusion and concern at one end of the spectrum to amusement and pleasure at the other end. Never, in the six-plus hours that we had been together that night, had I felt *fear*. In those minutes on the bed, however, all I felt was excruciating, debilitating terror. And reminders of my family turned the horror of the situation into the most forlorn homesickness.

Greg squeezed my cheeks harder as he barked in my face, "And what about lying to me about Jen, huh?"

It took me a second to figure out to what he was referring, and I didn't dare try and respond again.

"Uh-huh, that's right. I know you talked to her, Allie, because I can see all of her phone records. Why'd you lie to me about that, huh? Were you trying to play me? You think I'm stupid, *Allison*? Huh, do you?"

My eyes were wide with trepidation. Everything Jen had said came rushing back to me. She hadn't been lying at all. Greg was a monster, and I should have heeded her warning.

"Answer me!" he screamed and then released my cheeks to slap me as hard as he could.

I released the most bloodcurdling scream and started to fight back. With only one of his hands pinning my wrists and his body recoiling from the blow to my face, I was able to free one of my hands. Of course, once I got it free, I had no idea what to do with it so I just started pounding anything with which I could make contact. I hit his chest, chin, and finally his nose before he swiftly repinned my wrist with its mate above my head.

Then he lowered his face and hissed in my ear, "You like to play dirty, huh, Allie? You like it rough, don't you?"

I violently shook my head and screamed, "No, I don't. Get off me! Get off me right now, you son of a bit—"

The second blow was harder than the first, and it was executed with a fist rather than an open palm. I had never been punched in the face before. In the arm, sure; I had a big brother after all. But never the face. I guess maybe it wasn't exactly a punch as much as a closed-fist slap, but my cheek bone and jaw couldn't tell ya the difference. I immediately started howling a deep, guttural groan that was full of pain and regret.

"Now," Greg growled when my howling had dwindled to a whimper, "what *was* it exactly that little Miss Jen wanted to talk to you about, Allie? Huh? And this time, I expect you to answer."

My body had begun to reflexively respond to the stress and trauma of the situation by uncontrollably quivering, almost to the point of convulsion. The side of my face had started to swell, and I could taste the blood pooling in my mouth where the teeth carved into my cheek. The odds were definitely against me to be able to form a coherent thought, let alone articulation, but I knew I had to say something, or at least acknowledge him. As I carefully separated my lips to try and speak, a small voice inside my mind whispered once again, "You are my daughter."

Those four words brought me enough peace to steady my trembling voice and form the words, "She wanted to warn me, but I didn't believe her."

Greg glowered down at me, his expression unreadable. Was he mad? Confused? At that point, my left eye had all but swollen shut so there was really no use in trying to scrutinize the appearance of Greg's emotions. Honestly, at that point, I was in just enough shock to surrender entirely and allow whatever was going to be done, to be done. What was one more whack in the face or knee to the groin? What was one more bite of the ear or God-forsaken brush of invisible strands of hair off my forehead? By the following day, I would either be dead or alive, raped either way, and no amount of fear or bargaining or fighting was going to change the outcome.

Greg's hardened facial features softened subtly as he again depended on a one-handed grasp of my wrists while he encircled my face with his fingertips. "I told you she was crazy, didn't I? Heh, wanted to warn you. Of what? What a sleaze!"

Um, yeah okay. Of what, Greg? What could she possibly have to warn me of? Maybe the fact that you are a psychotic, abusive a-hole? Could that be it? Of course, I didn't say any of that, but I really didn't think I had to nor would it be in my best interest.

"You see, Allie?" he continued as he continued petting my forehead, cheeks, and lips like I was a freaking dog! "Jen has always been jealous of you. Of *course* she would try and "warn" you to stay away from me. She knows you already have my heart and I have yours. Tell me exactly what she said."

I couldn't speak. I didn't know what I could or couldn't say without being hit again.

"Oh, sweetie." He leaned down and pecked my lips over and over and over again. It was like listening to nasty people kissing on a soap opera. He was trying to be *so* dramatic and seductive. I wanted to vomit all over his face. "It's okay, baby girl, you can tell me what she said. She can't hurt you anymore. I won't allow it."

Was he for real? I knew I had to play this right if I wanted to somehow make this nightmare end, although I couldn't foresee a possible culmination anytime soon. I considered going along with the insanity and pretend as though I wanted to be with him as much as he did with me; I'd give into him sexually to just get the inevitable over with. At least then I wouldn't have to imagine the worst-case scenario when I rejected him yet again. I mean, I could take a few more blows to the face, but what if it got worse? What if he seriously injured me to the point that I ended up paralyzed or, the unthinkable, dead?

The thought of it made my eyes sting with tears once again as my time as a mother to Sam flashed before my eyes. My sweet, precious boy would never again feel the love in my embrace or hear the laughter of my voice at one of his squirrelly jokes. No amount of physical pain Greg could inflict upon me could compare to the absolute gut-wrenching emotional pain induced by thoughts of never seeing my angel baby again.

"Oh, sweetie, no reason to cry. Don't let Jen intimidate you, Allie. I told you, she can't hurt you anymore. I'm here and I'm not going anywhere, okay?"

Greg's derangement made the whole scene seem so unreal that my body responded in kind and released a bewildered sob so vehemently foreign to me that it was obvious I was in shock and was breaking down. My convulsions were only partly the result of extreme sorrow. They had transformed into a response of pure hysterical amusement. The situation was so incredibly unbelievable that, call it survival or what you will, my mind was somehow entertained. Of course, the howling noise coming forth from my vocal chords was obscure enough that Greg couldn't tell that I was actually laughing at him and his ridiculous charade. Who knows, maybe I should have let on that I was amused by him. Maybe he would have been appreciative of my levity and gotten the whole thing over with faster.

But somewhere in the back of my mind, I knew that I couldn't surrender to this beast and grant him permission to violate me, no matter how much easier and safer that would seem. More than the need to survive was a compelling compulsion to fight for what was authentic and honorable, no matter the cost. You read all the time about women who are assaulted or abducted. Those who make it out alive often tell stories about how they fought like hell, not knowing if their life was going to be spared or taken, but concluding that if they were going to go down, they were going down fighting! Friends, I was going to go down fighting. Sam needed a mom who, despite evidence to the contrary the previous year, stood up for what was right, just, and virtuous, even at the cost of her own life.

My resolve was reinforced right after my lunacy abated, and Greg soothed, "Oh, baby, that's okay. If it's too painful to talk about, you can tell me in the morning. For now, let's just quit talking with our voices and start talking with our bodies, okay? And I need to hear you say okay, and then maybe I can let go of your hands so you can touch my body."

With a split second of self-doubt and foreboding, my chin rose to initiate a nod of affirmation. It was in that nanosecond that the gentle voice I had come to revere more than any other person or thing in the world breathed, *My precious daughter, do not be afraid. Your suffering is a blessing, and I will restore you. I am with you. Do not fear.* I knew then that the voice I had been hearing was indeed from above, and I also knew what I had to do.

Instead of lowering my chin to complete the nod, I looked down my nose into Greg's eyes and hissed, "Get off of me now or I'm calling the cops!" It was a daring threat for sure, especially since he had yet to release my hands, but my mind and body were ready for anything he could hurl at me. Adrenaline was coursing through my body, and I knew that if he *did* remove one of his hands from my wrists to strike me again, I could and *would* break my arms free and start swinging. I was just that tenacious!

Unfortunately though, I didn't get the chance immediately because instead of assaulting me physically, Greg resorted to verbal desecration. *Bring it!* He attacked everything about me, from the physical to the intellectual. I was fat and ugly. I was emotionally immature and clueless; I was stupid and brainless. None of those things pierced my thickened skin to enter my soul. It was when he began berating my parenting and role as a mother that my esteem stated to wither a little. He could sense it too because his rant regained momentum, and he proceeded to choose a subject that would become my unraveling—my son.

In addition to insults about my son's appearance, behavior, and intelligence, Greg went so far as to refer to him as a "bastard." That stung. Bad. Say anything you want about me and my intelligence, appearance, and character, but don't you *dare* speak ill of the most important person in the world to me. My mama bear instincts kicked in full-fledged, and I growled like an angry tiger, kicking and thrashing on the bed. I tugged my arms as hard as I could, attempting to break free of his death grip and actually succeeded twice before being strung up like a sadomasochistic submissive yet again.

My reckless bravery enraged Greg, who had secured my wrists so tightly together after the second time I had broken free that the two radius bones were grinding together. His teeth ground together as he literally spit vulgar insults and swear words even *I* had never used. He began scouring the room frantically, searching for what, I did not know. Had he been less angry it would have been an ideal time to try and free myself yet again, but his fury made him stronger and his hold more determined.

"Come here!" Greg commanded and held my wrists firmly in one hand and grabbed a fistful of my hair with the other. He proceeded to drag me down to the foot of the bed and onto the floor where I wailed in pain. He pulled my hair straight toward the ceiling, forced me into a standing position, and led me toward my closet. Greg used his elbow to flip the light switch on the wall just inside my tiny walk-in.

"Where is a belt?" he demanded.

That simple question made my stomach lurch. He was going to beat me with a belt. "I…um…I don't have one," I lied.

"Bullshit!" he zapped. "Where is it?"

Through my newly developed tears, I cried, "Please don't whip me, Greg. Please?" I was full-out begging.

"You are so *dense*! Why are you always so incredibly stupid, Allie? I'm gonna tie your hands together since you can't seem to be trusted, you lying sack of sh———!"

I winced. "Okay, I have scarves. How about a scarf?" A scarf would certainly be more comfortable than a belt around my poor wrists that were already beginning to swell.

Greg widened his eyes and motioned with his head impatiently for me to direct him to my scarf collection. I slowly shuffled to a corner of the closet and pointed with my nose to a scarf hanger on the end of the rack, the scarves hidden from view due to the overcrowded clothing hung in front of them. He released my hair to tug one off the hanger, and when it came into view, I recoiled in angst. Of course, out of the five or six scarves on the hanger, Greg *had* to pick the one Chris gave me as an early birthday present before he passed away. It was pink with tiny owls printed on it, my very favorite of all wildlife.

Greg smirked at my obvious distaste for his choice and poked, "Aww, what? Did someone special give this one to you?"

My silent sobs prohibited me from using my voice, but I know he knew. He *knew* that scarf was a gift from my beloved—his "best" friend. Oh, what was Chris thinking now? I cried out his name in my heart, begging him to bring me some sort of peace. Would you believe that no sooner had I commenced my plea than this overwhelming sense of tranquility overtook my body?

It was short-lived as Greg yanked my hair so hard to pull me out of the closet that I ended up falling on my knees and being dragged the rest of the way to the foot of the bed. Once there, he ordered me to stand and resume my previous position. I did as I was told, and soon my wrists were joined behind my back and bound in venom by the very same scarf that was given in love.

Greg straddled me and reached his hands up over his head, grabbing behind him at the back of his shirt to pull off. He was sweating something fierce, and as I watched him swipe the beads off the top of his lip with his thumb, I was struck by how, if this were a consensual consummation with the Greg I thought I once knew, I would be extremely attracted to him. His torso was chiseled, his arms muscular to the point of displaying bulging veins. How different he would look if the darkness of *this* Greg was illuminated with the light of who I thought he had been. Instead, all I saw hovering over me was a big, sweaty monster whom I despised!

"Now, where should we start?" he sneered, undressing my entire upper half with his thirsty eyes. He then took the tip of his middle finger and placed it on my subtle widow's peak at the top of my forehead. He slowly and softly moved it down my forehead, over my nose, and halted on my lips. "Suck," he commanded. I clinched my lips as tightly as I could, refusing his authority. So in return I took another slap to the face.

He then placed his finger back on my lips and continued his pursuit, down my chin and throat, stopping right above my sternum on my neck. He tapped three times with the finger and then swiftly spread out his entire hand so that all five fingers wrapped around my throat. The tentacles constricted one, two, three, then released.

The pressure was enough to make me gasp and cough. Greg laughed his newly presented evil guffaw as I trembled. Clearly amused by the response, he repeated the trio of compressions four more times, allowing me to catch my breath in between each round. The man was choking me. He *was* going to kill me.

Finally, when he got bored of his strangulation game, he clasped his hands together over my face, turned them inside out, and stretched them toward the head of the bead, cracking each of his knuckles. "Whew, that was fun. Let's get down to business, shall we?"

My blood pulsed fury and hatred, and remembering my earlier resolve to fight back, I raised my head and spit on his smug face. Then I cocked my head back and swiftly catapulted back up to try and head-butt the fool, but my face caught the palm of his hand and he shoved my head back into the bed.

"Oh, you wanna play rough again? Huh?"

Greg proceeded to slap me two more times before literally ripping off my T-shirt. Then he got back up off the end of the bed and, in one swift motion, yanked off my pajama pants. Climbing back on the bed, he grabbed me around the waist and flipped me onto my stomach like a rag doll. My panties were clawed off next while my bra remained clasped, but forced up over my breasts as it would be futile to maneuver it past my tied-up arms. I could sense his impatience growing as his hot tongue rapidly flicked the back of my neck. And then finally my ears rang at the sound of his zipper. My soul wept.

26

I lay silent with my cheek pressed against the comforter, my ears begging to hear the sound of a condom wrapper ripping. The silent tears spilled over the ducts and slid horizontally across my face finding their resting place on the soft microfiber comforter that Chris and I had purchased together and snuggled under nightly. The dampened fabric against my cheek apple was the only sense of privacy I had. Greg could not see it nor touch it as he could the rest of my body. I protected that soiled space with the side of my face.

Greg's hands and lips were all over the back, sides, and underneath of my body. Unfortunately, my facedown position, for which I was originally thankful, exposed my hands to become available for his pleasure—a privilege on which Greg spared no expense. I knew the "main event" was imminent when Greg paused to compose himself by laying his head on my back and taking calculated, deep breaths, obviously in need of an interlude lest he prematurely crescendo.

My heart raced when he lifted his head from my back. I knew it was "go time," and all I could think about was my sweet husband watching this whole spectacle from heaven and weeping for me. I prayed hard that he could afflict a heart attack on Greg right at that moment. Alas, the heart attack didn't happen, and I felt Greg's devilish hands wrap around my hips and yank them upward while my head stayed pressed against the bed. He then clapped his hands loudly and rubbed them together like he was trying to warm them by a fire. I held my breath in preparation for the hell that was about to be cast down upon me.

When the hand friction ceased, I heard two more loud claps and then felt his hot fingertips, still pressed together, slide between the backs of my thighs, just above my bended knees. In one single motion, Greg hastily split apart my legs. Instinctively, I pressed them back together just as quickly; but after a mighty smack on my bare bottom followed by a much more painful separation of my legs (stretched as far apart as they could possibly go without literally tearing a tendon), I decided my efforts would be in vain.

"Good thing you practiced doing your splits earlier, huh? Got you good and stretched out for me," Greg heckled from behind me. He then nudged both of my knees inward, obviously realizing they were too far apart as well. I heard the shuffling of his knees as he inched closer and closer toward my backside and then felt his wicked hands clench the sides of my waist. One teeny tiny tear slid from the corner of my eye onto the dampened bed as I felt my integrity begin to slide away with it.

I closed my eyes and began singing a song into my head that I had sung to Sam so many times as an infant. The song is "He Knows My Name," and its chorus goes,

> He knows my name.
> He knows my every thought.
> He sees each tear that falls
> And hears me when I call.
> He hears me when I call.

I needed to drown out all other sounds and movements if I were going to survive this, and that particular song would melodically remind me that God in heaven knows. He knew exactly what was happening to me, how I was feeling about it, and what I was thinking. He *did* hear me call, and even if it I couldn't hear His answer yet, He heard my plea. And He watched me cry. Yes, indeed, God and Chris knew my supersecret, soiled spot on the bed. Greg would never get to see it, but my Heavenly Father and my beautiful son's father would certainly see it! I felt my lips curl just a bit and sensed a bouquet of butterflies dancing around my shivering, naked body.

I felt the top of Greg's thighs press against my butt, and my mind and heart cranked up the volume on the song. I clenched my bottom as hard as I could, hoping it would be too difficult for Greg to invade. And then I heard it. I heard the sound that could potentially perpetuate hope—if only.

Three quiet raps on the front door. I froze for half a second, wondering if I was auditorily hallucinating. But then Greg halted as well, and so I knew the sound *had* to be real. In every horror movie I have ever seen (which is embarrassingly very few), I always get so ticked off when the dumb protagonist knows someone is about to attack her and she just freezes; she doesn't scream or start running or anything. I'm always like, *Yeah right! In real life that idiotic chick would be screaming bloody murder and running for her life! This is so unrealistic.* Well folks, *I'm* idiotic. The whole thing was so surreal, almost like I was a teenager fooling around with a boy in my bedroom thinking my parents wouldn't be home for hours and then they walk in through the front door. For a split second, it was like Greg was my partner in crime, and we both had to be very still lest my parents catch us being naughty.

But when the knocks became a little louder, I snapped into sensibility and fully understood the opportunity at hand. I opened my mouth to belt out the loudest holler I could produce and actually got out the "He—" of the word "Help!" before my efforts were thwarted by Greg literally leaping over my back and turning my head to smash it into the covers. Then there were just my muffled attempts at a full-fledged wail.

Using only one hand on the back of my head, Greg continued to smother my face into the bed. I started to panic something fierce, no longer because I knew my plea for help was futile, but because I actually thought I was going to suffocate. I thrashed around as hard as I could, but Greg's full body weight holding me down made it impossible to break free. He said nothing as he lay there, slowly drowning me in my very own bed—the sign of a true psychopath.

When I finally stopped fighting, as I realized the flailing actually countered my efforts to take in oxygen, I tucked my chin into my sternum to create a small pocket of air and then lay completely still, praying my ears would detect the tapping sound once again, indicating the visitor had no retreated. *Who on earth would be coming to my house this late? What time is it?*

I had lost all recognition of time and space. For all I knew, it could be nine o'clock at night or three in the morning. I had nothing with which to gauge time, and the alcohol I had consumed earlier certainly didn't make it any easier. The doorbell rang, and at once, I tried to howl. But Greg was onto me and swiftly reached his hand around to cover my mouth before even a peep could escape my lips. I chomped down on his hand as hard as I could, but either the man feels no pain or he is just really good at receiving it in times of desperation because he didn't so much as wince.

I continued to make my muffled voice be heard, but I knew my efforts were in vain. After about three minutes of continuous yelling, my vocal chords were strained and hoarse, and I was extremely lightheaded. At any moment, I would pass out. I quieted my voice and concentrated on trying to take in what little oxygen filtered through Greg's fingers. It didn't matter anyway as I was fairly certain that after the first doorbell ring, not another was followed. That could only mean one thing: my one chance at salvation had left me for dead.

Finally, Greg decided it was safe to give me back my breath and released my mouth as he climbed off my back. I quickly turned my head to the side and gasped for air, realizing how close I had come to passing out due to hyperventilation when it took me a good minute to regain a normal breathing pattern. Greg too was breathing hard, but for a completely different reason. It was no wonder the person left as I had turned off all the lights in the house before trying to scare Greg coming out of the bathroom. If I only had that one act to take back…

Finally I said, "Can you untie me now and call it a night finally?" hoping to God that he'd had enough as well. Certainly he was sober enough by then to begin to see things more clearly and feel at least a little remorse for what he had done.

"Are you crazy? The fun hasn't even begun yet, Allie." He maliciously laughed. "And now we get to add another punishment for you screaming for help."

My body convulsed into a quiet sob. Never in my life had I been more scared and downtrodden as I was in that moment. Not even when Chris was literally on his death bed. My brain couldn't even begin to fathom how this whole thing was going to play out, not how it was going to end. So instead of lingering there in my mind, I just cried as hard as I could to distract my brain into nothingness.

Just as Greg had hoisted me back up into his favored position, I heard a loud shattering. Both Greg and I jumped at once and knew instantly that it was glass breaking somewhere in my home. Immediately, I became conflicted if I should take the opportunity to seek refuge from the intruder or commune with Greg for protection *from* the intruder. I mean, which was the lesser of the two wicked evils? I didn't have much time to internally debate those choices.

Luckily, I didn't have to when I heard the front door handle being jiggled and the word "dammit" flutter from the living room into my bedroom and kiss my ear. I have never been more joyful to hear any other word in my life like I was when I heard that curse word, because the lips from which it escaped belonged to someone whom I instinctively knew had come to save me. That person—that *man* was none other than my potty-mouthed big brother.

With a sense of relief I have never encountered in my life, I wailed, "Adam!" at a volume loud enough to have shattered the glass he had just broken.

Then I heard, "In her room, Dad!" and realized my daddy had come as well.

Greg jumped up off the bed and bounded to the bedroom door. He slammed it shut and locked it, then began darting his eyes around the room, looking for…I had no idea what he was looking for. He ran to the small bedside table and yanked it up just as my brother and dad reached the door and jiggled the handle.

Greg swiftly jammed the table up under the door handle and hurried over to the bed, pulling me up by the scarf tied onto my wrists. He forced me into the closet and slammed that door as well. Then his satanic voice penetrated the darkness: "Looks like we're gonna have to hurry this along, sweetheart!"

He forced me down onto my knees, my head resting on the carpet. There was barely enough room for him to crouch down behind me. My dad and Adam were banging on the bedroom door as I kept calling out to them to help me. Every time I did, I was struck on my back, my buttocks, my head, my side. I didn't care. My rescuers were so close I could almost touch them.

Not satisfied with my defiance despite his repeated blows, Greg must have spied the tip of a belt hanging below my shirts because he stood up and unhooked it from the hanger on which it hung. He crouched down right in front of my face, displaying the belt so that I could see him fold it in half. He then punctuated, "This is gonna hurt" and immediately stood back up.

I heard him snap the leather together a couple times just to taunt me, and then I knew it was imminent. I had been squirming around on the floor, trying to free myself until I knew the time had come. Then I just lay flat and still on my side, my back against one wall. Greg peeled me from my position and forced me into a kneeling position once again. I braced myself for a pain I had never known and then the delivering sound of glass breaking once again pierced the air.

Within seconds, both my father and Adam were standing in my closet doorway, my dad dragging Greg out of the closet in a choke hold. I collapsed onto the floor, unfazed by the fact that I was lying completely naked, save for the bra pulled up to my neck, in front of my father and brother. At that point, I couldn't care less.

My eyes faced the bedroom, and I saw what can only be described as a total beatdown performed by Daddy and Adam. Man, Greg tried to fight back and he really did put up a pretty good fight for the first minute or so, but the fury in the eyes of the most precious men in the world to me was not going to be waned until Greg was brought to his knees begging for mercy—which is precisely what happened.

Both my dad and Adam were already bloody when they reached me, having cut themselves significantly on the entrance in through the broken window. Their hands, forearms, shoulders, and legs were dripping blood at a slow but steady pace. Then after the "Greg Showdown," Adam had a swollen eye, and my dad's ear lobe was bleeding from where Greg tried to bite it off.

I witnessed things from the inside of that closet that I never could have visualized in my wildest imagination. My dad, for instance, holding Greg by the shoulders and kneeing him in the groin repeatedly. Adam punching him in the face and throwing him onto the bed, stomach down, and whipping him with the belt that Greg had almost used on me while my dad held his arms stretched taunt above his head so that he couldn't flip over. My dad wrapping his hand around Greg's throat and literally lifting him into the air, carrying him that way across the room and throwing him into the wall, all the while yelling obscenities and threats. I heard lots of references concerning me from both of my family members as they promised to kill Greg if he ever so much as *thought* of me again, let alone try and get a hold of me. My dad insisted Greg would be prudent to sleep with one eye open from now until eternity because the hatred my father would always posses for him could boil over at any second and he would drive to Greg's house and mutilate him.

I curled my knees up into my chest, reliving the nine months I had once spent in utero and began shivering uncontrollably. The shock was finally settling in, and when I saw Adam punch Greg in the ribs for the fourth time and heard the police sirens approaching, I bellowed, "Stop! Stop! Please stop! You're going to kill him!"

They both listened to my command from the tiny closet and spun around toward me with their eyes agape. I think they had almost completely forgotten I was still there. Greg lay face down on the ground, his position not too unlike mine had been in the closet when he had perched me up on my knees, face ground into the carpet. He was creating the most guttural whimper, like a cat being strangled. My dad was bent at the waist, his hands on his knees, catching his breath; while Adam was standing erect, looking from the closet to Greg and back again, as if he were mentally debating his next move. But as the sirens were obviously right in front of my house, he decided he would heed my wishes— right after one last kick in Greg's side. *Nice, Adam. Nice.*

Before the authorities entered the house, my dad found a robe in my bathroom and draped it over me. He then helped me up to a seated position, sat down next to me, and pulled me close, rocking me from side to side as I bawled like a circumcised newborn. My daddy had saved me. My brother had saved me. How had they known? These questions and many others would be answered over the next few days as I met with authorities, an attorney, and, finally, Jennifer Manis.

Apparently, the whole thing went down as follows: after Jen left my house late that Wednesday morning, she sat around and stewed as to what, if anything, she should do about the situation with Greg and the fact that I didn't believe her. She struggled with hurt feelings toward me and doing what was right, vacillating from one to the other, unclear of her next move. In one sense, the way I treated her coupled with the fact that she didn't know with 100 percent certainty that Greg would actually harm me convinced her that she would just be meddling by contacting my family. In another sense, she could completely understand why I had treated her the way I had and she felt she completely deserved it, which served as even more a reason to protect me at all costs. Luckily, the latter won out, albeit almost too late; and by nine o'clock, Jen was on the phone with my dad, insecurely expressing her concern for my friendship with Greg.

I guess my dad was so incredibly kind to Jen, never acting like anything had ever been amiss between the two of us (which is always my wonderful dad's MO) and spoke with her for over an hour, even staying on the phone with her while she drove past my house at ten o'clock and reported that Greg's vehicle was in my driveway yet all the lights were out. It was then that my dad became concerned, and after several failed attempts to get a hold of me by phone (I later found out Greg had turned off the ringer on both my home and cell phone sometime during the night), he phoned Adam, the two of them speeding down I-70 to get to me. It wasn't until after they had tried knocking and ringing the bell (my dad cursing himself a hundred times for forgetting the key he had to my house) and had circled the house, noticing the empty beer bottles and patio chairs splayed haphazardly, that they became concerned.

Adam, not having been the one to hear Jen's words firsthand, was not as convinced that something was amiss inside my house. He thought there was a distinct possibility that Greg and I were consensually making out in my bedroom and that their intrusion would be unwelcome. My dad, however, having heard the fear and trepidation in Jen's voice, knew something was wrong. He sensed it in his gut. Finally, on their way back around the house, Dad called Jen again to get Greg's phone number. Once on the front porch, he dialed it and through the living room curtain could see a light dancing on the couch's end table. Bingo!

They called the police and used one of my decorative Jayhawk stepping stones to bust through the living room window. Adam climbed through the window, cutting himself up pretty good before unlocking the front door for our dad. As soon as they heard my voice cutting through the silent air, they knew. They knew I was in trouble and charged to my room to save me.

Greg, however, didn't fare quite as well as I did. My hell lasted one night; his, twelve years. After having the crap beat out of him, he was arrested and cuffed in my bedroom. He was wearing only socks when he was formally read his rights, a sight my brother took immense pleasure in witnessing, followed by cryptic Facebook posts about the sight (not naming any names nor referencing the event because of the pending investigation). Only those of us who knew the details understood the wicked humor in his posts.

Jen and I met the Saturday after the event at her house and hashed out the whole thing, beginning with the first time Greg had spoken an unkind word to her and culminating with the traumatic experience that unfolded in my home. Our conversation lasted over four hours and included lunch. Everything she told me and I told her was also played out during Greg's trial.

Jen's hell began shortly after Annabelle was born. Contrary to Greg's report, while Jen *had* endured the typical postpartum baby blues, she had *never* reached the point of full-blown postpartum depression. She also swore on Annabelle's life (an action I found unnecessary) that my initial thoughts about her were true and that she had never, ever been weirded out by Chris and me being together. She had gotten over him long before we met up with her that night at the bar and had honestly been smitten with Greg from the get-go. There were no saved letters or photos of Jen and Chris. In fact, there never *had* been any letters, a confession that I believed, considering the fact that my late husband was many things but a heartfelt letter writer he was *not*! All of Greg's accusations were untrue, and Jen even went so far as to stand up from her kitchen table and demand I come search her house for any relics from her relationship with Chris or signs that she was lying about her feelings toward him. Bless her heart, of course I refused, but the gesture was so desperate and hopeful at the same time. She wanted to prove her innocence and clear her name. At least on the issue concerning my late husband and any jealousy toward me.

Greg's abuse began in the form of underhanded comments and controlling behavior. Jen, of course, contributed this negative behavior to the stress of his residency and subsequent practice. Unbeknownst to Jen at the time, but later revealed to her after Greg left, his hospital hopping at the beginning of his career (which he claimed was of his own doing because of the multiple offers he was receiving) was actually due to one affair gone awry and one pending sexual harassment charge. So all the time Greg was shouting "work stress" and berating Jen, he was actually just doing damage control to save his own a…er, reputation.

I remembered that time back in our friendship quite well, shortly after Chris passed. Should I have sensed something was amiss with Greg? Was I not paying close enough attention? I know I selfishly enjoyed the time that Greg was so crazy busy with hospital changes and the supposed "climbing" of ladders because I got Jen all to myself. But had I possibly suspected something at that time and just not mentioned it in an effort to keep myself happy?

I pondered this question as Jen detailed her marital journey and quickly came to the conclusion that in no way, shape, or form did I suspect a darn thing and the reason was actually selfish in nature, but not because of the aforementioned excuse. I was selfish because my husband had died, I underwent artificial insemination, endured a pregnancy without a spouse, delivered and mothered a baby, and dang it, I had every right to be selfish. So no, I wasn't paying a lick of attention to what Greg was doing, and I'm okay with that. And so was Jen. In fact, when I even tried to apologize for not recognizing anything bizarre about Greg's behavior, she immediately silenced me and brought up the exact same circumstances that would make it impossible to see anything beyond my realm of reality.

Greg's condescending hurtful behaviors did not take on a physical form until a month before Jen concocted the plan for she and I to take the trip to Omaha. Until that point, Jen just endured being made to feel inadequate and the eventual hateful insults about her appearance and personality, usually punctuated with curse words. Because of this slow fade into self-loathing, Jen became obsessed with Nick, or rather, Wesley—the *idea* of Wesley.

Like many women our age, Wesley represented something that we were either lacking in our lives or could use more of: a big, strong man who wanted nothing more than to take care of the woman he loved. Additionally, there was the fact that in the *Exemption* series, Wesley is in pursuit of rescuing a woman who is being severely abused. The story resonated profoundly with Jen, and the character of Wesley being someone who would take care of her—protect her from such a mean man and save her from her life of abuse—appealed to Jen like a juicy red apple to Eve.

Jen, however, didn't just want such a person; she desperately *needed* such a person. Whether that person come in the form of a man, woman, or God Himself, Jen needed a savior, and no one was there to save her. So instead, she allowed herself to become attached to and hopeful for this Wesley/Nick persona. The lines between fairytale and reality became blurred in her psyche, and Jen took it to the extreme. She confessed before me and in a courtroom full of people that she truly did believe that Nicholas Price would be the one to save her from her husband and the life that she no longer wanted to live.

Of course, Jen never got the chance to have Nick save her as Greg stopped allowing Jen to read any of the books, watch the movies, buy magazines, or look online *before* Jen had actually done anything tragically wrong with her affections. In fact, it was before we had even seen the first movie that Greg heard Jen talking on the phone with me describing the actor who was set to play Wesley. When he overheard her describe him as "looking pretty hot," Greg forbade her to go to the movie with me, but after Jen pushed back, using her only form of defense that we women sometimes become accustomed to using, a little manipulation, he hesitantly agreed to the first movie only. She told him that after she and I had talked so much about going, it would look suspicious if all of a sudden she couldn't go. The rest of the movies were in secret, another interesting fact of which I had not been made aware at the time.

As the verbal attacks heightened in both frequency and severity, Jen began escaping more and more into her own fantasy world, and that's when the e-mails to Nick and the Google searching began. As Jen had confessed the previous summer, Greg had indeed found out about all the e-mails and information Jen had been trying to obtain regarding Nicholas Price, and he *had* gotten incredibly angry. The part she had left out the previous year, however, is that his discovery of these items prompted the first beating.

Following the kicks to the stomach and the lashing Jen took to her back, one would think Jen would have either walked out on the bastard or stopped any and all thoughts or actions regarding Nicholas Price. She did neither. Instead, she stayed with Greg and pretended everything was hunky-dory for a whole month, all the while finding new and improved ways to be sneaky in her pursuit of Nick. By the time the trip to Omaha came around, Jen had gotten so used to lying to her husband that she was sure her airtight Omaha plan would go off without a hitch.

Her cousin Krista, who had made the hotel arrangements for us in Omaha, was an accomplice in Jen's guise, even though Jen lied to her about the reason for such discretion. Jen had cleared with Greg that she was going to go spend the weekend with her cousin in Omaha and after not hearing "boo" about Nicholas Price since he "shut her up," Greg bought her story hook, line, and sinker and had no reason to doubt her. Of course, being let out of the house, let alone the state, took some artful manipulation, but Jen had become a pro. Anything that could potentially contribute to Greg looking "bad" could be used against him in a test of wills, and he would cave.

All systems were a go after Jen and I arranged the trip and she had gotten "clearance" from Greg. It wasn't until Jen was in Annabelle's room quietly finalizing details with Krista while Greg and Annabelle had been in the backyard playing that all hell broke loose. In fact, Jen had just left the backyard after discussing the trip with Greg, immediately running upstairs and locking herself in Annabelle's room following his secession. Greg and Anna had just begun their game of TV tag, which Jen knew would take at least fifteen minutes, as Anna was not happy until she had been given enough chances to list her favorite television shows—all seventeen of them.

When Jen hung up the phone, she exited Annabelle's room, hopeful for her one-in-a-million chance to meet Nicholas Price and have all her problems whisked away at the touch of his hands. As she passed the bathroom that was accessible from both the hallway and Anna's room, she fleetingly thought it strange that the door was closed as they never had guests over and Anna was the only one who used it and she never closed the darn thing. Heck, she would pee on the side of the road if her mom would let her. The child had no modesty. The split-second thought, however, jogged Jen's brain into remembering that she had not only closed and locked Annabelle's bedroom door but also the door from her room into that bathroom. Most people would think nothing of it, but she was so close to fulfilling a months-long dream of meeting her "savior" that she could take no chances with things seeming out of place. She turned back toward Anna's room to also make sure she left no imprints on the bed or any other evidence behind, and when the room looked untouched by deceitful hands, she stepped toward the door, taking in a sight of Anna through the window in the backyard, playing by herself. *By herself?*

Jen said that at that instant she knew something wasn't right. The bathroom door being closed, Greg leaving Anna to play by herself alone, and just the twisting sensation in her gut relayed a message of caution as she twisted the bathroom doorknob to open it back up. The next thing she knew she was lying on her back, her heart pounding in her left eye as it almost instantly swelled shut. That was the second time Greg hit her.

When she called me to tell me the news that she couldn't go to Omaha after all, she relayed the story a little differently. I came to find out that the only reason she didn't come with me is because of the visible injury to her eye. Had it been anywhere else on her body, anywhere coverable, Jen would have gone to Omaha anyway. She didn't care anymore about herself or her marriage. She had viewed Omaha as her last chance at happiness. But with the evidence of abuse on her face—combined with the fact that she was just sure no one on earth, let alone Nicholas Price, would find her even remotely attractive in her state—Jen called the whole thing off.

Jen's accounting of the rest of the weekend and the weeks that followed were pretty much accurate with what I had already known and learned from Greg. She *had* been crazy with jealousy and speculation that weekend while I was in Omaha. She had played out various scenarios of me with Nick (scenarios that under any *normal* circumstances would be asinine) and kept herself up all weekend in a frenzy. Of course, she never admitted any of this to Greg, but he knew it from the moment she realized she couldn't go out of the house with the shiner that he had given her. In fact, he egged it on quite a bit, by razzing her with insinuations such as "Boy, wouldn't that be *crazy* if Allie and Nicholas Price got together and made *love*?" The more Jen would squirm, the more Greg would poke.

Then after Jen wrote the story, Greg hit her three different times. Finally she left him after the third time and tried to have him arrested, but the courts believed his side that she was just nuts and had evidence to prove it based on her obsession with Nick and her writing to the tabloids. My published account of events with Nick, Jen, and me didn't help her cause, a fact that inundated me with guilt. Greg told the courts that she was so nuts that she threw herself down the stairs in an effort to leave him and take Annabelle to be with Nick Price. After all, she was just *that* delusional.

In the end, she could do nothing about it—until after she freaked out when she saw me with Greg. He was so pissed that she came unannounced that he went to her house and beat the shit out of her. She was only to get a restraining order (which Greg managed to acquire against her quickly after), and another hearing was pending; but since the courts still thought she was nuts, they were dragging their feet. A neutral party had to take and deliver Annabelle since she couldn't. She feared for Annabelle, but Annabelle always reported that her dad was nothing but kind to her, and she was never around when Greg hit her mom.

Of course, everything changed the night Greg attacked me; and to spare you all the sordid details of his trial, in which luckily I only had a small part, let's just say that it was all finally taken care of and justice was served. Thank the Lord!

27

Even though Jen and I had a very pleasant heart-to-heart that Saturday, things between us were nowhere near back to normal. In fact, when I left I truly believed that we may never see each other again, apart from the impending trial that was set to begin in mid-July. Although I completely understood the rationale behind Jen's actions against me and had a newfound appreciation for her intense struggle, I still didn't trust her intentions when it came to my future happiness, and rightly so. I completely forgave her for hurting me, but she had indeed hurt me, and even knowing the circumstances that preceded her deceit wasn't enough to take away the implications of what she had done. What was done was done, but I was still suffering the consequences and was reminded once again of what those were when I left her house and noticed I had a missed call from an area code I would never forget: Beverly Hills, California.

I waited until I was in my house before I listened to the voice mail. Following the events of Wednesday night, my father and brother stayed with me until Sam came home from his friend's house the next afternoon. They offered to stay longer, but instead, I suggested that my dad take Sam home with him for a few days while I literally and figuratively cleaned up the mess that was left in the wake of Greg's torture. In addition to the legal action, I had to get bids on window repairs and a security system—all of which would be coming out of Greg's pocket.

When I was safely tucked inside my insanely secure home (my dad insisted that I get the most high tech security system, complete with window alarms and an alarm that was triggered by the sound of broken glass), I sat down on the couch and listened to Nick's voice stretching across several states.

"Allie, this is Nick. Hey, listen, we are set to begin shooting again this Wednesday back in Nebraska, and I've been told that I will not have even one moment on camera if those forms aren't signed. So can you *please* just sign them and then either fax them here by tomorrow afternoon, or to Omaha if it's later than that? Are you around tomorrow where you could do that please? Either way, call me back, and I will give you the fax numbers. Thanks."

I choked down my saliva. *Holy crap! He is going to be three hours away!* Of course, that really meant nothing as the distance between Nick and I was exponential, no matter the closeness of proximity. And of course, I had completely forgotten about the dumb papers and really wanted to run them by Adam before I signed anything, knowing he could read the fine print and advise me about how to proceed. But alas, time was of the essence; and honestly, I was too emotionally spent to even care about the damn papers, let alone my John Hancock at the bottom of each. Crap, I might even sign Sarah Alton's stupid requests. Getting sexually and physically assaulted really puts things into perspective. Nick was officially going to be out of my life. At that point, however, I really didn't care.

I retrieved the papers out of my carry-on that I had failed to empty out. I just planned on finding the X and signing without rereading anything on the pages, but of course, Nick's name typed out over and over again distracted me. I had thoroughly read through half of the first page when my cell phone rang. I jumped half a foot into the air. Slightly disappointed that the number didn't begin with the Beverly Hills area code, I answered before registering who it actually was.

"Hey, Allie, it's Jen. Listen, can you talk for a few minutes?"

I sighed, partly out of disappointment and partly out of annoyance for the distraction from thoughts of Nick. "You know, I was kind of in the middle of something, Jen."

"Oh. Um, okay," she said, her voice withering.

Dang it! Why couldn't I just be a heartless beast who let people wither?

"Wait, it's okay. Um, actually, I didn't tell you any of this today because, well, I really didn't get a chance," I lied. Actually, I really have no idea why I was even telling her then on the phone, except for the fact that I felt sorry for her and thought my sharing a little piece of my life might stave her off for a while, get her off the phone faster. "But I went to LA last weekend because Nick Price is back in the States and set to begin filming the next *Exemption* movie. In order to do that, his publicists want me to sign some confidentiality forms and papers that say I will not contact him."

I waited, expecting to hear something in her tone that indicated she still wasn't over the whole Nick thing but was pleasantly surprised when she responded apathetically, "Really? That sucks that they want you to do that. I'm so sorry, Allie. I know this is all my fault."

Jen wasn't trying to push for more information nor trying to manipulate me into feeling a certain way about the whole debacle. Instead, she was again accepting responsibility for her part in this mess. "It's fine, Jen. It really is. It's just kind of a mess because I have to get these papers signed like today and somehow get them faxed to either LA or Omaha by tomorrow, and I don't have access to a fax machine."

"Do you *want* to sign them, Allie?" she asked.

Hmm, that was a strange question coming from her. Instinctually, I assumed my earlier inclination was wrong and that her question was possibly loaded.

"What do you mean?" I huffed.

"Listen, I know I'm probably the last person you would come to for advice about this subject, but I read your story, Allie."

Okayyy? What is that supposed to mean? "Yeah?"

"Yeah, I did. Who would've thought you were a writer?" she joked.

In no mood to be cuttin' it up with the woman who sabotaged my shot at love, I snapped back, "What's your point, Jen?" It was harsh. Too harsh, but I no longer knew how to take the woman.

"Sorry, um, I'm just saying that I realized when I read your story just how much you really did feel for him. And I…I don't know, I realize that I ruined that, but knowing how serious you both were about each other, while it really hurt at first, now I know that it was real. Just based on what you wrote, I have a hard time believing you want to sign any papers that would keep you away from him."

I truly felt like Jen was up to no good, and I just wanted to get off the phone. I had no desire to be trapped by her sort of "crazy." No, she certainly didn't deserve what Greg did to her, but that didn't mean that she was vindicated of every single harmful thing she had done to me nor did it mean that I should trust her motives. "Well, thanks for your thoughts, but I really am done with the whole thing and have no desire to prolong the inevitable, so—"

"So what? You're just gonna give up? That doesn't sound like the Allie I know."

"Ugh, Jen, seriously? You know, I used to listen to your advice when I thought you really had my best interests at heart. And yes, with the events of this past week and our talk today, I realize that so much of your actions and behaviors had nothing to do with who you really are, but I'm sorry if I'm just apprehensive of your motives. I mean, I get why you felt the way you did and why you escaped, if you will, into a fantasy land in which you and Nick lived happily ever after, but that doesn't change the fact that you really truly tried to hurt *me*, your best friend. Or your old best friend anyway. I did *nothing* to you. I can see why you would want to hurt Greg, but I was completely innocent and always on your side and yet it was *me* you really went after. So I guess I just ask that you understand why I can't trust you right now…if ever."

Jen was silent for quite some time. My heart was pounding, yet I was very confident in my position and had no regrets for sharing my truth with her. Lord knows I had learned nothing if I hadn't learned the importance of truth. Finally Jen spoke, a little defeated. "I get it, Allie. I really do. But I really want to make it right and I really think that you and Nick had something that was real and it would be stupid of you to throw it away."

"Well, with all due respect, [Yes, I said that. Such a pompous literary thing to say. I totally wanted to say, "Frankly my dear, I don't give a damn what you think," but I actually said,] I stopped respecting what you think when you threw me under the bus."

"Deserved," Jen agreed. "Listen, I'll let you go, but I just have to say one more thing." She waited for permission to continue but was met with silence. She continued anyway. "I think you should go to Omaha to deliver the papers…unsigned."

Oh, the nerve of this girl. Why would she suggest such a thing?

"And I could go with you."

Aha! There it was. I knew it was too good to be true when she was all breezy at the beginning of the conversation. "You are insatiable, Jen! Unbelievable! You know what? Maybe I will go to Omaha to see Nick. In fact, I bet I could get him back and guess who *won't* be there when I do? *You*, Jen! *You!*" I hung up the phone.

I know, I know. A little harsh? Blame it on my frazzled state of mind. *I* sure do, but nevertheless, I had no intention of actually going to Omaha. I just wanted to sock it to her, hit her where it hurts. I try not to play catty, girly games, but sometimes I find that my double X chromosomes take over my mind and my mouth and make me say and do things that I probably shouldn't.

After hanging up on Jen, I paced around the house, frantic for something to ease my unrest. The anxiety that had been waxing and waning all week was in high gear, and I felt like I was going to rip my skin off my body.

For those of you who have experienced this debilitating anxiety, you know exactly to what I am referring. For those who haven't, consider yourself blessed. Imagine, if you will, a deep hole in the ground that you have suddenly been pushed into. Then, with no mercy whatsoever, the gravedigger starts filling in the hole with fresh dirt and clumps of mud. You scream for him to stop, but he can't hear you and so he continues piling it on and patting it down until finally you are immobilized and unable to breathe under the weight of six feet of dirt. You can't even blink, and you start to go insane. *That*, my friends, is what it feels like in the pit of anxiety. You feel trapped, imprisoned in your own mind, unable to escape. So what do you do?

Well, I called my mom. Yes, luckily there was a cell phone buried with me in my grave that day; it just so happened to be lying against my ear, and I spontaneously dialed my mommy. Many anxiety-ridden grave-dwellers aren't so lucky.

I had avoided speaking with my mom since the shakedown with Greg because I needed to be strong, and talking to her would have made me retreat back to the fetal position I had found myself in when I was in my closet and my brother and father were beating the crap out of Greg. I would have begged her to come stay with me and take care of me, and somehow I had the foresight to know that succumbing to infantilism was not what I needed to do to retrieve my sanity. It is like when a child learns to ride a bike and they fall for the first time. If the parent lets them forego trying for a while, they may never get back on the bike. If they give their child a quick hug and insist they get right back on and try again, the child has a much higher chance of success. The same applied to my sense of independence and security. Had I gone running home to Mommy, I might never return to my adult life in Olathe, Kansas.

I had let my dad do all the conversing with my mom, and even though I never told him that I didn't want her to come, I didn't have to. My dad lived by the same "rub some dirt on it and get back up" principle (in fact, he's the one who taught me); so when my mom tried to insist she come, he held her off. For that, I was eternally grateful.

But every dog has his day, and with the worst of my plight behind me, I felt confident enough in my ability to not fully crumble under her affection and so I called her. After four rings, the answering machine picked up right before I heard the receiver disengage. "Hello? Hello?" my mom barked against her own voice carrying on from the machine. "Oh, this damn thing."

It amazed me that the woman *still* had not fully figured out how to operate an answering machine, a gadget that by technology standards was already obsolete. "Mom?" I shouted above the chaos.

"Hold on, Allie. This damn thing." And then, not even trying to muffle her voice, she yelled, "Joe, I can't get this damn answering machine off! I swear, I don't know why we even need this stupid thing."

"Oh, Grandma, you said a bad word," I heard my little peanut reprimand in the background.

I knew by the beep that had sounded a few seconds earlier that my voice was now able to be heard on the machine, and so I chimed in, "Hey, Sammy! You're right. Grandma shouldn't be cussing, should she?"

"Mom?" I heard my excited son enquire in the background.

"Ugh, hold on, Sam. I've got to get this thing turned off." My mom was struggling not only with the answering machine but, by the sound of it, my son trying to pull the phone out of her hand.

The madness of it all made me start laughing. Here I was in total crisis mode, and my mom was clearly distraught over a 1980s answering machine. I was struck by the lunacy of the entire situation and could not control the hysterics within. I laughed and laughed until I cried and cried. Finally my mom figured out how to shut off the answering machine and asked, "Are you crying, Allie? Why are you crying?" She sounded impatient.

"Oh, Mom, I don't know. And I'm not crying, really. I'm laughing too."

"About what? What's so funny?"

"Oh, just you and the answering machine and how mad you get about it."

"I don't get mad. I'm just pissed off that the thing does that!"

I started chuckling again. "Well, isn't getting pissed off the same as getting mad?"

"Oh, whatever, Allie. What do ya need?"

"Oh, I get it. Now you're gonna be defensive, huh?"

"No, I just don't have time for this. Sam is running around like crazy, and I need to get him to eat something. I swear, that kid of yours doesn't eat anything of substance. You really need to be on him about this, Allie, or he'll end up—"

"Okay, okay," I interrupted. "I certainly didn't call to get lectured. I just was—"

"I am *not* lecturing you, Allie. I'm stating the truth, but never mind that. Excuse me that I don't drop everything to talk to you when *you* finally decide it's a good time to call me."

And there it was. She was bitter. If I had thought that my anxiety could be eased by a phone call to my mom, I was clearly mistaken. "You know what, never mind, Mom. I'm having a rough night, and I don't need to feel guilty to make it worse."

"I'm not making you feel guilty, Allie. I'm just saying there's a lot going on here. What's up?" Oh, she was the master of passive aggression.

"Nothing, it's just that Jen and I talked today for quite some time and it was good, but then I came home and had a missed call from Nick about those dumb papers that I needed to sign. I was reading over them when Jen called and we got to talking about it." I was becoming bored with my own story. "And I don't know, I just don't think I can trust her with anything to do with Nick. But she said I should go to Omaha and hand-deliver the papers to him, and then she had the nerve to suggest she come with me. So I'm just frazzled over the whole thing."

"Okay, so wait. Why would you go to Omaha to deliver the papers?"

"Oh yeah, well they are going to be filming the first part of the new movie there, and that's where he'll be."

"Then go," she said matter-of-factly.

"What?" I asked, confused. "No, no, that's not why I'm upset or whatever. No, it has nothing to do with that. I'm not going to Omaha. I'm just saying that the whole conversation left me feeling weird about Jen again."

"No, that's not why you called. You may *think* that's why you called, but in reality you called to get affirmation that you should go to Omaha."

What-the-what? Was that why I called her? I sat in silence, sorting through the muck and the mire in my brain and trying to locate a single fiber of intent that proved my mother right. And lo and behold, eventually I found it! That *is* why I called! Man, that woman is a genius. Maybe not technologically, but certainly intuitively.

"Mom, I think you're right. I think that *is* why I called you. Oh my gosh. That is the reason. That's crazy though, right? I mean, he already thinks I'm a stalker. If I show up there, it will just be proof!"

"Oh, Allie, I don't give a rip what he thinks or what anyone else thinks. What do you think? *Are* you a stalker?"

I had to think about that one. "Well, technically I guess I am."

"Oh, for crying out loud! No, you're not, Allison Belle! A liar, maybe, but a stalker, not at all."

I laughed. "Gee, thanks Mom."

"Well, does a duck quack?"

"Touché."

"Okay, so it's settled. You go to Omaha to hand-deliver the papers. Blame it on me if you have to or your brother. Tell him that it was against your lawyer's better judgment for you to mail such important documents such as these. Or crap, tell him you didn't have a stamp. I don't care what you tell him. You just be true to your heart and deliver those papers so that you get to see him at least one last time. After all, that's the reason you truly want to go to Omaha, isn't it?"

She was right. My signature on those papers made my relationship with Nick final. I was signing away my right to ever lay eyes on him in the flesh, and if I was going to do that, I wanted to do it in person. My good-bye had not gone the way I had wanted it to in California, and getting that last glimpse of him as I boarded the plane left so many unanswered questions that could only be properly answered face to face. I'm sure there was some sort of platonic explanation for his presence at my gate, but my heart begged to believe it was more than that.

"What about Sam?" I asked. "I mean, I can't very well take him with me."

"Oh, what on earth will you ever do?" she responded sarcastically. "I mean, if only you had two wonderful parents who *always* enjoyed watching your son for you."

"And again I say, 'Touché,' Mom. Touché."

I told my mom I would call her back once I found out when Nick would actually be in Omaha. I had no intention of telling him I was coming, but I *did* need to acknowledge his call and get the location of where I was supposed to drop off the papers. He had only told me to fax the papers and a fax number would not suffice for me to know his exact location, so I was going to have to be crafty with obtaining an address without lying to him once again.

When I built up enough courage, I called him back. He answered after the first ring. "Hey, Nick, it's Allie."

"Yes" was all he said.

I cleared my throat. "So, um, I got your message, and, well, that's fine and all. Well, I guess it's really not *fine* because I was hoping to get a chance to have my lawyer look over the papers, but oh well." I paused, hoping he would respond to my whine. When he didn't, I continued. "So anyway, just give me the address."

"What address? I told you to fax it."

Expecting this, I relayed what I had rehearsed, "Yeah, I know. Give me that number too, but I don't know if I will be able to find a fax machine in time so I could just overnight it." I inhaled and held my breath, waiting.

I heard Nick sigh and then say, "Well, hold on. I'll need to get the address of where I'm staying."

My throat clinched, and against my better judgment, I asked, "You're not staying at the same hotel as last time?"

Nick huffed and then remarked, "Yeah, it is, but sorry I don't have the address memorized."

Ouch. That stung. He was insinuating that I probably *did* have the address memorized. Oh, how I wanted to strike back, but instead I remained quiet while he fished for the address. As soon as he found it and relayed it back to me, I snarled, "K. Bye."

"Uh, aren't you forgetting something?"

Was I? "Uh, nope."

"I thought you were going to *try* to fax it if you could."

"Oh yeah. Right. Okay, what's the number?"

As he relayed the number, I realized I had forgotten to find out exactly when he would be in town. When he finished, I asked, "So when will you be there for me to make sure it's delivered?"

"It doesn't really matter if I'm there or not. Just send it to the front desk of the hotel with my name in the 'attention' spot. They will hold it for me if I'm not there."

Bummer. Oh well, I'd have to wing it. Either that or I wouldn't even go at all, what with his bad attitude and all.

"K. Bye," I said again, and this time I meant it as I hung up the phone. It quickly registered that the next day was Sunday, and thus, the mail wasn't even set to deliver. But I got what I wanted, and so if he tried to point that out, I would just play dumb and tell him I'd fax it instead.

As soon as I could think again, I remembered he had given me some sort of detail on his arrival when he had called before and left the message. I checked his voice mail again and identified that he hadn't actually said when he would be coming in to town. I knew he started filming on Wednesday, but it was Saturday. And I knew that if I couldn't fax the papers by the next afternoon to LA, then I'd need to fax them to Omaha. Of course, I had no way to know for sure if that meant that he would be coming to Omaha that Sunday as I'm sure the hotel would never in a million years release information about a guest as famous as Nick, so I would just have to take a shot in the dark.

Frantic to just go and get it over with, I decided I would drive to Omaha late the following afternoon. If he wasn't there by that night or early Monday morning, I would see it as a sign, leave the papers at the front desk, and leave the whole thing behind me. Once I was resolved, I phoned my mom back and asked if she and my dad could keep Sam until Monday evening, to which she obliged. And then I started packing.

28

With my bags packed and car gassed up, I left my house that Sunday afternoon with the unsigned papers in tow. I had secured a room at a nearby Holiday Inn, deciding it wasn't worth it to dip in to my fairly plush savings account for one night at a hotel at which I wasn't even positive the man I was intending on seeing would be there. In addition, if he was there and it didn't go down well, I definitely would *not* want to be staying in the same hotel as him. Although a part of me was feeling just a bit rebellious, considering the fact that I *hadn't* actually signed the papers and therefore was not held to any sort of legal obligation to steer clear of the great and powerful Nicholas Price. I mean, it's a free country, right? And after he was such a jerkface on the phone to me, the thought of pissing him off royally didn't sound entirely unappetizing.

It was a surprisingly mild summer day, and so I unrolled the windows and cranked up my Garth Brooks CD. Yes, I still owned CDs and had no intention of succumbing to popular culture and technological advance by getting an iPod. Not only was my vehicle not equipped for one (which really would only matter for another few months as I had planned on purchasing a more sturdy vehicle with the royalties from my book), but the CDs created a sense of nostalgia for me as Chris had introduced me to country when we first met and many of the CDs I still listened to were actually his. Some of them we had purchased together.

Oh, it felt so good to have the wind blowing through my hair as I recreated my tire tracks from the year before on my way to Omaha, Nebraska. The time flew by, and despite my large McDonald's Diet Coke, I only had to stop once to pee—a record for me! I had listened through two of Garth's albums and one Dixie Chicks CD. I don't care what kind of controversy those blonde chicks got themselves into, I was a loyal fan, darn it!

As I approached the hotel, my carefree attitude began to waver. Anxiety gripped at my stomach, and suddenly, I had to go to the bathroom yet again. I drove around the block and stopped at a Wendy's to use the facilities. While I was inside "taking care of business," I decided it might be best for me to drive to Plattsmouth, the location of the previous set. Surely they would be using the same set if they were back in Omaha, and that way I could check to see if production was at least beginning.

Surprisingly, I had to rack my brain to remember how to get to the old farmhouse. It was off a beaten path, and I actually drove right past it the first time around. Circling back, I paid close attention to my surroundings and recognized the makeshift gravel parking lot that had been created the previous summer for spectators. It was empty. In fact, there were no fences or walls up whatsoever, and I had a clear shot of the farmhouse where Nick and Sarah had filmed the scenes in the last movie. My stomach cramped.

I turned the corner where I had encountered the mean security guard that crazy summer day when my life changed forever. He was not there, of course. No one was. The gravel drive up to the farmhouse soothed my nerves, and when I reached the mailbox, I put my car in park mode and got out. The heat had cranked up a notch, so I grabbed my sunglasses and made my way to the set.

Of course, I felt a pang of defeat as the solidarity of that little old house meant that production had not yet begun and Nick would indeed not be in town after all. I walked completely around the perimeter of the house, and when I returned to the front porch, I jiggled the handle. Locked. Not to be overcome, I went back around to the back and tried to open that door. Locked as well. After jostling several boarded locked windows later, I surrendered to the fact that I was just *not* supposed to get into that house.

I really don't know why it bothered me so much except for the fact that I knew Nick had walked the old rickety planks in that house before. Maybe I just wanted to be a little rebellious and break onto a set or something, but truly, my heart longed to be closer to him—even if he had been snarky and mean to me earlier. I knew I wasn't going to see him at the hotel, so this house would have to serve as a symbol for my final good-bye, my closure. I contemplated just leaving the stupid papers on the front porch and hightailing it to Topeka to see my little man, but knowing my luck, they'd just blow away or get into the hands of some hillbilly from the sticks who would sell them on eBay and ruin my life and Nick's career once again.

No, with my stupid tail between my legs, I would take the papers back to the Hilton and leave them with the clerk at the front desk. Man, I sure hoped they would have a big envelope for me to use as, of course, I didn't even *think* about getting one myself. Duh.

I got in my car and started the engine. I had put in a CD shortly before arriving at the hotel that Chris and I had gotten from a friend's wedding. The bride, Hollie Bailey, was a family friend of Chris's and she had married a guy named Thomas Best. Their party favors included CDs for each guest entitled *The "Best" Wedding Album*. It was a clever little gesture, and Chris and I absolutely *loved* the songs burned onto the CD. It was such an eclectic mix of classics by artists such as Frank Sinatra to popular country hits by Tim McGraw with a little bit of Fresh Prince and Salt-N-Pepa sprinkled in.

As soon as I turned out of the driveway, the song "Like We Never Loved At All" by Faith Hill was on. Chris and I always loved trying to do a duet to the song, Chris of course being Tim McGraw while I busted out a little Faith. We sang that song so many times, but you know what? I really don't think I had ever heard the song until that day driving back into Omaha. Humor me for a second and check out these lyrics:

> How can you just walk on by
> Without one tear in your eye
> Don't you have the slightest feelings left for me?
> Maybe that's just your way
> Of dealing with the pain
> Forgetting everything between our rise and fall
> Like we never loved at all

Whoa, Nellie! That was just enough to tip me over the edge and nudge me into full-blown hysterics. I mean, was that song speaking to my situation with Nick, or what? He was just willing to sweep me away without even a second glance. This man, who had sent me flowers *every single day* for who knows how long had found it oh so easy to forget about me—like we never loved at all. Sigh.

Any primping I had managed to do before I left Olathe was all for naught as I made my way back to the hotel, mascara streaks down my puffy red face and snot—yes, literal snot—sliding dangerously close to my top lip. Had I been a five-year-old, I would have lapped that right up. But, being the sophisticated thirty-something lady I am, I wiped it with the back of my forearm. Who cared anyway? Nick wasn't even going to be in town, and no one else knew me in that God-forsaken town.

I turned into the parking lot of the Omaha Hilton and swallowed salty saliva. Oops, looks like either the tears or the snot made it to my tongue after all. Let's go with tears. Much easier to swallow, pun intended. I pulled into a parking space, and I'll tell ya, maybe a good cry was all I really needed because my nerves were totally stable. I had recreated that hotel in my mind so many stinkin' times over the previous year that even the thought of it made my heart pound, much like it did when I first approached it that day, before going to the set-that-wasn't. But something about that crybaby-fest managed to rid my body and mind of any anxiety whatsoever. It was as if my tears kidnapped all my fight-or-flight adrenaline on their way out. Oh, how good it felt.

That all changed, of course, when I stepped foot into the lobby. Memories as fresh as snow came flooding back into my soul like a tidal wave of longing. Holy cow, nothing had changed. Not that I should have expected it to, but you know when you have recreated something again and again in your mind how the scene is more surreal and vibrant? The colors are vivid and the lighting brighter in your mind's eye. The brass fixtures and knobs gleam in the light, and the hues pop off the rugs and walls. And then you reenter the actual space and you are struck by how muted it is, yet somehow it is more brilliant than even your imagination could build because it is home. Your entire sensory system is involved when you are actually *present* in that place that has brought you such distinct memories. The sounds, textures, and smells…oh, the smells! Presence does more for you to clearly experience those memories than your wildest dreams ever could. That, my friends, is exactly the phenomenon that took hold of me when I walked into that lobby.

I looked around, my eyes stopping on the entrance to the bar. The wooden doorframes encasing the beveled glass were so familiar I could almost smell the pine. Instinctively, I walked toward them, passing the receptionist desk. As I did, I heard a mature woman's voice call out, "Can I help you?"

Out of habit, I responded, "No, that's okay. I'm just looking," not even realizing until much too late that I was not in a department store. She said nothing else.

When I reached the beautiful doors, I ran my hand up and down the fine grain and stopped short of sniffing the wood. Instead, I took in the bar itself. Being only shortly after five o'clock on a Sunday evening, the stools were vacant, although gathering from the clanking behind the bar itself, I figured it must be open. I spotted the exact stools on which Nick and I had been seated and had half a notion to sit down for a drink to acquire the full effect of my nostalgia.

Thinking better of the idea, since I would be behind the wheel in another five minutes or so, I retreated from the bar entrance and slowly crept to the doors leading out to the pool. Oh, how my heart ached when I spied the slab of concrete where our bodies had been nestled next to one another by the water's edge. I could see us there, beer in hands, flirting mercilessly and longing to touch each other. My stomach flitted with those butterflies who had come back to roost as I visualized myself that evening and the astonishment I had felt sitting beside the enigmatic Nicholas Price. I was like a young schoolgirl, getting a chance to be with her ultimate crush.

When the fluttering morphed into nauseated regret, I turned away from the pool and headed toward the desk. I had a purpose for my intrusion, after all, as the clerk would soon find out. I stopped short of the desk, however, when I spied the elevator. Making a quick U-turn, I approached the elevator—the same one I had walked into with tears streaming down my cheeks the first night I ever met Nicholas Price. I remembered being too afraid to even look back at him to see if he was watching me because I ran the risk of losing my resolve of bidding him adieu after our one amazing encounter. I figured it was just too complicated, what with my "advanced age" and his insane fame and fortune. Not to mention the fact that I was a Midwestern mom with a child at home. Of course, the next morning, my resolve was kicked to the curb when Nick reached out to me, and thus began our painfully short yet insanely intense courtship. Man, now I *do* sound like I'm of an advanced age!

Literally maneuvering like I was being controlled by an unforeseen force, I pushed the button to call the elevator. I had a brief thought of my precious Sam and how he was quickly outgrowing the age in which he just *had* to push the buttons on an elevator. When he was a wee one, he would literally sulk in the corner of the lift if a stranger had pushed the button themselves. It was embarrassing, yet I remember a time when elevator button-pushing was equally as important to me and caused many a fight between me and my brother, Adam.

The elevator arrived in a flash completely empty, exactly as it presented itself that fateful night. I stepped in, reliving every motion as it cruised me up to the fifth floor. Exiting, it took me a second to get my bearings as the boring hallway was one place I actually *hadn't* burned into my memory. But then somehow, I remembered my room number: 507, which just so happens to be the first three numbers of Chris's social security number. I had forgotten about that connection that had struck me as a sign from Chris when I checked in the previous June.

I made my way down the hallway, passing rooms 515, 514, 513, and so on until I reached room 507. Of course, the door was shut, as were all the other doors, so I couldn't get a peek inside like I had hoped, on the off chance that housekeeping would just so happen to be cleaning *that* room at that exact moment. Yes, I know. I'm a dork and a half. If you were a fly on the wall in that hallway, I am 99 percent sure you would have seen my shoulders actually slump in defeat, like a five-year-old who doesn't get her way. I embarrass myself just picturing it.

I leaned against the adjacent wall to room 507 and noticed that the "Privacy Please" door hanger was hanging from the handle. Hmmm. I wondered if it was just left there from the previous guests or if someone was actually staying in the room and needed "privacy." Ooh la la! The hotel was truly a ghost town, so if I was a betting woman, I would bank on the former.

With my head tilted back, I closed my eyes and tried to picture the interior of that room. I remembered Nick's face in the doorway when he had been just as disheveled as I was after a night of no sleep from thinking about me. And then I remembered the beautiful bouquet of thirteen roses because we had known each other for thirteen hours. I let the memories infiltrate my soul with warmth. The floral fragrance tickled my nose; his bedhead hair and concerned expression tugged at my heart. If only…if only things had been different. If only I hadn't lied. Why had I lied? Would the truth have changed anything? Certainly not. Had he been privy to my knowledge of his fame he surely wouldn't have even given me the time of day. Oh, the heartache. Another deep inhalation and exhalation, and it was time to move on.

In, two, three, four.

Out, two three, fo—

The rattle of the handle attached to door 507 jolted my eyes open. *Oh crap! Oh crap!* I sidestepped to the right and then to the left, deciding what the hell to do. If I stay put, staring at the doorway, I will look like some crazy stalker to whoever resides inside. If I take off running in either direction, I will look like I was up to something and was bolting. There was no answer! *Oh crap!* (Of course, you realize that this was all taking place inside my mind over the course of a half second. Yes, my brain really does run that fast.) I decided my best course of action was to raise the stupid unsigned papers up under my nose, pretend to be thoroughly engrossed in the contents thereof, glance up, offer a courteous smile, and go right back on "reading." With any luck, the person would think I had just paused right outside of my own room to do some light reading. I mean, who really can read and walk at the same time? Am I right?

Or maybe I would act lost, as if whatever I was reading were directions to someone's room. Oh, but that wouldn't work because what if the person asks if they can help me find the room when in actuality there is no room? Oh, that'd be embarrassing, wouldn't it? I could just see myself being given a guided tour to an empty room and having to knock on a door that would never be opened. Or worse, it *would* be opened and then there would be a whole back and forth thing about which room I was looking for and the person in room 507 would still be trying to be "oh so helpful" and would take a peek at the papers in my hand and alas, they would find the God-forsaken forms that tell me to "Stay the hell away from Nicholas Price, you freaking stalker!" No. Plan A was definitely a better choice. (Once again, folks, it took half a second for both of those plans to formulate in my brain. Literally, the handle was only in midrotation as I had all of those thoughts and probably more.)

Sticking to my plan to just be nonchalantly reading some interesting pieces of literature, I turned slightly away from the door so that my shoulder was pressed against the wall. I allowed my hair to cascade down the side of my face so that he or she wouldn't even get a good look at me, as I was sure they would choose to use the elevator that was in the opposite direction. My heart thudded in my chest as the door creaked open. *Please just ignore me. Please, oh please.*

I heard what sounded like the tail end of female laughter and realized that the "Privacy Please" sign may have, in fact, been properly hung. The thought made me smirk but also caused me to feel even more embarrassed for myself and for the person/people in the room. How awkward to finish a little hanky-panky in a completely empty hotel only to find out someone has been standing outside your door. Luckily, I hadn't been here long enough to hear any of the goings-on. Or maybe the female was actually alone and on the phone. I'd soon find out.

I heard shuffling and then a manly sounding throat clear. Oh gosh, was I embarrassed for them. I wanted to be sucked into the wall. Since that wasn't an option, I studied the papers in my hands very intently, so as to look like I was in a whole other world and completely oblivious to anything sort of a charade going on in room 507. I even squinted my eyes, scrutinizing the text. It was then that I could sense the couple had crossed the threshold and entered the hallway, the door slamming behind them. It was also at that second that I realized my papers were turned upside down! *Oh, for the love of God!*

Trying to be as nonchalant as possible, as the copy was on both sides of each document, I slowly rotated the papers to their full and upright position. I chose that nanosecond as a good time to raise my eyes and give a courteous smile and nod, hopeful that my salutation would serve as a distraction from my upside-down paper snafu. I maneuvered so swiftly, not even meeting their eyes, that my fake focus was already back on the pages in hand before it hit me. Reflexively my eyes darted back up at the couple frozen in midstride. I swallowed strenuously as I tried to compute the scene before my eyes, even blinking impulsively several times like you might see a cartoon figure do when they literally *can't believe their eyes*. There, planted before me not five scissor-steps away, breathed the one and only Nicholas Price. And no, my dear friends, he wasn't alone. Nope, standing two feet beside him, with her mouth hung open wide enough for a bird to roost was my oh-so-former best friend Jennifer "You Little B——" Manis!

29

Someone please splash some ice cold water on my face before the steam billowing out of my ears and the scorching, too-hot-for-Lucifer flames shooting out of my eyes directly into Jen's soul catch these hypocritical, you-son-of-a-b— unsigned documents on fire and the whole hotel goes up in flames! For real, I tell you, Mama wasn't very pleased with the two ghost-white figures immobilized in front of her. That was, once the cylinders in Mama's brain started firing again and actually processed what it was that she was looking at. The recognition took a good ten seconds or more.

I have a short quiz for you. Picture yourself, if you would, in this exact position. I know, I know. What are the chances anyone on earth would be in this position? But I am living breathing proof that this exact position exists and yours truly had to endure it, so humor me if you will. What would you do? Okay, here are your choices:

A. Beat the frankenweenies out of Jen and then make a break for it.
B. Knee Nick Price in the groin and head-butt Jen and then make a break for it.

C. Scream "Rape!" at the top of your lungs for no apparent reason other than to draw unwanted attention to the two of them—and then make a break for it.

D. Fall to the floor, kick, scream, and throw a temper tantrum like a toddler, and then…

E. Crawl over to Nick, wrap your arms around his legs, and beg him to love you.

F. Pull the fire alarm..

G. Scream and yell every curse word you know at the two of them and then bolt.

H. Do all of the above.

I. Turn and walk away, wiping your tears as you hit the stairwell.

I bet you can guess that I chose the last one, immediately *after* I peeled my sunken self off the wall, the papers nearly dripping wet from my sweaty palms. Jen's voice was the first I actually heard, and though the loudest sound between my ears closely resembled a gong, I'm pretty sure I made out the words "wait," "explain," "good," and possibly "orangutan," but I could definitely be wrong about that last one.

I did not look back as I approached the door to the stairwell, although when the big steel door was closing behind me, I did manage to hear the two of them exchanging concerned words. Descending five flights of stairs would have usually caused a little panting and some dizziness, but this day, I felt as though I was floating down them. Maybe it was the shock protecting me from reality in the form of an out-of-body experience. Whatever it was, it continued as I exited the hotel through the side doors at the base of the stairwell and ran across the parking lot to my vehicle.

The tears were steadily streaming, but there were no sobs or convulsions. It was all contained right in my heart and just leaked out of my eyes. The sadness. The deep, deep sadness that *had* to be responsible for these tears. It wasn't sorrow or really even anger at that point. Just sadness. My mind was not capable of wrapping itself around the spectacle to which I had just born witness. It couldn't do it. It refused. I don't know exactly why, but my body was responding as it should, with the tears and all, yet the emotions that typically evoke such a response had yet to materialize. I felt nothing but a sensation of floating and viewing myself from the outside.

Now I'm not crazy, and I am not saying I had a near-death experience. I didn't physically *see* myself from the outside, but it was as if I was a present spectator to my life. My thoughts, though impossible to comprehend at the time, were perceiving my situation from an outsider's perspective. I knew to feel sorry for me and I knew I should be sad, but it was kind of like a dream. Your mind creates a whole dramatic scene without your actual body acting it out. You're just lying there, asleep, but in your dream you are running around, dancing, singing, playing, whatever. It was crazy, although at the time it was just surreal.

Like any normal person, I buckled my seatbelt, checked my mirrors, and backed out of the parking space. Once safely cleared on both sides, I shifted the gear into drive and slowly pulled out of the parking lot. These things I did, they were everyday, ordinary things that millions of people do without even thinking, myself included. The thing is, here I was performing the most ordinary of actions externally yet internally I was enduring the most extraordinary experience of my life. How was I able to keep moving forward with the knowledge of what just took place? I guess it is like those women who can literally lift a car up in the air if their baby is crushed underneath, or whatever that adrenaline-inspired urban myth says. I moved forward because I had no other choice.

It wasn't until I was on the outskirts of the Omaha city limit that my eyes actually saw what they were looking at in the rearview mirror. For all I know, I could have run over several small children within those first twenty minutes and never would have known. That's how out of sorts I was. I was literally just going through the motions of driving my car. Maybe it was some sort of curse that was only cast down on me in the city of Omaha because as soon as I crossed that city line, I became aware that Jen's vehicle was rolling down the highway right behind me. *Crap!*

As if it all happened at once, crossing that city limit and seeing Jen in my mirror jolted my mind and body into hyperawareness, and the appropriate range of emotion that someone in my predicament should feel came flooding into my being. Oh yes, the sobs and the convulsing began. The uncontrollable bouncing of my right knee made it impossible to keep the gas pedal depressed so I finally had to set the cruise control. And oh, the horrific sound coming straight from my gut and finding tone and volume as it passed through my voice box was akin to a panther in heat. Seriously, Google it! It's a thing. Oh, the wailing was so intense that there is no way on earth Jen could not see my fit as the *car* was literally shaking from it.

The emotions, which ranged from self-pity to serial killer rage and everything in between, were so intense that I actually feared for my life behind the wheel of the car. At one point, I was beating on the steering wheel so hard with my fists that my horn became depressed and stuck! Oh, for the love of Alex P. Keaton, are you kidding me with this? Seriously, did that really have to happen during my darkest hour? As if I wasn't shamed and embarrassed enough, then my hissy fit escalated to the point in which I was making a complete ass of myself as I continuously honked at everyone on the highway, including Jen behind me. And it wasn't a cadence like a car alarm being deployed. That would have been peaceful compared to what I had tripped. Oh no, it was a loud, endless, high-pitched blare that I tried desperately to terminate by actually ripping the plastic off the steering wheel hub. That did nothing to retard the sound.

I was frantically racking my brain for a solution while simultaneously searching for the nearest exit or at least a place to pull over. I really didn't want to have to pull over as then Jen would have me trapped on the side of the highway. At least if I could exit the highway, I might be able to lose her. Deciding that the steering hub cover was doing no good sitting in my lap, I began to jimmy it back on the column while managing to drive over the rumble strips in the shoulder twice. God bless the genius inventor of those rumble strips. I tell ya, nothing wakes you up when you're behind the wheel quite like a rumble strip.

By the grace of God, somehow while I was affixing the cover back over the horn button, the darn thing silenced. I exhaled in relief. At least one crisis averted! What would I have done if I had to go to an auto shop and try to explain what I fool I was over the loud shrill coming from my vehicle? Or worse, in speaking to my dad later about it, I found out that the horn continuously honking can drain the battery rather quickly.

I checked my mirror again to see if evil Jen was having a heyday with this one, fully expecting her to be laughing hysterically, as if screwing one of only two men I have ever loved wasn't quite enough. She wasn't laughing, however. She had her cell phone up to her ear, and when I glanced in the mirror, she made a grand gesture with her hand, pointing to the phone, obviously indicating that I was supposed to call her. Yeah right!

I did fish my phone out of my purse, however, and noticed that I had eight missed calls. How on earth did that happen? I never even heard it ring. Well, of course, horn-honking dummy, the ringer is off! I turned the ringer back on, and when it immediately started ringing, I just ignored it, making a mental note to block Jen's number when I got home and had time to figure out how. I scrolled through the missed calls, and surprisingly, only half of them were from Jen; the other half were from the heartless Nick Price. Seeing his phone number induced my chest to clinch yet again.

My phone began ringing as soon as I put it on the passenger seat, and so I glanced in my mirror again, not surprised to find Jen still gripping hers to her ear. *No chance, sister.* This went on for about five minutes until finally silence ensued. I checked the mirror once again and saw Jen still holding that dang phone to her ear, and so I anticipated another round of incessant calls. If I had to hear it ring one more time, I would probably chuck it out the window or, more realistically, silence it. But it didn't ring again. I watched her for a few seconds with the phone still at her ear. Her mouth was moving, so she was obviously talking to someone, probably Nick.

Oh crap! The papers! In my haste, I had completely forgotten about the stupid papers I was supposed to sign. My earlier anger that triggered the horn fiasco had resurfaced, and my knuckles turned white as they death-gripped the steering wheel. I looked in the mirror and saw that Jen was still blabbing on the phone, so I got an idea. The exit for Plattsmouth was two miles up ahead. I would scoot over to the fast lane, and of course, Jen would follow. Hopefully, traffic would be as consistent as it had been on the highway out of Omaha, and I could somehow lock Jen into the fast lane before scurrying over just before the exit.

Jen predictably followed closely as I cruised down the road, passing much slower vehicles on the right. Of course, as I inched closer and closer to my exit, the other vehicles on the road suddenly disappeared. I managed to speed up to a semi, however. A mere hundred yards from the Plattsmouth off-ramp and in an award-winning Dale Earnhardt Jr. impression, I pushed ninety miles per hour, cut off the semi, and crossed over onto the ramp in the nick of time, leaving Jen presumably scrambling for a solution. It was the first time I had smiled in thirty minutes, a devious little grin that felt surprisingly refreshing.

I formulated my plan as I traversed the back roads for the second time that day. My dad would have to be called and thanked following my scheme, as it was he who I needed to thank for always insisting three things were to remain in my car: jumper cables, a tool box, and mace. Luckily, the only item I would need would be the tool box, barely escaping the jumper cables and thus the mace, had my blaring horn drained my battery and caused Jen to gain access to me. Of course, I had always found these items silly because although my pops had shown me numerous times how to use the jumper cables, I was completely terrified of them and what might be the result of clipping on the wrong prongs or, worse, touching them together! The mace just seemed frivolous as until I actually met and had a "relationship" with a superstar, I had always been an "other people" type of girl. Everything always happened to *other people*, not moi. *I'd* never get mugged or raped—or assaulted in my freaking bedroom. *I'd* never meet a famous young actor and fall in love. Hmm, maybe it was time I changed my thinking, no?

And then there was the tool box. My dad was the handiest man I had ever met, which means I was the exact opposite. It was the classic case of the preacher's kid. Why learn how to do anything when your dad could do it for you? Oh, my genius father. He knew me better than I knew myself. Of course, there were also a few staples that I insisted never left my car: a first aid kit, baby wipes, tweezers, and lip gloss. Come on now, don't deny the chin hairs that can *only* be seen in the vanity mirror in daylight. My mom had given me a miniature sewing kit in my stocking one Christmas for my car because "you never know when you are going to need a needle and thread, Allie. Or a safety pin for that matter. I *always* kept one in my car when you kids were growing up!" Um, so yeah, I would have to dust that kit off, if I could even find it. That's how often it hasn't been used.

I found the farmhouse in the same state I had left it— abandoned. My tires spun out in the gravel as I yanked the steering wheel and turned into the drive. The anger inside was boiling, combined with the resolve of what I had to do. Coming to a screeching halt, I flung open my door, hastily grabbed the papers in my fist, and popped my trunk, not even bothering to close my door let alone shut off the car. Retrieving a hammer and four nails out of my tool kit (at least Dad picked out pink-handled tools), I went back around to the driver's seat and fished a pen out of my purse.

I stormed up the rest of the drive and the sidewalk leading to the porch. Certainly, Nick and the gang would be filming at this location come Wednesday so he was sure to see my correspondence. The fourth and final book in the *Exemption* series, *Resignation*, picks up right where *Liberation* drops off, so I felt secure in my plan. And hey, if some psycho got a hold of the papers and smeared Nick's name, all the better. I climbed the rickety porch stairs and stuck the heads of all four nails in between my lips. Flattening out the papers the best I could against the front door, I signed each and every one, even the one Sarah Alton composed.

As I was signing, I realized the pen I was using was the one I had taken from the Omaha Hilton hotel room in which I had stayed the previous year. I had kept it in my purse all these months, even transferring it when I changed purses. It was just a simple Bic black ink pen, but for the first few months after I had met Nick, every time I looked at that pen I was brought back to our time together. Eventually, the novelty wore off and I didn't think twice about it when I needed to use it for something, yet it still made the move from purse to purse. Well, the Omaha Hilton Bic pen had overstayed its welcome, and so I chucked it out into the brown patchy lawn.

I then picked up the hammer, placed the signed papers against the rotted out siding just to the left of the front door, and drove four nails through them, securing them to the side of the house. I stepped back to admire my handiwork and make sure it was clearly visible to anyone approaching the front of the house, and that's when I heard a not-so-distant vehicle crunching down a road nearby. *Oh crap, crap, crap!*

I literally jumped the four steps off the porch without falling and took off toward my car. The last thing I needed was to get arrested for vandalism on that crappy day. My car was still running, and I hopped in, hearing a dinging sound even after I shut my door. Confused, I looked around the console for what could possibly be making that noise, and I spotted my gaslight on. Of course. I had never actually tested to see just how many miles I could put on that baby between the light coming on and stopping to get fuel, but I'd assumed it was around twenty. Getting back to the highway would take a good ten minutes, and I was not familiar enough with the area to know how far to the nearest station.

The sound of the vehicle getting louder and louder caused me to not worry about the stupid gas and just get the heck out of there. I jammed the gear into reverse and gunned the gas, looking into both side mirrors to navigate. I was almost to the end of the drive when a black Nissan skidded to a halt, blocking the end of the driveway. I slammed on my breaks as hard as I could, coming within an inch of pegging that pristine two-door, tinted-window sports car.

I panicked. What were the chances that I would get assaulted twice in one week? I double-checked to make sure the doors were locked and then flung open my glove compartment, reaching for the mace. I eyed the car through my rearview mirror and could not see a lick through the tinted windows, and the driver had yet to emerge. With the mace in my left hand, I grabbed my phone with my right and pressed the number "9" and then "1" and hovered over the "1" to press again, should this crazy driver present himself/herself.

We sat completely still for a good minute, and the longer the seconds ticked by, the more anxious I became. I decided I would wait another minute, and then I was going to pull forward and see if the car followed me up the driveway or moved on. Either way I planned to just turn around in the dead grass and exit that way. Screw the driveway, although there was quite a ditch on both sides of the drive where it met the gravel road. I silently counted to sixty in my head, checking the mirrors obsessively. When I got to fifty-eight, I gripped the gearshift and depressed the break, ready to kick it into drive.

Just then, I watched the black Nissan shake a little, as if someone was moving inside; and then an interior light illuminated, the top corner of the driver's side door presenting itself just beyond the roof. *Oh no! Oh no! They're getting out!* In a panic, I picked my phone back up and of course had to wake it up to get it back to the dial pad, which had already rid of my previous two number. I dialed the nine and one again, gripped the mace tightly in my palm like a grenade, and stared at my mirror as I saw the top of the driver's head ascend from the vehicle.

I could tell immediately that it was a man based on the cut of hair, but I couldn't tell *what* man until he emerged entirely, exposing the top half of his body over the car's hood. My eyes widened in horror as I watched him slam his door and jog around the front of the Nissan toward my driver's side door. His jaw was clenched, his eyes squinted, and his hair a wreck! He looked pissed. More pissed than I had ever seen him look before. Slowing as he approached my door, he stopped and grabbed hold of the handle, only to find it locked. Then he crouched down so that his face was level with mine, and with the knuckle of his index finger, he rapped three times on the window and ordered, "Get out of the car, Allie."

30

I shook my head in protest, fully aware that in doing so I must've appeared like something akin to a reprimanded toddler. All I needed to do was cross my arms and huff and you could call me Michelle Tanner. This little charade went back and forth for a good thirty seconds before finally I realized that my car idling, even though in park, was doing nothing to conserve gasoline. Finally, with an exaggerated roll of my eyes, I shut off the car, which unlocked the doors; and I emerged from the vehicle, standing face-to-face with Nick Price. It was *then* that I folded my arms and huffed, even managing a tap of my foot. It felt so nice not giving a rip about what Nicholas Price thought of me. In this case, I had been the bigger "man," and I was so thankful he caught me during me pissed-off stage of the grieving process as opposed to the ugly, horn-blaring, sobbing stage earlier.

For the first time since he got out of the car, Nick didn't look so distraught. He even managed to crack a stupid grin.

I hissed, "What are you doing here, loser?" Yes, I know, if you're going to insult someone, "loser" is never your first line of defense. I guess I just wanted to add to my toddler persona.

He chuckled. "Might I ask you the same thing?" in his stupid, sexy Australian accent.

My response? I can't believe I'm going to admit this to you, but think of the most juvenile reply you could possibly come up with and I guarantee that is exactly what I said. Are you ready for it? Okay, here goes: "It's a free country." Yep. I said it. Sure did.

Nick snickered even more at that and countered, "It is indeed, Miss Allie, which is exactly why I am allowed to be here. Especially since this is the set in which I will be filming."

Finished with the back-and-forth nonsense, I finally quipped, "Yep, and your damn papers are on the front of the house. See ya."

I hopped back in my car and started the engine while Nick turned his body to try and see the front of the farmhouse. It was quite a distance away, and the side of the house was more visible from the angle. He turned back toward my car and rapped again with that damn knuckle. This time, I just unrolled my window and lifted my brows.

"What do you mean, *on the house?*" Nick asked.

"I mean *on* the house, Mr. Price. Not *at* the house. Not *in front of* the house. Not *in* the house. Not *over* or *below* the freakin' house. It's *on* the house. Like literally nailed *onto* the house. Now, can you please move that car so I can get home?"

Nick shook his head. "No, I cannot, Allie. I'm sorry, but I'm going to have to ask you to step out of the car again."

"Ha! Show me your badge and your sirens, and I will be happy to. Otherwise, go back to your girlfriend and leave me the hell alone. Now move your car or I'm calling the cops!"

Nick's expression remained amused, which was so darn insensitive. After all he had put me through, why was he patronizing and mocking me with his facial expressions alone?

"Allie"—his voice steadied—"I need you to hear me out, okay? I don't know what you think you saw back there but—" His hand shot up to stop me from speaking just as my mouth opened to do just that. "But, Allie, please give me a second before you respond, if you had actually picked up any of the calls that you got, you would have found out exactly what was going on."

I shook my head and pressed the button to roll up the window. In a flash, my hand was swiped away; and Nick's head and torso were through my window and over my body, and he turned off my car, taking the keys with him. Crap, *that* happened fast. I started to protest, throwing in a few choice words; but by the look on his face, I knew it was no use. I would have no choice but to sit and listen to the garbage he was going to try to feed me.

I stepped back out of the car and said, "Listen, I signed your dumb papers so you don't need to come here and feed me a line of bull so that I don't go telling everybody. I'm not like that." And then I got a little bold and quieter. "Contrary to your new girlfriend." I looked around the property, unable to meet Nick's eyes for that last dig. But hey, it was the truth. Jen *was* the one who ultimately sabotaged his career and my reputation. I had every right to bring her down in front of him. Especially then!

"Allie, I understand you are upset, and if you will just hear me out, you will realize that it is without reason."

I turned my back toward my car and leaned against it, crossing my feet and arms in an I-could-care-less-about-your-rationale position.

Nick wasn't thwarted as he continued. "What you saw back at the hotel was not what you think it was, okay? Jen came to see me because of—"

"Wait a second," I interrupted yet again. "How did you know I was here?" I pointed to the ground at my feet.

Nick inhaled and exhaled slowly, trying to collect his cool before, "If you will just listen for a few minutes, you will know, okay, difficult girl?"

Of course, my eyes got huge, and my teeth clenched. Oh man, I was ready for a fight, but Nick retracted his little insult immediately with his hands raised in surrender and then apologized seven times. I had no choice but to let it go before it had really even began. "Whatever. Just continue, would ya?"

Beginning yet again, he said, "I knew you were here because Jen called and told me. She had been following you while we both were trying to get a hold of you. I had this car coming to the hotel"—he pointed to the Nissan—"right at the time you stormed out, which is why I was leaving the room. I told Jen to follow you while I signed for this rental. We both kept calling you to explain what was going on, but you wouldn't answer. Then Jen told me about that naughty little move you made on the highway that could've gotten you both killed by the way, and when she told me the name of the exit I knew right where you were heading. So, I flew here, going ninety at my slowest. Thank God there were no cops."

He still hadn't gotten to the point at all, but the story was a little entertaining so I remained mum.

"Anyway, so here I am. Now, will you please walk with me up to the house?" Nick asked.

I was taken aback. What kind of question was that? "Um, no. Well, why?"

"Will you just trust me for a few minutes?"

"Ha!" I could barely contain my amusement at the irony. "Yeah, uh-huh. Oh yeah, I will *completely* trust you, Nick. I mean, why would I ever have reason *not* to trust you?"

"Oh, Allie, I would say 'touché,' but the truth is that only *one* of us standing here has ever lied to the other."

Ouch.

"Now listen, even if you don't trust me, please go with me anyway?"

I didn't verbally agree, but I suppose me taking the first steps toward the house was my nonverbal concession. We walked in silence the fifty or so yards to the house, and as we approached the stairs to the porch, I spied the Hilton pen I had thrown in the yard. The whole scenario suddenly struck me as completely asinine. Nick, the man I had longed to see right there in that exact spot was magically there; yet I felt grief, not nostalgia. I had longed to be in his presence, longingly look into his eyes, and had dreamt about it for months and months; yet here he walked, a mere half of a step in front of me, and I didn't *feel* any of those lovesick schoolgirl feelings.

Of course, things were a little unstable and fragile at that moment; but even if they hadn't been—even if he professed his love for me and I for him and we kissed in the kitchen of that old farmhouse—I don't know that there would be fireworks. Not because there wouldn't be chemistry. Oh, quite the contrary; the chemistry between us was so thick you could cut it with a knife, even then when I was mad at him for sleeping with my best friend and he thought I was some psycho stalker girl. No, the reason that there would be no fireworks and it would be nothing like my daydreams about it is because it was *real*. Being in the presence of Nick Price felt real to me. It felt warm, even when I was so mad at him my eyes could bleed, it still felt warm and comfortable— almost like we had known each other for years and years.

So everything I had imagined and longed for when I had come to the farmhouse earlier that afternoon was all just smoke and mirrors. Honestly, had the situation been different and had we patched things up and allowed ourselves to love again, I would have taken reality over the fantasy of what being in love with Nicholas Price should look like. I mean, I just kind of liked the guy. Not at that particular moment, but in general, had he been a regular old Joe Schmo from Topeka, Kansas, I would have felt the exact same way about him. Interesting.

Okay, so back to it, folks. Nick climbed the rickety stairs, and when I didn't follow, he turned and asked, "What?"

"Uh, I don't know. What? Am I supposed to go up there with you? The papers are right there. You really don't need me here. I wasn't lying about them," I defended.

"Come up here, Allie," he pleaded.

It was so strange. Nick Price had not been this nice to me since the previous June. In fact, every interaction I had experienced with him since had been nothing but negative. And here I finally had a reason to be mad and upset with him, and all of a sudden, he's Mr. Nice Guy. What was going on? I had just spoken with him the day before, and he was so incredibly short and rude. Maybe he was bipolar. Another mental note made: "Google 'Nicholas Price bipolar.'" Something was seriously wrong with this man. I mean, first he baits an older woman (a widowed mother, no less); and then he goes MIA for a year, comes back, is all "I'm going to restart my career and so you have to sign blah blah blah," and is mean and hateful about the whole thing. Next, he sleeps with the worst woman in the world who, if he had read what I had published, was psychotic in her own right and Googled naked pictures of him. Talk about a stalker! And now here he was being *nice* to me. Really, Nick? Really?

Allowing my confusion to simmer for a bit, I spat out, "It's locked, Nick. Even the great and powerful Wizard of Hollywood can't get in this house, so why do I need to come up there?" I really was confused, but also a little skittish. I guess the event with Greg *had* affected me more than I wanted to admit initially. Yet another mental note: "Make appointment with shrink. Possible PTSD."

Nick smirked again, and I was struck for the nineteen-thousandth time how amazingly beautiful this man was. I looked at my feet. "Oh really, Allie?" I looked up to see him turning the handle on the front door and opening it.

My eyes wide and mouth agape, it took me a second to formulate what I was going to say. "But I…but it…How did you do that? I was just here, and it was locked."

Nick stepped aside so that I could see the shine of a key poking out of the door handle.

"You have a key? Are you serious? Where did you get that? Do they know you have it?"

Nick chuckled yet again and spoke in a humdrum tone like he was talking to an annoying child with a bad case of the whys. "Yes, Allie, they know I have the key. They're the ones who gave it to me." Without the accent, he could've done a spot-on Ben Stein impression: "Buehler? Buehler? Anyone?" That's how bored he was by my naivety.

Curtailing any further questions, I corrected my posture to stand more astute as to be taken seriously when I stated, "Okay, well, good for you. Now can I go?" But oh, how I wanted to go in that house and look around. I had been dying to do it earlier, and now Nick was actually here, although I cared less about being in the home with him as I did about snooping around and scoping out familiar backdrops for scenes from the movie.

Nick sighed as he walked to the edge of the porch and then descended down the steps to meet me face-to-face. "Allie, I asked you to trust me for a few—" His phone began to ring, interrupting him. He pulled it out of his cargo shorts pocket, checked the screen, and then answered it.

Hmm, obviously someone more important than me.

"Yeah?" he answered. There was a few second pause and then, "Yeah, I know. I'm with her now."

Interesting. I could swear what little I could hear of the voice on the other end of the line sounded male, but Jen was the only plausible person he could be talking to who would understand any references made about me and she certainly didn't sound like a man, did she?

"No, that's okay," Nick continued. "Sorry about all that. I'll make it up to you, bro. Thanks, man." And then he hung up.

More confused than ever, I furrowed my brow questioningly.

"Okay, so are we ready to go inside?" was all Nick asked.

"Um, excuse me? First of all, you were starting to say something about trusting you and then you get on the phone and talk about me with someone? Uh, so, who was *that?*"

"Oh, that was just Stafford. Now will you *please* come here?" Nick asked as he climbed back up the stairs.

Completely bewildered, I followed behind, asking, "Wait, so Mr. Stafford knows I'm here? How does *he* know? Did you call him at home?"

Nick stopped at the doorway and turned to face me. "Nope, I called him in the limo. He's here in town. Well, he *was* here in town. Right now he is leaving Olathe, Kansas."

"What?" I actually yelled, my head shaking adamantly. "Wait, what did you say? Olathe? As in my hometown, Olathe? Why is he there? Did you send him there after you saw me? How could he have gotten there so fast?"

"Easy, girl. Let's just go inside, and maybe things will start to make sense."

My brain could not compute his words, so instead of insisting on clarification, I just followed Nick into the house like a little puppy dog. If I had been feeling out of my body before hand, this whole interaction caused me to feel like I was on the moon. I'm not one who is too keen on the unknown, and so I usually try to mentally map out my future. I remember when I first started my teaching career Terri would get so frustrated with me because as I asked so many questions about lesson plans extending through the end of the school year when it was only August. She would reprimand, "Allie, you don't need to know that yet. Just focus on this week. When this week is over, focus on next week. You can't eat an elephant in one bite. It takes several bites. You can't be working on step C before you conquer step A." Of course, I always countered that one of the seven habits from the Seven Habits of Happy Kids program our school had adopted taught kids to "begin with the end in mind." That's all I was doing after all by asking to see the big picture at the beginning of the year. Although taking both my stress level and that of Terri's at the beginning of the school year, I would suggest she may have been on to something.

My confusion was only compounded when I entered the old run-down farmhouse and immediately caught a whiff of tuberose.

Nick continued to walk through the foyer and into a room off to the right while I stood paralyzed in the doorway. A few seconds later he peaked around the wall and asked, "Are you coming?"

"What is that smell?" I demanded, sounding more paranoid than curious.

"Come on in here and find out," he teased and was out of sight yet again.

Certainly I was only imagining the smell. Why would my favorite scent be in this old farmhouse in Nebraska? I brushed the thought away and treaded carefully in Nick's path. When I rounded the corner, I was met with the most unexpected sight of my life. It would take a lifetime to explain the effect that the entire scene had on my mind and body, so let me just explain exactly what I saw and see if you can internally feel even a fraction of what I did.

There was a square table covered in a shimmery silver tablecloth with two ornate wooden chairs placed across from one another. Each chair had gold-ringed china place settings, complete with three forks and one knife on the left lined up on gold cloth napkins and two spoons on the right. At the head of each plate (which each cradled a matching salad plate), was an empty ornate glass snuggled next to a crystal wine glass, a knife tucked square underneath the top of the plate. Although the wine glasses sat empty, a bottle of expensive-looking Chardonnay nestled in an ice-filled bucket off to the side.

There was a pewter candelabra placed in the center of the table with twelve gold tapers burning silently in their sockets, and eight tiny water-filled glass bowls encircled the base, each containing various colors of floating *tuberose*! At the sight of this little detail, my eyes filled with salty liquid. I choked down a sob and continued to scan the display.

The remainder of the table was ordained with colorful flower petals, the type from which they were plucked I knew not. Resting on the place setting closest to where I was standing was a single red rose with a white tag tied around the stem with twine. The side of the tag I could see was embossed in gold with the name "Allie." Last but certainly not least was the haggard gentleman standing behind the adjacent place setting, his hands gripping the back of the chair. Finally, I met his eyes in complete and utter astonishment. Though my questions were many, I decided it may finally be time to let the man speak—uninterrupted.

I blinked several times to clear my clouded mind, thinking that with every blink the hallucinations would disappear and the image of the perfectly set table with the beautiful man standing behind it would clear. Surely, the aroma of my favorite flower would diminish if I just concentrated hard enough, and the newly discovered soft piano music playing in the background would quiet. *Focus, Allie, Focus!*

Each time I pried my eyelids back open, the backdrop was still the same, although after a few repetitions, with the tears gliding effortlessly down my cheeks, the blue eyes I was unable to turn away from became moistened themselves. I managed a bewildered smile and a cock of my head, indicating I was ready for an explanation.

And that is when Nick hoarsely said, "Please…sit down" while gesturing toward my chair. As I slowly stepped toward the table, Nick strode around from his previous post and pulled out the chair for me. Amazed, I glued my eyes to his as I sat lightly, allowing him to tuck my chair back under the table before releasing my full weight into it. With his hand still on the back of his chair and his fully glossed eyes peering back at mine, he paused for a good twenty seconds, letting whatever emotion was being unspoken between the two of us swell within our souls.

As desperate as I was to reach up and grab him, despite not having yet been given an explanation for the hotel incident with him and Jen, I kept my hands clasped in my lap until finally he retreated to the other side of the table, taking a seat himself. I adjusted my position to feel more comfortable and rested my left forearm on the table, scanning the utensils with my fingertips. Finally, Nick cleared his throat, and I looked back up into those alluring baby blues, bracing myself for whatever was to come next.

342

31

Nick positioned himself in a way that with both of his forearms on the table, he could lean in enough to close the gap between us a little, making the impending conversation seem more intimate. In a soft voice, still hoarse from the tears that had been wiped away with the back of his hand once they finally tipped over the edge, he began.

"I'm sure—" He cleared the croaking frog from his throat and began again. "I'm sure you are completely confused at this point, Allie." Nick paused, still looking into my eyes as if waiting for affirmation.

Of course, I was a fumbling fool and didn't realize that's what he was doing until a half second before he began again. It was like when you are really interested in someone's story, and they pause after they ask, "You know?" and you don't respond verbally or nonverbally because you are just so engrossed in the story and expecting them to go on.

But alas, I did nod, albeit a little after the fact, so he continued. "Let me just start by saying that Jen had no ill intentions in coming to see me today. I had no clue she was coming to see me, and it scared the s—— out of me when I got called down to the lobby to meet with someone who had come to see me. I got off the elevator, and there stood that disheveled woman who I recognized but couldn't quite place. I couldn't remember how I knew her, but the panic that I felt when I looked at her told me it wasn't a good acquaintance. Finally, she introduced herself, and I just about called the cops."

I chuckled the nasally laugh that comes out when someone is trying to cheer me up after a good cry. My sister Maggie is the queen of inducing this particular laugh. It always felt so good, and this time was no different. In fact, it struck me that this was the first time I had laughed all day.

"Seriously!" Nick continued. "I'm not even joking. That woman scares me!"

I laughed harder and harder, my eyes flooding once again.

Finally, when I could compose myself, Nick went on to say, "She was very quiet at first, acting afraid or something. I finally had to ask what she was doing here, and that's when she told me it was about you. I kind of panicked, thinking something terrible had happened to you. Well, something terrible *had* happened to you, but I thought you died or something. The lass at the desk was being quite nosy, and so I invited Jen up to my room."

"*My* room," I corrected, pointing at my chest.

"Oh, you noticed, huh? Yeah, *your* room. Actually, how about *our* room?"

My face flushed hot, and I looked back down at the rose in the center of the plate set before me.

Nick continued. "So anyway, when I brought her up to the room, I had her sit at the desk chair while I sat on the recliner. Neither one of us were ever on the bed, Allie, contrary to what you may have thought. I made sure that she didn't get any ideas because I really didn't know why she had come. But then she explained everything."

"Everything?" I asked.

"Yeah. She began her story back when she and you first got into the *Exemption* saga and how you were kind of incredulous in the beginning that anyone could bring justice to the character of Wesley, and even after you had seen my picture, you were still skeptical. That really made me laugh. Then she told me that while you both enjoyed going to see each movie together and chatting about the series, she was the one who was way more into it than you. She said you were far more grounded in reality and focused on your life with Sam. She also said that the idea to come to Omaha last year was all hers. Does this all sound pretty accurate to you?"

I simply nodded.

"So then she said that when you decided to come without her, after all of that crap with the louse of a husband she was married to, you weren't even thinking about me or meeting me, that you really *did* just need a break. She went on to tell me that you weren't some crazy lunatic fan who was stalking me, that the lunatic stalker title belonged to her." Nick grinned.

I remained unmoving, stunned.

"Anyway," he continued to say, "Jen was crying and going on and on about how you are truly an amazing inspirational person and that I would be crazy if I didn't try and get you back and that you only lied because you were caught off guard by actually meeting me. She told me about how accepting and including you had always been of her, even though she was your husband's ex and how you were the most selfless, caring woman she had ever known."

Tears toppled over my ducts yet again. I wiped them away with fingers.

Nick paused for a few beats, seeming to collect his breath and his thoughts. Finally, he looked down at his place setting as well and lowly said, "And she told me about what happened with that son of a b—— Greg." His jaw clenched, and I could see the vein within pulsing. After a few beats, he looked back up into my eyes and the dampness in his eyes illuminated the brightness of his blue eyes. I had never seen them so piercing before; even with the lighting and Photoshop tricks of Hollywood, no one had been able to capture the exact hue of those eyes I couldn't believe I was looking into. "Allie, I'm so, so sorry. If only I'd have known, I would have stopped him. I just…I just had to figure some things out and—"

I began vehemently shaking my head and cried out, "No, Nick. No, this wasn't your fault. There was nothing you could have done, no way you could have known. Why are you blaming yourself?"

"Because, Allie!" Nick was very convicted. "Because of me, you ran into the arms of that animal. Had I not turned you away in LA or, for that matter, last summer when I was in your home, you never would have been put in that situation!"

Oh man, I needed to step back a second. What on earth was going on? Everything had been turned on its head, and as someone who liked to know what the future looked like, I was certainly being met with changeups around every curve. One minute I am nailing stupid papers (papers that fall just short of a restraining order, mind you) on the front of an old farmhouse in Middle-of-Nowhere, Nebraska, while all evidence indicates that Nick is shagging my former best friend, and then the next minute I'm sitting in that same farmhouse with Nick himself who is showering me with apologies and affection. Nothing in my little corner of the world was making sense.

My bewilderment must have been portrayed on my face because Nick became quiet and scrutinized me for a second before asking, "Are you okay, Allie? Is this too much?"

Shaking my head, my eyes not focused on any one single thing in that room but rather on some make-believe place somewhere, I answered, "I…I don't know. Um, I don't understand what is happening. None of this makes any sense." I fiddled with the tag affixed to the rose stem, flipping it over. On the reverse side were more gold embossed letters. They spelled out "I'm sorry!"

"What do you mean? None of what?" Nick's tone and expression suggested worry.

"Um, any of this." I gestured across the expanse of the table and refocused on Nick's eyes. "Please understand that none of this makes sense to me. I mean, did *you* do this?" I gestured again to the scene before me.

Nick chuckled. "What do you mean? Of course I did this. Who did you think did it?"

"Okay, so you need to understand that while your brain may have been thinking or planning this for a while, my brain is going to need a little time to catch up. The last I knew you hated me and wanted me to sign my life away so as to never see you again. And then Jen's in your hotel room. And then now here you are. And then this…" I gestured one last time. I was so overwhelmed, and my shaky voice did nothing to betray that fact.

Nick's face changed with sudden understanding. "Oh my gosh, Allie! You're right." He reached across the table and grabbed my hand, his touch sending electric currents through my body. Was I dreaming? "Okay, so let me back up just a bit further, and maybe that will help clear some things up. Does that sound like a good idea?"

I nodded, my eyes transfixed on his warm hand enveloping mine, his thumb soothingly rubbing back and forth.

"Right after I left your hotel room in LA, I was sick with grief. Seeing you again brought back every pang of yearning and adoration I had felt the day I met you. I wasn't expecting that at all. I expected my anger with you and the feelings of betrayal would sustain my resolve for the duration of the time you were in town, but it was just too hard. I couldn't take it and I wanted nothing more than to be with you, so I decided I would go to the airport to see you off and confess all these feelings I was having. I thought it would be completely romantic…like something out of the *movies*!" Nick grinned, amused with his sarcastic, ooh-la-la movie reference.

I squeezed his hand in mine, encouraging his honesty and silly wit.

"I got to the airport with an hour or so to spare before your flight was set to take off because I figured you would have allowed plenty of time given that it is only, you know, the busiest airport in the world and all."

"Oh my gosh!" I covered my mouth with my unattended hand, suddenly recollecting the airport event. "That's right! I overslept, and Mr. Stafford literally had to wake me up. And I was so late, and then I saw you! I did, Nick. I saw you! Did you see me?"

Nick giggled and then presented his free hand, of which I was beckoned to take hold. With both of my hands nestled snugly in his, he continued. "Of course I saw you! I had been panicking that you were gonna miss your flight and then not make it home to Sam and then I thought maybe something bad had happened because I kept calling Stafford and he wasn't answering. I started running around the airport, thinking…*hoping* you just had the wrong gate. All the while, I was obsessively calling Stafford until finally he answered. He told me you were running really late and that he had just dropped you off and of course I was on the opposite side of the bloody airport by then so I ran like mad to see you off and was too late."

"No, you weren't," I interjected. "I *saw* you." I didn't even realize the tears were streaming once again. They were tears of wonderment and the gift of grace.

The two of us sat staring into one another's flooding eyes, silently communicating words that had been stored within for twelve months' time. Words of pain and regret. Words of forgiveness and healing. Words of love and admiration.

I was the one who finally broke the silence and asked, "Okay, so I don't get it. How did you even get into the airport? I mean, you were past security?"

"Oh, that." Nick gave me his sexy, sly grin. "Well, you see, plane tickets don't cost all *that* much…"

"You bought a flippin' plane ticket just so you could see me off?"

"Indeed."

I shook my head in disbelief and then asked, "Okay, well then, what was with the snarkiness when you called yesterday?"

"Snarkiness?" he asked, puzzled.

"Yeah, you know, you were rude to me!"

Nick laughed. "Oh, that!" He allowed his eyes to look all around the room, feigning innocence. "*That*, my dear"—his eyes met mine once again, and self-assuredly, he bragged—"was all part of my plan."

My eyebrows rose inquisitively.

"I needed to make sure you were going to be home today, and so I had to figure out a way to do it without tipping you off to my master plan."

"What are you talking about?"

"This," he said, mimicking my earlier gesture pertaining to the scene in which we sat. "I've been planning this since I left your hotel room in LA. I needed to find a way to see you again and tell you how I feel, and it *had* to be in person. After you left LA, I had a long conversation with Charlotte about you…"

It took me a second to figure out who Charlotte was.

"And she told me that you had asked about me. Oh man, I got so excited when she said that. I thought you hated my guts, but since you had asked about me and about the possibility of there being other gals in my life, I figured…well, I…" Nick's cheeks were flushing pink.

I smiled, his vulnerability both endearing and painfully sexy. So sexy, in fact, that I refused to let him off the hook and reveal that of course I still had feelings for him.

He squirmed a little in his seat and then, looking down at our interlocked hands, concluded, "I guess I figured maybe you still cared?" He squinted up at me like a child, unsure if they are about to receive a punishment.

Deciding I really wanted him to squirm for another few seconds, I answered, "Well, um, I don't know, Nick. I mean, whew, it's been a long year." I pulled my hands away from his and sank back into my chair, faking exhaustion and fatigue from the trying year. "Whew-wee, it's been a doozy. I just don't know if I *can* care anymore, ya know?"

I looked into his shell-shocked eyes and could not contain my amusement at his discomfort. I started howling in laughter, clapping my hands repeatedly. "Oh my gosh, you should see your face!" I exclaimed. "I got you *so* good, Nick."

He was grinning from ear to ear, shaking his hung head back and forth in disbelief.

"Seriously though, *that* is payback for the revolving door!"

At the reminder, Nick burst out in laughter as well. We laughed and laughed for what seemed like eternity until, almost as if on cue, our laughter tempered and we reached across the table to once again grab each other's hands. When we had laughed ourselves out, Nick picked back up his dissertation. "Okay, so where was I? Oh yeah, I had just gotten to the point where I knew you were still smitten for me, and so I decided to concoct this big plan." He winked and then continued. "Right after you flew out, I called my agent and told him the whole deal with those stupid contracts was off. I didn't want your signature on any of them, and I told him I had every intention of trying to get you back. Of course, we went round and round about this for a while, but like always, he came to see things my way."

"Wow, cocky much?" I chided.

"Only when I know what I want," Nick responded, cold-stone serious.

My heart literally stopped, and I could feel my loins—yes, I said my loins (though I don't actually know what loins are, but I'm fairly certain I could feel them)—constricting and pulsating.

"So once he was on board, I made the arrangements to come to Omaha and get the key to the farmhouse. We actually aren't set to begin filming for a few more weeks. I was banking on the signed papers being enough to indicate if you were going to be in town or not. I figured if you weren't, then you wouldn't have had the papers with you or been able to fax them. So then I flew in last night to get everything arranged here, and then I sent Stafford to Olathe to pick you up and bring you to me. Of course, *that* part of my plan got royally screwed when your friend showed up just as I was heading out to finalize the details here. And then *you*! Oh my gosh, when you showed up, I was so confused. I thought, 'Now wait just a second! There is no way Stafford could already be back with her!' I mean, he had only left an hour before. And then, well, I guess you kind of know the rest."

I was paralyzed by the substance and weight of all that was being revealed. I didn't even know what to say let alone formulate words to expel from my lips. I just kept slowly shaking my head from side to side, my eyes wide with wonder.

Nick cleared his throat and began yet again. "There is something I do have to tell you though, Allie. It's very important to me that you know this." He studied my eyes, obviously looking for affirmation; but I seriously was paralyzed, friends, incapable of a coherent response. He continued anyway. "I didn't stay away because of you. I mean, initially I *went* away because of you. I was so caught off guard and distraught over the whole thing. Allie, I had never in my life felt the feelings I had felt in the short time that I had known you. I went from zero to sixty in a matter of *minutes* when it came to falling for you. And then when it was revealed that quite possibly every single thing I had felt or thought was a lie, well, I just couldn't...I..." His voice cracked, and so he paused, trying desperately not to break down.

Finally, my dumbass self came *to* enough to try and comfort the man, albeit just in the form of my thumb rubbing the back of his hand. Hey, you get what you get, and you don't throw a fit, okay?

Composing himself, he restarted what he was saying. "Anyway, I couldn't deal with it, so I went home. I didn't plan to stay so long, but once I was there, I realized there were some things I needed to take care of before I came back. You see, when I found out you lied to me, it brought up a whole ton of crap that I'd never dealt with in regard to my pops. Without getting all 'psychological' on you, my dad was a huge dick when I was growing up. First of all, he was never around. Second, he cheated on my mom, and I was the one who found out first. He was secretly talking on the phone to this woman in secret, and I innocently picked up another phone in the house to call a friend. I heard all sorts of thing that a preteen boy should never hear. Anyway, in the end, my mom forgave him. But I never did…until I went back to Australia last summer."

Oh, this poor man. I had no idea that my betrayal was exacerbated exponentially by the fact that he had harbored past betrayals for a number of years. I didn't know what to say to bring comfort. Luckily, I didn't have to.

"But now, Allie…oh, Allie, now I realize what a tremendous blessing it was. I know this probably sounds so bizarre, but you lying to me was the best thing that could have possibly happened to me and my family. When I got home and I was heartbroken, my mom was pissed at you. Boy, was she ever pissed." He smiled and shook his head as I felt embarrassment and guilt. "See, I had already told her all about you, and she *knew* how intensely I felt for you. So when her little boy comes home heartbroken…well, you can understand, can't you?"

I knew he was looking for a response, and so I gave him the best one I could muster, "Well, I *do* have a little boy, and I *would* kill any girl who would hurt him so… "

Nick laughed and then said, "Okay, so you *do* get it! Well, Mum and I talked quite a bit about the whole thing, and to her dismay as well as mine, she couldn't make it better. My mum could *always* make things better. I honestly think she just got sick of my whining because one day my dad came into my room to talk with me. Of course, I didn't want to talk to him 'cause to me, *he* was the epitome of a betrayer. But in talking to him, things began to clear up in my mind. And for the first time since I was a boy, I realized how much I had missed the man and how remorseful he actually *had* been for what he had done. I learned so much from my pops this past year, and we spent so much time together just being and, well, healing. I forgave him, Allie. I *forgave* him! That was so huge for me. And he…" Nick's voice cracked again. He swallowed audibly and concluded, "He taught me how to forgive *you*! It's my dad, Allie, who has encouraged me to follow my heart and win you back!"

I inhaled sharply. *Win me back?*

"So here we are, and my plans got a little thwarted when Jen showed up to tell me all the reasons why I needed to run back to you. Of course I shared my already-in-place plan with her, and she was over-the-moon excited for you, not thinking you'd just show up yourself, of course. Jen and I had a really nice conversation and her story and the way she talked about you shed some light on some things. She really does love you, Allie, and I think she's actually beginning to feel the weight of her actions as she becomes more, what's the word, well, 'lucid', if you will. She is having a really hard time forgiving herself for what she did to you, which is why she came here. To try and fix it, make things better for you."

I was still having a hard time gripping reality as I sat motionless. I could tell Nick was getting a little antsy being the only one saying anything because every time he would pause for some sort of response only to be denied, he'd scoot around in his chair, tap his foot, or bite his lip. He didn't know how to read *me*, and *I* didn't know how to read the situation. It was all just so unreal.

When I finally couldn't take his discomfort any longer, I forced myself to seek answers to a few questions that had been nagging at me for quite some time. First, I asked, "Okay, so when you first called me about coming to LA and meeting with your

PR guy, did you want me back then? 'Cause you sure could have fooled me if you did!"

Nick snorted, obviously thankful for my involvement in the conversation. "Allie, I never *didn't* want you back! From the moment I met you until this very second, I have wanted to be with you. Now, was I willing to *act* on it at that point? Hmm, well, I don't know. I knew I wanted to see you and my PR guys really did need those papers signed but, well, maybe now is as good of time as any to confess that I haven't been the most honest person in the world either."

Taken aback, I began to pull my hands away from his, concerned about where this might lead.

"No, no. It's not *that* big of a lie. Well, actually maybe it is, but it didn't seem that way at the time. I just needed to see you, and those papers really *did* need to be signed. The thing is that they…well…"

Spit it out already!

"They didn't necessarily need to be signed *in person?*" He formed it as a question, although it was in no way, shape, or form a question. He shrugged his shoulders and gave the toothiest schoolboy grin I have ever seen, trying hard to keep from being in trouble.

I let it slide. I guess he owed me one.

"I thought that by seeing you," Nick continued, "it would make it easier to get over you, bring some sort of closure. I wasn't prepared to fall in love with you all over again."

Ding! Ding! Ding! The room went black for a split second, a cold sweat breaking out on my forehead.

"Oh my word, are you okay, Allie? You look terrified!"

"What did you just say?" I whispered.

"I said, 'You look terrified!'"

"No." I shook my head. "Before that."

Nick swallowed forcefully, suddenly aware of what I was referring to. Obviously, it had unknowingly just slipped out. "Um,

I, uh. Actually, you know what? I'm not afraid to say it again, damn it. I'm in love with you, Allie. I am! I fell in love with you the very night I met you, and a day hasn't gone by in which I haven't thought about you constantly. And that's the honest-to-God truth. No lies. No manipulation of the truth. No dishonesty. Allison Belle Holly, I am wholeheartedly madly in love with you, and I don't want another day to go by in my lifetime without you by my side."

Another minor blackout. Cold sweat. Heart pounding.

"How's that for honesty, eh?" Nick laughed nervously.

Breathe in two, three, four and out two, three, four...

EPILOGUE

"Mom, would you please hurry?" Sam yelled, extremely impatiently I might add. Nine has *not* been a pretty number on him. I remember when he was born everyone would warn me, "Oh, just wait until the terrible twos!" I prayed extraordinarily hard the week leading up to his second birthday because at eighteen months, he had turned into a holy terror. I couldn't even imagine what two would look like. Surprisingly though, two was actually easier than eighteen months. And then came three! Dun, dun, dun! By five, I realized, and confirmed with all my mommy friends, that the even numbers were worse for girls and the odd worse for boys. Nine is shaping up to be quite a doozy for Mr. Sam.

I shuffled down the stairs in my bathrobe and my hair wrapped in a towel. I couldn't even remember the last time I had enjoyed a nice, hot, leisurely shower lasting longer than four minutes. "What is it, bud? I'm soaking wet here!"

"I'm just sick of doing this. This is *not* how I planned on spending my spring break! All my friends get to go someplace cool like Hawaii or on a Disney cruise and I'm stuck here. It's not fair," he whined. Oh, it grated on my ever-loving nerves when he whined like that.

I was tired, too tired to have patience for a whiny nine-year-old, but I completely understood how he was feeling. And if I weren't so darned harried all the time, I might have taken the few seconds it would have required to show some compassion and sensitivity to my beloved oldest child, but alas, I did not. Instead, I countered, "Get over it, Sam. Sometimes ya just gotta suck it up!"

"Whoa, whoa, whoa, easy there, mean Mama," a sleepy voice said from the bottom of the staircase. "My main man's got a point, ya know? It isn't very fair, is it, Sam Man?"

Sam beamed up at his adoptive dad, thankful for the rescue.

"Easy for you to say, Mr. Snore-So-Loud-All-Night-I-Never-Hear-the-Babies-Crying!"

"What? Who, me?" Nick looked around the expansive hardwood living room, feigning ignorance. Of course, he got a rise out of Sam, who giggled so loud that baby Grace woke up wailing.

"And she's yours!" I exclaimed, pointing to Nick and heading back up the stairs.

As I padded across the catwalk, I looked down to see Nick unstrapping Grace from her bouncy seat, which had been in need of new batteries for over a week yet somehow not a single one of us had made the effort to replace them. Instead, I just made the grumpy nine-year-old manually bounce it when she got fussy, which was all the time!

Nick cooed and softly spoke in a high-pitched voice to sweet Grace, "Hey, baby girl. Who's her daddy's girl? Who's my beautiful girl?" while he rubbed noses with her.

He sat down next to Sam and asked, "All right, bud, what's on the agenda for today? I'm pickin' up what you're puttin' down about the lame spring break deal, okay. So let's make the best of it together, all right, mate?"

Sam curled up next to Nick, laying his head on his shoulder and placing his index finger in the palm of Grace's hand, which she would instinctively coil around his finger. "I don't know. I just don't want to sit at home all day."

"I hear ya. I hear ya. Here's the deal. I know this…well, right now this just kind of—" Nick looked around to make sure I was out of sight. He didn't bother to look up onto the catwalk. "It just *sucks*, doesn't it?" Ha. That stinker, using words I don't allow Sam to say to win him over.

Sam giggled and nodded profusely. "Yeah, it really does suck," he whispered.

When the cat's away…I had half a notion to holler a reprimand down to the both of them, but not wanting to interrupt their bonding, I remained mum. I still had to pinch myself time and time again to remind myself that I wasn't actually dreaming. This really *was* my life! Oh, how incredibly blessed I felt.

As I continued to witness the people I loved most on earth talk and tease each other, I reflected back on the previous two years. My memories traveled back to that sweet farmhouse in which I sat across from Nick as he poured his heart out to me. What I didn't know when I entered the house is that Nick had a whole team of people holed up in the kitchen waiting to serve us an amazing five-course meal complete with fresh lobster tail he had specially flown in from Maine that morning and the biggest, ripest, chocolate-dipped strawberries for dessert. Apparently, there was a trailer parked out of sight on the property where the food had been prepared. Nick thought he had more time as I wasn't expected to arrive after my "kidnapping" until the sun went down. When I showed up unannounced and his plans got thwarted, he sent Jen to follow me and communicate my whereabouts so that when he finally got behind the wheel, he could try and catch me.

He was none too relieved when Jen shouted on the phone that I had turned off at the Plattsmouth exit, knowing full well where I would be headed. For his scheme becoming such a mess, he was incredibly grateful that my sneaky move off the highway actually ended up in his favor. One way or the other, he was going to get me to that farmhouse, and alas, no kidnapping or high-speed car chases had to ensue to get that result. On the way to the house himself, Nick called his people and directed them to get ready because their performance had just been bumped up a few hours. Luckily, they stayed in the trailer until I was already in the house with Nick or else they would have scared the bejesus out of me when I was hammering nails into the house.

Part of what I came to understand that day is that Nick's feelings for me had never actually changed. He never actually read my publication until the flight back to the States from Australia. Since I was coming to LA to meet with him, he chose to finally read it, gathering as much insight as he could so he could make a truly informed decision about what he wished to happen with the two of us. Apparently, reading my story brought forth emotions he was not expecting, and it served to solidify his madly-in-love feelings toward me. The problem was that he didn't know how I felt. I had told him that I might bring a man with me to LA, and so he feared I had moved on. And of course, I offered him no real clues that weekend as to what my heart was feeling or if my affections had wavered. So basically, the two of us were just playing games with each other that whole weekend, trying to feel the other one out.

He *did* say that the accommodations made for me from the time I left Kansas City until my return were no accident. The flight crew as well as the hotel staff had very specific instructions on how to treat me and what I was to be served. Nick himself stocked the fridge at the hotel with my favorites. And as for the tuberose? Was it a coincidence or had he really known? I'll get to that in a second.

Sam looked up at Nick and sighed. Nick asked, "What is it, Sam Man?"

After a beat, Sam responded, "I don't know. I just…well, I'm just curious about something."

"Oh?" Nick asked.

"Yeah. Um…" Sam nervously chuckled, his face turning pink. Of course, my heart did all sorts of funky maneuvers. It clenched in dread for my son's discomfort and danced for the intimacy of two of the men I adored so much.

"It's okay, bud. Don't be nervous about it. You can ask me *anything* at any *time*. You know that, don't you?"

Sam squirmed. "Yeah, I guess. It's just that…well, do you… um, do you like me as much as you do them?" he asked, pointing to Grace who was back asleep in Nick's arms and to the empty baby swing across the room.

Yes, my friends, there certainly *is* a "them!" After Nick and I spilled our guts all over that table in the farmhouse, he proposed, although it wasn't an official proposal. He had purchased the most beautiful silver tennis bracelet with a carat weight I didn't want to know. Having been holding both of my hands throughout the duration of our soul-bearing love fest, he released one hand to adjust something in his pants. I figured either his phone was buzzing or he was being a typical guy who adjusts at the most inopportune times. When he brought his arm back up onto the table, I thought nothing of it until I felt something cold press against my knuckles. I looked down, and a shiny silver bracelet draped around my wrist, the sparkle of its diamonds dancing in the caught candlelight.

As I gawked in wonder, Nick slowly spoke, "Allie, I really do want to spend the rest of my life with you. I think promise rings are cheesy, and I refuse to officially propose to you before I meet your precious son and your family and have a chance to formally ask your parents for their blessing. But this bracelet *is* a symbol of my unending affection, and I would be so incredibly honored if you would give considerable thought to walking through this life with me by your side."

Talk about a whirlwind of a day! I had awakened that morning nervous about heading to Omaha, afraid he would call the police and have me arrested for stalking. Then the honking and the highway escape, the nailing on the house, and the impending "attack" by some mysterious stranger in a tinted-window black Nissan. And the next thing I know, Nicholas Freakin' Price is more or less asking me to marry him! Am I on crack or what?

The best part is that after he finished his soul-baring, I responded with, "I'll think about it."

Ha! How cruel, but I think he understood my intentions. I really *did* need some time to think about everything and communicate with my family about this sudden plot changer. In addition, I had some major soul searching to do in terms of Sam and what I really wanted for him and for *myself*! I mean, of course I loved the guy; that had never changed. But there's a lot more to marriage and family than love. (I know some of you hopeless romantics are out there screaming, "All you need is love!")

New love is wonderful and exciting and enticing, while familiar love is comfortable, safe, and secure. I had no doubt that Nick and I were capable of working out the details and kinks of our lives so that we could continue our new love and nurture it until it transformed into familiar love. *But*—and this is a big *but*!—I already had a main love in my life, and *he* was where my allegiance lied. My decisions no longer cast down consequences on me alone. Sam would have to reside in the shadows of my decisions, and so in making them, I needed to consider Sam and his wishes, thoughts, behaviors, and feelings actually *more* than my own. I'd already *had* my time in the throes of influence and experience. I'd been blessed with a phenomenal upbringing surrounded by the most incredible people in the world whose influence on me sculpted the woman I had become. I wanted nothing less for my sweet Samuel Christopher, and I *owed* him as much. I owed *Chris* as much. When I got pregnant with Sam, I made a vow to my heavenly husband that I would love and protect our child at all costs and would do my best to make the wisest choices on his behalf. Not even a crazy-hot, insanely famous movie star could come in the way of upholding those vows.

So I kept the bracelet, and when we finished our evening together, I assured Nick that my heart was in the exact same place as was his and he was more than understanding and accommodating with my wishes to take some time to process. We commenced the evening with the mind-numbing kiss that only Nicholas Price can give, and I drove home, contrary to his wishes that I get a room at the hotel. I had some big-time thinking to do.

Of course, the next day I could hardly contain myself and immediately called my sister Maggie, absolutely freaking out about the previous day's events. It literally took her three minutes to understand even one word I was saying because of the over-the-top shrill and pure speed of my words. Even as racy as I was speaking, it wasn't nearly fast enough to keep up with my thoughts. She finally had to actually *beg* me to stop talking and breathe in for four seconds and out for four seconds, during which time she asked, "Allie, are you in jail? Are you hurt?"

Ha! That's what she had taken away from my manic rant. She hadn't heard *one single word*. When I finally calmed down enough to relay as much as I could remember, Maggie became every bit as intelligible as I had been, shrieking and whizzing through her thoughts. Finally I let her go so that I could call our mom, which I knew I had to do immediately because Maggie could only hold on to gossip of this magnitude so long before she would burst into flames.

The rest of the day was filled with hashing the whole thing out time and time again with the various members of my family. My dad drove Sam home so that I could have the evening to talk with him about the whole thing, and while they were in transit, I called Jen. Man, did I owe that woman some fierce apologies, but she wouldn't have it. She completely understood where I had been coming from and was just so thankful that I finally understood her intentions for being in Omaha. By her voice, I could tell that she was thrilled beyond belief for me. While I had no intention of asking her to be my maid of honor, in that conversation I could see, for the first time in over a year, how our broken relationship could very well be mended. It felt so good to have hope in that friendship.

Sam was over the moon when I told him about my weekend and my rekindled romance with Nick (of course, I spared him any "That's embarrassing, Mom" details). He was especially excited to finally meet Nick, who would come to not only win Sam over but who was also instantly as big of a Sam fan as I was! The wit and compassion that I so admired in my young son was identified and commended by Nick the first time they met. How someone could not only pick up on character traits of a seven-year-old they had just met but could also then bring out the best in these traits was beyond me. But that was who Nick was: a man who never ceased to surprise me with his grounded intuition. Nick and Sam got along so well, in fact, that oftentimes it was yours truly who became the third wheel. After hitting it off immediately, the two of them continued to grow closer in their relationship and deeper in their understanding of one another, a result I could have never predicted in my wildest imagination. I always possessed a sense of hesitancy when it came to considering romantic relationships as Sam and I were so close and I was afraid a third party may not be a welcome addition. Moreover, I figured someone of Nick's caliber and young age would lack a certainly maturity that it takes to settle down and raise a family. Boy, was I ever wrong. In fact, sometimes I felt like Nick possessed more maturity and wisdom in his pinky finger than I did in my entire being. My two loves were so close in fact that when Nick asked for Sam's blessing to marry me as well as my dad's, Sam squealed, "It's about time!"

Nick and I officially got engaged on Christmas Eve that year in my parents' family room with my whole family in attendance. He finished taping *Resignation* in late September and moved into an apartment in Olathe. Making the sole decision that the

Hollywood life was not the life in which he felt called to immerse himself, he became very selective about the projects to which he committed and had strict demands written into each contract. Of utmost importance in those demands was that he was to never be away from home for more than five days at a time and would do absolutely no filming on weekends. In addition, Sam and I were to be not only allowed to travel with him but also to be treated as welcome guests on each and every set. If they couldn't adhere to his wishes, Nick had no qualms at all about rejecting the offer.

When he wasn't on location filming, he dedicated his time to opening a nonprofit performing arts studio for underprivileged kids, right in the heart of Kansas City. With my vast knowledge and experience with children and Nick's innate gifts of theater and music, together we opened the Christopher Holly Performing Arts Center on April Fool's Day in 2014. To date, we have given scholarships to over four hundred impoverished children in the greater Kansas City area.

As if that wasn't enough to keep us busy, two days after Nick proposed (complete with a five-carat diamond ring, lots of tears, and Nick on bended knee while the female members of my family swooned), we began wedding planning, the realization that five months was *not* enough time to throw together a wedding slapping me upside the head! Luckily, I had taken for granted the status of *who* I was marrying and was quickly ordained with two wedding planners, a stylist, and a personal assistant—not to mention my own two sisters, sister-in-law, and mother to see to the more personal details.

The wedding took place in my home church in Topeka, the exact location of my previous wedding to Chris. It was flawless to say the least. How could it not be with Hollywood's most prestigious planners and coordinators running the show and Hollywood's most talked-about stars in attendance? It was quite the amazing spectacle and completely overwhelming to this Midwestern mama, that's for sure. Luckily, Charlotte had come to give me daily massages the week before the wedding, and Nick, Sam, and I snuck in some alone time as often as we could.

Nick's family had flown in two weeks before the wedding, and they blended perfectly with my family. I couldn't have asked for a better communion. Nick and I had flown to Australia together over New Year's, and any fear or anxiety I had leading up to the meeting of his family was dispelled the moment I walked off the airplane and his mom literally *ran* to me and gave me the warmest, tightest embrace of my life. His family dynamics were so similar to mine that I knew there would be no problems bringing them all together for the wedding.

Nick and I wrote our own vows and bawled like babies throughout the whole ceremony. My sisters and Christy served as my bridesmaids while Sam, Stafford, and one of Nick's friends from his childhood stood up with him. Jen actually did have a small part in the festivities as I asked her to greet guests in the foyer and encourage them to sign the guestbook. Every word and deed performed during the ceremony was packed full of meaning and sentimentality and right after he "kissed the bride," Nick reached up into my hair and unclasped the white tuberose pinned above my right ear. He then affixed it behind my left ear, a Hawaiian gesture indicating I was officially taken. The crown roared with delight, and one by one, all stood to extend a standing ovation. It was hilarious and overwhelmingly heartfelt all at once.

At our over-the-top, only-in-Hollywood (but actually in Topeka) reception at the Ritz, we partied hard and danced into the night. People ate like kings and gossiped like crazy, and my sisters rubbed elbows with Nick's famous chums, some of whom were young enough to be their sons! And of course, in addition to the parting gifts in the form of two airline tickets *per person* to Maui, each guest also received a fragrant tuberose in a crystal bud vase, the weight of its meaning not lost on even one guest.

So the tuberose…

One thing I just *had* to know before I left the farmhouse was what, if any, significance should be attached to Nick continuing to bestow upon me my very favorite flower. I had to know if it was just a crazy coincidence or if he had indeed known that the tuberose held special meaning for me. At first he feigned ignorance, insisting, "What? That's your *favorite*? I had no idea!" But after threatening to throw the expensive bracelet at him and walk out, he finally knew the jig was up and spilled the beans. Apparently, sometime in the first few days after we met, when Nick had been showering me with roses, the count indicative of the number of hours we had known one another, he got the brilliant idea to try and find out what was my favorite flower. He jumped through hoops to track down my parents' telephone number, called my mom, and pretended to be a local florist new to town. He told her that in order to have on hand the favorite flowers of the locals, he wanted to know her preference. His first question was "What is your favorite flower?" and his second question was, "Do you have daughters? If so, what is their favorite flower?" Aha! Ingenious little devil, isn't he?

Nick, Sam, and I were three of the last ones to leave the reception. (Sam mentally had left three hours before as he was asleep on a love seat in the corner of the ballroom.) Nick scooped him up, careful not to wake him, and we piled into the back of Stafford's limousine. Sam's long, lean eight-year-old body was flanked across one couchlike seat while Nick in his tuxedo and me in my gargantuan wedding dress snuggled into the very backseat. I looked at my not-so-little boy, and my heart swelled with love and pride. Oh, how he had grown, and much more than just physically.

When Stafford started the engine, he unrolled the window, that separated the three of us from him. "Everybody ready?" he chipperly asked, clearly not half as fatigued as we were given the 3:00 a.m. reading on the clock. I looked up from the still body of my little man to Stafford in the front and...Wait a second! *Jen?*

Lo and behold, there in the passenger seat of the limo was Jen grinning back at me through the open window.

"Surprise!" she announced nervously. As fate would have it, unbeknownst to me and Nick, Jen and James Stafford had quite enjoyed each other's company at our rehearsal dinner the evening before. At the reception, they sought each other out and picked up their conversation right where they had left it off, capping off their evening in the back of our limo a mere twenty minutes before Nick and I loaded in. Of course, we hadn't known that little morsel of information until Jen told me after our honeymoon. James and Jen got engaged last month, and Nick and I will *never* let them live down the fact that they defiled our newlywed limo! In fact, we are already working on our toasts for their wedding reception.

So with Jen cheesing next to him, Stafford asked, "Where to?" as if there were any question. We were all exhausted, and I was more than ready to crash into my bed and fall asleep. I wondered if Nick would be down with waiting a night to consummate our marriage as I was certain he was every bit as exhausted as I was and surely we would *both* want to be awake for our first time together. Yes, ladies, as difficult as it was to keep my hands off his hot body, Nick and I both agreed that our first time together should be on our wedding night. It added a wonderful element of suspense leading up to the big day, but doggone it, a woman needs her beauty sleep!

I rested my head against Nick's shoulder for the long drive back to Olathe and replayed the magical day's events over and over again until the soft whir of the road beneath the tires and the beating of Nick's heart under my open hand lulled me to sleep. The next thing I knew, Nick was tenderly kissing the top of my head and whispering, "Sweet bride, we're home." Barely opening my sleepy eyes, I moved about the back of the limo to rouse Sam as Nick softly said, "No, don't wake him yet. Let's just get everything inside first. James will stay out here with him until we get back."

It would be easier to get him when I was out of the frilly cumbersome dress, so I agreed and exited the limo with Nick's help. As I finally stood upright and got my bearings, I realized that nothing in my line of vision looked familiar. I swiftly turned to meet Nick's delighted face and asked, "Where *are* we? This isn't my house!" I was too tired for games.

Nick planted the biggest kiss on my lips and exclaimed, "Yes it is!" opening his hand to reveal a set of keys.

Completely confused, I looked around in a daze until I halted in recognition. My eyes bulged at the sight set before me, and I took two steps back and leaned against the limo to catch my balance so as to not faint right then and there. We were standing in front of the most grand two-story redbrick home surrounded by at least an acre of land. I had seen this house before. I had coveted this house before. Nicholas Price had bought us a home in Arbor Farms, the very neighborhood in which Chris and I had dreamed one day of retiring in!

I melted in his arms as he scooped me up and carried me across the threshold of our new palace. James soon followed with Sam silently sleeping in his arms and carried him directly to his new bedroom, which was already furnished with Sam's belongings. The entire house, in fact, was completely furnished with all my belongings and those that Nick had brought with him to Kansas, in addition to amazing add-ons that were carefully selected and designed by Chris and a team of interior decorators prior to the wedding. The man had surprised me once again, and so as not to be outdone, I *did* make love to my new husband that night, as well as the next night and the one after that. Each time was better than the previous one and was filled with desire and longing, forgiveness and hope, love and redemption.

Yes, we made love as love was supposed to be made, and on one of those first few nights as newlyweds, our lovemaking culminated in the biggest surprise of all—a surprise that waited a little over a month to present itself and just over four months to *double* its blessing. Indeed, nine months after we said "I do," I gave birth to twins! Grace Elaine and Alexander Wesley were born on February 14, 2015. It seems only apropos that the fruits of our love be welcomed into the world on the day that the world celebrates love!

If I left my hair wrapped in the towel much longer, it would be a tangled mess to try and work through, but I just *had* to hear what Nick's response to Sam would be. Nick pulled apart from Sam just far enough so that he could see Sam's face and said, "Sam, I don't just *like* you. I *love* you! I know you have your daddy who is watching you every single day from heaven and who is so incredibly proud of you, but do you think it would be okay if *I* could be your daddy down here on earth? I'd like nothing more than that, buddy. And yes. in answer to your question, I love all three of my children equally."

Sam beamed with relief and joy and then reached up and hugged Nick's neck, causing baby Grace to stir. "Yes," my little man answered, "I would love it if you'd be my dad and if I could call you 'Dad.'"

"You got it, son. Now listen, what do you say you and I get out that crazy-looking stroller that your mom bought and take the two littles for a walk to the park. Your mom has been working so hard to take care of us, and she really, *really* deserves a break, don't ya think?"

Sam nodded in agreement and then added, "Yeah, I've never seen Mom look so tired *ever*! Have you seen those dark spots under her eyes? Kind of creepy."

Nick laughed as he stood with Grace still nestled in his arms. He lowered his voice and leaned in to Sam responding, "I've gotta be honest, little man, I've never seen a woman more beautiful than your mom, *especially* when she is tired and stressed and has bags under her eyes."

"Especially?" Sam was shocked.

"Yeah, man. Because that is the *exact* look of love! That woman…your mom, works harder at being the best mom and wife she can be than any other mom on earth. And it's pretty hot, if ya ask me." Nick laughed.

"Gross!" Sam exclaimed. "That's my *mom* you're talking about!" He then took off running toward the stairs, presumably to grab his shoes.

I bolted into my bedroom as fast as I could and hid behind the door lest he catch me eavesdropping. When he was safely in his room, I walked toward my bathroom to begin the daunting practice of ripping through the tangles in my hair. The sun was already shining bright outside, so I stopped by our sitting area to open the blinds and let the morning light fill the room with warmth. A piece of paper caught my eye, and I remembered that while Sam was lounging on our sofa watching cartoons while we tried to sleep that morning, he had been doodling or drawing something.

I picked up the paper and studied it, noting instantly that it wasn't a picture at all. It was a letter. When I saw the letter was written to "Dad," it registered that Memorial Day was right around the corner and we'd be taking our annual trip to the cemetery following our weekend at the lake. Obviously, Sam had already been thinking about it because here he had penned his yearly letter to be left on Chris's headstone. I swallowed hard as I sat down to read the letter. The damn tangles would have to wait.

Dear Dad,

Hi. So a lot has happened since the last time I visited u at your grave. Sorry we didnt come last year. Mom was getting to marryed to this famous guy named Nick and we had the honeymoon in Aruba. I got to go to and it was so awesome! You would have loved it. Well at least I think you would of. I mean, who wouldnt love a place like Aruba. Nick is so nice and fun and funny. Its kind of wierd but I think of him like a dad. I dont want you to be mad at me. Its just that I cant really help it. Iv never met you and I have met him and he treats me just like a dad should treat a son. And I love it. Im sure I would of loved you the same if you were still alive but since your not im really glad I have him. I havnt told mom this yet but when they got marryed mom had our last name stay the same. Grandma said she did it so that we could honer you or something like that. So im still Samuel Holly and mom is still Allie Holly. I dont want to make mom mad or sad but I really want to ask her if we can change our last names to match Nicks. Well and the babys. Yep we have babies. Two of them. They cry ALL the time and its annoying but they are really cute and mom keeps telling me that they will be fun some day. Ya right. Anyway. I better go. I hear 1 of the babys crying. I think its Grace because she cries nonstop. I need to pretend like im asleep or they will make me take care of her. Oh one more thing. Mom is doing great. Iv been taking really really good care of her just like I promised you I would when you came and talked to me that one night at grandmas. Do you know that the same exact night that guy who mom said used to be your best friend Greg hurt mom? He did. He basically beat her up. Its so weird that you came and talked to me that night and told me to take care of her and then that happened to her. Dont worry though. Papa and uncle Adam took care of her that night. And now she has me AND Nick to take care of her. We wont let you down.

Love, Sam Price (I like the way it sounds)

P.S. Mom always says that you gave her me as a gift after you died. I dont know exactly what she means but thank you! Thanks for giving me to her. She is the best person I know and I'm glad you didnt give me to anyone else because she is the mom for me! And please don't be mad, but since I can't have you here, I really think Nick is the dad for me too.